A
SEASON
IN HELL

Center Point
Large Print

Also by Easy Jackson and available from Center Point Large Print:

A Bad Place to Die

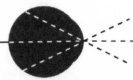

**This Large Print Book carries the
Seal of Approval of N.A.V.H.**

A
SEASON
IN HELL

A TENNESSEE SMITH WESTERN

EASY JACKSON

CENTER POINT LARGE PRINT
THORNDIKE, MAINE

This Center Point Large Print edition
is published in the year 2019 by arrangement with
Kensington Publishing Corp.

The text of this Large Print edition is unabridged.
In other aspects, this book may vary
from the original edition.
Printed in the United States of America
on permanent paper.
Set in 16-point Times New Roman type.

ISBN: 978-1-64358-268-9

Library of Congress Cataloging-in-Publication Data

Names: Jackson, Easy, author.
Title: A season in hell : a Tennessee Smith western / Easy Jackson.
Description: Large Print edition. | Thorndike, Maine :
    Center Point Large Print, 2019.
Identifiers: LCCN 2019015382 | ISBN 9781643582689 (hardcover :
    alk. paper)
Subjects: LCSH: Large type books. | GSAFD: Western stories.
Classification: LCC PS3610.A3496 S43 2019 | DDC 813/.6—dc23
LC record available at https://lccn.loc.gov/2019015382

A SEASON IN HELL

CHAPTER 1

Tennessee "Tennie" Smith Granger looked out the jailhouse window. With a Comanche moon shining above, she could see the sign on the butcher shop across the street almost as clearly as she could during the day. The saloons had finally shut down. The raucous laughter had ceased, and the loud banging of rinky-dink pianos had quieted. Everyone was asleep except the small shadows she could see scurrying in and out of the alleys.

Smoke began to billow upward from the middle of the road. The dark phantoms scampered to another spot in the street. A match was lit, and more smoke began to rise. Tennie left her place by the window and made her way to the jailhouse desk, stubbing her toe on its corner.

"Ouch," she whispered, hopping on one foot. Fumbling for the matches, she reached for the lantern hanging on the wall next to the windows. She lit it, taking another look through the glass. The flickering light showed only the reflection of a sleepy browned-eyed eighteen-year-old wearing a slightly vexed expression.

She headed back to the living quarters, passing through the hallway that held the staircase to the cells above, into the one large room

7

she and her stepsons lived in and the alcove where she slept. She glanced at their empty beds before drawing back the curtain to her bed. Pulling off her nightgown, she slipped into a dress, trying to hurry with her shoes and stockings.

A roll of thunder reverberated overhead. Tennie paused, remembering the cloudless sky she'd seen earlier. With one last twist, she had her shoes buttoned enough to stay on and went out through the office and onto the wooden sidewalk in front of the jailhouse.

A stench like rotten eggs filled the air. The smoke rising up and down the street was becoming so thick, Tennie could barely make out the inhabitants of Ring Bit exiting groggily from their homes, holding lanterns and making their way up the street to the "bad" part of town. A tall, rather lanky newcomer held himself away from the others.

The noise of rolling thunder increased, and the sound of hoofbeats could be heard coming from high above their heads. Tennie's eyes searched the sky and the tops of the store buildings. She couldn't see anything except an orangey moon and a few stars.

The murmurs of the crowd increased as acrid smoke filled the night air, and the smell of sulfur began to choke them. The voices of confused people became louder and louder until one woman, staring at the sky, began to scream between crashes of thunder.

"It's the death angels coming to get us!" she hollered, clutching her face. "The Lord is sending down fire and brimstone!"

"It's the end!" another woman cried.

Something belching smoke and rattling like the wheels of Hades rolled down the street while the hoofbeats coming from above became a frenzied stampede. People jumped away in turmoil, stumbling in the smoke. Women screamed, clutching their shawls and beseeching the heavens.

"Jesus save us!"

"It's the devil come to get us on his fiery horses!"

A rangy fellow, not quite sober from his previous revelries, beat on his chest, looking up at the sky and proclaimed, "I'm ready to meet the saints."

Another woman fell to her knees, clasped her hands together and began to pray. "Lord, I confess! That traveling salesman . . ." she cried.

"Tennie!" a stern voice said, cutting through the night and interrupting any more revelations.

Tennie's eyes searched until they found Shorty, the stationmaster from next door. In the glowing dark, she could see him getting ready to explode.

She turned to the tops of the buildings before he could really start yelling at her. "Rusty! Lucas!

Badger! You get on down here this minute. You stop that and get down here right now."

A small voice called from the roof of the butcher shop. "Aw, Miss Tennie," Lucas said.

"Don't you 'aw Miss Tennie' me," she yelled. "You get on down here and put these fires out."

Like a gassy mule after a whiskey and ginger treatment, the tension in the crowd released.

"It's just those gol-durn Granger boys again," a man grumbled.

The woman who had been about to confess her sins jumped to her feet.

"What's this here about a traveling salesman?" her husband demanded.

"That weren't me hollering," she said, looking innocent. "That were the widow over yonder. Everybody knows why she keeps her door hinges so oiled."

Tennie gave a sigh of relief when the husband pulled on his wife's arm. They would take the fight home, and she wouldn't have to worry about blood being spilled on the street.

People continued to cough and wipe their eyes. Pigs squealed, grunting and running in confusion at the commotion. The dogs and cats had fled and were hiding under buildings on the far side of town. The horses in the stalls and corrals next door began to make a racket as the smoke curled its way to the livery. The dark figure of the newcomer had long since headed in that

10

direction. He either didn't have a conscience or had nothing to confess.

"Do what Miss Tennie says," one of the merchants hollered at the boys. He stopped to hack smoke from his throat before adding, "You fork-tailed little infidels."

Tennie looked at the glaring eyes surrounding her, watching in dismay as the undertaker's wife approached, her lips in a thin, tight frown. Instead of her usual somber black dress, she clutched an expensive paisley silk robe to her stout frame. The colorful robe surprised Tennie, as did a head covered in a dozen or more rag rolls. At the moment, the rolls were shaking in fury, and that wasn't surprising.

"Mrs. Granger," the undertaker's wife said. "I don't know why the men of this town swore you in as marshal and have kept you in that position despite your obvious incompetence, but I can tell you one thing. You can forget about those disreputable stepsons of yours getting back into school."

Wincing as the woman flounced away, Tennie guessed it wouldn't do much good to remind the undertaker's wife that every male marshal preceding her had been killed or left town in a hurry to keep it from happening to them. She turned away, seeing the dark outline of a large muscular man just before he dived into the alley to escape notice. She didn't know why *he* had the look of someone guilty. It was her stepsons who had terrorized the town.

Looking up, she saw the boys scampering from the rooftops. Lucas looked as happy and proud as a roadrunner carrying a three-foot rattlesnake in its beak. Tennie wanted to cry.

Two days later, with the townspeople quieted down and the smell of sulfur dissipated, Tennie could once more appear in public. She swept the wooden sidewalk in front of the redbrick jail, stopping to push a strand of curly, light brown hair away from her face. Looking along the main street running through the town of Ring Bit, she saw drunks lurching from saloons, and a new wave of transient cowboys with their gun belts held low swaggering along the sidewalks.

Pausing the broom, she watched as one of the latest men to arrive exited a saloon, recognizing him as the tall newcomer who had observed the boys' smoke and thunder performance without comment and had left, she supposed, to check on his horse. He stood with ease, leaning one shoulder against a post and wearing a well-cut dark suit with a gray silk vest. A raven-haired man with a thick black mustache, his hat was also black and shaded his eyes. Nevertheless, the noonday sun outlined his somewhat coarse features.

Tennie noticed several men cross to the other side of the street rather than walk too near him.

The dogs in town didn't avoid him, but they didn't try to win a pat from him either. Even her three rowdy stepsons hadn't pulled any of the usual tricks they tried on new arrivals.

Shorty walked outside, peering above rimless glasses at the dawdling stranger before joining Tennie. "Why is it every time I step out the door, he's there?"

Tennie glanced at Shorty. A small, older man with slicked-back white hair, he looked perpetually aggravated. Wearing dark pants and a white shirt with a pocket watch hanging from his black vest, Shorty looked like a persnickety merchant who never handled anything more troublesome than a few drummers late for the stagecoach. Looks deceived the casual observer—he was a former Texas Ranger, and his glasses hid the glint of old and tested steel.

"I don't know what he's doing," Tennie said. "But that's been his favorite spot since he rode into town on a horse that looks like a million dollars."

"What do you know about horseflesh?" Shorty asked. "Or a million dollars, for that matter?"

"Nothing," Tennie replied. "But that's what Lucas said."

Shorty gave an almost imperceptible sniff. "He probably heard it from Lafayette."

Of the three stepsons she had inherited from a marriage that didn't make it through the wedding night, Badger, age six, was Shorty's favorite. Rusty, thirteen, and Lucas, ten, were the everyday cornbread while Badger was Sunday's light crust biscuit. Lafayette Dumont, the dapper owner of the ornate Silver Moon Saloon, stood way down on Shorty's list like hardtack, sometimes necessary but not particularly liked.

Shorty squinted at her. "Banned from school again?"

"Yes," Tennie replied. "Just when I thought the school board might let them back in, they had to pull that stunt."

Shorty's nose quivered and raised slightly. He had no problem making the boys behave when he felt like it. "Ashton let those boys run wild."

"He was ill, Shorty," Tennie said. "You know he had a bad heart."

A young cowboy wearing longish hair and cheap new clothes sauntered out of another saloon. He stopped to contemplate the man in black across the street. Glancing at the loafers in front of the saloon behind him, he grinned and crossed the road, approaching the man who leaned so unconcernedly against the post.

"Oh, no. Here it comes," Tennie said.

In Ring Bit, it was considered worse than pulling on a dog's ear to meddle in a fight, and even if Tennie had been a six-foot, two-hundred-pound male, people would still expect her to let the adversaries duke it out without interference.

14

But sometimes, men would start fights just to show off in front of her. Although she didn't think the young cowboy had noticed her standing behind Shorty, she started to go back inside the jailhouse to avert trouble before it began.

It happened so fast, she hadn't time to turn around. The young cowboy said something and made to pull his gun. Before it cleared leather, the man with the black mustache shot him with a blast that echoed throughout the street. The force of the bullet sent the young cowboy backwards and down onto the dirt with a bloody hole gaping in his chest, a look of surprise in his blank eyes, and a mouth hanging open from the last shock he would ever receive.

Tennie gasped and glanced at Shorty. Even he looked stunned.

"I've never seen anyone throw lead that fast," she said.

"He's a professional," Shorty said, giving the dark-haired man a speculative stare.

The new owners of the butcher shop and slaughterhouse across the street ran outside and gawked. The shop, painted white with a false second story, sat up high, with many steps leading up to a tall porch. The backyard contained a maze of pens and a cacophony of mooing cows and squealing hogs. The impressive bricked two-story jailhouse, a product of a failed attempt to capture the county seat, looked as incongruous in the neighborhood as Tennie did. With livestock across the street and horses on the other side at the livery, the air around the jailhouse at times became a hard burden to bear.

Tennie had hoped with the death of the previous owner, whoever ran the butcher shop next would be a lot nicer, but unfortunately, that hadn't been the case. "Maggot" Milton's younger brothers "accidentally" shortchanged customers, worked only when forced to, and often nipped from bottles they had hidden in various spots outside. Middle-aged, popeyed, and slovenly dressed, there was nothing to recommend the men. The rumormongers of Ring Bit claimed the only way one of them was able to catch a wife was when he told her he and his brother had inherited a thriving business.

Neither brother appeared too enthralled with the marriage, however. Inga Milton, square-jawed and statuesque, had deceptively smooth angel wings of blond hair on either side of her face. She gave orders to both men in low menacing tones that frightened Tennie so much, she never felt the least desire to be neighborly.

Inga left the men and walked across the street, facing Tennie. "Aren't you going to do something?" She spoke in a deep voice with Slavic overtones and towered over Tennie.

Tennie blushed. "It was self-defense, Mrs. Milton."

Inga snorted. "I could be better sheriff than you."

"I'm not a sheriff; I'm a town marshal. And you are welcome to the job if you want it." Tennie wasn't going to be one much longer anyway, and she wouldn't have to put up with the Miltons much longer either.

Inga glared at her in contempt. "You don't even wear a badge."

Tennie looked down at her pink dress covered in little gold flowers with its ruffles and tiny bows. She had forgotten to put her badge on again.

A crowd had gathered around the dead man. Tennie's three stepsons jockeyed behind them, trying to see. Rusty, a slender boy with sandy red hair and freckles, craned his neck around the men. Lucas, little and wiry, bent his dark head down low, gazing with sharp blue eyes through gaps between the men. Pudgy Badger, also dark-haired and blue-eyed, ran in a circle trying to see until he finally got down on all fours and crawled through the mass of cowboy boots and spurs, his little black and gray fur-ball puppy, Rascal, right behind him.

Two men picked up the body and headed for the funeral parlor with it. Tennie found herself trembling. The three boys watched for another minute, then catching sight of Tennie and Shorty, they ran toward them.

Inga saw them, too. "You cannot restrain your stepsons. I don't know why anybody would think you could restrain town, too."

"Nobody can rein in Ring Bit for long," Tennie said.

"Disgusting town, disgusting name," Inga said. "What does this *Ring Bit* mean?"

Tennie answered in a distracted tone. "It's a cruel bit they used to use around here to train unmanageable horses. Don't ask me why they chose it as the name of the town. I don't know."

Her stepsons reached her, out of breath with excitement.

"Did you see that, Miss Tennie?" Lucas asked.

"Don't interrupt when grownups are talking," Tennie replied automatically, but Inga was already leaving to return to her shop.

Lucas put his thumbs in his ears and made a face at her back. Badger did the same thing, sticking out his tongue.

"Enough of that." Tennie turned to Rusty.

He was older and had asked to dress like the cowboy he hoped one day to be, wearing his pants tucked inside his boots, just like they did. "We saw Mr. and Mrs. Payton a while ago. They asked if it was all right if they stopped by for dinner."

"Of course," Tennie said. "I'll set the table." She gave the disappearing back of the gunfighter one last look before she turned to go inside the jailhouse, trying to quiet the sick feeling in her stomach. She didn't know if she was sad or glad her stepsons were better at taking things in stride.

Tennie liked the Paytons. Mr. Payton had wanted to visit his family in Alabama one last time, and he'd agreed to bring back a bride to any decent, upstanding man in Ring Bit who desired one. He had allowed several exceptions and ended up bringing back quite a few women. She had been in a hurry to leave Alabama and had signed on to his wagon train, thinking she was joining a group of missionaries. Instead, she found she was to be a bride for a man in Texas desperate to provide a mother for his wayward sons. She had wanted to leave the wagon train, but Mr. Payton insisted it was too dangerous. Hardhead that she was, she'd planned on running away anyway. Instead, she saw Indians about to attack and warned the others. Winn Payton believed she had saved them, and he'd bought her a new dress and shoes out of his own pocket because hers were in such dire condition. And she agreed to go through with a marriage to a man she had never seen before.

Winn Payton's kindness stopped short of inviting her and her nefarious stepsons to live with him after Ashton Granger's sudden death, however. His answer was to get married again, and fast. He distinctly disapproved of her decision to take the job as town marshal over making a hasty marriage. But that didn't stop Tennie from liking the tall, slender old man with the gray muttonchop sideburns and his tiny whitehaired wife.

Because of the heat, they ate at the big table in the front office instead of in the back at the kitchen table. The jail cells above their heads were mercifully empty for the time being.

Winn Payton sat at the head of the table. "His name is Hawkshaw."

"Hawkshaw what?" Tennie asked.

"I don't know," Mr. Payton replied, sopping up potlikker with his cornbread. "He never goes by anything other than Hawkshaw."

"I wonder where he came from." Like most Southerners, Mrs. Payton was always interested in the genealogy of every stranger she met.

"I have no idea," Mr. Payton said.

"And the boy who tried to shoot him?" Tennie asked.

Winn Payton stopped eating long enough to give Tennie a stern look of disgust. "Just another loose cannon roaming the countryside, looking for trouble. He'd been in the saloon, listening to the local idlers talking up this Hawkshaw fellow and decided he'd be the one to take him down."

Tennie sighed. It seemed men spent their whole lives trying to prove something, and when they quit trying to move upward, they spiraled into the depths of a pit trying to prove how low they could go.

Mr. Payton broke into her reverie. "Tennie, have you heard from Wash?"

Before she could answer, Lucas bent his head low over his plate and began to quote dramatically. " 'My darling Tennie, my heart aches to see you, to feel the softness of your hair in my fingers, to gaze into those big brown eyes, to grasp your small back in my hands, and to feel the beating of your heart next to mine once more.' "

"You've been reading my mail," Tennie said. "Stop that!"

She looked at the Paytons and blushed. George Washington Jones was a silent and taciturn Texas Ranger most of the time, but when his lawyer oratory mode surfaced, he was prone to outbursts of extravagant speech.

Winn Payton had no desire to hear an argument between Tennie and her stepsons. He wanted to argue with her on his own. "You shouldn't have let Lafayette talk you into waiting for this elaborate wedding," he fussed. "Why in God's name Lafayette thinks you and Wash have to be married in the governor's mansion of all places is beyond me. No, I take that back. It's just like Lafayette to want to put on the dog."

"He thinks it will be good for Wash's career," Tennie said, not too happy about it either. "You know Wash has these aspirations of becoming a judge when he quits being a Ranger." And she secretly hoped it would help overcome her stigma of being raised in an orphanage from age ten and being forced into a profession that was looked on in horror as unseemly for a woman.

"They had different mothers, didn't they?" Mrs. Payton said, back on the genealogy trail. "Wash's mother was a Jones, and Lafayette's mother was a Dumont. And when they came to Texas, they took those names."

Tennie didn't even know what their real last name was; both said it was no longer important.

Before she could ask, Mr. Payton started on something else. "I don't know what kind of strings Lafayette had to pull to get you a wedding in the governor's mansion," he said, already knowing Wash and Lafayette's family history all the way back to the American Revolution and not caring.

"I'm sure it had something to do with the war," Tennie said.

The Confederate soldiers may have lost the war, but they created an exclusive fraternity out of it. Tennie reminded herself that Mr. Payton was in that brotherhood, too—he just didn't like being called General Payton.

"Before now, they haven't even seen hide nor hair of one another since Lafayette left home," Mr. Payton said. "What does Wash think about Lafayette killing their older brother?"

Tennie saw the boys' eyes grow big. She tried

to explain. "Mr. Lafayette and Mr. Wash had an older brother who thought Mr. Lafayette was paying too much attention to his wife."

"It wasn't no *thinking* about it," Mr. Payton said. "It was seduction."

"Now, Father," Mrs. Payton said.

"But Mr. Lafayette killed him?" Lucas asked.

"It was an accident," Tennie said in a hurry. "The brother challenged Mr. Lafayette to a duel, and Mr. Lafayette thought they would just shoot wild at one another and that would be the end of it. Instead, he realized his brother meant to kill him, so he tried to wing him, but he missed and accidentally killed him.

"Now don't be asking him about it," she warned. "That was a long time ago, and that's dead and buried."

Tennie turned to Mr. Payton. "Wash would just like to forget the whole thing. He said the brother's wife was always a little unbalanced, and Lafayette just got caught up in her web. He knows Lafayette didn't intend to kill their older brother."

"Lafayette is always going to be caught up in some unbalanced woman's web," Mr. Payton said. "Tennie, you are marrying into an old and well-respected Southern family, but they've got a streak of craziness inbred in them."

Tennie glanced at her stepsons. Other families spoke about such things in whispers and certainly not in front of children. Perhaps she was wrong to let them hear so much. But Mr. Payton never spoke anything in a whisper.

"She still wears heavy mourning," Mrs. Payton said. "The wife, I mean."

"Her family hates Lafayette," Mr. Payton said. "I can't say that I blame them."

"Would you care for some coffee?" Tennie said, rising.

"Yes, ma'am," Mr. Payton said.

She went to fetch it, hoping it would interrupt Winn Payton's tirade, but when she brought the coffee from the kitchen, he launched into another attack.

"I cannot believe Wash would leave you here as marshal in a town full of hot-blooded men," he said, pouring his coffee from the cup into the saucer. He blew on it and slurped it, giving a grunt of satisfaction.

"Now, Father," Mrs. Payton said again, taking a cup and saucer from Tennie.

"Lafayette convinced Wash that Ring Bit would be much safer for me than the ranch," Tennie said.

"Humph," Mr. Payton said. "I can't imagine any man in his right senses leaving a comely eighteen-year-old heifer alone in a jailhouse and working as a marshal in a town full of women-hungry men ready to kill for her. This whole scheme of Lafayette's to make you wait to be married and keep your engagement hush is ridiculous, and I can't believe either one of you agreed to it."

Tennie and Wash had been reluctant, but in the end, let themselves be persuaded by Lafayette. He had taken her aside and said, "My darling Miss Tennie, there are men in this town who will shoot Wash in the back in hopes of having a chance with you. Once you are married, it will be a done deal, but until then, it is in Wash's best interest to keep your engagement a secret."

"Father," Mrs. Payton said unexpectedly. "Tennie has a whole town full of men watching out for her. If one of them makes a false move, the others will be all over him like fleas on a hound. Lafayette was right to insist she stay here until they can be married. She can't live in his saloon. It wouldn't be appropriate."

"Hardly any more inappropriate than her being a city marshal," he retorted.

Tennie did not resent Mr. Payton's remarks. She knew he worried about her.

As they were leaving, Mrs. Payton handed Tennie an arithmetic primer. "From the undertaker's wife, Tennie dear. I think she feels a little guilty about the boys."

Tennie took the book, so shocked at first, she wasn't sure what to say. "Um, when you see her, tell her I said much obliged. I think."

Mr. Payton was never unsure about anything,

and he gave her one final word of advice. "Stay away from that new shootist in town. He's up to no good, whatever it is."

"I don't think you have anything to worry about," Tennie said. "I have no intention of going anywhere near him."

CHAPTER 2

That night, the sound of shots being fired increased, boisterous laughter was brasher, and it seemed the rinky-dink pianos played louder than ever before. Tennie sat at a table with her stepsons and tried to ignore the noises coming from outside. The town leaders wanted her to stay at or near the jail to open the cells to any miscreants they wanted to toss in. They also wanted her to feed the prisoners, to release them when they sobered, and to clean up after them. Anything else she could manage would be a bonus, and no one except Inga Milton seemed to expect it of her. The town paid her very little, but she had a roof over their heads and a stipend for all the food they needed.

While she patched holes in Badger's overalls, Lucas and Rusty took turns reading by the coal oil light. Wash liked to read to them, and Rusty, especially, tried to emulate his deep cadence.

A knock at the jailhouse door broke into Lucas's narration. Tennie placed her mending on the table, rising to hurry to the door. The boys followed her. Opening it, she saw a stout cowboy gripping an obviously intoxicated and much smaller one. Behind them, she caught a glimpse of a dark suit, and a man holding on to his upper arm.

"Pardon me, ma'am," the big cowboy said. "I'd take my hat off, but I can't let go of this here cork-puller."

Tennie nodded. The shorter cowboy was trying to focus his eyes on her and having trouble.

"I just started working for Colonel Lafayette," the taller one continued. "The name's Gid. Giddings Coltrane, but I ain't the Giddings Coltrane from down around the Nueces way. No ma'am, that ain't me."

"Uh, yes, Mr. Coltrane," Tennie said. "Did Mr. Lafayette send you over here with a prisoner?"

"Yes, ma'am. I know you be from the South, and that's where my people be from, so I know what kind of store we 'uns set on manners and such, but I'd be much obliged if you'd just call me Gid like most folks generally do. Calling me Mr. Coltrane adds a lot more to me than is really there, ma'am."

"Well, I doubt that," Tennie said, wondering why there seemed to be something familiar about him. "But I'd be pleased to call you Mr. Gid. And please call me Miss Tennie.

"Let me get a lamp," she continued, "and we'll put your prisoner upstairs." She fetched the keys from their nail on the wall and took a lantern from a hook. "Follow me, please." She led the way up the stairs.

The prisoner offered no resistance and said little, which piqued Tennie's interest. Usually, the saloon owners only sent the most violent rabble-rousers to be thrown into the jail cells overnight. She unlocked one of the three cells and stood with her back next the windows that faced the street while Gid more or less pitched his prisoner onto a cot.

He stood back while Tennie locked the door, explaining as he followed Tennie down the stairs. "He accused this here Hawkshaw feller of card cheating, taking a swipe at him with a blade, but Mr. Lafayette said he'd have him thrown in jail for a day or two to keep him from gettin' killed."

As Tennie came down the stairs, the light from the lantern illuminated below, showing her stepsons hovering in a corner and the man named Hawkshaw waiting at the bottom, holding a white handkerchief slowly bleeding red over his upper left arm.

Tennie remembered the flash of his gun and the dead young cowboy in the street. She didn't want to have anything to do with him, but she couldn't turn him away if he needed help. Hadn't she once been forced to kill a man who tried to harm her and her stepsons?

She turned the lantern on Gid. "Good night, Mr. Gid. I can take it from here."

This time, he did remove his hat. His head was square, its dark and curling unkempt hair thinning on top. He had large gaps between crooked teeth in a rather wide mouth, but he emanated innocent charm totally lacking in guile, and seemed eager to be friends.

"Don't worry. I'll be fine," Tennie said. "I'll be seeing you again, I'm sure."

"Good night, Miss Tennie," Gid said, giving a hard warning look to Hawkshaw before turning and disappearing. The sound of his spurs jingling through the night told Tennie he was heading back to the Silver Moon.

Tennie shut the door and held the lantern up so she could see her other visitor. "What can I do for you, Mr. Hawkshaw?"

"I hear you are a fair hand at doctoring. I need this arm sewn up." His deep voice held a hint of scorn for the rest of the world, Tennie included.

She nodded. "Follow me, please." Since the doctor had fled town, she had become something of an unofficial nurse in Ring Bit, having worked in a war hospital with her mother. Her stepsons' father had been a retired surgeon, and they had inherited his instruments. The women banded together to take care of one another, excluding Tennie. Anybody seriously ill had to go to Cat Ridge, the next town. But the single men in Ring Bit had come to rely on her to patch them up.

She helped Hawkshaw remove his coat. He hesitated at removing his shirt.

"Don't worry," Tennie said. "I've seen it

before, and I have my chaperones standing guard across the room."

He grunted a short laugh and unbuttoned his shirt.

"Sit down, please." Going to the stove Tennie poured hot water from a kettle into a basin, then took the basin to the table. She sat down and began to wash his wound—a deep but clean cut across the flesh of his upper left arm.

"Why are you doing that?" he asked.

"Their father," Tennie said, nodding toward her stepsons, "told me he had good luck with it during the war. It seems to keep down infections. I would advise you to keep it clean."

She took the needle and thread she had been using on Badger's overalls. "This is going to hurt," she warned. "I don't have any whiskey or laudanum."

"I'll be fine," he said, and did not so much as flinch when she poked the skin with the needle. He talked while she made small, even stitches. "I didn't think that yahoo was ever going to shut up."

"He was a talker, wasn't he?" Tennie said, concentrating on his arm. "I didn't realize you were bleeding so much, or I would have hurried him along."

"You can't hurry somebody like that."

"I wonder how there can be two Giddings Coltranes in Texas," Tennie said while she stitched.

31

"Probably it's his pa—they just don't claim one another," Hawkshaw said.

Tennie accidentally went in a little too deep with the needle, and he blinked.

"Sorry," she said.

He looked away. "That drunken fool upstairs better be glad he sliced my left arm and not my right, or he'd be dead."

"I've seen how fast you are with a gun," Tennie said, stopping to dab up blood. "I'm surprised they were able to stop you."

"I grabbed his knife and was about to slash his throat when that saloon owner, Lafayette, stopped me. He promised to keep him locked up for a while. I shoot with my right hand, and I would have killed the sorry skunk regardless of what anybody said if he had interfered with that."

"Glad I wasn't there," Tennie murmured.

"Every time some gopher starts losing at cards, he has to accuse the other fellow of cheating."

"Were you cheating?" Tennie asked, avoiding a small freckle on his white skin.

He snorted. "No. I don't have to cheat to win." His eyes roamed the room, taking in the back door, the cookstove next to it, and the windows on the side of the room.

Tennie glanced at him. She had seen that look on men before. It meant he was memorizing every place a man could come in or escape from.

"This is the strangest town I ever rode into,"

he said. "Everybody running around, trying to hold elections, find bank managers, see who's going to run what business. And to top it off, a lady marshal who looks like a picture out of a magazine."

Tennie blushed but continued to sew. She wondered if he was always so talkative. It crossed her mind that he was digging for information, but she put it aside. She liked conversation and was a naturally truthful person. "The men who hired me thought they could give the town a better image, and at the same time, hide their wrongdoings from someone who might be more suspicious. The Texas Rangers were investigating a widespread rustling outfit, and they narrowed it down as originating here. When they busted the gang, everything in town was shaken up."

"But the saloons are still going."

"Yes," Tennie said. "They are like you are about cards. Why make money illegally when they can make just as much legally? But I assure you, I am nothing more than a glorified cook and jailhouse janitor."

Hawkshaw gave a short laugh, an odd one that seemed to lack any warmth.

From the corner of her eye, she saw Rusty tugging on Lucas, but Lucas broke free and approached the table.

He stared at Hawkshaw. "My stepmother held a Navy Colt on the worst outlaw in these parts and told him to get on the stage or she was going to blow a hole in his stomach," Lucas said, driving his point home.

Hawkshaw stared back at the boy. "I have heard that," he said, dismissing him.

Tennie finished, knotting the thread and cutting it close to the skin. She wrapped a bandage around his arm, looking at his chest and torso, realizing the scar left from the wound she sewed would be joining others. She rose and began helping him into his shirt and jacket.

"Why isn't a beautiful young woman like you married?" Hawkshaw asked.

It was Rusty who spoke, having moved silently closer. "You ask too many questions, mister."

"Rusty!" Tennie said. "Don't pay him no never mind," she told Hawkshaw. "They're just afraid I'm going to get hitched to somebody they don't like."

Hawkshaw gave Rusty a stare while he buttoned his shirt but said nothing to the boy. "What do I owe you, ma'am?" he asked Tennie.

"Nothing. If I was a real doctor, I'd make you pay for my expertise. But I'm not. If you come back in a week, I'll take the stitches out for you."

Hawkshaw put on his hat. "I won't be here in a week," he said and left.

Three days later, the U.S. deputy marshal stopped by in time for the noon meal, as was his custom.

A slender young man with a mane of thick brown hair, he had straight bushy eyebrows set over lively green eyes, and a wide mouth hidden by an enormous mustache. Tennie was aware of the rumors that he had numerous sweethearts, and an ambitious one on the other side of Brushwood planned on roping him any day. He sat at the table, eating steadily, and only began to talk when Tennie served a green grape pie.

"I hear tell a man named Hawkshaw has been hanging around Ring Bit," the handsome marshal said.

"That's right," Tennie said. "But he said he doesn't plan on being here much longer."

The marshal made a noncommittal noise and began asking questions and gossiping about the other inhabitants of Ring Bit. When he left, Tennie followed him to the door and stood outside under the porch awning.

He stopped to look across the street at the butcher shop. "You know the Miltons blame you and Wash Jones for killing their brother."

"They can blame us all they want to, but their brother was running stolen cattle through that business. Besides resisting arrest, he came close to killing Wash and me. And they ought to be grateful. They inherited the business. I'm sure their brother never parted with a dime while he was living."

The marshal turned and called back into the

jailhouse. "You boys stay clear of those Miltons. They're sorry trash, and they won't have no qualms about getting even with you any way they can. The only reason they don't poison your meat is because they'd have Lafayette and the rest of the town down on them like hogs on a snake."

They hollered back, "Yes, sir!" as they fought over the last of piece of pie.

The marshal looked at Tennie. "How'd they do the rolling thunder?"

"Flapping a piece of tin they borrowed from the new blacksmith," Tennie said. "I should have known they were up to no good when one of the merchants told me they'd been in his store buying saltpeter and matches with their own money."

The marshal laughed, saying good-bye. He put his hat on and sauntered toward the saloons. Tennie turned, about to go back inside to do the dishes when she caught sight of a familiar figure walking toward her from the livery next door.

As far as she knew, the sheriff of the county had not set foot in Ring Bit since her arrival. A heavyset older man with eyelids that hung so low they kept half his eyeballs from being seen, he despised Ring Bit and made no attempt to hide it since most of the lowlifes inhabiting the town did not bother to vote. He halted in front of Tennie.

"They didn't hurt anybody with those smoke cans," Tennie said.

He gave her a puzzled look. "I don't know what you are talking about, woman."

"Oh. Why are you here?"

He turned red in the face. "I'm the sheriff of this here county, and I have a right to be here."

Tennie wanted to make a smart remark but stopped herself. "It's just that I've never seen you in Ring Bit before. That's all."

"You've got a man in this town with a lightning-fast draw, and I don't want him in my county," the sheriff said. "It's up to you to get rid of him."

"Up to me?" Tennie said. "Why me? But if you are talking about Mr. Hawkshaw, he said he'll be gone before the week is out anyway."

"Make sure of it," the sheriff said. "Which of the saloons does he park his hat in?"

Tennie wanted to say, "*You* tell him to get out of town," but instead, she answered his question. "Sometimes the Silver Moon, but most of the time he's in the one across the street."

The sheriff strode away while Tennie watched as he purposely avoided both the Silver Moon and the saloon across the street, going into a smaller one closer to the nicer part of town.

She shook her head, wondering why she questioned anything the sheriff did or said. If there was ever a problem in Ring Bit, she knew she couldn't count on him, or the U.S. deputy marshal, for that matter. Although she liked the marshal, he had a habit of always being someplace else when trouble came. The sheriff, who Tennie thoroughly disliked, thought Ring Bit deserved any tribulations it got and more.

When the sheriff returned, she was behind the jailhouse hoeing weeds, hoping to clear a patch to grow black-eyed peas. It seemed a silly thing to do, when she had every intention of getting married and leaving the jailhouse far behind.

"I heard about that stunt your stepsons pulled," the sheriff said when he reached her. "I'm warning you right now they better not try something like that in Cat Ridge. That oldest boy of yours ain't so young he can't be locked up."

Tennie stood up straighter, wishing she had guts enough to smack him with the hoe. "It was just a childish prank. And it was kind of funny when folks thought the Antichrist was coming to get them. We almost heard some juicy confessions."

"There weren't nothing funny about it," he snapped. "Don't forget what I said about that shootist."

Tennie stared at him, not openly defiant, but not compliant either. She had no intention of telling Hawkshaw anything.

The sheriff gave her a hard look from under those heavy lids. "And he's not the only one. I hear tell Ring Bit has taken yet another desperado to its bosom. I'm warning you if that trash spills into Cat Ridge, I'm complaining to the governor, friend of that fancy-pants Lafayette or not." The sheriff gave her another glare, turned on his heels, and stomped toward the livery.

Tennie hoped he'd get on his horse and leave town for good. "Why didn't I say, 'You go right ahead and complain. I'm sure they'd love to hear about all the help you gave the last time we had trouble.'" She muttered, "He probably would have slapped me. I'll be so glad when I can leave this job and never look back." She took her hoe and attacked the weeds.

She would marry Wash Jones and take her place in society as the wife of an up-and-coming attorney with ambitions of being a judge. She would leave behind the unpleasant odor of being a destitute orphan, of working in an unsuitable profession, of being a bride of one day to an old man she'd never met who died before he could do more than give her hair a brush with his lips. Wash would steady her stepsons and see to it they got a decent education.

"People in church will say, 'Will you sit here by me, Mrs. Jones?'" Tennie said out loud. "Instead of, 'We don't want you on our side of town.'"

A noise startled her, and she whirled around.

"Miss Tennie," Lafayette said. "Whatever are you doing standing there talking to a farm implement?" He laughed and gave her a gentle smile.

She smiled back, struck again by what a handsome man Lafayette Dumont was. Wash's older half brother had a fine head of dark hair, with wide gray streaks on the side. His face was thinner than Wash's, but they had the same lively blue eyes, except Wash's were slightly narrower from squinting in the sun so much. Their voices were different, too. Wash had the deep, distinctive voice of a born orator, while Lafayette's accent was much more Southern, and belied a little of the French blood he'd inherited from his mother.

Lafayette held out his arm. "Leave the farmwork behind, dear Tennie, and come inside with me for a while."

Tennie put the hoe down. She hesitated at placing her hand on the sleeve of his exquisite charcoal gray suit. "I'm afraid my hands are a little dirty."

He took her hand and placed it on his arm, smiling kindly at her. She smiled back and walked with him to the front of the jailhouse. He opened the door, allowing her to enter first. He followed her, leaving the door ajar to allow air into the hot office.

"Sit down," Tennie said. "I'll wash my hands. Would you like some coffee? I can make a pot."

"No, dear. A glass of water would do me fine."

She hurried to the back, washing her hands in a basin as quickly as she could, then poured two glasses of water and reentered the office. He was sitting at the head of the table, waiting for her.

"Here you are," she said, placing the glass in

40

front of him. She took a chair beside him and sat down.

"I hear your stepsons put on an entertaining show for the townspeople the other night."

"At the time, I was upset," Tennie said. "But looking back, it really was comical. The sheriff, though, threatened to throw Rusty in jail if he did anything like that in Cat Ridge."

"Rusty is too sensible to get caught doing anything like that in Cat Ridge, and Lucas is too wily to be caught by anyone but you. Badger just follows the other two." Lafayette paused a moment then continued. "And was the marshal angry about it when he stopped by?"

"Oh no," Tennie said with a laugh. "He just wanted to know how they did it. You know him. When he comes to Ring Bit, it's always at dinnertime. I don't think the man ever cooks for himself."

"Um," Lafayette said, fingering the glass. "I think the marshal might be as promiscuous with his affections as he is with his appetite."

Tennie laughed again. "I have heard that. Repeatedly."

Lafayette smiled, throwing back his head.

"I met your new helper," she said. "Is he another one of the soldiers who fought under you in the war?"

"Giddings Coltrane?" Lafayette asked. "Yes, he was a demolitions expert. He blew up many a

41

bridge for me. He's also a distant relative of my sister-in-law."

Tennie swallowed to keep from letting out a gasp. Was Gid kin to the wife of the brother Lafayette accidentally killed? Maybe it was another brother's wife.

Lafayette continued to talk in a natural voice. "After the war, when things got bad, it looked like Gid might lose his home. He foolishly joined his brothers in a train robbery. He wrote me from prison, saying he wanted to forget the past but needed help getting a new start somewhere else when he was released. He's young, stout as a mule, and has no brains whatsoever except when it comes to explosives."

Tennie took in a deep breath. "He must be the one the sheriff was referring to as a desperado. And he seemed so nice."

Lafayette gave a sardonic smile. "The only desperate thing about him is his desire that you not be angry with him."

"Why would I be angry with him?" Tennie asked. "I just met him."

"Because he's the one who told Lucas and Rusty how to make the smudge pots and brew up the sulfuric odor. He often sits and whittles behind the saloon during the day. When Lucas delivers the bottles he gathers to the back door of the saloon, he and the other boys like to listen to Gid reminisce about the war. Gid didn't realize they would try out some of his potions on the citizens of Ring Bit."

Tennie shut her eyes for a few seconds, trying to sort things out. She was only eighteen. She couldn't handle three rowdy boys. She couldn't handle a town full of men bent on raising hell either. She wasn't even sure she could handle marriage. "Lord help me," she said under her breath, opening her eyes. "It's not his fault those boys look for devilment wherever they can. But as long as they are not destructive to property or being cruel to animals, I'm not going to say too much. And I'm certainly not going to blame a war veteran for entertaining a handful of boys. Especially one who's gone through hell and wants a fresh start."

"That's my sweet girl," Lafayette said, squeezing her hand. "Despite Gid's faults, he'd do to ride the river with, as the cowboys say. Very well, in fact." He held on to her hand and rose from his chair.

She stood up.

"I received word from Wash today that he is wrapping up the rustler business and will be here shortly," Lafayette said. "We'll travel by stage to Cat Ridge, and from there, catch another stage heading south."

Tennie nodded, her heart filling with happiness, excitement, and fear.

Lafayette bent his mouth down to the hand he

43

still held, brushing his lips lightly against her flesh. "Tennie, dear," he said without looking directly at her, "I want you to be certain about Wash."

She found her heart beating faster. Her breath seemed to be coming out that way too, matching his. The electricity sparking in the air, the suppression of emotion in his voice and on his face told her he might be asking her to reconsider her choice of brothers.

Lafayette was handsome, successful, and like his brother, almost overpoweringly masculine. Tennie felt confused and couldn't for a minute seem to get her brain to work.

Both brothers had human frailties, but all she could think of was that Wash was 100 percent, whereas Lafayette was 98 percent. It was that two percent that bothered her. She knew she wasn't being logical and couldn't explain her reasons if asked. But her answer came from a sure heart and a sure brain, even if they were a little stirred up at the moment.

"Yes," she said. "I'm sure about Wash."

Lafayette nodded, kissing her hands before leaving. She followed him to the door, where he almost ran into Hawkshaw as he stepped over the threshold.

A frown crossed Lafayette's brow. "Do you make it a habit to eavesdrop on private conversations?"

"Listening to a middle-aged man making a fool of himself over a little prairie chicken is too entertaining to resist," Hawkshaw replied.

Tennie's mouth dropped open.

"My dear sir," Lafayette said. "I was about to accuse you of the same thing, lurking about and stalking our darling marshal."

"And what are you going to do about it?" Hawkshaw said, raising his voice.

They were beginning to attract a crowd. Tennie felt paralyzed, unable to understand what was going on. Lafayette had not been making a fool of himself, and Hawkshaw was not stalking her. Why would he pretend otherwise?

"I'm going to have someone break the knuckles on your right hand," Lafayette said, "if you bother this girl."

"Please . . ." Tennie said.

Neither man paid attention to her.

Hawkshaw continued to taunt Lafayette in an ever-louder voice. "Are you too cowardly to do anything to me on your own? You Southern gentlemen make me sick with all this empty talk about manners and protecting women."

Lafayette laughed at him. "If you think you are going to get me to engage in something as crude as a gun battle with you, you are sadly mistaken. If you want to fight, we will do it with swords or bare knuckles right here in the street."

"Please stop!" Tennie pleaded.

Hawkshaw looked at her and bowed. "As the lady wishes." He turned and walked away.

Tennie looked up at Lafayette. "What—?"

He laughed again and leaned closer to her, speaking low in her ear. "Don't worry. He's not going to do anything that might damage that gun hand of his."

CHAPTER 3

Tennie didn't have time to ponder about Hawkshaw too much; it was payday at Fort Griffin, and soldiers began pouring into town. Frequenting the saloons, they also wanted to experience at least one or two nights in Lafayette's elaborate gambling hall—the Silver Moon—pretending they were rich. All the soiled doves had fled town before the big shoot-out with the Rangers, but Shorty predicted it would just be a matter of time before more took their place.

Tennie had so many difficulties with the scarlet ladies, the thought depressed her, but in far-flung western towns with few women, prostitution was more openly tolerated than in places back East. Tennie could do nothing about it and preferred not to dwell on it. In the meantime, the soldiers filtered into the Mexican section of town where a few señoritas did not mind taking their money. If the men caused trouble, they were knifed and thrown back into the American section, and nobody knew anything.

Due to drunkenness and clashes with civilians, two soldiers from the saloons were dragged in by rough men who served at various times as strongarms for the smaller establishments. Cowboys didn't mind doing occasional work not on horseback as long as it wasn't considered permanent employment. Lafayette used numerous men at different times but always kept at least one on the payroll as his personal helper, usually someone from his past he trusted. She thought he must have great faith in Giddings Coltrane despite his regrettable lapse as an unsuccessful train robber.

Tennie had the cowboys put the prisoners in the farthest cell, having been instructed when she began the job to keep the soldiers separated from the usual town drunks. The two privates were noisy and boisterous, and it worried her that they weren't going to calm down. When the cowboys left to go back to the saloon, she could still hear the cursing of the soldiers as she walked into the living quarters.

It was late, but her stepsons were still up. None of them could go to bed early on the weekends. Six eyes were staring at her as they stood listening to the filth filtering down from upstairs. Tennie opened her mouth, but before she could say anything, she heard the sound of the front door being kicked open,

Gid's voice called to her. "Miss Tennie! Miss Tennie! I got a rounder."

They heard sounds of scuffling.

"And he's a contrary ole polecat," Gid said, raising his voice.

Tennie ran to the office. Gid had one elbow

around the neck of a belligerent soldier and the other twisting the soldier's arm behind his back. He squirmed, screaming obscenities at Gid. When he saw Tennie, he spat in front of her, grimacing and hollering in pain when Gid tightened his hold without regard to wrenched muscles and broken bones.

"Follow me," Tennie said. The lanterns hanging from their hooks were already lit, and grabbing the keys, she hurried up the stairs with Gid following, pushing his prisoner relentlessly as he fought with every step.

"Quit that, you ornery cuss," Gid's voice boomed behind her. "Before I bite off a chunk of your ear, dang your old sorry hide."

Tennie hesitated, not knowing what to do. The fighting prisoner coming up behind her galvanized her, and she opened the middle jail cell, unwilling to yell at the other prisoners to get back while she opened the door of their cell to put them together. She had no idea how many she would get in that night, but with only Gid to help her, she didn't risk opening the cell of two soldiers still in the throes of drunken madness.

Gid slammed the prisoner so hard and fast into the cell, he hit the back wall. Tennie shut the door as soon as Gid stepped out, locking it with shaking hands.

"That'll hobble your hooves, you kicking mule," Gid said to the prisoner.

A wave of profanity-laced bile spewed from the prisoner's mouth in response. Tennie ignored it, and Gid hollered at him to shut his trap.

"What has gotten into them?" she asked Gid as they walked down the stairs with curses screaming at their backs. "Three in a row in just a few minutes."

At the bottom of the stairs, Gid stopped to catch his breath. "They done had an Indian attack north of here a few days ago, Miss Tennie. They routed them, but one of the worst ones got away and holed up in a rock house. He killed several men trying to get at him. When night come, they snuck up on the roof and dropped a bag of burning rags soaked in turpentine on his head. He run out, and they riddled him, not realizing that some squaws and children had been in there with him. In the dark in all the confusion, they got killed, too."

"Oh my," Tennie said, looking up the stairs. "I guess they have a reason to be screaming and cursing."

Gid removed his hat and wiped his forehead with the back of his hand. "I reckon they're pushing for somebody to give them a licking over it for sure. I best be getting back, Miss Tennie."

She hesitated, wanting to ask him to bring a helper the next time he came. But to do so would be insinuating he wasn't capable of doing the job Lafayette gave him, a high insult in the West.

Besides, being the town marshal was her job, and she would have to manage the best she could.

"Thank you, Mr. Gid. I will probably see you later."

After he left, Tennie returned to the living quarters. "I guess we better go see if Shorty wants to play dominoes," she told her stepsons as one of the three men upstairs screamed of killing Gid and her.

The first time something like that had happened, the boys had cried and wanted to go back home to their dilapidated ranch. It had become less jarring over time but remained painful to listen to. In a twisted way, all the turmoil kept the boys from running around town after dark—that and Lafayette had ordered them from the very beginning to stay indoors at night in Ring Bit.

As she followed the boys out the door, Tennie muttered, "So much for being a darling marshal."

Looking back as they hurried to the station, a movement in the alley between the jailhouse and the livery caught Tennie's eye. "Go on in. I'll be there in a minute."

Rusty hesitated, but Tennie urged him to take the younger boys inside. When he complied, she crept silently back. Peering around the corner separating the two buildings, she gasped. Two Mexican men were dumping a third man into the alley.

They looked up, saw her, and halted. Three

jaws dropped. Tennie glanced at the body, sure by his dark clothing he was yet another soldier. She looked at the two Mexican men and realized she knew them. They were friends of Poco, a ranger who rode with Wash. They had built an outdoor oven for her behind the jail, encouraged by Poco because she had nursed him after he had been wounded in an Indian skirmish.

They realized she recognized them and began to speak softly in Spanish, making hand signals. Wash could speak fluent Spanish, but Tennie could only recognize a few words. She thought they were trying to tell her they had not killed the man but were just trying to get rid of the body.

"Poco's amigos?" she asked.

"*Sí, sí,*" they agreed.

"Vamoose," she said, waving them away and looking behind her to make sure no one else was watching. When she turned back, they had disappeared.

She knelt down, hesitantly placing her hand over the soldier's heart. The skin already felt cold, and she knew he was beyond help. She rose and hurried back to the station.

"Mrs. Granger!" a shrill voice called to her from across the street.

Tennie froze. She turned and saw Inga Milton striding toward her from across the road.

"I want to speak to you right now. Get over here," Inga said, pointing to the ground.

Reluctantly, Tennie took a few steps, meeting her in the street. "What is it, Mrs. Milton?" she asked, dreading the answer.

"It's that man. That Hawkshaw man. You must speak to him."

"Hawkshaw?" Tennie said, breathing a sigh of relief. "What—"

"Don't act so much like a moron. You must speak to him and order him to stop."

"Stop what?" Tennie asked.

"Stop snooping. Twice I caught him listening. Just now by the window, I saw him. You go find him and tell him you throw him in jail if he persists."

"Snooping?" Tennie remembered Hawkshaw had been listening to Lafayette speaking to her. And he was eavesdropping on the Miltons? It didn't make any sense to her.

"Do I have to tell you everything twice?" Inga said. "Go find that man and tell him you arrest him if he does it again."

Tennie shook her head clear. "I'm not going searching in the dark to find Mr. Hawkshaw this late at night, but I will speak to him in the morning."

"You better. You are sorriest town marshal in world."

"I'll find him tomorrow," Tennie said.

Inga stomped away, and Tennie went back to the station. Rusty and Lucas were waiting for her in the shadows. She said nothing but shooed them inside where Shorty sat at a table in the barren waiting room shuffling dominoes with Badger. A hundred-pound dog with long black and gray fur lay beside Shorty, his tongue lolling out and panting happily, saliva dripping from teeth that looked like a row of ivory bowie knives hanging from his jaw. Bear, like Shorty, never looked for a fight, but he never backed away from one either. The other dogs in town had learned a long time ago to leave him alone. Badger's beloved puppy, Rascal, Bear's son, lay beside him, tired out from following three boys all day. Shorty had high hopes of training Rascal to be like his father.

Shorty looked up and grimaced. "What did that Viking want?"

Tennie explained but said nothing about the dead soldier in the alley. Instead, she joined them at the table and repeated the story about the Indian fight.

Shorty pursed his lips together and glared at her. "A man has to learn to do his duty and leave the outcome to God. That's no reason to go on a bender and tear up everything and everyone in sight."

Tennie realized men like Shorty and Winn Payton had little patience with others who couldn't be as strong as they were. "I don't know why life has to be so stinking hard," she said.

Shorty gave a sharp glance at the boys around

the table. "Don't waste time asking why, Tennie. Save your energy for asking, 'What do I need to do today?' "

"I don't need to do anything tonight except try to beat you at dominoes," she said. "It's tomorrow I'm worried about. Mr. Slick Gun Hawkshaw is going to be laughing in my face. But I'd rather face him than Inga Milton."

"Tennie, were you abused by the matron of that orphanage?" Shorty said. "You'll stand up to any man, but you are terrified of women."

"That's not true," Tennie said. "I got along very well with the other women on the wagon train out here, thank you very much. It's these women in Ring Bit who give me the willies. No use talking about that," she said as she slid dominoes toward herself.

There were nice orphanages and not-so-nice orphanages. Tennie's fell in the latter category. When Ashton Granger had begged her to take care of his boys and not let them be sent to an orphanage, it had been easy to agree. Putting it into practice was another matter.

With her stepsons looking at her, Tennie looked through the opened door and into the street, and watched a group of cowboys riding toward the livery stable. She hoped they had come to Ring Bit to have a little fun—not destroy every saloon in the town and try to rob the bank all on the same night.

"It's just that Inga scares me," she said, turning back to the game. She thought about the dead soldier in the alley, saying a silent prayer for him and hoping the army wouldn't tell his mother he died in a drunken fight over some woman.

Gid came back with yet another intoxicated soldier, along with a helper. Afterward she asked Gid to take the body in the alley to the undertaker's. Gid had been in Ring Bit long enough to know that no explanations were necessary.

It was two a.m. before the brawlers in the jail cells above calmed down enough for Tennie and the boys to sleep.

"It's a good thing Shorty loves to play cards and dominoes," she said as the boys and their puppy hopped onto the beds on the far side of the room.

"It's a good thing Mr. Lafayette asked him if we could go over there when things get noisy here," said Lucas, who always took up for Lafayette.

Tennie agreed and went to her bed in the little alcove behind the curtain, saying her prayers, so thankful their jailhouse days would soon be over.

The next morning, a major arrived with two lieutenants to escort the imprisoned soldiers back to the fort. Tennie had prepared ham and biscuits for the prisoners to take on their journey, and as was her custom, invited the major to eat breakfast with her and the boys. A handsome young

West Point graduate with dark eyes and a clear complexion, far away from home and lonely, he readily agreed. Unlike many of the men of West Texas who refused to speak until they finished eating, the major remained voluble throughout the meal, telling Tennie the latest news from his sweetheart back East.

"I suppose you heard about the Indian attack?" he asked.

Tennie nodded.

"There's no way I can bring my fiancée out here," he blurted. "It's too dangerous."

Tennie forbore pointing out that *she* was living "out here." What happened between the major and his fiancée was their business, not hers.

"I tried to write to her about you, Miss Tennie, but, she . . . she doesn't . . . she can't—"

Tennie nodded, looking away momentarily.

He left his blunder behind and spoke of other failures to comprehend his life in the West. "The people back East have no understanding of what pioneers are facing. They solved their problems with Indians years ago, so they can sit back in their chairs and tell us without a qualm of conscience that the tales of atrocities are greatly exaggerated. If only they could witness what we have seen with our own eyes.

"And yet there are times when I feel so sorry for these people. So sorry that everything they know is vanishing and changing."

Tennie wanted to tell him Shorty's words of the night before, but she realized the major did not want her advice. He wanted her to listen. The boys must have known it, too, because they ate in silence, perhaps remembering their father, who was so traumatized by the war he quit doctoring and became a rancher.

After the major finished eating, and as he was leaving, Tennie did try to comfort him. "Just continue to do your duty with compassion, Major, and do not take everything so hard."

He grasped her hands in his and kissed them in gratitude.

Tennie smiled. "Get along now. I must get ready for another big night."

He smiled. "I fear so, kind lady." He doffed his hat to her, clicked his heels, and left.

"Shorty said you ain't never gonna get rid of these men if you don't quit feeding them," Badger said.

Tennie looked at the dishes on the table and wondered if she could get the boys to do them. It was going to be a battle to get them to do their other chores. "I cannot turn them away, Badger. Besides, the major helps me with the enlisted men and deserves some kindness in return. Now go help your brothers by bringing in some kindling."

"Aw, Miss Tennie!" The cries rose from the table.

"If you want to eat, you have to work. Now hop to it. I have to finish these dishes and go find Mr. Hawkshaw." She wondered when the man would ever leave town.

In a place where every building looked raw and new, the hotel managed to look like an old dump. Lafayette had grandiose plans for a new one to be built in conjunction with the coming railroad, but the railroad plans were stalling and so was the hotel. In the meantime, Tennie stood on the wooden sidewalk, looking at the unpainted, lopsided structure and hoping someone would come out.

A cowboy approached her on the sidewalk, coming from the west. "Ma'am?" he asked, tipping his hat.

Tennie smiled. "I need to speak to Mr. Hawkshaw. I usually see him on the street, but he isn't about today. Would you happen to know if he is in his hotel?"

"No, ma'am," the cowboy replied. "He's over yonder at the café."

Tennie gave him her thanks and turned to leave.

"May I escort you, ma'am?" the young cowboy asked.

"Of course. Thank you," Tennie replied. It was a little early for obnoxious drunks to be lurching from the saloons, but one never knew.

She made small talk about the weather until reaching the café. "Thank you," she said again, dismissing him in the kindest, firmest way. She was engaged to Wash Jones and did not need to be encouraging the attentions of other men. It dawned on her she would not need the major's goodwill much longer either, but she did not consider it encouraging his affections when all she did was listen to him moon over his fiancée.

She peered into the window of the café and spotted Hawkshaw sitting alone with his back to the wall and his face to the door and windows. There wasn't a woman in the crowded café. Seeing a bench near the entrance, she sat down to wait.

Men came out, tipped their hats and said, "Howdy, Miss Tennie."

She smiled, nodding in return, and continued to wait. After fifteen minutes, she resisted the urge to stand up and peek into the window again. Rusty, Lucas, and Badger joined her, hanging on to the posts in front of the café.

"Did you get the wood chopped?" she asked.

"Yes, ma'am," Rusty replied.

"Today is Saturday. It's bread day. Is there enough to bake bread?"

"Yes, ma'am, Miss Tennie," Lucas said.

"And what about Mr. Lafayette's bottles? Have you collected them?"

Badger leaned against her lap, staring up at her with his big round eyes. "We promised to help Lucas later."

"All right," Tennie said, rubbing his dark hair. "When Mr. Hawkshaw comes out here, keep quiet. Don't say a word."

They agreed, watching the men going in and out of the café without comment. Another fifteen minutes went by before Hawkshaw finally exited. The boys stood back but remained draped around the nearest post.

Hawkshaw paused, taking a gold watch from the pocket of his vest. He looked down at it and raised his eyes, giving an uninterested gaze up and down the street. Replacing the watch, he looked at Tennie. "Are you waiting for me, Marshal?"

"Yes," Tennie replied, thinking *only wealthy men carry gold watches.* She motioned to the spot next to her on the bench. "Will you sit down? Most people drop the 'Marshal' and just call me Miss Tennie."

He nodded, removed his hat, and sat down on the far side of the bench. When she had been close to him before, she had been concentrating on his arm with only a lamp for illumination. There on the sidewalk, she could see features made much sharper by daylight. His nose, ears, lips, and eyes were all large. His nose had been broken more than once, she guessed. His eyes were dark like his wavy hair and thick mustache. His skin was coarse like his features. Not an ugly man, but not a refined, handsome one either.

"Mrs. Milton has made a complaint that she has caught you twice by her window, listening to her conversations," Tennie said.

"She's lying," Hawkshaw said. "I listened once at the window and once by the door."

Tennie looked at him and made to rise.

He stopped her. "Wait a minute. Is that all you have to say?"

"Yes," Tennie replied. "I told her I would talk to you and I have."

He made a noise between a snort and a chuckle. "You aren't going to threaten to do anything about it?"

"I already have done something," Tennie said. "Everyone in town knows I have been waiting to speak to you, and they will worm out why from these boys fast enough. Having it known all over town that you are an eavesdropper is enough of a warning and a punishment."

"You are a hard woman, you know that?" Hawkshaw asked, and then he did laugh.

"No, I'm not," Tennie said.

He did not argue about that. "So, it is wrong for me to listen but not for your stepsons?" he asked, pointing his head in their direction.

"What happens to me, happens to them," Tennie said.

"I know something about you, too, Miss Tennie Marshal," Hawkshaw said. "I know you are secretly engaged to a Texas Ranger, and you are

62

afraid if it is known, someone in a jealous fit will shoot him in the back in the dark."

Tennie sat staring at him, not knowing at once how to answer. "If you are speaking of Wash Jones, whoever killed him would have to deal with Lafayette. And if he got to both of them, there would be others to contend with. In case you haven't noticed, both men like to surround themselves with people who are devoted to them."

Hawkshaw stared back at her. "And they are not the only ones who do that."

Tennie didn't understand what he meant. He had no friends; even the dogs left him alone.

"Are you still leaving soon?" she asked.

"Yes. Don't worry. You won't have to hold a gun to my belly and order me on the stage."

"Thank God," Tennie said, rising. "How is your arm? Do you want me to look at it before you go?"

"It's fine," he said, standing up. "Don't antagonize Mrs. Milton. She was once a guard in a Magdalene Laundry in Kentucky."

"I don't know what that is," Tennie said.

"A women's prison, more or less," Hawkshaw said. "It was and is a brutal place." He tipped his hat. "Good day, madam."

"Good-bye," Tennie said and joined her stepsons, glad to have that unpleasant task over with.

CHAPTER 4

Returning to the jailhouse, Tennie went into the kitchen to make her bread. As she kneaded the dough, she thought of Hawkshaw. She had trouble thinking of the right word. *Snoop?* She didn't believe he listened for the sheer thrill of it. And why would anyone want to listen to the Miltons? Rusty said they were just a couple of poor dirt farmers from somewhere around Waco. He detested the chore of going into the shop every morning to fetch their allotted beef and pork, saying Mrs. Milton was mean and bossy, while her husband and brother-in-law were cowed and sneaky. Tennie dreaded telling Inga about speaking to Hawkshaw because Inga would grill her over everything that was said.

Finished kneading, she left the dough for the first rise and went out the back door, expecting to see her outdoor oven still lying smashed on the ground. Corrupt men had destroyed it to discourage her from using the backyard and seeing the herds of stolen cattle and horses that were being sneaked into the corrals next door. They had demolished it and the brush arbor she and the boys had built near it.

To her amazement, the two Mexican men from the previous night were rebuilding the oven with mud and grass. They looked a little sheepish and avoided her eyes.

She said, "*Muchas gracias*," and went back into the jailhouse. She didn't want to tell them they were wasting their efforts; it wouldn't get much use because she would soon be leaving.

She prepared the jail cells for the next round of prisoners, dilly-dallying because she did not want to go out front and face Inga. By the time the dough was ready to be punched down, shaped into loaves to let rise again, she knew she couldn't put it off any longer. She left the dough to rise in pans and went out the front door.

The streets teemed with people, horses, and wagons as she sat under the tin awning on a bench in front of the jailhouse. When it became safer to be in Ring Bit on Saturdays, farmers and ranchers began bringing their wives and children into town without fear. She wondered how long that would last.

Tennie saw Inga come outside. Steeling herself, she stood as Inga crossed the street. "I talked to Mr. Hawkshaw this morning."

"Just forget that," Inga said. "It was mistake."

Tennie's eyes widened, but Inga continued without allowing her to speak. "And tell loudmouth stepsons it was misunderstanding. Only misunderstanding."

"All right," Tennie said, letting out a long and perplexed breath.

Inga didn't give her time to question her but turned and went back into the butcher shop.

Tennie talked about it with the boys at dinner.

"She's crazy," Rusty said, digging into the rice pudding.

"We told Mr. Gid about it," Lucas said. "Now we'll have to go back and tell him Mrs. Milton claimed it was all a mistake."

Either way, the story would be all over Ring Bit by nightfall.

On Monday morning, Rusty had to bang on the door of the butcher shop to rouse one of the Miltons to answer.

"It was Ozzie Milton, the one with the bug eyes. Bod is the one with the flat cheeks," Rusty told Tennie later. "He said Bod and Inga left town yesterday."

"Say 'Mr. Bod' and 'Miss Inga,'" Tennie corrected. "Where did they go? Are they coming back?"

Rusty shrugged. "Mr. Ozzie didn't say. He's lazy, and I don't much like him, but Mr. Bod is the one who really gives me the creeps. He's always asking me questions about you."

"About me?" Tennie said. "Maybe I'm glad they left town. But what are we going to do without a decent butcher? From what you've said, Mr. Ozzie isn't worth much."

"He said Miss Inga and his brother are going

to look for a buyer," Rusty said. "But I don't think that's the reason they left town. Mr. Ozzie kept shifting those buggy eyes around, and he only remembered to throw that in when I was leaving."

Tennie wondered if Hawkshaw had anything to do with their leaving.

When she mentioned as much to Shorty, he said, "Good riddance," peering over his glasses at the butcher shop. "If so, it appears we owe a debt to that cold fish."

By Monday afternoon, the jail cells had been scrubbed down, and the urine- and vomit-soaked blankets had been washed and were drying on the clothesline in the back. It was so hot, Tennie stopped to sit under the shade on a bench outside the jail, fanning herself with an old wanted poster. She knew she had been derelict in her duty by remaining hidden inside the jailhouse, afraid of the Miltons. But with Inga gone, she could once again walk up and down the streets in the early mornings, and sit out front in the afternoons, where just the presence of an eligible woman put men on better behavior, except when it came to fighting just to get noticed.

Shorty came out of the station, looking up and down the street. He saw Tennie sitting on her bench and walked toward her. "Have you introduced yourself to the new blacksmith yet?" he asked when he reached her.

"No, I haven't," Tennie said. "He's been paying Rusty to run errands and do chores for him, though. Right now, Rusty's with Lucas and Badger, I think. Sometimes they help Lucas collect his bottles to sell, and sometimes they don't."

"They're listening to that chinwagger Giddings Coltrane spinning one yarn after another, no doubt." Shorty snorted. "I don't know how Lafayette tolerates that continuous dysentery of the mouth."

"I don't think he does that with Mr. Lafayette," Tennie said. "I think he tells Mr. Gid to pull the drawstring on it, and he does. He has this idea Mr. Lafayette is still his commanding officer."

Shorty, looking down the street, did not answer, and when Tennie followed his gaze, she, too, fell silent. Hawkshaw was riding toward them. The horse was as dark as Hawkshaw's hair, and whereas the man was somewhat coarse, the horse was fine, full of muscle and spirit. Hawkshaw rode him that way, too, as a man who knew good horseflesh.

"He's leaving town," Shorty muttered. "Finally."

"He's headed in the direction of Cat Ridge," Tennie murmured as Hawkshaw gave her an unreadable stare in passing. He lifted his hat and bowed his head slightly in recognition.

Tennie stood up and walked toward him. He reined in the horse and looked down at her.

"Don't tarry too long in Cat Ridge," Tennie

said when she reached him. "They keep the law a different way than we do in Ring Bit."

He said nothing, not even a nod, just looked at her. Tennie had turned and was about to rejoin Shorty when an explosion rocked the buildings and a plume of smoke rose from behind the jailhouse.

No citizens rushed from their homes or businesses to see what was happening.

Hawkshaw merely said, "That's the third time this week, isn't it?"

"Yes," Tennie nodded in vexation. "I've warned them and warned them to be careful. I'm afraid they are going to lose a hand or an eye." She looked at the smoke, and raising her voice, called out, "Are you all right?"

Lucas's high reedy voice called back, "Yes, Miss Tennie!"

She turned back to Hawkshaw, but he was already riding away.

"Tennie!" Shorty bellowed, and she could almost see steam coming out of his ears.

"I know, I know," she cried.

Before she could say anything else, a voice thundered from up the street. "Coltrane!"

Shorty and Tennie exchanged glances. Lafayette rarely let any of the goings-on in Ring Bit bring him out of his saloon, and he seldom lost his temper. Tennie did not want to be in Gid's boots at that moment.

The boys did not come in that evening until supper was waiting on the table. Lucas trailed in last, keeping his head down. Tennie sat down, bowed her head, and asked the blessing.

She looked up across the table and stared at Lucas. "What happened to your eyebrows? And why does the hair along your forehead look like a sheep's been grazing at it?"

Rusty sniggered. "It got blasted off. I told him to stand farther back."

Tennie threw down her napkin. "Okay, that's it. No more blowing up stuff. Why do you want to learn to blow things up anyway? It will be over my dead body before I let you blow up a railroad track to rob a train, I can tell you that right now."

Lucas opened his mouth, but Tennie interrupted him, ranting in the same vein for several minutes. When she finally wound down, she took a big breath of air and clamped her mouth shut, continuing to stare at Lucas.

"We were just learning how to blow up stumps, Miss Tennie," Lucas said. "Farmers will pay us good money to come on their property and get rid of stumps for them."

"You're going to have stumps instead of hands if you aren't careful," she said. "How are you going to make a living with no hands?"

"We told him, Miss Tennie," Badger joined in. "Mr. Gid told him to get back."

"That's right, Miss Tennie," Rusty said. "Mr. Gid said later he knew it wouldn't hurt Lucas, but maybe it would teach him a lesson."

"I'm going to teach Giddings Coltrane a lesson—" Tennie began, but three voices interrupted her.

"Mr. Lafayette already jumped all over him," Lucas said.

"That's right," Rusty added. "Some of the champagne glasses fell off the shelf and broke, and Mr. Lafayette got real mad."

Tennie looked down and rubbed her forehead.

"Don't fuss at Mr. Gid, please, Miss Tennie," Lucas pleaded. "He's just trying to help us learn about things."

"Why in the world do you need to know how to blow things to kingdom come? Answer me that." Tennie shook her head. "No, don't. I don't want to hear it." She felt like crying. "I promised your poor old pa I'd look after you, and I'm doing a sorry job of it."

"You're not that bad, Miss Tennie," Lucas said. "Honest."

Lucas looked so sincere, she burst into laughter. "Thank you, Lucas.

"Oh well," she said as she took a piece of cornbread. "Mr. Hawkshaw left. He probably got so tired of hearing those booms, you could say you blasted him out of Ring Bit. He just better be careful in Cat Ridge. I bet the sheriff wouldn't have any conscience about getting rid of somebody with a shot in the dark."

"That's right, Miss Tennie," Lucas said. "We got shut of him without shooting him in the back. Ain't that right, Miss Tennie?"

"That's right," Tennie agreed. "But don't say *ain't* all the time, and don't talk with your mouth full. Nobody can say that we aren't polite here in Ring Bit."

"That's right," Badger echoed. "That's what Mr. Gid said. He said we are the politenest bunch of wildcats he's ever seen."

"I'm glad he recognizes it," Tennie said.

Tuesday was always the slowest day in town. Soldiers were back at the fort. The cowboys who had jobs were back at the ranches, and outlying ranchers had done their business in town on Saturday. Because the soil was not suited for it, there were very few farmers around Ring Bit, and they, too, had done their trading on Saturday.

When the front door kicked open that night, and Gid hollered he had a prisoner, it took Tennie by surprise. She jumped up and ran to meet him. He was behind the prisoner with his arms under the man's armpits, holding on to his throat.

Tennie gasped. "Don't kill him!"

"I'm not." He loosened his grasp on the other's throat.

The man came alive and grabbed Gid's arm and bit it so hard, blood spurted. Gid knocked him in the back of the head with his forehead and grasped his gullet again. He began to move the prisoner toward the stairs. The man tried to struggle, kicking his feet, but he was having trouble breathing.

Tennie passed them, running to fetch the keys from their nail on the wall. As she raced up the stairs with Gid behind her, a nauseous odor caused her to look back. The prisoner was defecating all the way up the stairs. Gid didn't seem to notice or care. Speechless, Tennie turned and hurried to the second floor, throwing open the door to the first cell she came to. Gid pitched him in, and while the man hit the cot, holding his throat and gasping, Tennie slammed the door and locked it.

She turned to Gid. "What is his problem?"

"Oh. He threatened to kill Colonel Lafayette."

"Kill Mr. Lafayette? Whatever for?"

"Drunks don't need no reason, Miss Tennie. You know that. They get something in their head, and there it is. He probably won't even remember it come tomorrow."

Blood dripped from his arm. "You better let me tend to that arm, Mr. Gid."

"It'll be all right," Gid assured her. "I'll throw some whiskey on it when I get back to the saloon, and it will heal up. I done been bit many a time."

He removed a faded blue bandanna from his neck and wrapped it around his arm.

Tennie didn't have the heart to fuss at Gid for teaching the boys about explosives. Maybe she felt like Gid owed her something, though. She wasn't sure but found herself blurting out a question she wanted to know the answer to. "Are you related to Mr. Lafayette's ex-sister-in-law? The wife of the brother who . . . died?" She didn't want to say, "The one Lafayette accidentally killed." That might not be common knowledge.

"Oh, yes, ma'am. We be kin, but it's so distant we could get married and have normal children without ever having a peck of worry over it," Gid said. "They look down their noses on our side of the family, anyhows. They tries to pretend they don't even know us."

He took a breath, and Tennie started for the stairs.

But he began again. "Yes, ma'am, I told my mama I was coming out here to work for Colonel Lafayette. But I said, 'Mama, don't you be telling nobody where I'll be. You know, they still hold that mess against the Colonel.' She said, 'Don't you worry son. I won't tell none of them highfalutin kin of ours.' But Mama's getting old and forgetful. I sure hated to leave, but I couldn't stand to stay around my brothers when they gets out of the pen."

"They're not out yet?" Tennie said, conscious

of the awful odor rising from the stairway even if Gid wasn't.

"Oh, no, Miss Tennie," Gid said. "They doing more time. The judge let me off easier 'cause all I did was blow up the tracks. I didn't partake of that there train robbery. No, ma'am. I was innocent of that. Nab is at home taking care of my mama. Although Nab is getting on up there in years, too. I didn't want have to listen to my brothers whining about the Yankees and how the war done messed their lives up."

"Mr. Gid," Tennie interjected. "You better go see about that arm. You're dripping blood."

"Oh, yes, ma'am. Sorry about that." He turned and started for the stairs, still talking. "Mama said, 'You gonna look for Pa when you get to Texas?' and I said, 'No, ma'am. Not after the way he done us.'"

Tennie stood at the head of the stairs and watched him as he smashed one boot down in total unconcern on something brown that had fallen from the prisoner's pants. She hesitated, loath to step in urine and filth. Gid realized she wasn't behind him and turned, looking at her. In a few seconds, it dawned on him that she was reluctant to step in what hadn't bothered him a bit. "Hold on there, Miss Tennie. I'll help you."

He stomped back up the stairs, and before she knew what he was doing, he picked her up and slung her over his shoulder like she was a sack of pinto beans. He tromped down the stairs with Tennie bouncing on his shoulder.

"I guess I best go get shamped tomorrow," Gid said. "Colonel Lafayette told me to watch out. Men could grab my hair in a fight, but I told him not to worry. It's so thin, it'd slip right through. But the colonel don't want no shaggy employees in the saloon, so I—" He broke off in midsentence when they were three steps away from the bottom floor, his body tensing.

Tennie twisted around to see what the problem could be.

A young man with a lean body, hard blue eyes, and a scar running downward across both lips stood at the foot of the stairs, holding a Peacemaker pointed at them. Gid stared at him with a stony expression so harsh it frightened Tennie.

She squirmed from Gid's hold. "It's Mr. Lafayette's brother, Mr. Gid," she cried. "Wash! Wash!" She began toward Wash but stopped midway between the two men when she realized the hatred coming from Wash's eyes wasn't just directed at Gid.

She grew solemn. "Wash, this is Giddings Coltrane," she said, making her voice quiet and even. "He works for Lafayette. He brought in a prisoner tonight who . . . had dysentery going up the stairs. Mr. Gid was trying to keep me from having to step in it."

Wash's nostrils flared. He did not put the pistol away, and he and Gid continued to breathe invisible fire in each other's direction.

Wash glanced at Tennie. "We've had this discussion before," he said between gritted teeth.

Tennie felt her temper rise. "If you can't trust me," she exploded, "then get out! Turn around, walk out that door, and never come back in here again!"

Wash wavered, exhaling deeply. Giving up, he put the gun down and replaced it in his holster. "Aw, shucks, Tennie. You know I trust you. Come give me a hug."

Tennie ran, jumping on him, hugging and squeezing him as tight as she could while covering his face with kisses. He smiled, responding in kind. When he put her down, he looked at the boys, who had, of course, witnessed everything.

"You boys go clean those stairs for Miss Tennie." He smiled at Tennie again. "We've got a lot of catching up to do."

To Tennie's surprise, the boys didn't raise a howl. They scurried to the kitchen for hot water and a bucket.

Wash shot a look at Gid. "Much obliged to you."

Although his tone was noncommittal, Tennie nevertheless knew he wasn't enthralled with Gid. Neither was Gid enchanted with him. He

77

removed his hat, nodded, gave them a short good-bye, and left.

Smiling and happy inside, she stared at her weather-beaten, scarred-up Texas Ranger sometimes lawyer and thought Jesus Christ couldn't have looked any better.

CHAPTER 5

Although Tennie believed Ring Bit would be better off with a tougher town marshal, she did feel guilty for chucking the job away at a day's notice. However, Lafayette assured her he would handle everything.

The stage line that ran from Ring Bit to Cat Ridge was part of a main artery running across the nation. The stagecoaches on the line were top notch, the latest in style and comfort. When they left Ring Bit, Tennie sat on one side with Wash and Badger, while Rusty and Lucas sat across from them with Lafayette, the stagecoach rocking back and forth as the wheels turned in the direction of Cat Ridge.

Both Lafayette and Wash had warned her that the various stagecoaches they would have to catch on their way to the capital would not be as comfortable. But she was so happy, she wouldn't have cared if she had to ride in the back of an oxcart to Austin. Lafayette was full of plans for the wedding.

"I don't have a proper dress, though," Tennie said. There hadn't been much available in Ring Bit.

"Don't worry," Lafayette assured her. "The governor's wife has her dressmaker on standby."

As he went on about candlelight and champagne, Tennie let herself be drawn into his design, fantasizing about the beautiful wedding she would have, so happy she was leaving Ring Bit behind and all the worry and slights she'd suffered along with it.

Wash let Lafayette ramble, squeezing Tennie's hand occasionally under the folds of her skirt. When Lafayette paused, Wash asked him about Gid. Lafayette repeated the story about Gid robbing a train and writing him before being released from prison.

"He said he didn't rob the train; he just blew up the tracks," Tennie said.

Lafayette looked amused. "Is that what he told you?"

Tennie nodded. "Yes."

"No, my dear," Lafayette said. "Gid was right in the middle of it with his brothers. He told you that fib because he worries so much about your opinion of him."

"Oh, for goodness sakes," Tennie said. "How did he get released from prison before his brothers did then?"

"I think the judge liked him and realized he had been lured into something he never would have done on his own," Lafayette explained.

The boys were looking at Tennie with anxious eyes. They didn't want her to think badly of Gid.

She smiled. "I reckon he's learned his lesson. I hope."

Wash shook his head in mild disgust but said nothing. Tennie didn't worry about it—they may never see Gid again. Wash hadn't made up his mind if he wanted to go back to a practice in San Antonio, or open one in Ring Bit, or stay with the rangers for a while longer.

Tennie wondered what the boys had brought along in their burlap tote sacks. Badger was still mad that Shorty had insisted he leave Rascal behind for the time being, saying he was too young for such a trip. She hoped Badger hadn't tried to sneak the puppy into one of the bags.

Lafayette asked her what she would prefer for her wedding supper, pheasant or roast beef, and she forgot all about the secret treasures her stepsons were hoarding.

She knew only two people in Cat Ridge, the sheriff and the attorney who had handled Ashton Granger's affairs for her. She liked the attorney and wouldn't mind seeing him, but she decidedly did not want to see the sheriff again. Ever. It was so late, however, when they arrived in Cat Ridge, there was only time to clean up before supper. Wash had gotten her an upstairs room with an adjoining one for the boys. He would stay in a separate room with Lafayette.

"Freshen up and rest for a little while," Wash said. "I'll either come back here to fetch you, or you can come to our room. It's the last door at the end of the hall on the left."

She nodded. He kissed her before smiling playfully, turning her around and telling her to skedaddle.

The boys wanted to go outside and look at the horses, but Tennie told them to hold off until after supper. "Get cleaned up first. And we probably should rest."

She knew they were too wound up to rest. She tried stretching out on the bed but jumped up after five minutes. She knocked on the adjoining door to their room.

Before she could turn the handle, Lucas called out, "Just a minute!" and she waited until he opened the door. He smiled at her. "This station is something else, isn't it? You won't have to cook supper or wash the dishes."

She knew she should be suspicious about what they were up to, but she was too happy to look for trouble and wanted to be with Wash. "Let's go see if Mr. Wash and Mr. Lafayette are ready for supper."

They followed her down the hall, poking one another and giggling. Tennie gave them a look but didn't question them. The door to Wash's room was open, and they could hear the two men in an intense discussion.

Tennie paused, unsure of what to do. The boys stood silent behind her as Wash's strong voice carried out the bedroom door and into the hall where they stood.

"You're serious? You have another group of whores coming in next month?"

"Yes, little brother," came Lafayette's weary reply.

"Fay, you know I'm not a prude," Wash said, "but how in the hell can you stand living like that? Didn't you learn your lesson with that last crazy whore you had living with you?"

"I have to," Lafayette replied. "The men need it."

"Then do like Winn Payton did and go back East and bring them some brides."

Tennie didn't know what she should do. She didn't want to eavesdrop, but she didn't know if she should walk in or go back to her room.

"Look, Wash," Lafayette was saying. "I'm not like you. I don't want to go traipsing after criminals, and I couldn't stand working in a courtroom. The only thing I'm any good at is playing cards. And I either have to roam all over the countryside, or I can have my own establishment and give men like Gid Coltrane jobs to keep them out of prison. And that means providing entertainment."

"It's your life, Lafayette," Wash said. "You do want what you want."

Tennie turned and looked at the boys, shooing them back to their rooms.

Wash came and got them a little later, but Tennie said nothing to him about what she heard.

The boys did not mention it either. At one point, Badger looked like he might say something, but Rusty hushed him with a poke and a hard glance.

It was wonderful to sit down at a table and be waited on by someone else, but Tennie found herself exhausted and troubled. It wasn't very long after they had finished eating that she requested they excuse her.

"Please do, Miss Tennie," Lafayette said with a smile. "You were about to nod off into the soup earlier."

Wash walked with her upstairs, saying he would bring the boys later.

At her door, Tennie turned to him. "Wash, let's get married now. I don't want to go through with all this fuss."

He stared down at her, taking her by the hands.

She squeezed his hands in return. "I know this sounds silly, but at the dining table, I was overcome with the feeling that this trip isn't going to turn out well."

"Tennie, sweetheart," Wash said, choosing his words carefully. "I don't want all the fuss either. But you know we are doing this first and foremost for Lafayette's sake, don't you?"

"If you say so," she nodded.

"I do. He killed our older brother because of a woman. And he thinks that by stepping aside and not trying to court you himself, and by giving us the most magnificent wedding he can come up with, he can somehow atone for his past sins."

"That's foolish," Tennie cried. "You've forgiven him; God has forgiven him."

"I know," Wash said. "But I can't take this away from him."

Tennie gave in, placing her forehead on Wash's chest. "I know. I understand."

Wash lifted her chin and kissed her. "It won't be long, and it will be all over. And then our life together can begin."

The next morning, they boarded a smaller and less comfortable stagecoach as they began their journey south. The dusty dirt was unpleasant, but Tennie had experienced that on the wagon train out West and was prepared for it. When Lafayette began talking about the wedding again, she found she had no enthusiasm for it, but she tried not to let it show. When Badger remarked they hadn't seen Hawkshaw in Cat Ridge, Tennie was grateful for the diversion.

Wash gave him a sharp glance and turned to Tennie. "Hawkshaw?"

"He was some shootist who was in Ring Bit for a while," Tennie said. "But he left before you got back."

"Was he a tall man, dark hair, dark mustache, dressed well but looked a little rough?" Wash asked.

"That's him to a tee," Tennie said.

"What was he doing in Ring Bit?"

"Spying on people," Lucas said. "Miss Tennie had to get on him about it."

Tennie blushed. She had eavesdropped on Wash and Lafayette just the evening before. Before anything else could be said, something outside the window caught Wash's attention.

"There's a rider coming up fast," he said.

Tennie joined him at the window.

Gid, riding a swift horse better than Tennie could have imagined him capable of, caught up with the stage and stopped it. "They's a fire at the Silver Moon, Colonel," he said, breathing heavily and sweating as much as the horse. "Men are trying to put it out, but it sure don't look good."

Lafayette's face blanched. "Drive on to the next stop and hurry," he called out the window to the driver. "We'll get fresh horses at the next stop," he told Gid. He pulled back in, looking at Wash. "You and Tennie go on ahead. Once I find out what the damage is and take care of it, I'll get a fast horse and catch up with you as soon as I can."

Wash nodded as the stage lurched forward, the driver cracking his long whip and hollering, "Giddy-up now!" to his horses.

They weren't far from the next swing station, and the stagecoach had barely stopped when Lafayette leapt out the door and hurried to rent a horse to take him back to Ring Bit.

They all got off the stagecoach at the station

that was little more than a log cabin with a corral. The boys hung on to their tote sacks, but excitedly explored the corrals and looked the horses over. As soon as a fresh team of horses had been hitched, they were called to hop aboard the stage again.

As excited as the boys were to be going on a journey, the rocking motion of the stagecoach soon had their heads nodding.

Tennie, feeling sleepy herself, smiled at them. She turned to Wash and smiled at him also. "Thank you for taking them on, too."

He nodded, taking her hands in his and looking at them before speaking. He rubbed her knuckles lightly with his thumb. "I think it will be for the best, Tennie. Truth is, I'd like to continue being a ranger for a year or two more, and I couldn't bear to leave you all alone for weeks at a time. But with the boys there with you when I have to be gone . . ."

She sat up and stared at him. "I thought you had other aspirations."

"I do. It's just that I want to do what I've been doing a little while longer. I don't want you back in Ring Bit. I have a little house on the outskirts of San Antonio. It's a nice place. It's built sturdy, made of rock. There won't be any Indian problems that far south. You and the boys will be safe there. I have good ranch hands; I have good neighbors.

"You don't mind, do you, Tennie?" he asked. "I'm just not ready to retire into the courtroom entirely."

Tennie shook her head. "No, I don't mind. Not if that's what you want."

He turned her hands over and kissed her palms.

"Wash," she asked, feeling a little embarrassed. "Does this have anything to do with Lafayette? We overheard in the hall what he plans on doing."

Wash leaned back in the seat, looking upward and taking a deep breath. He turned his head and spoke to Tennie in lower tones to keep the boys from awakening. "Yes, maybe. Tennie, those kinds of women are all over the West in every town. Sometimes it's a poor soul who has been abandoned by some man and has nowhere else to turn. But out here, things are different." He looked down at his hands as if trying to decide how to continue.

"Mr. Payton told me the fallen women who land in Ring Bit are the hardened ones who don't want to live any other way," Tennie said. "He said Lafayette would use them until they got diseased or old, and then he would put them on a stagecoach to somewhere else. Is that what you are trying to tell me?"

"Yes," Wash said, nodding. "To be frank, it hurts me to see Lafayette turning himself into some kind of a pimp. And it will not end well for him."

Tennie wasn't sure what *pimp* meant, but she had an idea. "He's right about one thing, though. The money he has made has helped a lot of people, including me."

"I know. But promise me one thing, Tennie. Promise me that if something happens to me, you will not under any circumstances let yourself be drawn into the life Lafayette is living. He would never hurt you intentionally, but sooner or later, you would find yourself burned."

"I promise." Tennie looked across at the boys and saw a flicker of Rusty's eyelids, and she thought one of Lucas's, also. She would be glad, though, if they had overheard. It was best for them to face the truth, too.

The station they spent the night in wasn't as grand as the one in Cat Ridge, but it had a roof and four walls, so Tennie didn't complain. The boys groused a little about the food when the stationmaster was out of hearing, but Wash laughed and told them they were spoilt by Tennie's good vittles. Everyone, including the old stationmaster and his wife, slept on cots in one big room.

The novelty of riding a stagecoach wore off the next day, and the boys began to squabble. Badger cried, saying he was tired of always sitting in the middle. Tennie moved closer to Wash and set Badger by the window next to her. He leaned his head out so far, Tennie had to grab the back of his overalls to pull him back in. It was nice, however, to have an excuse to sit closer to Wash and enjoy being near him.

Wash began telling stories about outlaws and Indian skirmishes, quieting the boys. Tennie talked about the orphanage a little. She described being loaned out to work during parties in mansions as an assistant to the cook, of peeking through doors and watching lovely ladies and gentlemen as they dined at sparkling tables. When she realized she was describing the life Wash lived as a boy, she stumbled over her words and fell silent.

"Tennie," Wash said. "That life was built on the backs of slaves, and I'm not sorry to be shut of it."

She was embarrassed. Embarrassed he had seen the envy she had for those fine homes and elaborate parties, and ashamed of herself for coveting something that wasn't worth it. At first, she was at a loss of what to say.

"I'm glad you feel that way," she said finally, and changed the subject to the wagon train with Winn Payton and the other women who'd become ranch brides to men at Ring Bit. Wash wanted to know more about the Indian attack, and the boys, who had already heard most of it, begged her to repeat it.

When they tired of telling stories, they began to

sing. Wash, used to the desolation of the prairies and cross timbers, had memorized many songs. Badger, who sometimes had the attention span of a gnat, began hanging his head out the window again. Tennie, tired of pulling on him when he leaned too far, was about to ask Wash if he had a rope she could tie to the back of Badger's overalls when the boy suddenly gave a cry.

"It's more riders coming up behind us!"

Wash looked out his window, while Rusty and Lucas stuck their heads out of theirs. Tennie tried to see past Badger, but before she could, Lucas cried, "It's Mr. Poco and Mr. Ben!"

Tennie felt something as heavy as a Clydesdale's horseshoe sink to the bottom of her stomach. Wash called out to the driver to stop the coach.

"What could they want?" she asked, fearful of the answer.

"I don't know; we'll find out," Wash said.

As the stagecoach came to a halt, and before Wash could exit, the two rangers were at the window.

"We need you, Wash," Ben said. "Senator Wetzel's daughter has been kidnapped. We've got a horse for you. Come on!"

Before Tennie could take in what was happening, Wash was pulling a wad of folded bills out of his vest pocket and placing it in her hands. "We're not that far from Waco. You and the boys wait for Lafayette there. I'll try to get word to him as soon as I can."

"Wash—" Tennie began.

He gave her a swift, firm kiss on the lips. "I have to go. I'll see you as soon as I can. Wait for me or Lafayette in Waco."

She nodded, but he didn't see it. He was already climbing out the door. She heard him speak to the driver and the helper who rode shotgun but couldn't understand what he said except to hear the word *Waco* again.

Tennie scooted over to the window and looked out in time to see him jump on a horse and ride away in another direction with his two men. The stagecoach driver did not tarry but cracked his whip and hollered at the horses to giddy-up, calling them by name and urging them to get going.

The stagecoach gave a lurch, and Tennie fell backward in the seat. She stared at the boys, tears coming into her eyes.

Lafayette was always going to be chasing after money, and Wash was always going to be chasing after lawbreakers, and she was always going to be left behind to hold down the fort.

"Don't cry, Miss Tennie," Lucas said.

"He'll be back," Rusty assured her.

She tried to stop her tears. "We must pray for their safety and the safety of the little girl," Tennie said, sniffing. Another sob escaped her throat.

Badger stared at her with solemn eyes. "You always said we can't be depending on nobody but ourselves, Miss Tennie. Don't you believe that anymore?"

She looked at the boys, biting her lower lip.

"It's rule number one, Miss Tennie," Lucas reminded her. "Never expect help from anybody. Be glad when you get it, but don't expect it."

Why did the boys always have to throw back things she said just at the time she didn't want to hear them? She forced herself to stop wallowing in self-pity. "Well, praise the Lord and pass the ammunition. I guess we'll just have to take care of ourselves for a while."

Tennie, grateful for Wash's thoughtfulness in one area anyway, stuffed the roll of money into the front pocket of Badger's overalls, buttoning it securely. "Don't lose that. If we get robbed, maybe the thieves won't think to look there."

In the meantime, Wash was her betrothed, and he had told her to wait in Waco.

"I heard they have an ice cream parlor in Waco," she said.

"What's that?" Rusty asked.

"A place where they sell ice cream," Tennie said.

"What's ice cream?" Badger asked.

"You've never had ice cream?" Tennie asked. "It's frozen cream with sugar. You'll like it."

Besides a possible ice cream parlor, Waco had

saloons galore and a reputation for being a rowdy town. Also known as "Six-Shooter Junction," it was split by the very religious and the very bad, mostly bad. Tennie had the feeling she would once again be the outcast stuck on the outside of the circle.

"Come on. Let's practice our arithmetic while we're trapped in this stagecoach," she said.

The boys let up a howl, but she interrupted them. "What if the people in the ice cream parlor are crooked? Do you want to be taken for a fool?"

Lucas looked at Rusty. "She's right. Remember what Mr. Gid said about measuring powder."

Tennie gave him a sharp look. "What did he say?"

Lucas looked at Rusty, and Rusty answered, coloring a little as he did. "You have to know the right ratio of powder to sulfur and things like that."

Tennie wanted to wring Gid's neck at the moment, but she said in an even voice, "See. Arithmetic is important in a lot of things. Now Badger, what is one times one?" She felt an irrational anger at Gid for coming for Lafayette, and an even stronger anger at Poco Gonzalez-Gonzalez and Ben McNally for dragging Wash away from her. It was stupid to be mad at the messenger when she was really mad at Lafayette and Wash for leaving her alone in a bumpy, dusty stagecoach with three bored boys. But what good did it do to be mad? There was a reason for everything under the sun. Besides, she told herself, she would have hated it if Lafayette was a slothful business owner like the Miltons, or if Wash had a heart of stone and refused to help a little girl in distress. How could she be mad? Except at Gid. She decided she could be mad at Gid over his smoke cans and tree stump explosions. It made her feel better to be angry at him.

CHAPTER 6

They made a short stop at another swing station. The boys picked up sticks to practice sword fighting. Rusty swung too hard and hurt Lucas's arm. Tennie looked at it and decided it wasn't quite as bad as Lucas was making it out to be. Back in the stagecoach and on their way, the boys began to bicker about it again, erupting into a fistfight with Tennie yelling at them to stop while she and Badger tried to stay out of the way.

The driver stopped the stage, and his young shotgun rider hopped down. He stood menacingly at the window, holding gun in hand and spitting his chaw of tobacco onto the ground before speaking.

"You boys don't stop that fighting, y'all be walking the rest of the way to Waco."

"Yes, sir," Rusty said, begrudging the words. Lucas, with a similar pout, repeated the same thing.

After giving the boys another hard look, the guard got back up on his seat, and the stagecoach started again. Tennie shut her eyes, giving in to the rocking motion of the stage. She opened one eye a slit and saw the two boys across from her nodding their heads. Badger was propped up on her side, already asleep.

She wondered about the fire at the saloon. Perhaps Lafayette's new cook had accidentally started it. Or more likely, someone had shot out a coal oil lamp, and it caught Lafayette's lavish drapes on fire. And the poor kidnapped girl. Tennie racked her brain trying to remember what she'd read in the newspapers about the senator. What she recalled didn't make sense. Why would anyone want to kidnap the daughter of an East Texas backwoods politician who had twelve children and probably a mortgage on his farm? They hit a large bump in the road, but she was so sleepy she hardly felt it.

Tennie didn't know how long she slept before becoming aware the stagecoach had stopped again. In her groggy state, all she could think of was that the boys hadn't been fighting, so she didn't know why it had stopped. She sat up and tried to clear her head.

Rusty looked out the window. "Hell's banjo! It's the Miltons."

Tennie looked out the window as two masked men held rifles on the driver and his helper, ordering them to throw down their weapons. "How can you tell?" she whispered.

Rusty lowered his voice. "I'd know those holes he cuts out for his corns in Bod Milton's boots anywhere."

The two men on top of the stagecoach reluctantly threw down their weapons. One of the masked men dismounted and approached the door of the coach, throwing it open.

"You!" he said, pointing to Tennie. "Out!"

Tennie didn't budge, and he reached in, pulling her roughly from the stage. He pointed his gun on the boys. "Get back!"

He shoved Tennie toward his companion. He grabbed Tennie and held on to her arms, but not before she had seen his bulging eyes above his mask and knew he was Ozzie Milton.

"Ride on to Waco!" Bod yelled. "We got men posted on every ridge ready to blast you to hell if you stop this stagecoach before you get to Waco."

"Miss Tennie!" Lucas cried. Behind him, Badger was sobbing.

"Go to Waco," Tennie cried. "Wait for Mr. Lafayette like Wash told you!"

Ozzie shook her and told her to be quiet.

"Move it!" Bod said, pulling a pistol from his belt and firing it in the air.

The stagecoach driver gave an agonized look at Tennie.

"Hurry!" she screamed. She wanted the boys away from the insane Milton family as quickly as possible. The driver popped the reins and the stagecoach sped away, with three boys hanging from the windows, looking back at Tennie with tears streaming down their faces.

The two men waited until the stagecoach was out of sight before shoving Tennie toward a wooded area filled with underbrush.

"What do you want?" Tennie asked.

"Shut up," Bod said.

The fire at the saloon, the wild-goose chase deep into East Texas—how had the indolent and somewhat simpleminded Miltons thought of all that, much less executed it? And for what reason?

They reached a clearing containing a wagon. In the wagon sat Inga Milton, and suddenly, how they planned it made sense.

Pulling the bandannas from their faces, they propelled Tennie toward the wagon while Inga watched.

"Tie her hands first," she said. "Then push her in wagon bed and tie feet."

Tennie's mind raced. Whether to run or fight? Did they intend to kill her? If she fought, she couldn't win. If she ran, she might get a back full of buckshot. Hawkshaw had told her not to antagonize Inga.

"Hello, Inga," she said, forcing herself to be calm.

Inga looked at her and smirked. "Little Mrs. Granger has more courage than perhaps I gave her credit for." She looked at the men. "Hurry up. Stagecoach driver may not believe story about men waiting to shoot if he stop."

Bod twirled Tennie around and seemed to make a show of roughly tying her hands behind her back. He pushed her into the back of the wagon, forcing her down. He took her feet and tied them together. Looking to see if his wife was watching, he ran a quick hand up Tennie's leg when Inga glanced at the direction from whence they'd come. Tennie drew back but said nothing to him.

"What do you want, Inga?" she asked.

Inga looked at her. "Did you search her for money?" she asked the men, ignoring Tennie's question.

Bod felt all over her skirt until he found a pocket. Reaching a grubby hand in, he pulled out the small bag that Tennie had brought along, emptying the contents. A comb, a handkerchief, and a twenty-dollar gold piece.

"That's all you had?" Ozzie said, leaning over the wagon and looking disappointed.

"My fiancé carried all the money I needed," Tennie said. The rest of the money she carried was in her other pocket, but Bod hadn't thought to look there.

"Hurry up. Let's go," Inga said.

Tennie looked at Ozzie. She had bought the comb, a nice one, with her first earnings. "Will you put my comb and handkerchief back in my pocket, please?"

"Leave it," Inga ordered.

Ozzie cringed, but as soon as Inga turned her back to take up the reins, he scooped up the comb and handkerchief and shoved them back into Tennie's pocket, squeezing her thigh as he did and making her wish she hadn't asked.

Ozzie and Bod got back on their horses as

Inga urged the mule forward. Tennie lay still in the wagon bed trying to assimilate what was happening. She thought she better try to raise up enough to see where they were going. Wriggling herself against the side of the wagon, she managed to push her shoulders upward.

Inga hit her across the neck with a whip. "Get down," she ordered.

Tennie slumped back down. She looked up at the cloudless sky and found the sun. They were heading west. They left the clearing, and on either side of the bumpy road they were following, trees leaned over the wagon and brushed against its sides. Finding a large crack in the boards of the wagon bed, Tennie looked downward. If they were following a road, it was one that had been little used in the past. Grass brushed against the bottom of the wagon bed.

They didn't appear concerned about covering their tracks. From the sounds of the horses and the wagon, Tennie thought Bod and Ozzie were riding in front. If they spoke, she couldn't hear it above the creaking of the wagon. They entered a shallow and sandy stream, heading north, following it wordlessly for a distance, the wagon jarring every time they hit a hole. Inga urged the mule onto a flat bank, and they followed what could only be described as a wide Indian trail for some time before Inga again drove the mule into the creek. The creek bed was smoother this time, but they only followed it a short time before coming out on the opposite bank. The mule again picked up a trail heading south, and Tennie realized they were backtracking to the road.

They began heading west again, the grassy road dotted with occasional weeping tree limbs giving way to harder, rockier ground before the wagon came to a sudden halt.

Inga stepped down. "Get her out," she ordered.

Bod and Ozzie came around to the back of the wagon bed. Bod took Tennie by the feet and jerked her out, shoving her upright.

Tennie had to fight to keep down the rising hysteria that threatened to set her off screaming. She swallowed hard and looked around.

They were at an old cabin that sat two or three feet off the ground on top of precarious stumps. The whole structure looked like it might blow over if they all exhaled at once. A nearby barn, oddly enough, was in slightly better condition.

Tennie swallowed again, determined to keep her temper. "However did you find this place?"

"It's the Milton old home place," Ozzie said with pride.

"Shut up, Ozzie," Bod said.

That was how they knew to get to it in a circuitous way, Tennie realized. Looking at what was little more than a shack, she could imagine a pack of lazy hounds lolling in the cool under the porch and skunks wallowing their way underneath a house with no underpinning. She thought she saw a shadow flitter by the window. Someone else was in the house. Perhaps it was an older Milton, the father or the mother.

Inga ordered her untied. While Bod worked on the ropes on her hands, touching her buttocks as covertly as he could, Tennie tried to sway away every time he did. Ozzie untied the rope at her feet, running his hands around her ankles. Careful not to express anger, she looked down and kicked at his hand slightly, letting him know she did not appreciate his caresses. He drew back with the ropes.

She was a pawn used to punish her and Wash Jones for killing their brother. She looked at Inga's hard face and realized it was more than that. It had to be money, and the person with money was Lafayette.

Bod shoved her toward the house. Tennie tried to take in her surroundings as she stumbled toward it. They were in a clearing on a wooded ridge. It would be difficult, but not impossible, for anyone to get to the cabin without being seen.

She staggered up the steep steps of the porch as Bod shoved her again. He was purposely provoking her, but she was determined not to let an emotional outburst give them an even stronger upper hand.

"Bod, you ain't got to be so rough with her," Ozzie said.

Inga told him to shut up. She flung the batten door open and stood aside. Tennie felt immeasurably safer outside and did not want to enter. Bod's hand on her back gave her no choice.

She took in an old table, decrepit chairs, a rude kitchen containing empty shelves and a row of meager supplies. Bod pushed her farther into the room, and a noise like a heavy breath escaping caught her attention. She looked behind her.

Next to the door stood a tall man with dark hair, his mustached lips curved in a faint and mocking smile. "Mrs. Granger," Hawkshaw said, with an insolent tip of his hat.

"You!" Tennie said, breathing fire. She remembered her resolve and clamped her mouth shut, but she couldn't stop the flaring of her nostrils or the flashes of uncontrolled hatred coming from her eyes. She took a breath and forced her voice to come out evenly. "Would you mind telling me what is going on?"

Hawkshaw moved a step closer. "Yes, I mind. Put her in the storeroom."

Ozzie, who had heretofore been the nicer of the brothers, decided to show how tough he was in front of Hawkshaw by jerking Tennie toward another batten door. He pushed it open and shoved her roughly into a small room that was the size of a large pantry minus the shelves.

With the door shut, the light in the room dimmed. When Tennie's eyes adjusted, she saw slits of light coming from between the boards of the door. The room was so ill-built, there was light coming in from cracks in the outside walls. The floor was rotting and had holes in it. Someone had recently swept it out, but there wasn't a bucket, a plate, a can, or a scrap of anything else in the empty storage room.

Tennie could hear voices coming from the other side of the door. "I don't have a waste bucket," she cried.

"Use corner!" Inga yelled.

"What about water?" Tennie said.

"Tomorrow! Shut up!" Inga said, her voice so rough, Tennie slumped to the floor. The jailor had become the jailed. She placed her back to the door and heaved in and out, trying to keep from screaming or melting into tears.

Surely the stage drivers would go to the law. What was happening with her stepsons? The stagecoach drivers would see that they had a place to stay, but what then? If Lafayette tarried long, they would get into trouble. They would run through Waco so wild, Rusty, and possibly Lucas, would be thrown into jail while Badger would be shipped off to an orphanage. She shut her eyes, and after much effort, forced herself to pray inside her head in clear, concise words instead of a jumble of fear.

She leaned against the door, shutting her eyes again while she tried to concentrate on what those idiot Miltons were telling that traitor Hawkshaw. She wanted to strangle him. But it went back to rule number two, never expect gratitude for anything. She forced herself to forget Hawkshaw and listen.

"He'll pay up, won't he?" Ozzie asked.

"Of course, he will," Inga said. "She is to be his sister-in-law."

"I think we should have asked for more money," Bod said.

"No," Inga replied. "We ask only for what he can get easily. If he has to get loan, too many people get involved."

"That's right," Ozzie said. "The sooner we get this over with the better."

"Have you forgotten about Creed?" Bod thundered. "They shot him."

Creed? Tennie wondered. *Who was Creed? Oh. That must have been Maggot Milton's real first name.*

"I ain't forgot," Ozzie said. "But Creed, he weren't no good to us nohow."

"Shut up!" Bod roared. "He was our brother."

"So, we get even the best way," Inga said. "Money in exchange for life of no-good brother."

It sounded like she was putting food on the table and Tennie could hear chairs scraping against the floor. Hawkshaw had remained silent, but she believed he was still there. Whether it was because of Inga's realism, or the desire to satisfy hunger, they stopped arguing.

Tears came to Tennie's eyes, and she brushed them away. She wasn't hungry, but her throat was parched, and she was covered in road dust. The light coming in through the cracks began to fade. Night was falling. The murmur of voices receded, and Tennie fell asleep against the door, praying over and over that God would get her out. She was so near hysteria, she couldn't finish the rest of the sentence, only that she wanted out.

Sometime in the middle of the night, she thought she was at the jailhouse, and Rascal, Badger's puppy, was pestering her. "Get away, Rascal," she murmured, and pushed him away. The second time it happened, she pushed harder and something small hit the wall. She awoke with a start, jumped up and screamed. "Mice! Oh God, there's mice in here," she said, turning to pound on the door. She kicked at what she couldn't see with her shoes, cringing when they made contact.

"What is it?" Inga demanded.

"There are mice in here!" Tennie said, and she began to cry. Where there were mice, there were snakes, and she had already almost died once from a snakebite. This time, there wouldn't be anyone to save her.

Inga laughed. "So little Mrs. Granger isn't so brave after all," she taunted.

Tennie beat the door with her fists as hard as she could, wishing it was Inga's head. Inga only laughed louder. Tennie quit pounding on the door and turned around, leaning against it. She spent the rest of the night standing up, intermittingly kicking whether she felt mice running across her shoes or not.

At dawn, she opened her eyes. The mice were gone. She slumped to the floor, unable to stop herself from lying down.

Later, she felt someone push at the door behind her.

"Get away from door," Inga ordered.

Tennie scurried to the far wall, crouching in the corner. If they wanted to shove her around, they would have to pick her up first.

Inga opened the door and set a bucket inside. Along with it, she placed two pieces of cornbread on the floor. Sneering, she left the storeroom, but before the door shut, Tennie could see Bod and Ozzie staring at her, with Hawkshaw watching in the background.

Tennie went to the bucket. It contained two inches of water. She put her hand in and drank thirstily. The cornbread looked edible, but she wasn't hungry. She debated on what to do with it, but decided she'd better eat it to keep her strength up. Besides, she didn't want to leave anything to attract more mice.

In a little while, Inga again ordered her to back up, opened the door, and removed the bucket. Tennie was glad she had swallowed most of the water. She realized she wasn't going to get any more that day. Again, she saw the three men watching her before the door shut. The look in Bod and Ozzie's eyes sent shivers down her spine. It said they wanted more than just a quick feel of her buttocks and legs.

That afternoon, they began drinking. Tennie could hear them talking and ordering one another to pass the jug. She was fairly sure Inga was drinking with them, but she wasn't sure about Hawkshaw. Occasionally, he said a word or two that proved he was still there. How had he gotten mixed up with the Miltons? He must have overheard them discussing their plans and demanded to be in on it. Hadn't he already shown a grudge toward Lafayette? Tennie wanted to talk to him but realized it would be hopeless even if she could.

Toward late afternoon, the voices began to slur even more, making it hard for Tennie to understand what they were saying. The door rattled, and Tennie again went into the corner.

Inga opened it, her eyes red and bleary. "The men, they want you out here," she said, slurring her words.

Tennie refused to move, staring at Inga who was beginning to rock back and forth.

"I will watch. I like to watch." Inga gave Tennie a frightful smile. "But maybe I will join in. Would you like that, little Mrs. Granger? The men and the woman kissing and licking your breasts? No?"

Hawkshaw walked forward, putting his hand on the door. "If we harm her, Lafayette, if he lives, and her fiancé, and her fiancé's friends, and all the single men in Ring Bit will hunt us down like dogs and kill us. If we let her go unscathed, they will pay the money, be glad they got her back, and eventually forget about us."

Inga stared at him. "You are right, Mr. Hawkshaw," she slurred. "You are always right. Perhaps, you would enjoy something with me. Yes?"

Hawkshaw shut the door, locking Tennie in, and she breathed a sigh of relief. She did not hear Hawkshaw's reply. Bod said he had another jug somewhere, and after that, they began to argue over how they would spend the money. Hawkshaw abstained.

Tennie knew she was going to have to escape. She couldn't wait for Lafayette to pay the money or to rescue her or anything else. She had to get out. Staring at the rotten floor, she put her hand in the biggest hole and pulled. The boards squeaked. She stopped. They were drinking so heavily, she thought they would soon pass out. At least, she hoped Hawkshaw was drinking as heavily as the Miltons were.

She went back to her place by the door, peeking through cracks into the room. The Milton men were leaning back in chairs. Inga was sitting nearby in a rocker. Her head lolled to one side, but her eyes were still open. Tennie moved from crack to crack, but she couldn't see Hawkshaw.

Bod sat up with a crash. "We don't need him," he hollered, pulling a gun out from his belt. "And we don't need his preaching about what to do with that gal, either."

Inga sat up, but her head wobbled. "We can get money and kill her."

"By God! We can do what we want to with her right now and kill her any time we take a notion." Bod slapped the table.

"Hawkshaw . . ." Ozzie began.

"I ain't afeared of him," Bod roared.

"A broom handle," Inga said, ignoring the men and gazing at something unseen. "A broom handle brings exquisite torture."

Ozzie sat, looking befuddled. He breathed heavily and said to no one in particular, "We ought to have brung one of those young'uns back with us. I like little boys, too."

"Shut up, Ozzie," Bod said.

The front door opened and Hawkshaw entered, carrying a jug in his left hand.

"Did you find that other jug?" Bod asked.

Hawkshaw handed it to him in silence. He took a chair and placed it in front of the door, where he could easily watch the others. Turning the chair around, he sat down, resting one arm on the chair's back and leaving his gun hand free.

Bod lifted the jug to his mouth with one hand, his other still holding on to a pistol.

"Reckon they is out looking for us right now?" Ozzie said.

"No," Inga said. "Remember note said not to search or we kill her."

Ozzie looked perplexed. "Note?"

The jug paused in Bod's hand. He stared at his brother. "Ozzie, you handed the stagecoach driver the note, didn't you?"

Ozzie shook his head, looking as if he was about to cry. "I thought you were going to give him the note."

Inga, shocked into sobriety, jumped from her chair like a panther. "You did not give them ransom note?" she shrieked. "You fools! You utter, utter fools!"

She began to pace back and forth across the room in anger, clutching a small pistol by her side. The Milton men shrank from her wrath, but she had ceased to pay attention to them. Hawkshaw said nothing but kept his eyes on her.

She came to a sudden stop. "I will take note to Waco at daylight and see Lafayette gets it. They will not suspect woman. I will say in note to give me the money or the girl dies if I do not return with it."

"But what if they follow you?" Bod ventured, looking more in fear of Inga at the moment than Lafayette and his men.

Inga turned to Hawkshaw. "Hawkshaw will accompany me. He will kill anyone who tries to follow us."

The three Miltons stared at Hawkshaw. He met their gaze with cool eyes and responded. "Sounds like a plan to me."

"Good." Inga stood staring at the floor, opening and closing her free hand in a fist. "They won't find us. They will search robbers' nests east, not west where there is no one." She turned and looked with scorn at her husband and brother-in-law. "Drink up, you fools. Tomorrow, I will be the one to do the job. You will stay home and sleep like dogs."

Tennie felt so sick, she was afraid she might throw up. It would not surprise her if Inga ordered the men to kill her after she and Hawkshaw left. Inga was no longer drunk, but sitting in her rocker, alert and brooding. They did not light a lamp, and darkness was creeping in, covering the cracks so Tennie couldn't see. Wiping tears from her eyes, she scooted over, taking off one of her shoes, ready to tackle any mice and use it as a lever to raise the boards as soon as she thought they were sleeping. As she looked over her shoulder at the door, Hawkshaw's duplicity stabbed her.

She turned back around and waited, watching the hole in the floor with her shoe poised and ready.

CHAPTER 7

Just as the increasing darkness would soon make it impossible to see anything, Tennie spied something black with a curved head begin to rise slowly through the hole in the floor. She gasped, raising her hand to smack what she was sure was a snake as hard as she could with her shoe. A split second before she did, she realized what was rising up through the hole in the floor was a crowbar, not a snake. She grabbed it, set it aside, and looked through the hole.

"Lucas!" she whispered, catching sight of pale skin and dark hair underneath the house.

He drew close to the hole. "We're going to set the barn on fire. When they go outside to look, use the crowbar to pull up the floor. We have horses on the east side of the house, hidden in the trees."

Tennie knew she should order them to get away, to go home, the Miltons were too dangerous, but they wouldn't listen anyway, so all she whispered was, "All right. Be careful." She had no doubt whatsoever that her stepsons could set a barn on fire if they set their minds to it. And if anyone was capable of squirming out of trouble, they were.

She heard the sound of a chair crashing and

the floor on the other side of her door shaking. Racing to the side of it with the crowbar raised, Tennie stood ready to bash in anybody's head who opened the door.

Instead, Inga called out, "What is noise?"

Tennie saw a chance and took it. "I'm hitting mice with my shoe." Maybe if they did hear her pulling up boards, they would think she was warding off rodents.

Inga sniggered. "You cannot imagine how happy the thought makes me." She walked away from the door, telling the men, "I go to bed. Don't bother me."

Tennie lowered the crowbar and breathed a sigh of relief. Sitting down, she hurriedly put her shoe back on, ready to tear a hole in the floor the minute the fire was discovered and praying harder than a soldier caught in the crosshairs of an enemy's rifle.

For five minutes, she sat waiting with every muscle tense. With Inga supposedly in bed, the Milton men and Hawkshaw said little. She knew by the occasional word spoken or the scraping of a chair they were still there.

Just when she thought her nerves would snap from waiting, the front legs of Bod's chair hit the floor. "Do you smell smoke? Ozzie! Wake your sorry ass up! I think something's burning."

"Huh?" Ozzie said, sounding groggy.

Someone walked to the front door, and it made

a creaking sound as it opened. She heard boots on the floor and someone running back into the room.

"Ozzie! The barn is on fire! Inga, wake up! The barn is burning like a son of a gun."

Tennie heard Inga's groans, the sounds of rushing feet, a thud as if a chair hit the floor, and the sounds of more boots on the front porch.

She began to attack the floor with the crowbar. The nails squeaked loudly as they were pulled up, and the screeching of wood as it broke sounded like thunder in the night, but no one rushed into the room to stop her.

When she believed the hole big enough to shimmy through, she thought of the mice, snakes, scorpions, and other creepy things living under the house, took a deep breath, clutched her crowbar tighter, and put her feet into the hole. Her dress caught on the jagged wood, and she had to let go of the crowbar. With fumbling fingers, she ripped at her dress, making her way down.

Rusty, Lucas, and Badger were waiting for her at the wall's edge.

"Come on, Miss Tennie." Lucas bent down, urging her as he and the other boys shot fearful glances in the direction of the barn.

Tennie left the crowbar and crawled as fast as she could to where they stood. Rusty reached in, pulled her out, and helped her stand. While

Tennie gave the barn a backward glance, he began pulling her in the opposite direction, clutching a rifle in his other hand.

They had made a fine job of the fire. While it roared, Bod and Ozzie jumped up and down, screaming expletives. With little time to look at the blaze for more than a few seconds, Tennie and the boys pounded across the hard, rocky ground, plunging into taller grass toward a mott of trees, the smell of smoke filling their nostrils and the sound of furious cursing filling their ears. In the dark, she could see the shadowy outlines of horses hidden among the oaks.

They reached the horses, Rusty still grasping Tennie's hand. He stopped so short, Lucas and Badger ran into Tennie's back before they could halt. Rusty stood staring, breathing heavily, and Tennie followed his gaze.

Hawkshaw stood waiting for them.

Tennie gasped but realized he was standing next to his saddled horse, holding the reins in his hand.

"Saddle up if you want to get out of here," he said.

Tennie could feel Rusty's hesitation. She looked at the other three horses. "Which one's mine?" she asked Rusty.

Rusty guided her toward a horse with a saddle. He turned to Lucas and Badger, helping them onto a bareback pony.

As Tennie put her foot in the stirrup of a dried, cracked leather saddle made sometime before the War of 1812, Hawkshaw murmured, "Don't try to ride sidesaddle."

Tennie nodded and straddled the horse, grateful for the dark so Hawkshaw couldn't see clearly how clumsily she got on and how high her skirt got hitched doing so. With lives at stake, it seemed a stupid thing to be thinking.

Hawkshaw eased smoothly into his saddle, reining the horse toward Rusty. With one swift motion, he took the rifle from Rusty's hand. "I don't aim on getting shot in the back." He turned to Tennie. "Follow me."

With Hawkshaw winding them through underbrush and thick stands of trees, Tennie followed behind Lucas and Badger while Rusty insisted on bringing up the rear. Hawkshaw seemed to know exactly where he was going, and they followed blindly, crashing through brush and brambles they could scarcely see. Tree branches ripped at Tennie's skirt, but they were traveling so rapidly, she dared not take the time to tuck the folds around her legs. She wondered if the boys, who did not know the evil the Miltons were capable of, thought it was more of an exhilarating adventure.

Barely able to tell direction by the position of the sun during the day, Tennie was completely baffled riding on the back of a swiftly moving horse on a cloudy night. She had no idea if they were heading toward Waco or not.

After what seemed like hours of riding and becoming so tired she could hardly stay upright in the saddle, they approached a clearing. She could make out the shapes of another smaller shack and a corral. They had arrived at the spot Hawkshaw had been leading them to.

He slowed the horses to a walk and took his time approaching the corral. At the gate, he got down and signaled for them to dismount. When Tennie's foot hit the ground, she almost fell the rest of the way. Hawkshaw led his horse into the corral, and the Grangers followed, too numb to think. There was a water trough half full, and after getting their tack removed, the horses went straight to it. Tennie went to one side and seriously considered hopping in, she felt so dirty.

"There's a well and bucket over yonder," Hawkshaw said. She didn't know if he sounded gruff because he was mad or just exhausted.

Tennie nodded, leaving the horses. Lucas and Badger went outside the corral and plopped to the ground. After drawing the bucket, Tennie drank thirstily before proceeding to wipe the dirt from her the best she could.

Hawkshaw and Rusty approached, Hawkshaw throwing the almost empty bucket into the well and pulling it up again. He drank his fill and handed the bucket to Rusty. Lucas and Badger had fallen asleep on the ground.

Hawkshaw didn't speak, but Tennie spoke her mind. "I'm not sleeping in that shack if there are mice and snakes in there."

"The snakes that are outside would have no problem curling up under that pretty dress of yours tonight, but there weren't any in the shack when I was here last."

Her tired brain tried to make sense of what was going on. "So, you planned to bring us here? Are we still kidnapped?"

"You state everything as baldly as a skinned onion, Mrs. Granger," Hawkshaw said. "You are free to go whenever you want, but since the Milton men will soon be after us, you might want to stick together."

"Would you stop with the Mrs. Granger? I was Miss Tennie in Ring Bit, and I'm Miss Tennie out here." She looked down at her ragged dress and mourned. "And my dress is no longer pretty. It's so torn up, it will have to go in the rag pile when this is over."

She went to the sleeping boys and picked up Badger, while Rusty helped Lucas up then followed Hawkshaw into the small shelter. Rusty commented that it looked like a cowboy's line shack. Hawkshaw did not respond.

Tennie thought of something else. "You said the Milton men would be following us," she said to

Hawkshaw as he stood at the door. "What about Inga?"

"I slit her throat before leaving," he said, opening the door.

Tennie stood still. After a pause, she spoke. "No use being a hypocrite by saying I'm sorry. Why didn't you shoot the men?"

"In the back? I don't operate that way. I killed her because she figured I was the one who set the fire and was about to shoot me with that little derringer she carried."

"But you were ready with a knife so it wouldn't make noise," Tennie said, surprising herself for being able to put two and two together when she was so tired.

"I won't say I'm sorry she tried to kill me," Hawkshaw said. "Maybe a comment I made about how fast a little coal oil can start a fire in a haystack made her think I had something to do with it. Now, are you going to come inside or not?"

"Yes. I'm much obliged." For what, she wasn't sure. The questions she had for him and the boys would have to wait.

Hawkshaw left them in the shack, saying he would stay outside on guard.

He roused them at predawn, throwing a rope to Rusty. "Tie the horses so they can get their fill of grass. I brought a little feed they can have later."

121

He tossed each person a stick of jerky, ordering Lucas and Badger to catch half a dozen rabbits. "I heard you kids bragging in town about killing rabbits. As soon as it gets light enough to see, prove it. I'll gather some wood and get a fire going."

"I'll help," Tennie said.

"No, you won't," Hawkshaw said. "Because if you see a snake, you'll start screaming."

"Well," Tennie said, trying to maintain her dignity, "if you'd been bitten by a rattler before, you'd be scared of it happening again, too."

"Get off your high horse," Hawkshaw said. "When daylight comes, you can start filling canteens. We've only got two. I didn't know I was going to be rescuing an army of midgets."

"In town, you hardly said two words to people," Tennie said, following Hawkshaw out the door. "Out here, you just keep bossing like you're some kind of general or something."

He didn't bother to answer, and she sat down to wait for daylight on a stump someone had placed next to the wall of the shack.

Later, as they sat crouched around a campfire, eating roasted rabbit, Hawkshaw glanced at the horses grazing in tall grass.

"Where'd you get the crowbaits?" he asked Rusty.

"We rented them from a livery in Waco," Rusty said. "We went with the stagecoach drivers to the sheriff to report what had happened. He brushed me off when I tried to tell him I thought it was the Miltons."

"He said it had to be outlaws hiding out east of Waco," Lucas said, tossing a bone over his shoulder and reaching to take another rabbit off the makeshift spit. "He said nobody lived out this way except a few poor whites and some Mexicans."

"The posse wouldn't let us ride with them, anyway," Rusty said, "so we decided to rent some horses on our own. These are all the liveryman would let us have. And it was only when the stagecoach driver vouched we were friends with Mr. Lafayette that he would let us take these."

"He tried to cheat us, Miss Tennie." Badger looked up. "Just like you said somebody might. Rusty counted out his change, and he made him give us the right money back."

"Well, I declare," Tennie said. "I was just flapping my jaws, and it really did happen."

"How'd you find us?" Hawkshaw demanded.

Rusty flushed. "We remembered that the Miltons came from around Waco, so we started asking around if they had a place here." He grew bold and blurted, "When I get older, I'm going to become a Texas Ranger."

Hawkshaw grunted. "Looks to me like you've already got a head start over some of them. Did anybody think to wire Lafayette?"

Rusty and Lucas looked at one another.

"We didn't," Lucas admitted. "We were in too big of a hurry. But the stagecoach drivers will see that it gets back to him."

Tennie finished eating, throwing the bones in tall grass for some other critter to feed on. Things weren't adding up right, but she had no desire for a confrontation at the moment.

The boys had made short work of the rabbits. Hawkshaw rose and began kicking dirt on the campfire. "I didn't have anything to do with the fire at the saloon or the telegram saying the little girl was kidnapped," he said, not looking at Tennie.

"But why didn't you stop them?" she asked.

He shrugged. "I didn't think they would really go through with it. When I crossed paths with them outside of Waco, I realized what was happening and thought it best to go along with them."

He didn't wait for her to ask more questions but ordered the boys to get the horses ready. Taking two sticks, Tennie fished out a lump of coal from under the dirt and threw it into the water bucket, where it sizzled and hissed. As soon as it cooled, she fished it out and began rubbing it over her teeth.

"What are you doing?" Hawkshaw demanded. "Come on. We need to hurry."

Tennie stood and threw her lump of charcoal down. Despite Hawkshaw's demands to make haste, he took his time with the horses, brushing them down and picking up hooves, poking around the frogs with a knife to rid them of dirt and pebbles. He ordered them to drink plenty of well water; reminding them again they only had two canteens.

"But it shouldn't take that long to get to Waco," Tennie said. "I had to ride in the back of that wagon several hours, but not all day."

Hawkshaw, who was bent over to examine a horseshoe, raised his head and stared at Tennie. "We can't escape in that direction. Too easy of a target. We'll have to zigzag our way back, and I don't know how long it is going to take."

Tennie, seeing the troubled look on Rusty's face, shrugged her shoulders. Rusty nodded in return but kept his eyes on Hawkshaw. While Tennie waited, she watched the horizon for signs of Bod and Ozzie Milton.

It was dread of Bod and Ozzie that made her get astride her swayback horse without complaint, even though the insides of her thighs were sore from the previous night's ride.

As the morning wore on, they did as Hawkshaw said, alternately riding west and south. He refused to return the rifle Rusty had bought in Waco, even though he admonished him to keep his eyes open and watch their rear. At first, Tennie examined every tree and bush for fear a Milton would pop out at her.

They stopped only to let the horses rest, or coming across a shallow stream, to drink. In the late afternoon, Tennie's discomfort became so acute, she no longer bothered to examine her surroundings.

None of the boys gave trouble; their fear and suspicion of Hawkshaw was too great. They rode without complaint, but when Lucas and Badger slipped from the back of their pony because they had fallen asleep, Tennie begged Hawkshaw to stop.

"There's probably a creek on the other side of this rise," he said. "Keep moving."

When Hawkshaw turned back around, Rusty shot a dirty look at his backside and helped his brothers back on their pony.

Correct in Hawkshaw's prediction, a creek flowed lazily at the bottom of a gently rolling slope. Tennie was so grateful, she almost cried. She slid from the horse, hanging on to the saddle horn until she could trust her legs.

After watering the horses, she removed her hairpins, wrapping them in her handkerchief. "Mr. Hawkshaw, would you happen to have a bar of shaving soap in your saddlebag that you would be so kind to loan me?"

He started to say no, but looking at her bedraggled appearance, he must have felt sorry for her, because he lifted the flap of his saddlebag, drawing out a round bar of soap and tossing it to her. She missed the catch but picked it up eagerly from the grass. Going slightly upstream, she walked into the water, and after diving under and thoroughly wetting every hair and cotton cloth on her, began to scrub. The boys jumped in the water, too. Not to bathe, but to swim.

Hawkshaw, after hobbling the horses in tall grass, walked downstream and out of sight. In a little while, they heard a rifle shot. A stab of fear went through Tennie, and she hurried out of the creek. It frightened the boys, too, and they got out beside her, standing and waiting, looking in the direction from whence Hawkshaw left.

He walked back carrying a beaver that must have weighed thirty pounds.

"Are we going to eat that?" Badger asked.

"Yes," Hawkshaw said. "Unhobble the horses."

"Why? We're not camping here?" Tennie asked.

"No. Up the hill. Too many mosquitoes when the sun goes down."

Tennie, dripping water from head to toe, put her shoes back on. She went to Hawkshaw's saddle and slipped the soap back into his saddlebag without looking inside. But she refused to get back on her horse and began leading him up the hill.

Rusty joined her while Hawkshaw and the other two boys rode ahead.

"He's leading us deeper and deeper west," Rusty said.

Tennie turned to stare at him. "What do you mean? We were zigzagging south, too."

"I know," Rusty said, keeping his eyes on Hawkshaw. "But each time he led us farther west than he did south. A lot farther." He paused then spoke again in a low voice. "And another thing. He keeps telling us to hurry, but he's really taking his sweet time out here."

That part Tennie knew. She stared at Hawkshaw's back. "He's up to something. I believe that. But if push were to come to shove, I think he'd be on our side."

"I hope so," Rusty said.

Hawkshaw halted on a flattened ridge in a small mott of oaks, announcing they would make camp there. They hobbled the horses again so they could graze, Hawkshaw saying they would tie the horses to a string line later.

They watched as he dressed the beaver with a sure hand and a sharp knife, as if he had killed and eaten beaver every day of his life.

"I've never had beaver," Tennie said, and the three boys echoed the same thought.

Hawkshaw didn't respond; it was as if they weren't there. He threw the pelt aside, and Tennie rubbed her hand gingerly over the soft fur.

She lifted it up and kissed it. "Thank you, Mr. Beaver, for feeding us," she said softly, and the boys laughed at her. She smiled in return.

"Fetch some firewood," Hawkshaw growled, as if their laughter angered him.

While the beaver roasted, the boys decided to

128

build a lean-to using fallen trees. Tennie didn't want to get dirty again, so she sat near the campfire, combing her hair and watching the boys work. It wasn't the first lean-to they had ever built; they had made many on the ranch before their father died. Nevertheless, they had a lively discussion over which two trees to build it between and how to place the logs. Badger wasn't much help but hung around the older boys as they worked.

Hawkshaw stared at them as if he wanted to say something, but he would turn his head away without speaking. He refused to look at Tennie and did not invite conversation.

When the boys finished the lean-to, he spoke, saying the words like he was pulling a bent nail from a board. "You gonna sleep under that?"

"Sure," Rusty replied.

Hawkshaw paused. "Cut some branches from that cedar tree yonder to lay on. It'll keep you off the ground and repel some of the bugs." He immediately turned away from them and concentrated on the roasting beaver.

Tennie didn't understand him. The longer they were around him, the less communicative he became, as if he didn't want to get too close to them. She kept her thoughts to herself, however, and enjoyed the succulent beaver tail he cut into pieces for them.

When darkness came, Tennie and the boys

prepared to curl up under the lean-to, while Hawkshaw sat off to the side by himself, resting against a tree. The cedar boughs were scratchy and had a strong odor, and since Hawkshaw's back was to them, Tennie shimmied out of one of her petticoats, spreading it over the branches. They lay in a row, Tennie, Badger, Lucas, and Rusty.

All four were almost instantly asleep.

CHAPTER 8

Tennie heard rapid gunfire and thought at first she was dreaming. She bolted upright, breathing heavily. Looking in the direction of Hawkshaw, she saw his shadow scramble behind a tree, fire and smoke spitting from his pistol as he fired in rapid succession in the direction of the creek.

A hail of return fire met his, looking like gigantic fireflies flashing in the night. Tennie heard the whistling of bullets and the splintering of the tree next to her. She grabbed Badger and pushed him as far back into the lean-to as she could, shoving Lucas in at Badger's feet. The barrage of gunfire deafened her ears, and she threw herself across Badger while Rusty did the same thing with Lucas, their backs to the creek and facing as far into the lean-to as they could squeeze. Bullets landing in the ground spewed dirt on their feet and backsides.

A sudden scream from the direction of the creek stopped the volley of fire. A voice somewhere else shouted, "Ozzie! You hit? Ozzie!"

"It's the Miltons," Rusty said. Lucas tried to squirm out, but Rusty thrust him backwards. Badger began to cry.

"Shhh," Tennie said, whispering in his ear. "Be brave."

Not a sound could be heard but the return of katydids singing in the trees and bullfrogs jumping into the creek until Bod Milton began to shout, "Hawkshaw!"

When he got no response, he hollered again, "Hawkshaw, answer me."

Tennie raised her head enough to see Hawkshaw pick up a rock and throw it far from him. It landed with a thud loud enough for Bod to hear.

"Listen, Hawkshaw. You give the girl to me. You can take those boys and hightail it out of here, but I want that there girl."

Tennie again wiggled up to look through the cracks between the logs. She saw Hawkshaw's shadow holding a rifle in his hand and creeping away from the tree. A stab of fear slashed through her heart so intense it left her breathless. Was Hawkshaw abandoning them?

"She ain't gonna be nothing but trouble for you," Bod said. "Lafayette will hunt you down and shoot you just like he would me. You might as well let me have her. Hawk—"

The sound of rifle fire interrupted him. While the rifle sang out repeatedly, Bod fired back, and Tennie's head went down, trying to shield Badger the best she could.

As quickly as it started, it ended, and the katydids ruled the night once more. The four of them huddled under the lean-to, each hearing the other's breath going in and out. A minute passed. Rusty jumped up and began a running crouch in Hawkshaw's direction.

"Stop!" Tennie cried in a whisper, but the boy never slowed.

They heard a single rifle shot. After that, nothing.

"Rusty!" Lucas cried, jumping to his feet.

Tennie grabbed him to keep him from running to his brother.

"It's all right," Rusty called. "It's over."

They scrambled from the lean-to and raced to Rusty and Hawkshaw. Hawkshaw was hunched over, clutching his thigh. Rusty stood in front of him, holding the rifle and looking down at the dead body of Bod Milton.

"I guess I owe you one, kid," Hawkshaw said, and collapsed against the tree.

"He's been shot!" Tennie hurried to him, grasping his arm. "Help me get him away from here," she told the boys. "Let's move him under the lean-to."

With their help, Hawkshaw was able to limp to their lean-to. Tennie guided him to her petticoat and helped him down. His leg was already swollen bigger than his waist. Without hesitation, Tennie shimmied out of another of her petticoats. Handing it to Rusty, she asked him to cut a strip from it to wrap around Hawkshaw's leg, then he helped her apply the tourniquet.

Tennie ran her hand as gently as she could over Hawkshaw's thigh, front and back. "I don't think the bullet hit an artery. It's not bleeding enough for that. But the bullet's still in there. Do you think it hit a bone?"

He gave a slight shrug, closing his eyes in pain.

Tennie didn't know what to do and prayed for guidance, pressing her lips together as she stared into the shadows at his face. She was stuck out who knew where with three children and a wounded man. She shut her eyes, and an image of the women on the wagon train praying over a sick girl came into her mind. One of the younger ones had come down with fever. Besides doing everything physically possible they could, the older ones had laid their hands on her forehead and prayed. She'd passed away regardless, but she died a peaceful death.

Tennie did not want Hawkshaw to die. She needed him to live. "Put your hands on his head and pray," she instructed the boys. Placing her own hand on Hawkshaw's forehead, she prayed out loud. "Jesus, heal this man."

"What are you doing?" Hawkshaw shouted weakly, brushing their hands aside. "I don't believe in that shit."

"Well, we do," Tennie yelled back. "And we need you alive, so you just shut up."

She turned to Lucas. "Would you bring me a canteen?"

He nodded and fetched the canteen. She had Rusty cut off another piece of petticoat, and she wet it, using it to wipe the dirt and sweat from Hawkshaw's face.

"Stop," he said, but he didn't yell.

She desisted. "Do you want some water?"

He nodded. "Yes." He took the canteen from her hand, drank, and handed it back to her. "In the morning, you're going to have to take the bullet out. I can't risk riding or moving around too much. It could travel and sever the artery."

"Mr. Hawkshaw," Tennie said, dismayed. "I've never removed a bullet."

"You watched doctors removing bullets from soldiers when you were a kid, didn't you? During the war?"

"Yes, but, that was years ago," she cried.

Rusty swallowed hard. "Miss Tennie, we watched our pa do it lots of times. We'll help you."

Tennie looked up at Rusty. He'd had to kill a man that night, and tomorrow, he was going to have to help her operate on another. She shook her head and looked away. Boys had to grow up fast in Texas, and she guessed girls did, too. Growing up during a bloody war, being sent to an orphanage later had been hard, but it had only begun to prepare her for what her life in Texas was like.

"Try to rest," she told Hawkshaw. "When it gets daylight, we'll do what we can."

135

They spent a restless night, on edge because of the events and not totally sure Ozzie was dead. Hawkshaw didn't like them too near him. Tennie slept on the far side of the lean-to while the boys slept outside it. In the early morning hours, Hawkshaw became feverish. The boys brought more water from the creek.

"We found Ozzie," Lucas said. "He won't be bothering anybody anymore."

Tennie nodded. She asked them to gather all the knives and lay them on the ground for her to examine. Unbeknown to her, they had scavenged all of Bod's and Ozzie's possessions.

"Is this your twenty-dollar gold piece, Miss Tennie?" Rusty said, holding it out.

"Probably," Tennie said. "Will you keep it for now? I don't want to touch it until after it's been in your possession for a while. I don't want anything that was in Bod's or Ozzie's pockets to rub off on me."

"I'll put it in my tote bag," Rusty said.

"You boys still have those?" Tennie asked idly while she looked over the blades.

"Their guns aren't much use," Rusty said. "Just some old homemade conversion models."

"They worked well enough on Mr. Hawkshaw last night," Tennie said.

Hawkshaw stirred. "Get on with it."

"All right," Tennie said, knowing she was putting off the inevitable. "We don't have

136

anything to dig the bullet out with, and I'm afraid to use a knife for fear of nicking the artery."

"What if I whittled down two sticks that were kind of narrow and flat like forceps?" Rusty asked.

"We can try it," Tennie said. "But hurry." She pointed to two knives with the skinniest blades. "Lucas, which one of these is the sharpest?"

"This one," he said, picking one up. "Let me hone it against a piece of leather."

Tennie nodded. "Find a piece for Mr. Hawkshaw to bite down on, too."

Lucas went to one of the saddles they had claimed from the Miltons, cutting off a flap from the fender. While he ran the blade up and down the leather, Tennie washed her hands. After he finished sharpening the knife, she washed it with Hawkshaw's shaving soap. Going to him, she knelt down and ripped his pants to expose the wound. Looking at the round, bloody, gaping hole made her feel almost faint. She washed the wound with soapy water, praying God would guide her hands. Rusty came back with the sticks.

Tennie shut her eyes and thought of the times she had witnessed surgery in the war. Who had been the best surgeon? An image of a kindly gray-haired doctor rose in her mind. In her mother's opinion, he'd been the best in the hospital. Tennie pictured him removing a bullet from the leg of a wounded soldier, replaying in her mind everything she had seen him do.

"I'm going to have to probe for the bullet with my fingers, Mr. Hawkshaw, so be prepared for pain. Lucas, put that piece of leather between Mr. Hawkshaw's teeth, please."

He did as she asked, and she turned to Rusty.

"Stay up there by his shoulders, so you can watch me and hold him down if you have to. Lucas, you and Badger hold his legs down."

"Lay over his legs, like Pa had you do before," Rusty said.

When everyone was in position, Tennie reached her fingers for the wound. Closing her eyes, she let her fingers probe the path of the bullet as the good doctor had done. Hawkshaw flinched but showed remarkable fortitude in what had to be agonizing pain.

"I found it," she said. "Rusty, the knife."

Rusty handed her the knife, and she held it over the wound. Tears sprang from her eyes, and she brushed them away with her arm. "I'm going to cut into the wound so I can get to the bullet," she told Hawkshaw.

She looked up at Rusty, and he nodded. "Pa always cut bold. That way it only hurt them once."

It had been the same with the army doctor. He believed in going in as quickly as possible and getting out as fast as he could.

"For Mr. Hawkshaw," she muttered under her breath, and made a swift clean cut as close to the bullet as she dared get. "Quick, the sticks."

138

They were clumsy to use, and Hawkshaw bit down hard on the leather, but Tennie was able to wriggle the bullet out. She threw it beside his leg and exhaled.

"There will be a piece of cloth in there from his pants, Miss Tennie," Lucas said. "Don't you remember, Rusty? Pa always said to get that out, too."

"He's right," Rusty said.

That meant she had to go fishing inside the wound again. Tennie nodded, using the sticks to scrape inside the wound as gently as she could until she wormed out the piece of blood-soaked black fabric. She looked up and saw Hawkshaw had passed out.

After washing the wound again, she bound it with more strips of her petticoats. When done, she threw herself down on the ground beside Hawkshaw and stared at the logs of the lean-to above her, breathing so heavily she thought her heart would burst.

Hawkshaw stirred, and she removed the piece of leather from his mouth.

"You finished?" he asked.

"Yes," Tennie said. "Close your eyes and rest."

She got up and walked to the cold embers of the previous night's campfire where the boys were standing. "Thank you."

They nodded and Rusty spoke. "Bod and Ozzie are beginning to swell, Miss Tennie. We ought to do something with the bodies. There's a gully we can push them into and try to throw rocks over the bodies to cover them."

Tennie nodded. "Can you boys handle that by yourself?"

All three nodded. "Yes, ma'am. We'll do it."

"Be sure and wash your hands when you are done." She sat down heavily, not knowing what their next course of action should be. She didn't have a pot to even boil water in.

They ate some of what remained of the beaver. It was smoky, tough, and chewy, but it would probably last them another day or two, it was so dried out like jerky. As they sat in front of the lean-to, Tennie looked up and thought she saw a flitter of white behind the distant trees.

She wondered if she had really seen it, or if it had been a trick of the sun. She saw another, disappearing almost instantly. "Boys, I think somebody is watching us."

Rusty and Lucas went for the guns.

Tennie said, "Steady now. It may be someone friendly who is just wondering who we are. Or it may be nothing at all."

Whoever or whatever it was disappeared and did not show again. Hawkshaw was feverish, and Tennie spent most of the afternoon worrying over him and trying to get him to drink water, even though he disliked her hovering over him and couldn't stand for her to touch him. The boys tended the horses, which included Ozzie's old flea-bitten gray mare that looked like she had given birth to one mule too many. Bod must have traded his along the way for a young Appaloosa with a dark body and a blanket of white spots on its backside.

Tennie had heard of the breed, but never seen one up close. They were generally scorned as being an Indian horse, and she supposed Bod had made a good trade for it. Rusty made fun of the horse, but Lucas and Badger were enchanted with it. Rusty declared its eyes were probably so weak, it would never make much of a night horse, but Lucas replied that Bod had ridden it to find them, hadn't he?

The horse appeared gentle and allowed the two younger boys to climb all over him, riding him back and forth to the creek. Maybe he was grateful the boys had led him out of the barn before they set it on fire.

"Don't y'all be going out of sight," Tennie admonished. "We don't know who might be hiding out there in the brush."

She went back to Hawkshaw, sinking on her knees beside him. The swelling in his leg had gone down some, but she knew all was not going well.

Darkness came, and Tennie spent a fitful night. Hawkshaw would moan in his sleep, and because she knew he had a high tolerance for pain, she realized it had to be terrible. She would go to his side, but only so close. If he awakened, her nearness would upset him.

By morning, even the boys knew things were bad. Tennie prayed for a miracle. Tired of beaver, they turned again to rabbit. The boys would come upon a rabbit hiding in the bushes and drop a knife on it to kill it without wasting bullets or having gunfire draw attention to them. Tennie was tired of beaver and rabbit but didn't complain. When they had finished eating, they sat staring at one another, wondering what to do.

Lucas stood up. "Miss Tennie, look!"

Tennie turned, jumping up to see the strangest sight she thought her eyes had ever beheld. A Catholic priest in a long brown robe was leading a group of Mexican men clad in white cotton clothes and large sombreros straight for them. The other boys stood, drawn together in apprehension while they waited for the men to approach. When she could make out the features of the priest, Tennie got another surprise. He was taller than the others, slender and handsome with curly dark hair and large kind eyes—a man in his thirties.

He smiled and bowed, speaking to them in English with a Spanish accent. "Please do not be afraid. I am Father Francisco, and this is my little flock. We heard gunfire and thought we might be of assistance."

Tennie exchanged glances with the boys before speaking. "We were followed and attacked night before last. The men who attacked us are dead, but the man riding with us was wounded."

The priest nodded. "We would be honored if you would accept the hospitality of our village. It is across the creek and in the hills just a few miles away."

Tennie looked at Hawkshaw. "We took out the bullet yesterday morning. I'm afraid to move him."

"We will be gentle," the priest said, his voice persuasive.

Tennie again exchanged glances with the boys. They were as unsure as she was.

"There is a woman in the village who is a good healer," the priest said. "Her methods are perhaps peculiar, but they are effective."

Tennie nodded, wondering how an obviously educated priest landed in such an unlikely place. But they needed to do something for Hawkshaw, for she feared he would die otherwise. "We would be honored to be your guests, Father."

In Texas, Tennie had had very little contact with Mexicans, besides Poco, the ranger who rode with Wash. Mr. Payton had told her most Texans would be friendly to a man right up until the time they decided to kill him and warned her of the importance of being polite in her dealings with them, explaining that was especially true of those of Mexican descent. "They set quite a store on that, Tennie," he'd said.

Father Francisco turned to the men and said a few words in Spanish. They removed some of the long poles from the lean-to, being careful not to disturb Hawkshaw.

Tennie went to him, kneeling down to explain. "There is a group of Mexican men led by a Spanish priest who are going to take us to their village not far from here. Supposedly, there is a woman there who has a reputation for being a healer."

Hawkshaw looked at her as if he thought he might be having a dream. He shut his eyes and leaned his head back. Tennie stayed with him while the men built an H-framed travois out of sinew and horse blankets. They hitched it behind the Appaloosa, while Rusty and Lucas saddled the other horses and readied them for their move. On the spur of the moment, Tennie ripped a piece of her dress and tied it to one of the remaining lean-to poles.

"Will you walk beside me for a while?" the priest asked when they were ready to leave.

"Yes, of course. I'm sorry I did not introduce us." She proceeded to do so, walking beside the priest while holding the reins of her horse.

"The man is not your husband?" Father

144

Francisco asked. His query was so gentle and without judgment, Tennie found herself telling him the entire story. He listened, nodding his head.

It embarrassed her that she had talked so freely to someone she'd just met. To change the subject, she asked if he had been at the village long.

"No, only a few weeks. I usually come once a year, stay for a week, and then leave for another parish to marry, to christen, to pray over the dead."

"But you are staying longer this time?" Tennie asked.

"Yes," he replied. "We must walk downstream to a shallower spot in the creek to cross."

Tennie nodded, following the Appaloosa and hoping Hawkshaw was not being bounced around too much. They came upon a section where the creek ran over a sandbar, and the water was only a few inches deep. Tennie waited on the bank while the men crossed with Hawkshaw. She looked down at her dress, the skirt so shredded and torn by brambles and limbs as to be almost useless. Without hesitation, she ripped another piece from it and tied it to a tree limb. Surely Lafayette, and Wash when he learned of it, would come looking for them.

Getting on her horse, she rode it into the water, crossing the creek to the other side and dismounting to talk to the priest about the village he was taking them to.

"The people are very superstitious," he said. "Do not stare at their children for too long. If the child sickens, they will think you gave it the evil eye. If you say a child has pretty hair, you must also touch it; otherwise, you will have cursed the child. But, you do not speak Spanish, and I am the only one who speaks English, so that will not be a problem."

"Oh dear," Tennie said. "I hope I do not step on any toes."

The priest smiled gently. "Do not worry, Mrs. Granger. You do not realize it, but we have been praying for a miracle, and you and your stepsons and friend are the answer to our prayers."

"Pardon?" Tennie thought she misunderstood.

He smiled again. "You are tired. Get back on your horse and ride for a while. I will explain everything to you later."

She stared at him for a moment. "First, I must check on my patient." She left the priest and quickened her steps until she had reached Hawkshaw's side. She touched his forehead—his face was burning. "Will you stop, please?" she asked the men.

They gave her looks of incomprehension until the priest called out a word in Spanish to them. They halted immediately.

Tennie fetched the canteen from Rusty and took it to Hawkshaw. Leaning beside him, she held out the canteen. "Mr. Hawkshaw, you have a fever.

You need to drink as much water as you can."

He was conscious enough to put the canteen to his lips with her help. Water dribbled from the sides of his mouth as he swallowed. After a few sips, he pushed the canteen away, turning his head.

Tennie stood back and nodded for the men to go on. She hoped the woman healer was as good as the priest claimed.

She got back on her horse. Following the travois, her horse took advantage of their sluggish gait to go even slower. On either side of the path they were following toward the rocky hills grew fields of corn, squash, and beans. Little boys in sombreros were watching a few cows and donkeys graze in a meadow. The ground hardened as they approached the hills, and soon they were traveling through a narrow gap between tall rocky outcroppings. Looking up, Tennie could see small boys peering down at them, as if sentinels of a fort. She halted the horse until the priest caught up with her.

"Father Francisco, is this the only way into your village?"

"Yes, it is the only way. It is at the end of a box canyon."

"We will probably have men searching for us. Will they be allowed to come in? They won't be shot at, will they?"

"My people have no weapons other than a few

bows and arrows," the priest said. "They would probably be unable to stop them in any case."

Ahead of her, the going was not as smooth for the travois, and Hawkshaw groaned. After winding through the boulders, they came upon a clearing dotted with trees. Ahead lay a row of cottages made of mud and straw bricks, each with a thatched roof. There were lean-tos against some of the houses, walls and roofs made of more bundled straw. In the center of the village stood a small church made of mud bricks and stucco, its gabled windows covered in wooden shutters. A cross stood in a cutout spot in the arched gabled front.

Chickens clucked in the street, and small children ran to hide behind their mother's skirts when they saw them approach. The men, children, and some of the women were dressed in coarse white cotton fabric, the men in pants and long-sleeved shirts. The women wore long-sleeved dresses, some of them in faded calico covered in white aprons, their long dark hair tied in braids on each side of the dark heads. Brown eyes stared in solemn curiosity.

Tennie followed the priest's advice, trying to look friendly without resting her eyes on anyone too long.

The men stopped the Appaloosa in front of a small house, the thatched roof extending out to create a shady retreat in front. The dirt around the house looked swept and packed down. A woman taller than the others came to the door and stood. Tennie dismounted and waited beside Hawkshaw for the priest to introduce them to one of the most beautiful women she had ever seen.

CHAPTER 9

"Mrs. Granger, this is Lupe," Father Francisco said. "She is the healer I spoke of. You and your party will be her guests while you are here."

With large dark eyes, full dark lips, and a voluptuous figure, the woman looked mature, perhaps in her late thirties.

Tennie nodded her head and said, "*Gracias*." She turned to the priest. "It is one of the few Spanish words I know."

He spoke a few words to Lupe, and she nodded, motioning for the men to take Hawkshaw inside.

The men carried him into the house with Tennie following. At the threshold, she turned to look at her stepsons. They would be on their own. "Take care of the horses, please," she requested and followed the men inside.

The room was clean with a homemade bed by one window. A crude table and chairs were in the middle of the room. On the other side were shelves and more beds. The men took Hawkshaw to the bed beside the window, the cornhusk mattress rustling as they placed him on a brightly patterned blanket.

The priest lay his hand on Tennie's arm, warning her to stay back. She obeyed his command and watched as Lupe looked Hawkshaw over. To

Tennie's surprise, she saw scars covering Lupe's hands. She tried not to stare, however, as Lupe spoke a few words in Spanish, and the men removed Hawkshaw's boots and gun belt, placing them under the bed along with his hat.

Lupe sat down on a small chair beside Hawkshaw and began removing the bandages from his leg, grimacing at the sight and shooting Tennie a look of disgust. Tennie got the distinct impression she would never be very high on Lupe's list.

Lupe removed a downturned glass from a saucer sitting on the little table beside the bed. On the saucer lay a white slab covered in black and green flecks. She took it and placed it over Hawkshaw's pestilent red wound.

"Is that moldy bread?" Tennie asked the priest in surprise.

"Yes," he replied. "We are lucky she had been using it to treat another patient, and your friend did not have to wait for the bread to mold."

Tennie kept her mouth shut, watching as Lupe took wide green leaves and placed them over the moldy bread. Hawkshaw was conscious but submitted to her ministrations without comment. She wrapped the wound and its poultice of bread and leaves with a clean cotton cloth.

Lupe rose, and Tennie thought she had finished, but she called for something else. A woman came forward and placed an egg in her hand. The house had become so packed with bystanders, the air became thick and claustrophobic as they pressed closer, watching with eager faces.

Taking the egg, Lupe rubbed it over Hawkshaw's body. When she was finished with the front, two men came forward and rolled him over, where Lupe proceeded to rub the egg over his backside. To Tennie's surprise, he again submitted to this without agitation. When Lupe finished, the men rolled Hawkshaw onto his back.

Cracking the egg on the rim of a glass of water on the table, Lupe slipped it from its shell carefully into the water. An older woman, her wrinkled hands looking at least a hundred years old, handed her a piece of straw. Lupe fashioned the straw into the shape of a cross. As she moved toward the glass, it seemed the crowd drew closer and held their breath. Lupe placed the straw gently on top of the yolk. It immediately broke, and thrilled gasps escaped the people, the old woman grinning toothlessly while Lupe looked around the room in triumph.

Tennie regarded the priest with questioning eyes. In English, he whispered as if out of respect for their beliefs. "Someone put the evil eye on your friend, but the immediate breaking of the yolk means that Lupe has taken the evil away."

Tennie raised a brow, and the priest shrugged. She said nothing more, however.

The priest spoke to the crowd of people, and they began filing out of the house.

Tennie followed him to the door. "I must see about cooking something for my stepsons and Mr. Hawkshaw to eat, Father Francisco."

"No, no, while you are here, the women of the village will feed you. Go back into the house, lie on one of the beds, and rest, Mrs. Granger. You look exhausted. Your stepsons will be fine."

When Tennie walked back into the house, she went to Hawkshaw first. He lay on his back staring at the ceiling and did not turn to look at her when she approached. Lupe stood beside him like a guard, eyeing Tennie with an inscrutable face.

"Mr. Hawkshaw, I'm going to lie down across the room. If you need me, all you have to do is call out."

He nodded his head without taking his eyes from the ceiling, and Tennie let him be. She lay down on a bed directly across the room from him, lying on her side in order to watch him. Lupe carefully placed her chair so she obstructed Tennie's view. Tennie did not protest, but shut her eyes, falling asleep and dreaming of fish.

When Tennie opened her eyes, Lupe was gone, and the priest was by Hawkshaw's side. He had moved the chair, enabling Tennie to see Hawkshaw. Father Francisco was leaning over him, talking earnestly. He placed a compassionate hand upon Hawkshaw's shoulder. Hawkshaw stiffened, his fist clenched. The priest withdrew, saying a few more words of comfort before leaving.

As Tennie rose and went to Hawkshaw, Lupe entered the house. When she saw Tennie she went to the shelves and busied herself there.

"Are you all right?" Tennie said, leaning over Hawkshaw.

He nodded, and Tennie asked if she could get anything for him. Behind her, Lupe made a loud noise. Tennie turned to look, and Lupe shot her an angry glare.

Turning to Hawkshaw, Tennie said, "I'm going to check on the boys." She went outside and stood under the shade of the thatched straw. Lucas and Badger, seeing her, ran to her side.

"This is a great place, Miss Tennie," Lucas said. "They know how to catch catfish just by reaching up under the bank with their hands. They are teaching us how to do it."

Tennie grimaced. "I guess we'll never go hungry as long as we are near catfish then. Are you and Rusty taking care of the horses?"

"Yes, ma'am," Lucas said. "All the girls are following Rusty around, giggling at him. The father already had to have a talk with him about it."

"Good heavens," Tennie said. "Don't cause any trouble. We are guests in this village."

"Oh, we're not causing trouble," Lucas said, putting on his best angelic face. He turned to race back down the street to join a gaggle of little boys, Badger following.

Tennie hoped Hawkshaw would hurry up and get well before her stepsons did something that would get them run out of town.

Tennie could not understand the attitude of the villagers. They regarded them with awe and esteem, all except Lupe, who fawned over Hawkshaw, ignored the boys, and treated Tennie as an unwanted interloper. She had no idea what she had done to earn Lupe's disrespect or the reverence of the rest of the people.

The children were shy and sweet, unwilling at first to approach her as she sat under the arbor. Cautiously, they crept toward her, first standing near. The girls were fascinated with the lace she had carefully sewn on one of her petticoats—plainly visible through the rips in her dress. They gathered enough courage to touch it, pulling their hands back swiftly. Tennie smiled at them, realizing they had never seen lace before. When she'd understood how much Wash Jones loved her and wanted to marry her, she had bought the lace and sewn it on her best petticoat. It had been intended for his eyes only, but it was being admired by girls who loved beautiful things.

The little boys wanted to get close to her. She had been without a hat so long, the sun had streaked her hair blond, mesmerizing the children. One small brave lad with large brown eyes gingerly touched her hair. He smiled at her, and she smiled back.

She stayed under the arbor in front of Lupe's house, sitting on a bench with the children and observing the rest of the village. As she watched the women busy in a communal outdoor kitchen in the center of the town, she thought they looked like those in any other place. But as she continued to gaze, it came to her that there were no young men. Only little boys and old men. Father Francisco was the only man in his age-group she saw. When she thought about it, she realized the men who had brought them to the village had all been hardened, but gray-haired. There weren't even any teenage boys. Where were all the men?

That evening, before dark, Lupe brought in a bowl of food for Hawkshaw and one for Tennie, placing it sulkily on the table.

Tennie, who felt guilty for not helping despite the father's instruction not to, said, "*Gracias*," and sat down at the table while Lupe took Hawkshaw his, glancing over her shoulder at Tennie.

Tennie picked up a spoon made of cane and took a bite. Tears sprang into her eyes. The food was screaming hot with spice, but rather than spit it out, she swallowed it whole, causing her to choke. Lupe, watching her, smirked. Hawkshaw

156

was having no trouble eating his. Tennie picked up her bowl and went outside to join her three stepsons as they crouched on haunches, eating with the other children under the arbor.

She watched them gobbling their food. "That's not too hot for you?"

"No, ma'am," Rusty said, while Lucas shook his head.

"I can't eat mine; it's too hot," Tennie said.

Rusty finished his bowl, and she offered him hers. He took one bite and spit it on the ground. "Whoa!"

"Let me try; let me try." Lucas took the bowl and spooned a bite into his mouth. Spitting it out, he made an awful grimace. The other children took turns, trying food from the bowl, making a contest of who was able to swallow and who had to spit theirs out.

One of the older women saw what they were doing and came over to question the children in a sharp voice. They explained, and the next thing Tennie knew, the woman had grabbed the bowl and entered Lupe's house, screaming rapid sentences at her. The old woman stomped back to her pots, returning with a fresh bowl for Tennie.

"*Gracias*," Tennie said once again, trying to keep from crying. She took a bite of the much milder and savory food, saying *gracias* twice more.

As it began to grow dark, she reluctantly

157

reentered the house. Lupe ignored her. Tennie went to Hawkshaw. Whatever faults Lupe had, being a bad nurse was not one of them. Hawkshaw's leg already looked better. His color was coming back, his breathing deeper and more even. Tennie didn't hold much faith in the egg treatment. It had been too much of a dog-and-pony show, but she was intrigued by the use of the moldy bread.

Tennie left Hawkshaw and went to bed. The house filled with people—people all over the beds, lying on the floor, curled in the corners. Tennie felt guilty she had a bed all to herself. The boys slept outside under the arbor, using horse blankets to lie on. As Tennie lay listening to the sounds of breathing and muttering around her, she brushed tears from her eyes. She wanted Hawkshaw to be well so they could leave and go to Waco. She wanted Wash or Lafayette to come get them. She wanted Lupe to stop hating her. She wanted the cornhusks in her mattress to stop making so much noise when she turned.

Although Hawkshaw appeared on the mend in the morning, he still refused to look at Tennie, staring at the ceiling when she spoke to him.

"Don't speak to me when Lupe is in the house," he muttered without turning his head or his eyes. "She thinks you are talking about her."

"All right." Tennie tried to give his arm a reassuring touch, but he grimaced and turned his face away. She rose and left him, feeling all alone in the world.

She walked outside, and not wishing another incident over food, decide to brave walking to the outdoor kitchen. The women clucked over her, handing her something wrapped in what appeared to be a flat pancake. She wondered if it was the tortilla Poco had described to her.

"Tortilla?" she asked, holding it up.

"*Sí, sí,*" they said, their pretty faces smiling.

It tasted delicious, and she tried to make hand signals telling them how much she liked it. They smiled and nodded in return, but Tennie couldn't help get the impression they were respectful, in awe, and wished she would get away from them.

She found her stepsons racing horses with the village boys. When Lucas reined the Appaloosa next to her, Tennie smiled.

"Having a good time?"

"You bet!"

"That's good, but make sure you leave Mr. Hawkshaw's horse alone," Tennie said. "Brush it, feed it, take good care of it, but don't ride it."

"Oh, we won't." Lucas nodded.

"Don't even get on him," Tennie said.

Lucas flushed, and she knew her arrow had hit home.

"Yes, ma'am," he said.

"Badger," she said, looking over at the younger boy, who was munching another of the tortilla wraps like she had eaten earlier, "you mind your brothers."

He swallowed. "Yes, Miss Tennie."

She smiled and left them to their playmates, returning to her solitary spot on a bench by Lupe's front door. She was under no illusions about their conduct. If they weren't afraid of possibly facing the wrath of Hawkshaw, there was no telling what they would be doing and saying. At the same time, the remembrance of their incredible cunning and bravery in coming to her rescue made her ready to forgive any future lapses in behavior.

She spent the next hour waiting. The little girls interrupted her vigil. They were fascinated with her rubber comb, so different from the porcupine tail they used on their hair. She found herself letting them comb her hair and put it into braids. Her mother had detested lice and issued dire warnings to Tennie about loaning her comb to anyone. But her mother was dead, and she was stuck in the middle of nowhere. Besides, she could delouse herself later if she had to. So, she combed the little girls' hair and tried to put it up with her pins, but it was so thick, it was hard to get them to stay in. That turned into another session where they combed her hair out again and tried to put her hair up with the pins.

Lupe came outside and spoke to them in Spanish. They scattered, and Lupe left the house, walking to the center of the village. Tennie waited a minute before going inside.

"Are you feeling better?" she asked Hawkshaw again.

He turned his head to look at her. "Yes. Don't go anywhere. Stay near this house."

Tennie shook her head in bewilderment. "Mr. Hawkshaw, I'm not going to leave you here alone."

"I know that," he snapped, as if cross with her because of it.

"You don't have anything to worry about with me. Father Francisco is the only man in this whole village under the age of fifty who's also not under the age of twelve. Something strange is going on here."

"Just do what I ask, please."

Lupe came back in the house, staring at her. Tennie didn't try to give Hawkshaw any reassuring pats but nodded her head and went back outside again to wait.

Later, Lucas came to check on her. He paused by the door and stared inside. The intentness of his gaze made Tennie get up and look. Lupe was leaning over Hawkshaw, crooning and caressing his forehead with a damp cloth. A shot of anger went through Tennie. Hawkshaw got upset with her for even patting his arm, and he was letting Lupe stroke his forehead.

"Mr. Hawkshaw can't stand anybody touching him, can he?" Lucas whispered.

Tennie opened her mouth to object, until she saw Hawkshaw's white knuckles clutching the blanket. She motioned Lucas to come away from the door.

"No, he can't." And she added almost to herself, "He didn't mind me sewing up his arm, or taking a bullet out of his leg, though."

Rusty had walked up and heard them. "You weren't trying to show him any feelings or wanting anything from him. As long as it's impersonal, he doesn't care."

Tennie shook her head. "I just want him to get well so we can get out of here."

"Aw, heck." Rusty laughed. "It's not so bad."

Tennie gave an exaggerated curl of her lip and a sideways scowl that made him laugh.

The boys walked off, smiling and laughing. Tennie stared at the door. Hawkshaw would be the perfect candidate to visit one of Lafayette's ladies of the night. He could pay them and leave, without any emotion being expended on either side. Tennie was willing to bet he had never been with the same woman twice in his life. She blushed at her own crudeness and sat on the ground against the wall, crossing her arms and putting her head down to dream of Wash Jones.

At supper, the women of the village solved all problems by sending two little girls over with Tennie's food. She smiled her thanks to the girls, and turning her head, smiled and nodded her thanks to the women at the kitchen.

The mob of boys and girls around her lost their shyness and chatted happily. When Tennie finished eating, she listened for a little while, then looking at them, she picked up her spoon and said, "Spoon."

It didn't take them long to figure out that she wanted them to repeat the word to her in Spanish, and they spent the rest of the time until dark picking up things and repeating the Spanish name for her, laughing as they did.

Even though she had done nothing all day, Tennie was tired. She went inside to lie on her bed, soon falling asleep amidst the noises of other people retiring for the night.

She dreamed Lupe had her hand against her throat choking her. She began to cough and gasp, rising from the deep sleep she had been in to realize she was being strangled. Her eyes flew open, seeing Lupe standing over her by the dim light of the moon coming in through the door and windows, one hand on her throat, the other grasping a raised knife.

With a burst of strength fueled by terror, Tennie pushed her off. Lupe came at her again, and picking up a nearby clay pot, Tennie smashed it against her head, sending her reeling backwards.

Pandemonium broke out in the room. Candles were lit, screams were heard. In less than a heartbeat, the house filled with snarling people. More candles were lit and the room became illuminated. Two women held back a growling Lupe. On one side of the room, a group of angry people with homemade knives drawn glared at a group on the other side ready to attack with *their* homemade knives. Lucas took one look and fled.

People began screaming and spitting at one another back and forth across the room. The women took turns seeing who could shriek the loudest, while the men brandished knives back and forth. Tennie backed up against the wall, wishing a hole would open up and swallow her. Rusty and Badger squeezed through the mob and stood beside her. Lucas came hurrying back with Father Francisco by his side.

The priest spoke strong commands to the crowd. They reluctantly put down their knives. Tennie began to breathe again. What had happened to the nice, peaceful villagers she had seen the day before? It had become a battlefield inside the house.

Father Francisco came over to Tennie. "I am sorry this happened."

"I should sleep somewhere else, Father," Tennie said.

"No!"

Everyone stopped what they were doing and saying to look at Hawkshaw. He had raised up on one elbow and was looking like murder.

"No, she'll stay right here." He gave Lupe

as hard a look as any man ever gave a woman. "Lupe's not going to cause any more trouble for Mrs. Granger."

Lupe understood what he meant. Everyone in the room knew what he meant. Lupe cast her eyes downward in submission.

The father spoke to the crowd, shooing them out of the room. He addressed Lupe, who refused to look up and meet his eyes. She nodded understanding instead.

"Come, Mrs. Granger," the priest said. "Go back to your bed. I will stay here for a little while if it will calm you."

Tennie nodded and went back to bed. The priest sat in the chair beside Hawkshaw's bed, taking a pipe from his pocket and filling it with tobacco. He ignored Hawkshaw and said nothing to anyone. Tennie had intended to stay awake until morning, but the soothing presence of the priest soon had her asleep.

The next day, it was as if all was forgotten. Lupe didn't cause Tennie any trouble, and Tennie took care to stay out of her way, trying not to aggravate her. Outside, Rusty and Lucas ridiculed the older woman's obsession with Hawkshaw.

"The kids make fun of her," Lucas said.

"How do you know?" Tennie asked. "You can't understand that much Spanish yet."

"Because they point to her and smooch their

elbows and bat their eyes, holding their hands over their hearts, muttering *Hawkshaw*."

"Yeah," Rusty agreed. "She's even worse after he laid the law down to her about you."

Tennie sighed. "Nothing like obedience to foster love."

"Good luck to her with that old chunk of ice," Rusty said.

"Rusty!" Tennie chided, but she laughed. "She's so hot-blooded and beautiful, she just might be the one to turn him into a warmhearted human being."

"Shorty would say 'when pigs fly,' " Lucas said. "But Mr. Hawkshaw's better, isn't he?"

Tennie nodded. "He's sitting up. If he keeps going like he has been, we should be leaving here soon."

"Aw, this place is fun," Lucas repeated, but it lacked his earlier conviction.

The night before had them all thinking about moving on.

Lupe went down to the river to wash clothes, taking the children with her. When she was out of sight, Tennie walked back into the house. Hawkshaw was getting up.

"What are you doing?" Tennie asked.

"I want to sit outside. I'm sick of this house."

Tennie followed him, not daring to offer to help. He found a bench next to the house under the arbor and sank down. Tennie sat down beside him, but not too close.

"Well?" he asked.

"Well . . . ?" she asked back. "Why did you bring us so far west?"

"Because I wanted to lure Lafayette here to kill him."

CHAPTER 10

Tennie wondered why hadn't she seen it coming. "Who hired you?"

"The brother of his ex-sister-in-law, Raiford Beauregard," Hawkshaw said. "I'm sure you know the story. She walks around dressed in mourning, raising hell. She keeps moaning as long as Lafayette is alive, her life is ruined. Her brother thought if Lafayette was dead, she would get over it."

"Why did you take the job?" Tennie asked, uncomprehending why anyone would want to be a hired killer.

"Look, besides having an affair with his own brother's wife and killing him over it, Lafayette is a saloon owner and a razor-sharp gambler. He pimps out whores. There had been newspaper articles even in that part of the country about the young woman he seduced and infuriated into killing a famous singer."

"She was a prostitute he picked up in New Orleans, and he hoped the singer could humiliate her into leaving," Tennie said. "He didn't realize she was so crazy she would kill the poor woman in a jealous fit."

Hawkshaw shrugged. "I could see right away Lafayette is no fool," he continued as if Lafayette's morals didn't matter anyway. "I couldn't use the usual methods to rile him enough to get him to draw a gun on me. I knew the only thing I could use to upset him enough to try to kill me would be you. When I overheard the Miltons' plan, I went along with it, waiting for the right time to rescue you."

"And then what?" Tennie asked.

"Then, I would take my time getting you back to civilization, and we would be alone together long enough for there to be talk, and I would fuel that talk until I infuriated Lafayette into feeling like he had to kill me to protect your honor."

Tennie sniffed. "In Ring Bit, there are always people ready to believe the worst about me. They don't need you for that."

Hawkshaw took a deep breath, looking so weary she felt sorry for him.

He shook his head. "Nothing went the way it was supposed to anyway. I didn't plan on your stepsons arriving like the cavalry. And I thought with Inga dead, Bod and Ozzie would leave the countryside in a panic before they tried to follow us. I left them alive because I wanted to use them to scare you into flight. It surprised the hell out of me when they showed up."

"Why are you telling me all this?" Tennie asked. "I'm not going to let you kill Lafayette."

"I don't know why I'm telling you. Maybe because you sewed up my arm. Maybe because you took a bullet out of my leg. Maybe because you and your stepsons haven't deserted me in this hellhole."

Any other man would have thought he had landed in paradise, but not Hawkshaw. He touched the bandage on his leg, turning his hand over to stare at his palm. He looked over to her. "Do you have any idea, woman, what it would do to my reputation if I don't kill Lafayette? If I just return the cash and say *sorry?*"

"What reputation?" Tennie asked. "You have no reputation, except as a shootist, and who wants a reputation like that?"

"And what am I supposed to do?"

"I know you have money, Mr. Hawkshaw," Tennie said. "Don't try to tell me you don't have money in banks all across the whole United States, probably. Retire and be a rancher. Every man who comes to Texas wants to own a ranch."

"I don't know anything about cattle and don't want to," Hawkshaw said. "The only thing I know about is how to draw faster than the other hombre. And I don't want to sit around Texas waiting for some young glory hunter to come looking to do me in."

"And horses," Tennie said, not to be deterred. "You can have a horse farm. Sell the glory hunters a horse they can brag about. 'I bought this horse from Hawkshaw, the famous shootist,' is what they will say."

"It's too late for that," Hawkshaw said.

"It's never too late." She wanted to talk more, but Lupe was coming back. Tennie turned and asked one last question. "The senator's daughter?"

"Never happened," he said, looking toward Lupe. "Inga had a friend working for the senator who faked the telegram." He got up and went back inside the house.

Tennie walked to the far side of the arbor, leaned against a post, and wondered where Wash Jones could be.

That night, the air was heavy with excitement, almost fear. Tennie did not know if the villagers were hoping for another fight, or if there was something else causing their anxiety. She took a blanket, planning to sleep underneath the arbor. Lupe's knife attack had smacked of the same theatrics as her egg performance, but Tennie was taking no chances. If Hawkshaw didn't like it, he could lump it.

But nothing happened during the night.

The next morning, Hawkshaw again walked outside and sat down on the bench under the arbor. Lupe banged things as loudly as she could in the house to show her displeasure, but neither Hawkshaw nor Tennie spoke.

The priest emerged from the church, his robes flowing as he walked with purpose in their

171

direction. He stopped under the arbor and said a cheery, "Good morning."

Tennie returned his greeting; Hawkshaw just looked at him. The priest stood at the door and spoke a few words to Lupe.

The children, sensing something might be about to happen, crowded underneath the arbor. Lupe exited the house, refusing to look at Hawkshaw or Tennie, pushing aside the children and striding to the communal kitchen, where she turned to stare at them. The father spoke to the children, and they scattered. All except the Granger boys, who refused to budge.

Father Francisco did not object. He took a short stool from the house and set it down in front of Hawkshaw and Tennie. "Mrs. Granger, do you remember on that first day when I said you and your party were an answer to our prayers?"

Tennie stirred. "I remember it now, but I had forgotten all about it."

"Does this have anything to do with the fact there are no able-bodied men in this town?" Hawkshaw asked.

"You noticed that, did you, Señor Hawkshaw?" the priest said. "Yes, it has everything to do with that. If you will permit me to explain?"

Hawkshaw stared steadily, and Tennie nodded her head.

"These are a poor people, as you can see," Father Francisco said. "But they are industrious.

They have raised livestock and planted gardens. Over the course of time, bandits from the South have made yearly raids on their village. At first, they only took a few things, so it could be tolerated. But in the past few years, the raids have become increasingly violent as a new leader took over. This last time, the women were raped, the older children taken to be sold into slavery. They snatched some of the women to take with them, abusing them to the point they collapsed, and they were left for dead along the way. Lupe is one of the few who managed to make her way back. The men who fought back were killed or taken to be sold as slaves."

Tennie immediately regretted all the harsh things she had been thinking of Lupe.

"Do they always come at the same time every year?" Hawkshaw asked. "Why don't the people just leave?"

"Because they learned from previous years, not only would they be chased down, their homes and everything they have built up would be destroyed," the father said. "They were planning on departing this year, even knowing they would probably be hunted down and killed. The leader of the banditos is cruel, and he does not care. They have been praying faithfully, my friends. When they heard your gunfire, they knew you had enough *pistolas* to fight the banditos, Señor Hawkshaw."

Tennie glanced at Hawkshaw. He sat staring at the priest, and even though he did not move a muscle, she knew he was filled with a cold fury so intense it frightened her.

"And why did you allow Mrs. Granger and her children to stay here, knowing that?" he asked.

Even the calm priest seemed disconcerted by Hawkshaw's hatred. He took a breath and continued. "Because, they would have somehow learned of her existence and possibly tracked her down anyway."

"And when do you expect these banditos?" Hawkshaw said.

"Always on the last quarter moon during this time of year. Possibly tomorrow. I have received word they are near," the priest said. "I did not tell you sooner for fear you would leave."

"And you expect me to wage war on how many banditos? Twenty? Fifty? With just myself, a woman, three boys, and a few guns?"

The priest faced Hawkshaw's wrath with courage. "If you do not, they will kill you and take your friends hostage. Mrs. Granger's stepsons will be sold as slaves. I do not have to tell you what will happen to Mrs. Granger."

Tennie felt sick. She swallowed and willed herself to remain calm. The boys were whispering among themselves.

Rusty walked forward. "Excuse me, Father, I must tell Mr. Hawkshaw something." He went to

Hawkshaw and whispered something into his ear.

Hawkshaw shot his head around and stared at him. Rusty nodded.

Hawkshaw looked back to Father Francisco. "Preacher, you just got saved from having a bullet hole put in your skull."

A sudden dawning came over Tennie. "Did you bring those explosives with you in your tote sacks? Did you?" she yelled at Rusty.

He owned up. "Yes, ma'am."

"You could have blown us all to kingdom come. You know that?" Tennie ranted.

"Shut up," Hawkshaw said. "Now is not the time."

The priest looked shocked. "Señor Hawkshaw, that is no way to talk to a woman."

"Don't pay any attention to him," Tennie said. "He was raised by an old mama grizzly."

Hawkshaw ignored her. He sat breathing heavily. Tennie sensed he was fighting an inner battle—to stay or to leave.

"Do they always come through that little canyon?" he finally asked.

"Yes," Father Francisco nodded.

Closing his eyes and exhaling, Hawkshaw gave in. "Have your people bring as much livestock and food back here as they can. Tell them we are going to blow up the bandits in that canyon. Warn them that we may cause a landslide that will seal us in here, so make sure they have plenty of food and water in case it takes us a while to dig our way out."

"Of course," Father Francisco said, rising. He bowed. "Thank you, señor. My people are not entirely helpless. The men are excellent with bows and arrows. But unfortunately, their arrows are not able to stand up against so many revolvers and rifles."

Hawkshaw nodded but did not waste time on niceties. "Keep Lupe and the others away from here while we discuss the best way to handle the explosives. Miss Tennie, go with the priest."

"No," Tennie said. "You are not shutting me out."

"You better let her stay, Mr. Hawkshaw," Lucas said. "Sometimes she has some real good ideas."

"I don't have any ideas," Tennie said. "I only know I'm not going to let you shut me out."

"You just don't want to be left alone with Lupe." Hawkshaw glanced at the priest. "Vamoose. I'll send for you when and if I have any questions."

After Father Francisco left, Hawkshaw looked at Tennie. "Do you know how to fire a gun?"

"Just barely. Rusty and Lucas were born with rifles in their hands. In target shooting, they could hold their own with you." She paused and continued. "I realize they have to put the explosives together, but my job is to protect them. You can detonate the bombs, and I will help you."

Hawkshaw stared at her. "You and me against an army of cutthroats?"

Rusty stepped forward. "You won't be alone. Lucas and I aren't going to become slaves without a fight."

Hawkshaw stood up and began to pace, dragging his leg, muttering curse words under his breath. He sat down and covered his forehead. After a few minutes, he looked up.

"We'll have to get a volunteer to detonate the bombs, one of the older men. I'll be high up in the center of the canyon, picking off bandits that live through the explosion."

He looked at Rusty. "You and your brother can be toward the canyon head to shoot whoever tries to leave. That will be the safest place because they'll have their backs to you, trying to escape. The village men can be ready deeper in the canyon with bows and arrows to shoot whoever gets past the explosions and tries to enter the village."

He moved his eyes to Badger. "You and your friends will have to take care of our horses. They aren't going to like the noise. Think you can do that?"

Badger nodded. "Yes, sir."

"And me?" Tennie asked.

Hawkshaw took a deep breath. "Can you stay with me and reload my guns?"

Tennie nodded. "I can do that."

They began to discuss what to use to make the most destructive bombs they could.

Tennie, thinking about the men and the horses they would be destroying, couldn't stand to listen. She got up and walked to the other side of the arbor. She railed against circumstances that made children have to behave like men, and yet, when Rusty declared he would not be made a slave without a fight, she could think of no other way out. If they let the men into the village, separated them from their horses, somehow managed to get them into a building away from everyone else . . .

But that was hopeless, too. They would ride into the village and begin plundering immediately, grabbing women to assault, shooting at whoever they felt like.

"Rusty!" Lucas exclaimed. "We can build a land torpedo. Don't you remember Mr. Gid telling us about that?"

"He told you how to build one of those?" Hawkshaw asked.

Lucas nodded. "Yes, sir. He said he did it twice before they made him stop. They said it was too inhuman."

"Inhumane," Rusty corrected.

"Inhuman or inhumane, it would be the best way for us with the amount of powder we have," Hawkshaw muttered, thinking out loud. "You sure you remember what he told you?"

"Yes, sir, we can do it," Rusty and Lucas both exclaimed.

"What is *it?*" Tennie asked.

"We'd build a trench down the canyon floor, Miss Tennie," Rusty said. "Filling it with explosives, and gravel, and any bits of metal we can find. We'll set up a tripwire, and when they ride over the tripwire, it will set off the explosives down the canyon."

"We'll be high up, hidden in the rocks of the canyon, when it goes off," Lucas said.

Tennie looked at Hawkshaw. It was brutal warfare. "You better have guards posted to warn any innocent people who happen to come by not to go into that canyon then," she told the boys.

They discussed it in detail before taking it to Father Francisco to explain to his people. As soon as they heard the plan, the village became alive with activity. Men, women, and children filed into the canyon to dig a long trench. Others went to a gravel bar near the creek to haul the gravel that would be used as projectiles. It would have to be spread and baked in the sun to be perfectly dry. Still others gathered pieces of broken glass and metal left over from the metal hoops surrounding the supply barrels the visiting priests had brought to them. It was harder to find the right size wire, but that too was eventually discovered.

The men used the shovels; the women got on

their hands and knees and used whatever they could find to dig in the dirt, Tennie alongside them. The irony that her savior might indirectly be a loquacious country bumpkin whose only skills were bouncing heads and blowing up bridges was not lost upon her. Tennie asked God a hundred times to forgive her for ever being mad at Giddings Coltrane about anything.

Hawkshaw, crippled and still not completely well, could only watch. Tennie would see his eyes scanning the rocks above them relentlessly, looking for hiding places. When remembering what Gid told them and putting it into practice proved harder than Rusty and Lucas had thought, Hawkshaw had to help.

"He knows more about explosives than he let on," Lucas whispered to Tennie.

Tennie looked over the trench to where Hawkshaw stood in discussion with Rusty. "I'm not surprised. He plays everything close to his chest."

Father Francisco translated instructions and helped to dig and spread gravel. Just before sundown, boys were posted at the entrance of the canyon, ready to sound the alarm or to warn off any lost travelers if need be. Hawkshaw sent Tennie, along with the villagers, back toward the village while he, Rusty, and Lucas strung the tripwire. The villagers, reluctant to leave, stood at a safe distance where they could still see. Father Francisco got down on his knees, to pray, and Tennie, with the other women, joined him. Tennie kept peeking, though, and when it came time to make the final connection, Hawkshaw sent Rusty and Lucas away, and he did it himself.

When he finished and walked toward them, a collective and silent "amen" was breathed. They trudged back to the village, exhausted and hopeful. Tennie walked alone, leaving Hawkshaw to his thoughts and the boys to their friends.

Father Francisco fell into step with her, speaking in a low, even tone while an owl began to hoot in the dusky night. "You think it is odd that a priest would encourage such warfare?"

"The thought did cross my mind," she said.

"As a child, my sister and I were captured by the Comanche," he explained. "I helped her to escape. For my treachery, I was castrated and left to bleed to death. A group of Spanish missionaries happened upon me and saved me. They were educated men who had renounced lives of wealth and ease to work and live in poverty to help others."

Tennie's steps slowed. "I'm sorry that happened to you."

"It was many, many years later that I found my sister. She had made her way to this village."

The handsomeness of both brother and sister suddenly struck her. "Lupe is your sister, isn't she?"

"Yes, and I am once again trying to rescue her."

Tennie took a deep breath but kept walking in step with the priest. "And the men who are coming? Are they Mexican or Indian or white?"

"Mostly Mexican, some with more Indian blood than others. We Mexicans are a mixture of Spanish and Indian, you understand," the priest said. "A few of the villagers traveled to Waco to beg the Anglo sheriff for help, but he refused to come."

After listening to Rusty's and Lucas's description of him, Tennie could believe it. It was probably not in his jurisdiction, and he had not bothered to tell the men to seek out the U.S. marshal or approach the rangers.

"I am sorry for that, too," Tennie said.

"The problem is not race or color, Mrs. Granger. The problem is sin."

"Then I hope we are not sinning by trying to kill somebody before they kill us," Tennie said.

"To save a child or let it be killed? I am willing to take that risk."

The priest moved ahead, and Tennie lagged, turning to look at Hawkshaw. Badger and his friends had gone for his horse so he would not have to walk back. They, along with Rusty and Lucas, surrounded him. Tennie wondered if he would be able to stand the attention and closeness until they reached the village.

She slept fitfully outside with the children, in agony that something might go wrong. In the few hours before dawn, she fell into a deep sleep, dreaming of the Indian attack that happened on her way to Texas. She had found herself under a wagon next to an old scout, handing him ammunition as he fired his rifle to protect them. In her dream, she knew she would be doing the same thing the next day.

In the morning, everyone arose early. They would be hiding in the cliffs of the little canyon to wait in the sun all day, perhaps for many days, if necessary.

Before she left, she begged Father Francisco to stay with Rusty and Lucas. "They can handle firearms. That part I'm not worried about. But they are inexperienced and will put their heads up when they should stay down. It appears Mr. Hawkshaw does not trust anyone but me to act as his legs, and I must stay with him in case of an emergency."

The priest patted her arm and smiled at her indulgently. "Never fear, dear lady. I will be on that end of the canyon anyway to make sure our lookouts do not show themselves or get so distracted they forget to do their duty." He paused for a moment before asking, "Señor Hawkshaw avoids human contact, does he not?"

Tennie nodded. "Yes." It did not seem necessary to add more.

"Yet, he has asked me to send some men up to

his lookout point to kill any snakes that might be hiding among the rocks because you are deathly afraid of snakes."

Tennie nodded. "I came close to losing an arm, at the least, with a snakebite once. A drunken Indian saved my life. Mr. Hawkshaw's main concern is that I not get hysterical near him if I see one, not that I get bit."

The priest laughed. "Perhaps, but the men are also clearing away snakes from the area where your stepsons will be staying."

"You've been very kind, Father," Tennie said, and she felt herself grow quite calm.

Because of his leg, Hawkshaw rode his horse as high as he could go, with Badger and his friends following with packhorses. The women had prepared skins of water, baskets of food, and anything else they could think of that might make their vigil more comfortable.

When Badger left with the horses, Hawkshaw went over and over with Tennie which cartridges went into which firearm and how to load them. "Yesterday, you were a wreck with worry. Why are you so steady today?"

Tennie stared at him. "Who knows that we were not brought here for this purpose? If that be the case, then the outcome, too, will be in God's hands, not ours. All that is required of me is to do my best."

Hawkshaw shook his head. "If you get

hysterical, I cannot promise you that I won't smack you so hard you fall backwards, hitting your head on a rock and dying."

"I accept that might happen," Tennie said. "I hope it doesn't."

"There is something else I haven't told you," Hawkshaw said.

CHAPTER 11

Tennie continued to stare at Hawkshaw. He intended on admitting something he hadn't wanted to; she was sure of that.

"We don't have enough powder to do real damage," he said. "We have rigged the explosions so that when one goes off, it triggers another and another down the line. What we are trying to do is create mass confusion that will allow us time to shoot them with our guns. If I get shot, you must take the rifle and kill them."

Tennie nodded. "You keep saying 'we.' Does that mean the boys understand this?'

Hawkshaw nodded. "We didn't tell you earlier for fear of worrying you too much. I'm telling you now so you know if you do not shoot as many of these men as possible, you will be putting your stepsons in greater danger."

"Are you going to give me a gun so I can fire?"

"No, I am a faster and better shot. It will work smoother if you are here to reload for me."

"All right," Tennie agreed.

"We'll just have to wait," Hawkshaw said.

Tennie had plenty of practice in waiting. Waiting as a child for the men in agony at the hospital to either get better or develop lung fever and die. Waiting for her father to come home from the war. Waiting at the orphanage for the abuse to stop. Waiting for something to happen that would put her in a different situation. Waiting for saloon strongarms to bring her prisoners. Waiting for prisoners to calm down and fall asleep. Waiting for Wash Jones.

Now without Lupe and seemingly all the time in the world to discuss anything they wanted, Tennie and Hawkshaw did not speak.

A howling dog broke the silence.

"I hear a dog barking," Tennie said. "I didn't see any dogs in the village."

"That's our signal," Hawkshaw said, lying down on the rocks and steadying his rifle. "Get down and be ready to reload. Remember to put the right cartridges in the rifle or you will have made it useless."

Tennie could hear the beating sound of many hooves. Unable to stop herself, she peeked over the rock she hid behind. At least thirty-five men rode on ragged horses, dressed in cheap white cotton that seemed covered with every kind of gun and knife imaginable. Under their sombreros, the brutish lines on their faces told of every possible degeneracy. After a split-second glance, Tennie fell back to her place, looking at the cartridges and praying she would not get them mixed up.

The buried bombs exploded just as Hawkshaw had said they would, creating deafening roars as the gravel, shards of metal, and glass spewed everywhere. He rose and fired so rapidly, it seemed that only seconds passed before he had thrown the rifle down and was reaching for a pistol. Tennie grabbed the rifle and reloaded it as fast as she could. He threw the gun down, taking the rifle from her hands, and she did the same with the pistol.

He had not described the sounds of carnage, of men and horses screaming in pain. On one level, her fingers flew, only occasionally fumbling, knowing she could not pause. On another level, she listened for Rusty's and Lucas's gunfire to her right, for as long as she heard it, they were alive.

At times, Hawkshaw was faster than she was. He would take another pistol because she wasn't ready, and every one of them took different cartridges. After the first wild confusion of bombs exploding, the bandits began to fire back, and as Tennie reloaded, bullets and splintered rocks ricocheted around them. Hawkshaw moved like a machine, firing round after round with a speed that left the guns he was using smoking so hot, they burned in Tennie's hands when she took them to reload. If he had shown any weakness at all, she realized she would have faltered. But he did not, and she kept up with him as best she could.

Was it three minutes or was it an hour? When

the firing stopped, she stared at him, her fingers still trying to place a cartridge in his rifle. He crouched, regarding the scene below, but Tennie was afraid to look. A noise came from her right, and Rusty and Lucas bounded toward her, surrounding her and hugging her as tightly as they could. They were trying hard not to cry. She could only stare at them. Father Francisco followed, crossing himself and mumbling prayers.

"Don't look, Miss Tennie," Rusty said, his arms hugging her shoulders.

Lucas had his arms around her waist, hiding his face in her bosom. "Mr. Gid didn't tell us it would be like this."

Tennie hugged them back, overcome with gratitude that they had not been hurt. Even though they were upset, she could feel a thrill running through them. She did not share their blood rush; she felt only numbness.

Hawkshaw ignored them, trying to distance himself from such an obvious display of excitement and sentiment.

"Badger . . ." Tennie began.

Rusty and Lucas jumped up. "We'll go find him." They turned to Hawkshaw. "We'll bring your horse, Mr. Hawkshaw."

Hawkshaw nodded and rested his back against a rock, shutting his eyes. He did not see the boys passing Lupe on their way down. She stopped at the top to stare at Hawkshaw. Father Francisco spoke to her, and taking her by the arm, led her downward to the village.

Tennie followed Hawkshaw's example and shut her eyes.

The boys brought horses as far as they could. Hawkshaw allowed Rusty to help him down the rocks. Tennie knew if she dared touch him, he would slap her hand and tell her to get away for fear she might burst into a welter of tears next to him. When they reached the horses, Rusty stood slightly back, allowing Hawkshaw to get on his horse by himself. Lucas helped her onto hers, making her feel grateful she was not a man and didn't have to prove anything.

On the way down, Tennie avoided looking into the floor of the canyon. When they drew closer to the village, she could see horses with bloody legs and barrels wandering around, some of them already eating grass and oblivious to everything else.

"Don't worry, Miss Tennie," Rusty said. "The villagers will take care of the horses."

She nodded. They stopped at Lupe's arbor, and Hawkshaw instructed the boys to keep their horses close. Father Francisco rushed to them and looked about to give Hawkshaw's hand a vigorous shake.

Hawkshaw circumvented him with a cold look in his eyes. "We'll be leaving as soon as most of the bodies are out of the way. We'd appreciate it if you would have one of our horses packed with food and water."

The priest looked slightly taken aback. "Of course, Señor Hawkshaw, but you are welcome to stay as long as you like."

Hawkshaw shook his head. "No, we are leaving today."

Tennie didn't say anything, although she knew it would be better for him to stay off his leg for another week at least.

At the moment, the villagers were intent on coping with the dead. If any of the bandits had survived, their reprieve would be short-lived in the hands of a vengeful mob, and Father Francisco probably knew it would be useless to try to stop them. But when they finished with their gory tasks, they would want to have a celebration and shower Hawkshaw with unwanted attention.

Lupe had disappeared. While Tennie waited, she went inside Lupe's house and removed her lace-covered petticoat, folding it carefully and placing under Lupe's pillow.

Hawkshaw refused to take Ozzie's old mare with them and told Father Francisco anyone who wanted her could have her. When the rest of their horses were ready, and the dead bodies of men and horses had been stripped and thrown into a communal grave some distance away, they made preparations to leave, arrangements that put an end to the numbness Tennie had been feeling.

"What's the fastest way to Waco?" Hawkshaw asked the father.

"Follow the creek, señor," the priest said. "It will lead you to the Brazos, and the Brazos will lead you to Waco."

"Much obliged," Hawkshaw said.

Father Francisco left Hawkshaw and took Tennie by the hands. "Thank you, Mrs. Granger."

"I hope we meet again one day, Father," she said.

He drew closer, smiling gently and staring into her face. "May I tell you something, Mrs. Granger?" he said so low his voice was almost a whisper.

"Of course," she replied.

"When I look at you, it makes me wish I was not a priest, that I was a full man once again."

She smiled and felt her face blushing. "Thank you."

She got onto her rented horse. The children surrounded her, touching her legs lightly to say good-bye. She felt in her pocket and brought out her comb, handing it to one of the girls with a smile and making a circular motion with her finger to indicate it was for all of them. As she picked up the reins and was about to move forward in the saddle, a little girl ran up to her and thrust a porcupine comb in her hand.

Tennie grinned, kissed it, and called, "*Gracias!*" waving good-bye.

"*Adios!*" they cried as they left. "Good-bye, Father Francisco!"

A herd of children crying "*adios*" followed them for a good while before turning back. When Tennie looked over her shoulder, Father Francisco was still watching them. She raised her hand to him, and he held up his in return.

She realized that, given Hawkshaw's condition, it was going to be a slow ride.

As they approached the creek, Hawkshaw began to question her as the horses made an unhurried and steady plod to the path that would lead them to Waco. "What were you giggling about with that priest?"

"I was not giggling," Tennie said. "Just smiling."

"Humph," he grunted. "Mexican men can charm the birds off trees and then turn around and beat their women without batting an eyelash."

"Oh, shut up. Father Francisco wouldn't beat a fly. You broke Lupe's heart back there. You know that?"

"You're awful forgiving of someone who tried to kill you," Hawkshaw said.

"She wouldn't have really killed me," Tennie said. "Maybe put a scar or two on my face, but not kill me."

Hawkshaw didn't laugh out loud, but he smirked with the corners of his lips curving upward. They crossed the creek to follow the trail, but when Hawkshaw said he wanted to return to their old camp for nightfall, the rest of them agreed. Tennie glanced at the clothes he wore, thinking of the weight he had lost.

She noticed that his watch fob was missing. "Where is your gold watch?"

He gave her a cool look. "Next to the lace petticoat you left under Lupe's pillow."

Tennie grinned but did not tease him about it. She joined the boys, still full of talk about the fight. She supposed they would be talking about it the rest of their lives.

They found their old lean-to and replaced the logs that had been taken from it. With the sun going down in the trees, they made a campfire. None of them were hungry, but the boys were too excited to sleep and wanted to stay up talking. Hawkshaw lay against his saddle, exhausted, letting the boys and Tennie tend to everything. She was so happy to be free from the constraints she had been under, she was almost giddy.

Noises coming from the trees and brushy growth behind them put an end to their exultant reflections. Tennie let the log she was about to put in the fire drop. Hawkshaw rose, pistol in hand. Rusty picked up his rifle. Badger drew closer to Lucas. More noises came.

In the fading light, Tennie made out three riders, one of them wearing a familiar gray suit under a Stetson. "Lafayette!" she cried and raced toward him.

He dismounted his dark bay, grabbing her and holding her close. "Tennie, Tennie, thank God," he whispered in her ears, kissing her hair.

She returned his hugs and leaned back to smile. Shorty rode toward them on a sturdy little strawberry roan, with Gid behind him on a brown horse with a chest the size of a pickle barrel.

Lafayette looked her up and down, and Tennie suddenly realized how truly tattered her appearance was. A cloud came over his face, and he turned to stare at Hawkshaw, whose arm hung down, the pistol limp in his hand.

"You bastard!" Lafayette yelled. He pushed Tennie aside and drew his pistol.

"No!" Tennie screamed, grabbing his arm. "No, he saved us."

Lafayette stood with gun in hand, shaking with fury. Hawkshaw made no move against him. As Tennie continued to entreat him, Lafayette reluctantly put the pistol back into his holster. Hawkshaw slowly did the same.

"What has happened?" Lafayette said.

"Get off your horses," Tennie told the other men. "Come to the fire, Lafayette, and let us explain."

But it was she who had to clarify their odd situation. For once, she did not have to chide her stepsons about interrupting. Lafayette's unexpected rage had silenced them. Hawkshaw did not offer a word of explanation.

195

By the time her story wound down, darkness had come. Lucas grew bold and asked how they had found them.

Lafayette, still distraught and trying to digest everything, told them. "Every man in the countryside is searching for Tennie. We joined the others east of Waco but were getting nowhere. Someone happened to mention that three boys had been inquiring about the old Milton place. As soon as we heard the name *Milton,* we knew.

"We couldn't find anyone at their farm. We were about to give up when Shorty found a scrap of Tennie's dress caught on some brush, and we realized she had probably been trying to escape."

Shorty and Gid had been throwing sharp looks in Hawkshaw's direction ever since they'd arrived with Lafayette, but they let him do the talking.

"We thought we heard something and felt a faint rumble beneath our feet," Lafayette said. "Gid said he thought it was an explosion. That put the boys immediately to mind, so we followed the direction we thought it had come from."

"And Wash?" Tennie asked. "Have you heard from Wash?"

Lafayette paused to exchange glances with Shorty and Gid. "No, we haven't heard anything."

"Nothing?" she said, and when they reiterated they did not know anything, her eyes fell downward. She withdrew from the circle of fire so they could not see her tears.

196

She had seen that day the kind of men Wash faced. If he ran across outlaws so depraved they had nothing to lose . . . he might never make it back. Her heart contracted, and she stifled a sob in her throat. What was she to do? "Oh, God," she muttered under her breath.

Lafayette drew close to her. "Tennie, don't worry, my dear. Wash can take care of himself. Return to Ring Bit with me."

"You still have your marshal job in Ring Bit," Shorty interjected before she could even think to answer. "We merely told people you were on a personal errand. You can return anytime."

She wanted to scream she didn't want to be the marshal of Ring Bit. She was tired of being a joke, a laughingstock, a pariah, all those things rolled into one. She bit her lip and tried to calm herself. Wash had told her to go to Waco. There might be word from him there. And if there wasn't, she would have to go back to Ring Bit. Once again, God would be putting a real ring bit in her mouth, forcing her to do things she didn't want to do.

"I think I should go to Waco and wait a few days," Tennie said. "Wash thinks I am there. If I don't hear from him, I'll return to Ring Bit." And because Wash had warned her not to get too close to Lafayette, she would return as marshal, bitter medicine that it would be.

They made a quiet camp that night. Tennie was exhausted and troubled.

• • •

When Lafayette examined the horses from the livery in Waco the next morning and learned how much the boys had paid to rent them, he became irate. "Not another penny. If they ask for any more money when you deliver these broken-down nags, refuse to give it to them." He looked at the swayback, knock-kneed specimens and frowned. "I will give them a piece of my mind," he declared. "Robbing children."

Hawkshaw said nothing and seemed to withdraw into himself. As they traveled, following the creek until it ran into the Brazos River, the boys did not fight amongst themselves, but watched the older men, trying to imitate the way they rode, how they sat in the saddle and handled the reins. When Shorty explained different ways of finding the best place to cross a river, they listened attentively.

Tennie sat glumly, wishing she could recapture her earlier giddiness. The men from Ring Bit were at odds with Hawkshaw, giving him cold glances that cast a heavy pall over the rest of them. He appeared oblivious to their stares of dislike. But he had not raised his gun to Lafayette, and they realized Hawkshaw could have killed them all if he had wanted to. When they pretended it was for her sole benefit they traveled slower, with frequent stops, not because of Hawkshaw's wound or Shorty's breathlessness, she did not contradict them.

Despite his insistence on being unhurried, Lafayette was unable to hide his worry over his business or his anxiousness to get back. The fire at the Silver Moon had been quickly put out, but there was still damage to contend with. He accidentally let it slip he had several freight deliveries coming in with new fixtures for the saloon and no one he could trust to accept them. Shorty, too, was concerned about his job, having delegated it to a helper he had little faith in.

On the second morning as they broke camp under a rustling canopy of cottonwood trees, Tennie begged Lafayette and Shorty to go on ahead without them. "You can make much better time, and we'll be fine in Waco for a while. Just tell us which hotel or boardinghouse to stay in."

"My dear Tennie," Lafayette said. "I wouldn't dream of leaving you and the boys alone out here in the wilderness or in a town such as Waco."

"I'll be with them for a while," Hawkshaw said, seeming to almost talk to his horse. "I have to wire back the money I was paid anyway."

Gid looked at Hawkshaw, opened his mouth, shut it, and turned to Lafayette. "Colonel, you and Shorty go on ahead. With your permission, I'll stay with Miss Tennie and these young'uns and see that nothing happens to them. You can count on me, sir."

Tennie could see Lafayette wavering and the

relief on Shorty's face. "See there, Lafayette. We'll have Mr. Gid and Mr. Hawkshaw with us. We'll be fine for several days or a week. And after that, if I haven't heard from Wash, we'll go back to Ring Bit."

Both Lafayette and Shorty shot Hawkshaw a look that said they wouldn't trust him to look after the Virgin Mary in Waco. He was still concentrating on getting his saddle right as if they weren't there.

Shorty turned to Lafayette. "I believe she is right, Lafayette. As long as Gid is with them, I don't think any harm will come."

"Yes, sir, Colonel," Gid said. "I'd be pleased to. You don't even have to pay me no wages. I'll do it for free. I don't mind a bit. Not one bit, sir."

Lafayette took a deep breath. "Calm down, Gid. You'll get your regular wages." He turned to Tennie. "Are you sure, though?"

She nodded. "I'm sure. I would feel terrible if I knew I was holding you back, keeping you from your work."

"All right, then." Lafayette spoke to the boys, who had been lingering in the background, listening to every word. "You boys mind Miss Tennie, hear now?"

"Yes, sir!" Rusty said, with Lucas and Badger repeating it.

Before he and Shorty left, Lafayette took Tennie aside, pressing money into her hand. "I know Wash gave you some money, but I want you to take this. He would skin me alive if I didn't. You have to have new clothes, and hotel living is expensive. I want you to stay on the square in Waco. That's where the best hotels are, and you will be surrounded by respectable businesses. Do not venture anywhere else."

Tennie nodded. He didn't have to tell her twice. She had once been kidnapped in Alabama and thrown into a brothel, escaping through a window before anything could happen. She had no desire to relive that experience.

"Tennie," he said, drawing closer to her. "About this Hawkshaw person . . ."

She tried to reassure him. "You've had customers in your saloon who didn't like anyone to get chummy with them or touch them in a personal way, haven't you?"

"Yes," Lafayette said, looking at her to continue.

"He's like that," Tennie said, fumbling, trying to find the right words to express Hawkshaw's peculiarities. "He can tolerate a person trying to fix a wound on him or something like that, but he can't handle someone wiping the sweat from his brow in compassion. He can't stand us getting too close to him. If he thought I was going to get hysterical and start crying or something, he'd go dig a hole and bury himself in it if he had to. But at the same time, he did save my life, not to mention stopping those awful Miltons from abusing me. You don't have to worry about him."

Lafayette stared at Hawkshaw's back. "I have seen snakes with warmer hearts than his. All right, my little Tennie. Go to Waco and wait for my brother." He kissed her cheek before turning to get on his bay. Once in the saddle, he moved the horse toward Gid. "Giddings Coltrane. Keep your hands to yourself. Do not touch Miss Tennie in any way for any reason without her permission. Do you understand me?"

"Yes, sir," Gid said, and Tennie thought for a moment he was going to salute.

Shorty, after getting on his horse, gave the Granger children a severe look. "Boys." He did not have to say more. One word said it all. He looked at Tennie. "Tennie, you have been through an extraordinary ordeal. Rest in Waco."

"Yes, Shorty," she promised.

After more directives from Lafayette about getting added money from the bank in case of an emergency, having their luggage delivered to the hotel he wanted them to stay in, and promising to call off the posse looking for her as soon as they reached Waco, the two men left.

CHAPTER 12

Tennie sat down on a fallen cottonwood log. There was no hurry. If Lafayette met Wash in Waco, he would send him to them. If he wasn't there, they would have to wait anyway.

With Lafayette and Shorty gone, Rusty and Lucas began to fight over who would ride the Appaloosa.

"It's my turn," Rusty said.

"You didn't even like him at first," Lucas said. "You just want to ride him now because I won a horse race with him."

It became an increasingly louder shouting match until it turned into a fistfight.

Badger began to cry. "I want my Rascal," he sobbed. "I want my dog."

Tennie tried to console him. "We'll see Rascal soon."

He was having none of it. "I want my Rascal right now!" he cried, throwing himself on the ground. He lay on his back, proceeding to have a screaming fit, kicking his feet and flailing his arms.

Tennie stared at him in dismay while Rusty and Lucas threw violent punches at one another, causing blood to spurt from noses and eyes to be blackened. Gid, without a word, picked Badger up and tossed him as far as he could into the muddy Brazos, creating a tremendous splash that put a halt to Rusty and Lucas's fight.

As pudgy as Badger was, especially after all the tortillas he had cadged off the Mexican women, he could still hold his own swimming with the rest of the boys. Tennie walked to the river's edge, just to be sure that a current didn't take him under, but he swam with ease to the shore. She helped him out of the river, and they walked back to the others.

"Are we going to reach Waco today?" she asked Gid.

He shook his head. "Probably not, Miss Tennie."

She turned to the older boys. "Rusty, you can ride the Appaloosa today, and tomorrow, Lucas can ride him into Waco."

"Well now, that sounds like a plan," Gid said. "Say, what's that there horse's name anyhow?"

"I want to name him," Rusty said.

"No! He's mine, and I'll name him," Lucas insisted.

"No! Me! Me!" Badger cried.

"I'll name him!" Tennie yelled, trying to circumvent another argument. Everyone stared at her. "His name is . . . his name is Apache John!"

Lucas and Rusty looked at one another.

"Apache? That's a good name for a horse," Rusty said, and Lucas agreed.

Tennie closed her eyes and shook her head. When she opened them, she was surprised to see Hawkshaw had not fled.

"Who's Apache John?" he asked.

"He was an Indian who saved my life with a mad stone when I got snake bit," Tennie said.

"I thought you didn't believe in that stuff," Hawkshaw said.

"That I believe," Tennie said. "I'm just a little skeptical of a raw egg being able to take any of your evil spirits away."

Hawkshaw laughed.

Tennie shook her head again, giving up trying to understand this strange man. "Listen," she told the boys. "That horse really belongs to any relatives of the Miltons."

"No, he doesn't," Hawkshaw said. "There aren't any."

That settled that.

As they made preparations to leave, Tennie realized they now had an Appaloosa to feed in addition to a gray dun, a buckskin, and a mule back in Ring Bit. She was sure she was going to be horse poor.

Once on their way, Gid began to talk about his mother, who was in ill health; his no-account brothers, two who were in prison and two more who were out roaming the countryside causing trouble; and his snooty relatives who included Lafayette's disastrous former love interest.

Just when Tennie thought she knew more than she could ever possibly want to know about the Coltranes, Hawkshaw said, "Don't you ever shut up?"

Gid gave him a hard look. The horse Gid was riding whinnied as if he had been holding it in, waiting to get a word in edgewise. "Ain't nobody complaining but you, gunfighter. You can hightail it out of here any time you're ready."

Tennie reined her old nag closer. "No, he can't. His leg still hasn't healed, and he doesn't need to be off by himself somewhere else in case he falls sick."

Gid gave Hawkshaw a snort. "Some folks ain't got no manners."

"Appears to me like you're the one with no manners," Hawkshaw taunted. "Where's that politeness you Johnny Rebs are always bragging about?"

Tennie sighed. Hawkshaw was an expert needler. She started to say something to break them up, but Gid spoke first.

"Blue belly, wasn't you?" Gid said, making it sound like something shameful. "I reckon I should have known that."

"Gid was an explosives specialist. It's because of his expertise that we were able to blow our way out of trouble," Tennie reminded Hawkshaw.

Despite anything she said, Hawkshaw and Gid continued to jab one another. Neither came off the victor or the loser because each held the unassailable belief he was right. To make matters worse, the weather had begun to grow hot and sultry.

Tennie moved away from the bickering men, riding off to one side by herself as she wondered if Wash Jones had forgotten about her or had decided he didn't really want to marry her after all. Why should he? She wasn't and never had been like the soft southern belles he grew up with. She was just a nobody.

She wiped sweat from her brow. Her dress was wet with perspiration, and her horse dripped with it.

"The wind is changing. It's going to storm," Gid said, breaking off the squabbling. "We best get away from this here river and find someplace safe to make camp."

They rode for some time, looking for shelter. The trees were near the river. Beyond that was a sea of stirrup-high grass.

"We're getting into this goldang black gumbo, too," Gid said. "If it rains, we'll be up to our eye pits in mud." He told them they would have to find a small grove of trees surrounded by larger ones. As clouds with dark underbellies rolled closer, and the scent of rain could be smelled, they found something not too near the water. They set about building two lean-tos.

Hawkshaw stated he had no plans of sleeping

anywhere near Gid, and Gid replied he wasn't about to let Hawkshaw out of his sight. Hawkshaw gave in, and Tennie could tell by his paleness that his leg was bothering him. He gimped around somewhat but couldn't do the work Gid and the boys did. She tried to help, too. As wind began to whip her skirts, and fat drops of water hit her face, predicting what was in store, she tied branches to the lean-tos in hopes of tempering a soon to be driving rain.

Thunder rumbled and lightning began to strike. Gid ordered her and the boys to get under the lean-to and not crowd too close to one another.

Thus began a miserable night. Their lean-to offered a minimum of protection. Hawkshaw and Gid had blankets they insisted on giving to Tennie and the boys, but they were soon soaked. Thunder crashed, and lightning struck a tall tree in front of them, lighting up the night as it ripped through the trunk, splitting it in two and making as loud an explosion as the gunpowder they had set off in the canyon. It looked and sounded like the devil was after them. Sleep didn't come until far into the night, when the thunder and lightning stopped and the rain slowed to a steady miserable drizzle.

By dawn it had let up, but they awoke hungry and feeling wretched. Hawkshaw and Gid immediately began to argue. Hawkshaw accused Gid of snoring louder than a freight train, and Gid accused him of buzzing like a sawmill.

"Let's just go," Tennie pleaded. "We can find something to eat later."

They had to stay in the trees near the river. The thick roots were the only thing that kept the horses' hooves from sinking in black mud. When they began to see acres of cotton growing, they knew they were getting close to Waco. Despite the crops, there were no signs of humans.

The storm seemed to have scared off every living thing. Rusty and Lucas asked permission to try *bagre* fishing as the Mexican boys had taught them. Tennie didn't trust rivers, especially after a rain. If it had stormed upstream, a wall of water could come down the river at a few seconds' notice. She was also afraid of cottonmouth snakes.

"I ain't seen so much as a rabbit to kill around here," Gid said.

Tennie gave in when he promised to watch the boys and keep Badger on the bank.

"You go on over yonder with your back to that there tree so these young'uns can strip down," he ordered.

"All right." She looked at Hawkshaw. "Will you join me, Mr. Hawkshaw? I think you need to sit down and stretch that leg out for a while."

He nodded and she followed him to a massive cottonwood tree trunk. She didn't try to help him down, and when he was seated, she sat down on a protruding root some feet away.

"How is your leg?" she asked.

"Tolerable," he answered. "That idiot is eating all this up. He's nothing but a big kid himself."

Tennie thought of the look in Gid's eyes when he had faced Wash holding a gun on him. "Don't underestimate him. If we weren't putting up with him, we'd be putting up with Lafayette and Shorty pacing around, panting at the bit to get home to business. And if you think you are low on Gid's list, you are at the bottom of Lafayette's."

"I don't give a rat's ass," Hawkshaw said, and Tennie realized that just about summed up his life.

They could hear the boys squealing and hollering, but it sounded like happy noises.

"What are you going to do now?" she asked.

"I don't know," Hawkshaw said, letting out a long breath. "I'm thinking about taking the money back to Beauregard instead of wiring it, just to put the fear of God into him. Otherwise, he may put a bounty on my head, too, just out of pure cussedness."

"Right now," Tennie said, "all I can think about is getting to Waco, taking a bath, and throwing this dress and all these filthy petticoats into the trash." She was happy to see a sardonic look cross his face, replacing the despondency.

"Ladies don't talk like that to gentlemen, Miss Tennie Marshal," he said.

"I'm all right then, because you aren't a gentleman."

"Miss Tennie, Miss Tennie," Lucas called. "Come look and see what we got."

Tennie tried to rise, but tripped over a root, landing palms down. She grimaced and stood up, wiping her hands on the massive tree trunk. A thought darted across her mind that it had become abnormally quiet in Lucas's direction.

She stepped out from behind the tree and gasped. Two lowdown ruffians had appeared, one holding on to Lucas and Rusty while the other had a chokehold on Gid's neck with one arm, holding a gun to his head with the other. A petrified Badger had strapped himself to Gid's leg, while Rusty held a gigantic catfish, both he and Lucas looking surprised at suddenly being manhandled.

"Well, would you lookee here now," one of the ruffians said when he saw her.

Tennie reasoned fast. Hawkshaw would rise and come around from behind the tree. As soon as that thought popped into her head, Rusty dropped the fish and he and Lucas stomped on their assailant's feet, escaping his grasp.

"Hit the dirt!" Tennie yelled and fell facedown.

Lucas and Rusty did the same, followed by Badger, still clutching Gid's foot. Hawkshaw came from around the tree and fired two shots so fast, Tennie wasn't sure which man he hit first.

The one who had been grasping the boys got it in his chest. The one holding Gid received his between the eyes.

Tennie rose as Gid shook his head. "Gosh dang it," he said, popping his ear with his hand. "That flew by so close, I think it busted my eardrum. I can't hear a thing out of this here ear."

"Who were they? Road agents?" Tennie gasped.

"Yep, I reckon so," Gid said, his hearing impairment not affecting his voluble tongue. "Come from out of nowhere."

"What are we going to do?" she cried. "Do we have to take them with us to Waco?"

"Oh no, we'll just chuck them in the river," Gid said. "Ain't no use in taking them to Waco and causing a stir."

"Can we see if they have any money on them first?" Lucas asked.

"Lucas!" Tennie said, but no one paid her any heed.

"Why sure, boy." Gid leaned down and began to strip the bodies of their possessions with the precision speed of an expert.

"What about their guns?" Rusty asked.

Gid picked one up, eyeballed it, and tossed it aside. "Can't keep that one. Got his initials carved on it. Last thing we want to do is ride into Waco carrying a dead man's gun. Some of his kinfolks might recognize it." He examined the other one. "This one will be all right. We can keep it."

Tennie turned to Hawkshaw and gave him a questioning stare, but he just shrugged his shoulders.

"What about their horses, Mr. Gid?" Lucas asked.

"Go fetch them and let's have a look-see," Gid said.

"Shouldn't we get out of here?" Tennie asked.

Gid rose and saw the look on her face. "Don't you worry none, Miss Tennie. We'll slit their lungs, throw 'em in the river, and they'll sink like cannonballs. Then we can take our time roasting this here nice catfish."

Tennie didn't know whether to cry or throw up.

Rusty and Lucas came back leading two nondescript horses. Gid ransacked their saddlebags, but finding nothing of importance, announced the saddles were trash and not worth keeping. "We'll chuck them in the river, too. These here horses ain't nothing but scrub, so no use losing any time even giving them a thought. We'll turn 'em loose."

Tennie, feeling like a ghoul, turned away. She looked at Hawkshaw and shook her head in resignation. Despite being nauseous, she was still hungry. "Isn't the wood going to be too wet to catch fire? I can't stand raw fish."

"Miss Tennie," Hawkshaw said. "You underestimate the skills of former soldiers, blue and gray. Help me gather some firewood."

213

Tennie thought it impressed Hawkshaw that Gid never acted like he even wanted to complain Hawkshaw had risked his life shooting someone so close to him. Gid grumbled about his ears ringing from the sound of the bullet exploding so close to his head, but his faith in Hawkshaw's aim appeared unquestioning.

Later on, as Tennie sat on her haunches eating delectably roasted fish, she thought how cheap life was on the frontier. But she couldn't help that and said, "I sure hope we can make it into Waco without anything else happening to us."

"Oh, that weren't nothing but a little tussle," Gid said.

Tennie thought it was more than a tussle, but she didn't contradict him. "I look a sight. I'm going to be embarrassed riding into Waco looking like this. I know menfolk can take baths in barbershops, but will they let women bathe there too?"

Hawkshaw shook his head. "We'll have the hotel bring you up a tub and some hot water."

"I hope Mr. Lafayette remembered to have our bags taken to the hotel," she said.

"We can get two rooms side by side," Gid said. "You can stay in one, and me and the boys, and Hawkshaw can stay in the other."

Tennie raised her eyes to look at Hawkshaw, but he continued to eat and made no protest about sharing a room. Gid would flop on any bed and have no problem sharing it with three squirming boys, but Tennie was willing to bet Hawkshaw would kick everyone off the bed and tell them to sleep in the corner. But he wasn't talking about dumping them the minute they hit Waco.

The first thing they saw as they neared Waco was its new suspension bridge. With tall turrets, it looked like an illustration out of a book of fairy tales. The boys had never seen one, and it fascinated them. To their left, hundreds of cattle grazed, waiting for tired drovers to herd them across the bridge and onto stock cars that would take them to Houston and beyond. There was a small fee to cross, and the robbers left behind with the fishes in the Brazos paid for that with some left over. As she crossed the bridge, looking down at the wide, muddy Brazos, Tennie felt a little light-headed.

They were soon across, riding straight toward the town square. Hawkshaw and Gid declared they would see her settled in a hotel before taking the horses back to the livery. Every neck except Hawkshaw's craned at the bustling crowds and the big buildings that looked like grand dukes on the prairie. Gid had ridden horseback to Texas, staying to the north and bypassing Waco, but Hawkshaw had taken the train. None of it was new to him, and being well traveled, Tennie doubted he was overly impressed the first time he saw it.

Too embarrassed by her ragged appearance to stand around in the lobby for long, she stayed outside the rather impressive hotel while the men went in to see about rooms.

When the men returned, they reported Lafayette had remembered to make reservations and have their bags brought over. A maid had been instructed to take a tub and hot water to Tennie's room.

"Was there a letter from Wash?" Tennie asked. "Any word at all?"

Gid shook his head. She gave him a small smile and a nod, determined not to ruin anyone else's fun by fretting over Wash.

By supper, Tennie had cleaned and luxuriated in a sumptuous room she never would have dreamed of renting herself, but Lafayette had already made arrangements on what she should have and that the bill be sent to him. She had forced the boys to bathe and put on clean clothes—although Rusty still dressed like a cowboy and the two younger boys remained in overalls—the idea being they would buy fancier wedding clothes in Austin.

Going downstairs, the four of them met Hawkshaw and Gid in the lobby. They went to the door of the hotel dining room and peeked in, finding it full of white tablecloths and sparkling crystal.

Tennie looked at Hawkshaw and Gid. "Is there a café nearby?"

Without a word, they turned and herded the boys outside.

The café they followed Hawkshaw to was nicer than the one in Ring Bit, but the tablecloths were blue checkered homespun, not linen. He led them to a table on the side, where he could sit with his back to the wall, facing the windows and door. They hadn't had anything but fish all day and fell hungrily on their food. Hawkshaw hardly spoke. Gid, being new to Texas, wasn't as silent as most men when he dined; nevertheless, he was serious about eating.

After supper, Gid wanted to have a beer in one of the saloons, and Hawkshaw said he wanted to check to make sure the stableman had followed his instructions about his horse. They left Tennie and the boys on the hotel veranda, where they could watch the rest of Waco until nightfall.

Gid and Hawkshaw had been gone about five minutes when Tennie caught sight of a square-faced man with a drooping gray mustache. Not a big man, he wore a nondescript gray hat, pants tucked into his boots, and a leather vest with a star pinned on the shoulder. He looked as if he was purposely heading their way, and Tennie held her breath, wondering if he was bringing news of Wash.

He stopped on one of the veranda steps, placing one hand on the post. "Mrs. Granger? From Ring Bit?"

Tennie remained seated but leaned forward.

217

"Yes, sir?" she asked, aware the boys were nearby and listening.

"I'm the sheriff of McLennan County. I'm also a friend of the sheriff in Cat Ridge."

Cat Ridge? Tennie wondered. What did the sheriff in Cat Ridge have to do with Wash?

"I'm here to warn you that I run a tight town," the sheriff said.

Tennie forbore replying that Waco had a reputation of everything except being a tight town.

He continued. "We license all our saloons and the houses on Second Street."

Tennie knew she looked confused. Why would she care if he licensed houses on Second Street? And why not houses on all the streets? Nothing he said was making sense.

"I don't want no trouble in this town. And you've caused enough already. I've heard about those stepsons of yours, and if they so much as look cross-eyed at a stray cat in this here town, I'm running them and you out."

That she understood.

The sheriff looked at her. "What's the matter with you? Are you deaf?"

Tennie sighed. "No, just tired. They'll behave."

He didn't know what to make of her or how to take her. He finally threw her a cross look and stalked away.

Tennie looked at her stepsons. "No trouble."

"Yes, ma'am," they agreed.

218

CHAPTER 13

The next day, Tennie looked in the stores, shopping for a new dress. Along the way, she counted ten law offices on the square, many of them in partnerships. Ring Bit didn't have any attorneys, and Cat Ridge only had one. The boys found the ice cream parlor, and she stopped to eat ice cream with them, laughing at them for licking their chins to catch every drop.

Later, dissatisfied with the quality of dresses she found, she decided to buy the fabric and make her own. It would give her something to do while she waited in Waco. She picked another pretty pink calico. The petticoats in Waco were of a much finer make, however, and she was able to purchase those.

Once at the hotel, she rang the bell in the lobby for the clerk. He appeared, emerging from a room behind the desk, a slender nervous man with his hair parted down the middle and a thin mustache across the upper lip of his beleaguered face. She asked about sending the fabric out to be washed and pressed so it could be shrunk before she cut it, but he gave her a frazzled look and proclaimed he was shorthanded.

"I'm so sorry, Mrs. Granger," he said. "You can wait a few days, or if you'd rather, you can take it to the washerwomen who live in shanties down by the river. They'll do it for you."

He gave her the names of a couple of women to ask for. "You'll be safe heading in that direction during the daytime, but please avoid going south."

She nodded and, after thanking him, asked the boys if they wanted to walk with her.

"We'll go part of the way," Rusty said. "But can we stop at the livery and wait for you there?"

"I don't see why not," Tennie agreed.

They walked together, and leaving them at the livery stable, Tennie continued on to the river. As she neared, she saw row after row of crude hovels, so ill-built she couldn't understand how they could manage to stay standing in a strong breeze. Dirty and half-dressed children ran in the muddy streets that were little more than trails like dogs and coyotes made. And the dogs she saw looked like mangy skeletons. Women went about their business, leaving the few men there sitting in doorways. They were sickly looking, almost all amputees.

She stopped some children and inquired about the women the hotel clerk had told her about. They led her to a shanty that looked like all the others, where a bent woman was standing over a fire, stirring clothes with a stick.

"Excuse me, ma'am," Tennie began, explaining that the hotel clerk said she might be able to wash and iron a bolt of cloth for her.

The woman agreed, sounding as if she had just come down from a mountain deep in the Appalachians. As Tennie listened attentively, she looked carefully at the woman. She saw that her hands were knobby, and she was bent because she couldn't stand up straight. Her long arms hung by her stunted torso, her large, wide mouth downturned and sad. With a shock, Tennie realized the woman was probably only a few years older than she was.

She was telling Tennie she would deliver the fabric to the hotel before nightfall. The hotel clerk would pay her and charge it to Tennie's bill.

Hesitantly, Tennie reached into her pocket for some coins. "I want you to do a special job on it. So, I'm tipping you extra now." She thrust the coins into the surprised woman's hands, leaving the fabric with her before she could mutter much more than "Thankee, ma'am."

Tennie left the shantytown as quickly as she could without attracting undue attention. Almost unable to breathe, she walked, looking straight forward. As much as she hated being the town marshal of Ring Bit, as much as she hated the cursing and violence of the prisoners, the messes they left for her to clean up, her life was nowhere near as hard as that of the washerwomen.

She realized what lay south of town, what Second Street was, and she thought of the women there. Would she have the courage to turn herself into a drudge rather than live the softer life of a prostitute? She thought of the abuse heaped on them by others and by themselves. Nothing was easy.

All she could do was follow her own way, to walk the path she thought was right.

The fabric was delivered to the hotel as promised, and with it, Tennie spent the next few days cutting and sewing. Many times, she sat in one of the big rockers on the hotel veranda, stitching in better light and talking to whoever happened by. Hawkshaw, trying to stay off his leg, often sat in a chair away from hers and never interacted with anyone. Gid made the rounds in Waco, visiting the liveries, the stores, the banks, and the saloons. He knew every doctor, lawyer, gambler, and blacksmith in town. When he wasn't out gossiping, he was talking to Tennie or entertaining the boys with fantastic stories of his experiences, many of which Tennie wondered if he had made up. But then again, once they were no longer in Waco, Gid's story of Hawkshaw shooting a man next to him between the eyes would become part of his repertoire.

Rusty and Lucas stayed busy making friends with the Waco boys, earning extra money cleaning out stables and running errands for shopkeepers and businessmen. Badger divided his time between following them as much as they would let him, hanging around the hotel with Tennie, and occasionally going with Gid on his rounds.

Tennie finished her dress and sent it off to be pressed. Afterward, she found her favorite rocker on the veranda and sat down to look out over the square. Hawkshaw joined her, sitting several feet away as was his custom. They caught sight of Gid, shambling toward them with his head down.

"I wonder what's wrong with him?" Tennie said.

"The beer wagon must have met with an accident," Hawkshaw said.

Tennie turned and shot him a look. "He hardly drinks at all."

Gid removed his hat when he reached the veranda. He stood in front of Tennie, fiddling with the brim.

"Mr. Gid," Tennie said. "What is it?"

"I been over yonder talking to some Texas Rangers. Near as they can figure, when Wash and his men got close to the senator's farm, somebody come out to meet them. Instead of saying it had all been a hoax, they said it had been taken care of."

Tennie tried to digest what that meant. Hawkshaw, seeing her confusion, told her. "It means he didn't have a clue it had been a setup."

Tennie threw him a grateful glance then turned back. "What else, Mr. Gid?"

"Well"—Gid looked down and shifted his

weight from one foot to the other—"he got sent down to this here Nueces Strip where there's bad trouble going on."

"Nueces Strip?" Tennie asked.

"It's a strip of land between Mexico and the Nueces River. They's always having problems down yonder. Bandits, raiding Indians, all kinds of horse thieves and outlaws. It's a rough place, sure 'nuff," Gid said.

"He's gone to this Nueces Strip?" Tennie said. "And he didn't send any letters?"

"Oh, yes, ma'am," Gid assured her. "He done sent a whole passel of letters, but the mail bag got robbed. I reckon he don't know nothing about what happened to you, Miss Tennie, and he thinks you done been getting all his letters."

Tennie put her head down and rubbed her forehead. Remembering her manners, she thanked Gid for relaying the information. She knew he had pumped the rangers for every scrap of information he could get out of them.

"They was going to come over here and tell you they self, but I said I'd pass the word along to you," Gid explained. "They said there ain't no use in you sending him no letters down yonder. He ain't going to get them nohow."

Tennie tried hard to keep from crying. "Thank you, Mr. Gid." She looked over the square, feeling so forlorn she didn't know what to do. She saw the boys running toward them.

Rusty had something in his hand, and after a span of a few seconds, she realized it was a telegram.

"Oh, no, more bad news," she said with a gasp, and Gid turned to see what she was talking about.

The boys reached the veranda, but the telegram was for Gid, not Tennie.

Gid took the telegram and looked at it, holding it far away from his eyes, frowning at it. "I can't make head nor tails out of this." He thrust the telegram back in Rusty's hands. "Here, you read it."

Rusty cleared his throat. "MA DEAD STOP BROTHERS HIRED SHYSTER LAWYER STOP" He looked up. "It says it is from Nab Coltrane."

Gid threw his hat down, tears coming in his eyes. "Aw, shucks! Ma's dead," he cried. "Them good-for-nothing brothers of mine are trying to cheat Nab and me out of the farm."

"How do you know?" Lucas asked.

" 'Cause Ma willed it to me and Nab before I left," Gid said. "I told Nab to look after my share. And now our sorry brothers are trying to get it and kick poor old Nab off the farm."

"Mr. Gid, I'm so sorry . . ." Tennie began.

Gid went off on another tear about his brothers. While he was bemoaning the death of his mother and the blackheartedness of his family, Lucas and Rusty appealed to Tennie.

"Miss Tennie, can't we do something to help Mr. Gid?" Lucas asked.

And Rusty whispered, "Miss Tennie, Mr. Gid can barely read and write. He'd be no match against scoundrel lawyers."

"I don't know what we can do," Tennie said.

Hawkshaw made a noise, and she turned to look at him.

"When I return the money to Beauregard, he's going to hire someone else to come here and kill Lafayette." It was as if he had been waiting for the right moment to tell her.

"Miss Tennie," Lucas cried. "We have to do something."

"I don't know what to do," Tennie cried. "We can't go roaming all over the South trying to help Mr. Gid and keep some old man from getting revenge."

"But we have to do something," Rusty pleaded.

"Ain't that your job as marshal?" Lucas asked. "You're still the marshal, ain't you? Shorty said you were."

"Let me think," Tennie cried. "Just let me think on it a while." She rose and went back upstairs to her room.

Walking to the lace curtains, she looked out the window over the town. In his letters, Wash would have advised her what to do. But his letters hadn't come. Would he be furious with her if she left Waco and went off with two men and three boys hundreds of miles away from Texas to try to solve something that was beyond her capabilities anyway? Lafayette would be horrified.

On the other hand, there could be no telling when Wash might return. It might be months before he was free to come back. And the thought of going back to Ring Bit to wait for another assassin to arrive to kill Lafayette was abhorrent.

Round and round her thoughts went. How would she like it if Wash went off with two strange women? She would hate it. It dawned on her that Wash probably ran across lonely and needy women like Lupe all the time. He expected her to trust him. Shouldn't she expect him to trust her, too?

If only Wash was there with her. He would take care of everything.

She looked down at the street and saw her three stepsons in a whispered conference. They stood up and hurried away, out of her sight. She was too caught up in the dilemma facing her to wonder too much about what they were up to.

At supper, everyone but Gid was silent. He complained about his family, cried over his mama, wondered if he should find his father and tell him, and bemoaned that his hands were tied, making Tennie feel even guiltier. Her stepsons, however, kept their eyes on their food and left off their pleading.

227

Tennie went to bed, praying for wisdom and guidance as she fell into a fitful sleep.

The noises outside began to filter into her room, interrupting what little rest she had. It seemed the whole south side of town had erupted into a volcano of noise and activity. Guns were fired off more so than usual. Loud curses and screams filled the night. Just when the uproar seemed to be dying down, someone began to bang loudly on her door, and she heard a man hollering her name.

"Mrs. Granger, Mrs. Granger! Open this door."

She got up and reached for the robe she had bought before leaving Ring Bit. "Just a minute." Poking her arms awkwardly through the sleeves as she hurried to the door, her heart gave a lurch, worrying that something had happened to one of the boys. She tied the cord and opened the door.

The sheriff stood in the dimly lit hall, his face angry and as red as a rooster's wattle. Gid and Hawkshaw came out of their room. Rusty, Lucas, and Badger hovered in the background. The sheriff ignored them and the eyes peeking from behind cracked doors up and down the hall.

"What is it?" Tennie asked, pretty sure she didn't want to know the answer.

"I told you, woman, I told you," the sheriff yelled. "I said if those stepsons of yours so much as caused one inch of trouble in my town, I was kicking them and you out of this here town."

"Uh," Tennie began. "What did they do?"

"What did they do? What did they do?" He was so apoplectic, Tennie feared he was going to have a heart attack.

"Do you need a nitroglycerin tablet or something?" Tennie asked.

"Shut up! No, I do not need a nitroglycerin tablet," he roared. "I need you to take those little hellions of yours the hell out of my town. I have never in all my born days seen such an uproar as they caused. Rats put in beer barrels. Dead snakes on the sidewalks. Street signs switched. Horses moved all over town and saddles put on backwards."

"They didn't hurt the horses, did they?" Tennie asked.

"No! But isn't that enough? Isn't it enough they wrote, 'Waco, home of the clap,' on the sidewalk in front of every brothel in town?"

"What is the clap?" She remembered almost as soon as the words left her mouth, causing her to blush so much she thought blood would exit her pores. She hastily changed the subject. "How do you know it was my stepsons?"

The sheriff got right up in her face. "Because only trash from Ring Bit would dare do such a thing," he said, his breath coming out hot and foul. "I don't want you or your stepsons in my town any longer."

Tennie raised herself up and spoke with as

229

much self-respect as she could muster. "We will be happy to leave tomorrow. Now I must ask you to let me get back to sleep."

"Aarrghh," he growled. He turned on his heels, stopping to give Hawkshaw and Gid a momentary glare before stomping away.

"You didn't do anything here in the hotel, did you?" Tennie whispered.

Her stepsons shook their heads vigorously. "No, ma'am, only on Second Street."

Tennie stared at all five of them. She set her eyes on Hawkshaw. "What time does the train leave for Dixie?"

"One o'clock tomorrow," Hawkshaw answered. "I already have the tickets."

Her eyes moved to Gid. Hawkshaw saw it. "Don't accuse me of having sympathy for anybody else's troubles. When I go in dragging you and these kids behind me, no one will blame me for returning the money and refusing to do the job."

"It's so nice that one always knows where one stands with you." She looked at the boys. "Go to back to bed. We have a big day tomorrow." She went back into her room and shut the door.

Due to circumstances mainly beyond his control, Wash had left her stranded in a Waco hotel. She couldn't wire Lafayette for help or advice. He would insist on accompanying her. Not only did he need to take care of his own business in Ring Bit, he would probably unintentionally instigate another duel. She put her forehead against the door and shut her eyes. Hawkshaw was out to save his own skin, and Gid would only aggravate his own relatives.

She beat her head against the door frame. "I can't do this. I can't do this. I can't do this," she whispered. She stopped the banging and wiped away the tears that sprang into her eyes. She would have to try.

Going back to bed, Tennie fell into a deep sleep.

In the morning, she began writing—facts, not accusations. She would leave a letter for Wash in the general delivery box in Waco. As far as she knew, he was still her fiancé, and she wrote of her love and longing for him.

While she was agonizing over what to write Lafayette, to tell him where she was going without him trying to follow her, Badger rushed into the room.

"Miss Tennie." Breathless, he leaned his elbows on her knees as she sat at the desk. "Mr. and Mrs. Payton are downstairs sitting on the veranda, and they want to talk to you."

Surprised, Tennie rose. "Thank you, Badger," she said, following him out the door and wondering what the Paytons were doing in Waco.

"We heard about your troubles, Tennie," Mr.

Payton explained as she sat down by the couple on the veranda. "We had a cousin who died, so we thought we'd come here and settle his estate in person and check on you at the same time."

Tennie murmured her thanks and sympathy, wondering just how much land the Paytons already owned. They dressed and lived simply, but she had the feeling there were piles of money to back up anything they felt like saying or doing. They wanted to know about the kidnapping, and she explained about that.

"What's this I hear about you running off on the train to save Lafayette's hide?" Mr. Payton demanded when she finished. "Let him take care of his own problems. I told you before, Tennie, Lafayette will do everything he can to get you to feel obliged to him."

"It's not that," Tennie said, explaining about Wash. "Shorty told me I am still the marshal of Ring Bit. I either go back to Ring Bit and wait for the next hired gun to show up, or I try to put a stop to it now. I don't have anywhere else to go. I don't know when Wash is coming back, and the sheriff is kicking us out of Waco."

"Humph," Mr. Payton said. "The sheriff's just trying to get you out of town hoping Hawkshaw will leave, too. He's afraid of him."

"I never thought about that," Tennie said. Her anger at the sheriff softened somewhat. "It doesn't make any difference, though."

"If I could get my hands on Wash Jones," Mr. Payton threatened, "I'd lay down the law to that boy."

"It's just the way it is," Tennie said. "He told me on the stage coming here that he wants to continue being a ranger for a while yet. He doesn't want us to stay in Ring Bit. He wants us to live on his San Antonio ranch. But we're not married yet, and he's not here."

The boys were in the background, hanging on to Winn Payton's words. Their faces were full of worry, hoping Mr. Payton didn't change her mind about helping Gid. She thought perhaps Hawkshaw and Gid had gone into hiding.

"That's another thing," she said. "Will you talk to Lafayette for me? And convince him that we'll be fine with Mr. Gid and Mr. Hawkshaw as escorts? And if Wash gets back soon, I'm sure he'll try to join me. If Lafayette goes, he could start another family war and that many more duels."

"I don't care what happens to Lafayette," Mr. Payton said. "But I agree you'd be better off without him. I'll talk to him if you are dead set on going."

Tennie breathed a sigh of relief, thinking he had finished with his fussing, but she was wrong.

"But this Coltrane business," he said. "Tennie, do you have any idea what those people are like? They live up in those hills feuding with one another. Somebody will probably take a potshot at you before you ever reach the house."

"All the better for us to have Mr. Hawkshaw with us," Tennie said.

Mrs. Payton interjected in her gentle way. "Tennie, dear. It's not wise for you to travel alone with two men, even if your stepsons are with you. You may trust them, but other people will be suspicious of you. You certainly won't be received in the South. You really need a female chaperone with you."

"You mean, they won't talk to me?" Tennie asked.

"Oh, no, they'll speak to you. They just won't ask you to stay in their homes."

Tennie shrugged. She had been ostracized for so long, it never occurred to her to think otherwise. "I don't know anyone here in Waco . . . unless you would want to go with me?"

"Oh no, dear. I'm sorry," Mrs. Payton said. "It's taken it out of me just making this trip."

"I don't want you interfering in some kind of legal hassles with the Coltranes," Mr. Payton added. "That crazy branch Lafayette got mixed up with will be bad enough, but the Coltranes . . ."

Tennie felt like crying. She knew they were right, but she didn't know what else to do.

Mrs. Payton sat with an introspective look on her face. She turned to her husband. "Father, didn't the son of the judge there serve in your unit during the war? Why don't you write a letter of introduction to the judge for Tennie? That may solve many of her problems."

He nodded and turned to the boys, surprising Tennie. She hadn't known he realized they were behind him.

"Make yourselves useful and go fetch me a pen, ink, some paper, and something to write on. And if you boys don't mind Miss Tennie on this trip, I'm personally coming up there to haul your behinds back to Ring Bit and make the preacher take care of you."

"He won't. He hates us," Lucas said, adding, "sir."

"He will if I say so," Mr. Payton said. "And he doesn't hate you. He just can't stand you. Now hop to it. You have a train to catch."

Before they left, Mr. Payton asked how she was paying for the trip. She was reluctant to tell them most of it was being paid for with money taken off the bushwhackers at the river. Instead, she explained she still had some of her own, plus the money Lafayette gave her. "I won't touch what Wash gave us unless we are starving."

"How much money was on the Miltons?" he asked.

Tennie paused. "About forty dollars, I think."

"There should have been more. They sold the butcher shop."

"I don't know," Tennie said. "They probably gave most of it to Inga."

"Lafayette said they didn't find her body," Mr. Payton said.

"They probably buried her and the money before coming after us," Tennie said, not wanting anything more to do with what the Miltons might or might not have had. "Mr. Hawkshaw bought our train tickets in exchange for showing we are a big part of the reason he decided not to go through with killing Lafayette."

Mr. Payton grimaced. "He may be a cold-blooded devil, but he does have brains. If you get broke and stranded, Tennie, wire the bank in Cat Ridge. I'll see that they send you something."

She almost cried again, hardly believing how kind the Paytons were to her.

CHAPTER 14

When she found out the amount the livery was going to charge for stabling the Appaloosa, Tennie drew back and gulped, but the boys promised to pay for part of it out of the money they had made running errands in Waco.

Gid apologized multiple times all the way to the train station for not hearing them sneak out to raise havoc the night before, but Tennie assured him it had worked out for the best. She knew very well Hawkshaw understood exactly what they were up to even before they did it, but he said nothing and so did she.

Horses and buggies filled the street. At the train station, people were lining up next to the tracks. Farther down, drovers were herding cattle into livestock cars, their long horns clashing. It was exciting and scary watching the men with their long whips, cracking them above the cattle's heads, using the noise to jolt the frightened animals into moving in the direction they wanted them to go. One second of getting too close could mean death to man and horse, and many of them looked only a few years older than Rusty.

Tennie found herself suddenly afraid of the iron horse belching fire. She looked at Hawkshaw. At least he had ridden a train before, and Gid knew how to rob them, or not, since he had failed. Hawkshaw had had the café prepare four baskets of food for them, along with canteens of water. He explained that although riding a train was much faster, it lacked certain luxuries a stagecoach provided. They would be stopping to take on firewood and water during the trip, and people were expected to exit the train and make quick use of that time to take care of necessities.

"I want to ride in the caboose," Lucas said.

"Me too, me too," Badger repeated.

Hawkshaw ground his teeth in impatience. "You can't. That's for the brakemen."

The conductor began calling for them to board, and Tennie found herself feeling much like a longhorn steer being led to slaughter. She wedged in between Hawkshaw and Gid, with the boys following behind.

As they stepped up into the car, Tennie, remembering Hawkshaw's idiosyncrasies, murmured, "Where do you want me to sit?"

"Sit with the boys in the middle of the car. I'll sit on one end, and Coltrane can sit on the other end. If there's any trouble, we'll have both ends covered."

"Trouble?" Tennie said, her lips trembling, but since she had reached the middle and Hawkshaw indicated for her to take a seat, she said no more.

Badger wanted to know why he couldn't sit with Gid.

238

"Because he doesn't want you pestering him to death," Rusty said.

Tennie looked around uneasily. "Let the car fill up and get going. Then if there's room, you can sit by Mr. Gid for a while. We have a long way to go."

Several of the cowboys who had been driving the cattle took seats near her, their spurs jangling on the wooden floor. When the whistle blew, there were only two other women on board, and they were obviously with husbands.

As the afternoon progressed, it was as Hawkshaw said. Dashing to get off the train at stops and a rush to get back on so one didn't get left behind. The grating and squealing of the iron wheels on the track made a tremendous noise, and cinders and ashes blew over them from time to time. Tennie did not blame Mrs. Payton for not wanting to endure it. They were entering cotton country again, miles and miles of cultivated river bottomland. Tennie had expected her stepsons to act like little firebrands, but beside the presence of so many hardened men who looked like they wouldn't put up with trash from anyone, much less a troublesome kid, the boys refrained. Besides, they were tired from their nocturnal Waco activities.

Tennie leaned her head back and closed her eyes. The cowboys behind her talked of nothing but cattle and horses. Keeping her eyes shut, she thought they knew she was listening to their excited talk of going to South Texas in search of a different breed of horse especially good for working with cattle. The boys, when they were not asleep, kept quiet, listening to the older boys talk of cattle and horses like it was a romance.

The only person who gave trouble was Gid. Sweat poured off him, and he fidgeted constantly.

Badger ran back and forth to report to Tennie. "Mr. Gid can't stand riding on the train. He says he feels boxed in."

And later, "Mr. Gid says he's about to go crazy. He's ready to jump out the window."

To Tennie's surprise, it was Hawkshaw who made the boys fill the canteens at every stop. It was Hawkshaw who stood on the steps making sure they were back on the train. Gid shot out at every stop, resting one hand against the boxcar while he bent over gulping large amounts of air. Instead of watching over the boys and helping them, they had to take Gid by the hand and lead him back onto the train. He was in shambles.

It was dark when they pulled into Hempstead, the last major stop before Houston. The train took a long time before starting up again. Hawkshaw disappeared.

When he came back, he held a brown bottle, halting by Gid and pressing it into his hand. "Drink it all and pass out. Maybe you won't wake up until we get to New Orleans."

Tennie fell asleep listening to the *click-clack* of the train wheels and the snoring of the other passengers.

When they stopped in Houston, the cowboys exited, and the railroad workers took off the livestock cars and added others. Almost everyone woke up during the loud clanks and short tugs of the locomotive, except Gid, who continued to snore loudly in the corner with his mouth open. Badger lay against Tennie, while Rusty and Lucas sat up sleepily to see what was happening.

After a long interval, they were back on their way to Louisiana, and Tennie fell asleep again. When she woke up, it was dawn, and they were in New Orleans. As the train screeched and jerked to a slow halt, she rose and gathered with the rest of her companions around Hawkshaw, crowding as close as he would let them.

"We're changing cars here," he said. "Get out and we'll fill these food baskets. But be careful. There are a lot of pickpockets in this town. If someone bumps into you, it's almost a sure thing they are trying to pick your pocket."

They exited the train, and Tennie gawked at the ornate streets, so different from anything she had ever seen before. Women with chocolate-colored skin walked with baskets balanced on their heads, chanting *"Belle Calas*! *Tout chauds*! Beautiful *calas*! Very hot!"

"What is that?" Tennie asked.

"Fried rice cakes," Hawkshaw said, stopping to buy some.

Hawkshaw and Gid filled their baskets with sausages, bananas, and sandwiches stuffed with fried shrimp and oysters.

"There might or might not be a dining car on this train," Hawkshaw said. He told Tennie there was no need for the men and boys to ride first class, but it might be more comfortable for her if she did.

"They're hooking up a Pullman car. You can sleep a lot better."

But Tennie shook her head. She wanted to stay with them.

Hawkshaw bought a copy of the *Picayune*, and they climbed aboard. When he finished the newspaper, he handed it to Tennie, and she and the boys took turns reading it out loud above the roar of the train.

"Listen to this, Miss Tennie," Rusty said. " 'Daring Dandies strike again.' "

Tennie and Lucas crowded closer to Rusty, looking over his shoulder as he read the story to them. A group of train robbers known for their flashy attire had held up three trains in the last six months.

"It says they always use a different modus operandi, Miss Tennie. What does that mean?" Rusty asked.

"I think it means method of operation,"

Tennie said. "They've blown up tracks, held up stationmasters at out-of-the-way stations, and also gone on board ahead of time and pulled out guns when their cohorts forced the train to stop."

"Maybe it's a different gang each time," Lucas said.

"No, they are always dressed in expensive, eye-catching clothes," Rusty said. "It says so right here."

"Do you think they'll rob our train?" Lucas asked, his face avid.

"I don't want to be in a train robbery," Badger cried.

"Don't worry," Tennie said. "I doubt if they rob us." But she looked at Hawkshaw and Gid.

Nevertheless, the thought of being robbed scared them. Tennie kept very little money on her; most of hers was sewn up in the pockets of Badger's overalls. Rusty decided to hide his in his hat band, while Lucas tucked his money inside his shoe as Gid had done.

When they left the last station on the coastline, entering deeper into Mississippi, the boys returned to the train with glum faces.

"What's wrong with them?" Hawkshaw asked.

Tennie glanced at the three boys. "I think they're disappointed the Daring Dandies didn't strike."

Hawkshaw gave a snort and shook his head.

"They'll get to see plenty of bullets flying where we are going, no doubt, and they won't be shot by dandies, I can guarantee you that."

The next day, they rolled into Alabama, stopping in Tennie's hometown. The station was impressive, built on a high bluff overlooking the river.

Gid leaned over her to look out the window as she stared at the bustle of people. "This here is your old stomping grounds, ain't it?" he asked, swallowing hard and trying to appear normal.

Hawkshaw joined them as Tennie nodded. "Yes, this is where I'm from."

"Do you miss it, Miss Tennie?" Gid asked. "Are you sorry you left?"

"No. If I could be with my parents again, it would be different. But they're gone." She was reluctant to leave the train. "Just before I left, a man pretending to be my uncle kidnapped me and dragged me into a saloon to work. I jumped out a window and ran away." It had been more than a saloon, but Gid and Hawkshaw understood what she meant.

"Ain't nothing going to happen to you now," Gid said, holding out a clammy hand to help her up.

"If you say so," Tennie said.

They had only a short time to buy more food. Gid was being especially careful, since despite

Hawkshaw's warning, his pocket had been picked in New Orleans. Since he carried most of his money in his boots, it hadn't been a great loss, but he didn't want it repeated. After purchasing food, they went inside the station to wait for the all-aboard call.

As Tennie looked out the front windows, a wave of homesickness overcame her in spite of what she had said to the others. She had no family, no real friends there, but it had been the home of her parents. Maybe she had been unwise to run away to Texas.

The conductor called for them to board, and she turned to join the others.

As they left the inside of the station and walked back to the tracks, she caught a glimpse of a familiar face. She stopped abruptly, hardly believing her eyes. The man who had abducted her was about to get on the train.

"What is it?" Hawkshaw said.

"It's that man, the one in the black derby," she said. "That's the man who kidnapped me! And he's getting on our train!"

"Are you certain, Miss Tennie?" Gid asked.

"Yes. It's him," Tennie cried. "Oh, no." She didn't want to ride on the train with him. She turned to ask Hawkshaw if they could take another one.

He was staring at the man, and before she could ask, he spoke. "He's not getting on with us." He

245

walked up behind the man, pulling his gun out of his holster and pointing it in his back. "You're not taking this train, mister," he said softly.

The man turned, opening his mouth to speak. He looked at Tennie and recognition spread over his face. "I think you are mistaking me for someone else, sir," he said, twisting to see the gun in his back.

"I don't think so," Hawkshaw said.

Gid moved slowly, putting himself between the man and the train, staring at him as if he wouldn't mind at all if the stranger tried something.

He gave up. "Another train will do me just as well. If it means so much to you."

Gid left him and returned to Tennie, escorting her onto the train as the man backed away.

When she had reached the top step, he called her name.

"Tennessee, wasn't it? Tennessee Smith. The job is still there if you are ever without your goons."

Tennie looked at him but didn't answer. She turned and stepped into the railway car.

It wasn't until she sat down that she began to tremble over his covert threat, thinking God had a funny way of telling her she hadn't made a mistake. An image of Wash Jones came to mind, as if a gentle reminder that going to Texas had been exactly the right thing to do. She said her prayers for Wash and tried not to let her thoughts be consumed with worry over him.

Gid stayed green and had to sit by the window or he went to pieces, but he managed to sleep the rest of the way without old man barleycorn. The cowboys who had gotten on at Waco, although talkative among themselves, had been shy around Tennie and had not approached her. She figured they had heard gossip in Waco and knew who she was traveling with. But other men didn't know that. Some of the saucier ones grew bold, ignoring the glares of Rusty and Lucas as they attempted to draw her into unwanted conversation.

Gid, though ill, was still capable of leaning over in his seat and yelling down the aisle of the train car, "Miss Tennie! Y'all need any help down yonder?"

Between the three of them, nobody bothered Tennie.

Hawkshaw sat in a far corner by himself, and as far as Tennie knew, spoke to no one. Only when the train ran absolutely full did anyone have the courage to sit by him after receiving one of his icy stares.

When they finally reached their destination, Tennie was so tired of sitting on the train, if it had looked like Death Valley, she wouldn't have complained. But the morning sun glistened on verdant hills and valleys covered with trees that made the ones in Texas look like stunted bushes. Rolling fields of lush emerald grass contained nary a cactus or a bull nettle. The station platform they alighted on was in a big town, but not so large as to be frightening, with sedate and settled buildings full of quiet charm on clean streets.

Tennie wanted to find out from the sheriff what was happening on the Coltrane Farm, but Gid was in a panic to rent horses and ride immediately to Nab's rescue. She expected Hawkshaw to find a hotel or tavern and stay put until they finished Gid's business, but to her surprise, he went along willingly with Gid's straightforward plan.

The men at the livery knew Gid well, but if they were aware of what was happening at his farm, they kept it to themselves. Once off the train, Gid had become so voluble, it would have been hard for them to get a word in edgewise in any case. They outfitted them silently with good horses, looking at Tennie and the boys with furtive curiosity and with outright suspicion at Hawkshaw, but they did not question Gid. He was too distraught over Nab to give coherent introductions or explanations anyway.

Instead of riding down closer to the river, they began ascending into the hills. There were small, pretty farms close to town. As they went higher and higher, it began to be cabins placed farther and farther apart. Nothing changed the breathtaking view, and Tennie wondered how Gid could bear to leave such a beautiful home to come to Ring Bit, Texas, where the most interesting thing in the landscape was a dried cow skull bleaching in the sun.

Neighbors came out on porches to watch them ride by. Gid would nod to some; others, he ignored.

One old man in clothes full of rips and wearing a hat with large holes in it called out to them, every word accentuated in a slow drawl. "Giddings Coltrane, you best keep them young'uns down yonder by the gate."

"Much obliged," Gid called back while the Granger boys exchanged glances with one another.

The man's warning scared them, as did the obsessive compulsion propelling Gid to ride on without stopping to gossip with his neighbors.

Tennie looked at Hawkshaw, but if he had any concerns, they didn't show on his face.

It took them almost three hours to reach the end of the road and the old, but professionally painted, sign at the gate that read COLTRANE FARMS. The wooden fences were in perfect condition. Horses dotted the rolling hills carpeted with rich grass. The barns and paddocks on the hill were unpainted, but otherwise strong and well built. The house, however, was another matter. The roof sagged, the structure leaned, and shingles were missing from the roof. Not to mention a collection of broken chairs, old washtubs, and a hodgepodge of miscellany cluttered the porch.

As Tennie took it all in, she realized she had been under a mistaken impression—the farm Gid co-owned did not deal in vegetables, tobacco, or cotton, but horseflesh.

A man came out of the house onto the porch and fired a shot in their direction. The horse Tennie was on skittered and neighed.

"You cut that out!" Gid hollered. "I got women and children down here."

She was the only woman, but Gid was so upset, he couldn't be blamed for getting mixed up.

In answer, the man on the porch fired again.

Tennie looked at Hawkshaw. "Shouldn't we move back?"

"He's firing above our heads," Hawkshaw said in unconcern. "He can't hit us at this range anyway."

Meanwhile, Gid was hollering that he wanted to see Nab.

"Nab's in the house, Gid," the man said. "The boys are locked up in the barn. They's going to stay thar until Nab signs this here paper we done had the lawyer draw up."

"Is Brother in there with you?" Gid hollered. "Is Brother in on this?"

"Yep, he is'm, and me and Brother is going to get our fair share of this here farm and sell it and go to Californy, and you and Nab ain't stopping us."

"I ain't signing no paper and neither is Nab," Gid hollered.

"The lawyer said you ain't got to sign cause you done give Nab the power of the attorney."

Gid and the man on the porch, who Gid cursed and called a "no-account brother," continued to spar with one another. Tennie's attention was drawn to Hawkshaw, who had dismounted and wandered to the fence. He stood leaning with one boot on the lower fence rail, looking at the horses with interest.

Tennie alighted, and leading her horse, walked to Hawkshaw. His eyes remained on the horses, and Tennie followed his gaze. At first, she couldn't understand his interest. They were just horses to her. But as she stared at them longer, she realized what huge, wide jaws they had, along with perky small ears. They were layered in heavy muscles, especially in the hindquarters, like the horse Gid rode in Texas.

She turned to Hawkshaw. "This is why you didn't faunch about coming here, isn't it? You wanted to see these horses."

He gave her one of his mocking stares. "I know you were listening to those cowboys behind you on the train. They were talking about going to South Texas to see if they could buy some Billy horses. Sometimes they are called Steel Dust or Bull Dog horses," he said, returning his gaze to the animals. "That's what these are."

"What is so special about them?" Tennie asked.

"They are good racers on short tracks, and

evidently they make good cattle horses," Hawkshaw said. "Almost every man in Ring Bit has tried to buy Gid's gelding from him."

Gid was still exchanging yells with his brother. "I'm going for the law," he hollered.

"Law ain't going to help no Coltrane," his brother hollered back.

"I got me a friend what got a letter of introduction to the judge," Gid said. "We'll get this straightened out."

In answer to that, his brother fired another shot.

"I want to see Nab before'un I leave here," Gid shouted. "You bring Nab out on that there porch, or I'm coming in there shooting."

After hassling over this for a while, the brother went back into the house. When he came out, Tennie realized she had been under another mistaken impression. Nab wasn't a man, but a woman almost as tall and big as Gid. The faded dark skirt that flowed from her large waist was huge, as was the man's shirt she wore. On top of her head was a black hat with a floppy brim, and Tennie was willing to bet it had holes in it, too.

"Nab, you all right?" Gid hollered.

"Yep," she shouted in a deep voice. "I ain't signing nothing."

"Don't you worry none, Nab. We be leaving, but we'll be back. I got the law with me from Texas, and we'll straighten this out with the sheriff and the judge."

Tennie looked at Hawkshaw and rolled her eyes. Poor Gid! She could only hope her letter of introduction to the judge might help. Being the town marshal of Ring Bit wasn't going to do a bit of good.

When they headed down the hills, Gid hollered at his neighbor that he'd be back. He was going for the law.

The old man laughed. "I reckon your dogs will be barking up a coonless tree, Gid. Law ain't gonna get involved in no Coltrane feud."

"I reckon they will," Gid said, his jaws shaking in belligerence as he slowed his horse but kept him moving. "I done got the law from Texas with me, and we done got a letter to the judge."

The old neighbor looked Hawkshaw over. "Maybe so, Gid. Maybe so."

With a start, Tennie realized the old man thought Hawkshaw was the law from Texas. And that Gid knew he thought so and did not disabuse him of that notion.

Hawkshaw's face, as usual, remained a cool slate.

Nevertheless, Tennie knew he was up to something. She just didn't know what.

CHAPTER 15

When the horses carried them into the town, Tennie and her stepsons were exhausted and starving. Still, Gid insisted on pressing on to the sheriff's office. Unlike Ring Bit, which kept its jail at the edge of town, the sheriff's office was in a courthouse dominating the town square. As they tied their horses to a hitching post out front, Tennie stood and gazed upward. It looked like some kind of Greek temple with huge pillars in front rising to three stories if one counted the basement. Gid led the way, and since neither he nor Hawkshaw told the boys to stay outside, Tennie didn't either.

They walked single file into the imposing edifice with cool marble floors beneath their feet. Walls still dark from the soot of smoke contained blank spots where paintings of Confederate generals once hung. They trailed Gid to the back of the building. A door to the left stood open, and he charged in with the rest of them following. As a volley of convoluted sentences flowed through his excited mouth, Tennie stared at an older man behind a desk in front of an opened window.

He had white hair and a white mustache, and when he saw Tennie, he rose, removing a new gray hat and throwing it casually onto a bookshelf to one side of the window. He wasn't a heavy man, neither was he a long slender bag of sinew and bones like so many of the men in Texas. He bowed his head slightly to Tennie. She nodded and took the chair he indicated while Hawkshaw took another. The sheriff sat back down. Standing with hat in hand, his fingers kneading the brim, Gid had never stopped talking.

"They's trying to cheat us, Sheriff," he said. "They got Nab and them grandsons hostage. You know Nab ain't got nobody but them grandsons. Her old man and her boys done got kilt in the war. And Ma left that place to us, Sheriff. She done made a will and everything."

"Gid," the sheriff said. "Who are these people?"

Gid stopped with his mouth hung open, his brain working to get back on another track. "This here is Miss Tennie and her stepsons, Sheriff," he said when his jaws functioned once again. "And this here is Mr. Hawkshaw. Miss Tennie done got a letter of introduction to the judge from some friends of hers back in Texas."

The sheriff leaned forward in his chair. "May I see the letter, Miss Tennie?"

Tennie dug in her pocket and brought out the letter, placing it in the sheriff's hand.

He examined it without opening it while she sat back down. He turned to the window. "Hey, boy," he called, and a little black head poked up. The sheriff handed the letter to him through the open window. "Here now, take this letter on up to the judge's chambers and ask him if he wants us to come up yonder or if he wants to come here, but we need to speak to him. Hurry up now, and don't dawdle."

"Yessir," the boy said, stretching the words into a long drawl. He jumped up and ran around the side of the building.

Tennie looked through the window at the jailhouse next door, thinking the county was wealthy enough to hire a jailor so its sheriff could have a nice office in the courthouse.

The sheriff leaned back in his chair. "You run that will through probate, Gid?"

"Probate?" Gid said with a blank look on his face. "I don't know. Nab's got it. And they done got Nab hostage wanting her to sign some no-account paper."

The sheriff rose heavily from his chair, letting Gid trail off as he exited the room.

Gid swallowed. "I don't know nothing about no probate."

Before Tennie could say anything, the sheriff returned with a ledger, setting it down on his desk. He got back in his chair and opened the heavy book, running his finger down the pages.

"Gid, taxes haven't been paid on that place in years. The county is going to sell it as soon as it can get a buyer."

"Taxes?" Gid said, thunderstruck. "But Ma

wrote to me in prison and said not to worry, everything had been taken care of."

The sheriff grimaced. "Gid, she told you that so you wouldn't break out of jail and try to rob another train. And I can't get Nab to understand it ain't like the old days. These taxes have to be paid."

"How much is they? I ain't got that much money on me."

The sheriff looked down at the ledger and read off a figure that made Gid's eyes roll back in his head.

To Tennie's surprise, Hawkshaw spoke. "How come nobody's come in here before now to pay those taxes to get that farm? That land and those horses must be worth quite a bit of money."

The sheriff looked at Hawkshaw as if deciding how much to tell him. Gid, realizing that, assured the sheriff Hawkshaw was indeed a friend of his.

"People expected Gid's cousin Raiford Beauregard to pay them to get the property for himself. The Beauregards are still a powerful family in this here county, and nobody wants to get crossways with them. But perhaps you know that?"

"Then why hasn't Beauregard come in here and paid them?" Hawkshaw asked.

"I don't know. You'll have to ask him yourself," the sheriff said.

A small old man wearing a black robe came in.

Tennie noticed an immediate change in Gid. An attitude of respect came over him, and he stood up straighter. Tennie turned back to the judge. He had sharp blue eyes and longish white hair. She thought how odd it was that young men kept their hair so short, and old men wanted theirs long. Gid remained standing, while Hawkshaw stayed seated.

Glancing out the window, Tennie saw a little black head slide down and out of sight. He would listen, later telling his people about what the white folks had said, and they in turn would share it with every other person of color they came into contact with until Gid's business became known all over the county in black circles. The sheriff must have known he was still there, but he did not appear to care.

The judge greeted Gid.

"Judge, this here is Miss Tennie and Hawkshaw," the sheriff said. "Miss Tennie, Judge LeRoy."

"How do you do, Judge?" Tennie said as politely as she could, wondering if her penchant for always sucking up to the most powerful person in the room was based on self-preservation or just a disgusting habit.

The judge smiled, his face kind. "Proceed," he ordered the sheriff as he sat down to one side to observe.

"I was just telling Gid here somebody's got

to pay the back taxes on the Coltrane farm or nobody's selling anything," the sheriff said.

"I'll pay them," Hawkshaw said. He looked at Gid. "And sell the farm back to you for two studs and two mares of my choosing."

Gid gulped and looked from face to face. "I don't know about that." He shuttered. "Nab, she always takes care of the business end. I can't go agin Nab."

"Gid," the sheriff said. "You are in a tight spot, boy. You better take this here fellow's offer because you ain't gonna get a better one today."

Gid moved from one foot to the other, his eyes darting about in agony.

Tennie felt sorry for him. "Mr. Gid, how much is the most money you and Nab made selling a horse?"

Gid grew even more flustered and unwilling to part with information. It appeared that while he could understand the formula to figure explosives, when it came to business, calculations fled his head.

"Tell Rusty and let Rusty multiply it by four," Tennie said. "Rusty can tell you if Mr. Hawkshaw's offer is fair or not."

Gid swallowed hard, and out of the side of his mouth, he mumbled an amount to Rusty. Rusty knew the answer immediately, but he paused, unwilling to make a mistake in front of adults. By his eyes, Tennie could tell he was refiguring.

"It's purt near the same amount," Rusty told Gid. "Maybe just a little bit in your favor."

"See there, Mr. Gid," Tennie said. "It's fair."

"It ain't just that!" Gid blurted. "Nab, she's awful particular about what horses she keeps and what horses she sells. I can't give Mr. Hawkshaw permission to take any horse he wants. Nab would skin me alive."

Hawkshaw stretched his legs out and examined his hands. "Oh well. I don't have a pasture for them in Texas anyway."

Rusty opened his mouth and leaned forward. He didn't say anything but stared at Tennie with beseeching eyes. She nodded her head.

"Mr. Hawkshaw, we've got a ranch we lease for cattle grazing," Rusty said, "but I don't imagine they'd mind if you put your horses up there for a while till you found a place of your own."

"That's mighty kind of you," Hawkshaw said, so nicely that Tennie wondered what he was playing at. "But I don't know how we'd get them back to Texas, anyhow. They have to ride the rails and stop halfway for a rest. Nab probably doesn't know anything about shipping horses, anyhow."

"That ain't true!" Gid roared. "Nab knows more about shipping horses than any man in these here parts. She sends a couple of them grandsons of hers to ride in the stock car with them horses. That's part of the deal. She don't let nobody ship her horses unlessen they agrees to pay for a couple of her boys to ride as hostlers. And that's a fact. You ask anybody around here." He stopped, looking miserable.

The judge stirred. "Take his offer, Gid."

Gid nodded, relieved to have the decision out of his hands. He could tell Nab the judge made him do it.

"Now then," the judge said, looking at Hawkshaw and Tennie. "What's your real business? You didn't come all this way to save Gid's horse farm."

Tennie wasn't sure what Winn Payton had written in his letter. He had sealed it, and she hadn't opened it.

The sheriff eyed Hawkshaw. "Haven't we seen you around here before? Here while back?"

Hawkshaw nodded but did not elaborate.

The sheriff, however, continued to study him under half-closed eyes. "You the Hawkshaw gunman from Kentucky?"

"That's right," Hawkshaw said.

"How come you buying horses here then, boy, instead of Kentucky?" the sheriff asked.

Tennie tensed. Hawkshaw was anything but a boy, and she knew the word in this case had been meant to insult.

Hawkshaw answered even enough. "Because they won't let me back in Kentucky," he said, staring the sheriff in the eye for so long, the sheriff turned to Tennie.

"What's your story, young lady?"

"I'm engaged to a Texas Ranger. He goes by the name of Wash Jones, but Jones is his mother's maiden name," she said, stumbling over words. "Mr. Beauregard sent Mr. Hawkshaw to instigate a fight with Wash's brother Lafayette and kill him. Mr. Hawkshaw, after assessing the situation, declined to do so and wants to return the money. I'm here to convince Mr. Beauregard to stop this insanity."

Tennie stopped to gasp. She knew her explanation was garbled.

"Why didn't your fiancé or his brother come? Why send you halfway across the country with two strangers?" the judge asked.

Tennie thought perhaps Mr. Payton's letter had spelled all that out, but the judge wanted to hear it from her lips. "Wash is in South Texas chasing bandits and knows nothing of this. And I convinced Mr. Lafayette not to come for fear it would just provoke more trouble. Mr. Gid and Mr. Hawkshaw are not strangers. Mr. Gid works for Mr. Lafayette, and Mr. Hawkshaw saved my life."

"Miss Tennie is the law in Ring Bit, Judge," Gid said.

"Really?" the judge's eyebrows went up.

The sheriff's eyebrows were up, too. "I heared they did things different down in Texas, but I didn't realize they were so savage they made their womenfolk manhandle criminals."

262

"I don't manhandle criminals," Tennie said as fast as she could. "Mr. Gid and other men like him do that. I just feed the prisoners and clean up after them."

"Don't you be so bashful, Miss Tennie," said Gid, her staunch friend. He turned to the judge. "This little gal got more gumption than a porcupine got quills, Your Honor. Yes, sir, Miss Tennie ain't a-feared of facing the devil hisself."

"Gid," Tennie pleaded. The first time the U.S. deputy marshal met her, he said he had been expecting a drunken, sometimes prostitute, dressed in men's clothes and chomping on a cigar. She wanted to disassociate herself from that image as far as she could.

"You are embarrassing the young lady, Gid," the judge chided with a trace of a smile on his lips. "And what is your plan for convincing Raiford Beauregard to leave your future brother-in-law be, young lady?"

Tennie flushed. "I don't have one."

The judge gave another small smile and looked at the sheriff. The sheriff picked up the hint and sat up straighter, leaning forward in the chair. "Well, let's get this tax business straightened out, Gid."

"But Sheriff, we got to go rescue Nab," Gid said. "She's being held prisoner. The boys is locked up in the barn. I don't know how many days they done been in there."

"They'll survive," the sheriff said. "I'm not riding out and getting there roundabout midnight in the pitch dark. Nab can wait until morning."

"Gid," the judge said, "you best leave yourself just enough money to get back to Texas and give the remainder to your brothers so they can go on to California and stay out of Nab's hair. Not to mention the rest of the county's."

Gid swallowed hard, but he said, "Yes, sir, Judge."

"Boy!" the judge said, throwing his voice to the window.

The little black head popped up again. "Yessir?"

"You go tell Miss Viola to expect one young lady and three hungry boys for supper," the judge said. "Tell her to fix up some beds. They've been traveling and will want baths and their clothes cleaned."

Tennie blushed again. She had tried to wash all the train dirt and soot from her face, but she was still covered in dust. "Judge, sir, we couldn't possibly impose on you."

"Nonsense. These here men can take care of themselves. But a friend of Winn Payton needs a clean bed to sleep in."

Like Gid, Tennie found herself falling in line with the judge's wishes. Gid approved, and Hawkshaw made no sign or comment whatsoever. The boys didn't look too happy. They wanted to stay with Gid, but at the same time, they were hungry and tired of waiting for food.

The judge told Hawkshaw and Gid to continue with their business. He rose and escorted Tennie and the boys out of the courthouse, pointing to a large brick house south of the square. "I'll have your things sent over. Viola will show you where to get cleaned up for supper. I'll be there directly."

Tennie felt so grateful. "Thank you, Judge LeRoy," she said with a relieved smile. She turned and followed the boys down a respectable side street to a big house on a large lot surrounded by a thigh-high wrought-iron fence. The grounds were immaculate. The house, although old, projected stability and comfort. There was nothing like it in Ring Bit.

The four of them walked up to the shady porch on a sidewalk paved with bricks, straight and level without a dip in it. The white front door had glass on each side and a transom above the top. The black shuttered windows on the porch went all the way to the floor.

Before they could knock on the front door, it was opened by a black woman in a calico dress and long white apron. It was hard for Tennie to tell her age because her skin was so smooth and wrinkle free. But gray hair peeked from underneath the white scarf wrapped around her head, and Tennie thought she must be well past middle age.

"Miss Viola?" Tennie said. "I'm Tennessee Granger and these are my stepsons, Rusty, Lucas, and Badger. The judge sent us here."

"Yes, ma'am, I know," the older woman said. "Come this way, and I'll show you where you can wash up." She held the door open for them.

Tennie and the boys entered, all of them impressed with the polished wood floors, the gleaming staircase, the rooms with ornate trim around the doors, and the thick carpets within them. Viola shut the door, and they followed her down a long hall to a door in the back of the house that led to a porch where washbasins, soap, and towels awaited them. An expanse of wide lawn stood in front of them.

"You can sit in these chairs while you wait for the judge," Viola said.

Tennie nodded and gave her thanks. Viola disappeared back into the house, and Tennie looked down at her stepsons. "Well, don't just stand there gaping. Let's get cleaned up."

While they sat on the back porch waiting for the judge, the little messenger boy came around the back and began talking to Tennie's stepsons. He wanted to know all about the black cowboys in the West. Before long, Tennie began seeing signs that meant only one thing. "No wrestling until after supper," she warned.

Fortunately, the judge walked onto the porch

before that could happen. He was smiling and seemed happy to see them. He held his arm to Tennie, and as he escorted her into the dining room, his other hand reached out and rubbed the top of her hand. She was a little surprised by his unexpected gesture of familiarity, but it pleased her to be so welcomed.

When they entered the dining room, she wondered if her eyes were as big around as the boys'. A silver candelabra stood on top of a gleaming white cloth. China, crystal, and silverware were at each place setting. When she had been loaned out by the orphanage to work in big houses for parties, Tennie had washed plenty of expensive dishes and utensils, but had never eaten off any of them. She doubted if her stepsons had ever seen them.

The judge motioned for her to sit next to him, and she could only hope she did not look as gauche as she felt. She thought of the scarred table in Ring Bit, and she was almost overcome with desire to own something much better, dazzled by the sparkling array of beautiful things.

At the supper table, however, the judge encouraged the boys to talk, asking innocent questions about hunting and fishing. Before long, in between shoveling food like there was no tomorrow, they were telling him of Tennie's kidnapping. They weren't shy about sharing their role in rescuing her and fighting banditos.

The judge showed the proper amount of curiosity and appreciation, although the tale sounded so fantastic, Tennie didn't know why anyone hearing it would believe it. Urged by the judge to continue, the boys described the train ride and how Gid hung his head out the window being sick most of the time. When Rusty told how Hawkshaw didn't like anyone sitting by him, the judge responded by rubbing his upper lip and saying, "Interesting."

"We thought the Daring Dandies were going to rob the train, but they didn't," Badger informed him.

"My, what a disappointment," the judge said, smothering a smile.

When the boys had just about run out of tummy room and words, Tennie apologized to the judge. "Most men in Texas refuse to say two words while they eat, but I'm afraid they have picked up the habit of talking too much from me."

"Nonsense," the judge said. "I haven't had such an enjoyable conversation in a long time. Boys, you may go out onto the back porch, and Viola will bring you dessert. I'd like to talk to your stepmother alone for a while."

"Yes, sir. Thank you, sir," all three of them echoed, and Tennie was happy they at least knew a few manners. She just hoped they didn't tear up the lawn, wrestling.

"Are you acquainted with Wash and Lafayette, Judge?" she asked after they left.

"Oh, yes. Not perhaps so much Wash. He was very young the last time I saw him—a serious boy with a keen sense of right and wrong, if I remember correctly. Both he and Lafayette were excellent swordsmen. Wash's skill allowed him to escape an appalling blow with only a scar across his lips."

Tennie nodded and the judge continued.

"It was a terrible business with Lafayette and his brother. Maribel was always a problem."

"Maribel?" Tennie asked. "Is that the woman . . . ?"

"Yes, Raiford's sister and Lafayette's sister-in-law."

"Can you tell me something about Raiford Beauregard?" Tennie asked, feeling hesitant about digging into the reputation of a man who was so far above her socially.

The judge frowned. "He's a pompous, over-bearing little jackass still living in the Middle Ages."

"Oh, fabulous," Tennie muttered. She caught herself and blushed.

"Don't worry, my beautiful little Texas girl," the judge said with a smile. "You will utterly charm him. If not, then he is beyond redemption."

Tennie laughed. "Not sure about that, but thank you." Southern men did have a way with words.

He rose, leading her into the parlor, again squeezing her hand. The carpet underneath their feet was so thick, it muffled the sound of every footfall. The room was unlike any she had ever seen, since her services had only taken her into the kitchens and dining rooms of expensive homes. The highly waxed furniture created a soft glow in the room. A fireplace with an elegant mantel graced one wall, while tall bookshelves filled with leather-bound volumes covered another. Hurricane lamps made of exquisite glass sat on small marble-topped tables. Tennie felt it was the most enchanting room in the world.

The judge led her to a velvet-covered chair and took his place in another near her. He insisted she tell him all about herself, from her upbringing to how she got to Texas. His eyebrows raised when she told him Ashton Granger had died almost immediately after the wedding, before they could even spend one night together. She worried she was being too frank.

"And Wash, my dear?" the judge asked delicately. "He has not presumed upon you, I hope?"

"Oh, no," Tennie said, feeling her face burning a flaming red.

He leaned forward and patted her knee. "I'm sorry. I didn't mean to embarrass you."

"Oh, that's okay," Tennie assured him. "We kissed, but that's all." And she blushed again, chastising herself for blurting out whatever came to mind.

Viola appeared at the parlor door. "Miss Tennie's bathwater is ready, Your Honor," she said.

The judge rose, taking Tennie's hand to assist her from her chair. "Yes, child. You are exhausted, and I have selfishly kept you talking."

Tennie, walking with him to the door, assured him she had enjoyed their conversation very much. She left him and followed the silent Viola into the large kitchen. The arrangements of pots and pans hanging from hooks on the wall, the large fireplace, and equally massive cookstove had her exclaiming with pleasure.

Viola held up a large sheet in front of a washtub. "You slip out of your clothes, Miss Tennie, and get into this here tub. I opened your bags and brought down your gown and robe."

"Oh, thank you, Miss Viola," Tennie said. There had not been much privacy in the orphanage, but it still embarrassed her a little to strip in front of Viola. She did, however, and dropped into the tub quickly. Viola handed her a thick washcloth and a bar of milled soap. She stayed busy in the kitchen while Tennie started washing from the top of her head downward.

As Tennie scrubbed, Viola began to talk. "The judge, he like having young ladies in the house."

"Really?" Tennie answered. "He's very nice."

Viola kept talking without looking directly at her. "Yes'um, he miss his wife a lot."

Tennie poked the washcloth in her ear and brought out black soot, grimacing when she saw it. "Has she been gone long?"

"Oh, a few years now," Viola said. "He miss her a lot. He miss having the comforts a woman brings." She paused. "Especially a young one."

CHAPTER 16

Tennie's hand stopped in midair. She swallowed, thinking of the caresses on her hand, the pat on her knee. "Is he going to come into my bedroom?" She took a deep breath.

"I puts a chair in your room," Viola said. "You puts that chair under the doorknob, and he won't force hisself in."

Tennie's hand relaxed. "Thank you."

"Unlessen, you might like to be the mistress of a house like this 'un."

Tennie looked around the kitchen, thinking of her few old iron skillets in Ring Bit. "I would love to have a house like this almost more than anything in the world. But not that way."

Viola nodded. "I'll mix up some vinegar and water to pour over your hair. It will cut the soap and make it nice and shiny."

While Viola mixed vinegar and water in a bucket, Tennie bit her lip. "Miss Viola, can you tell me about the Beauregards?" And because she was tired and worried, tears came into her eyes. "I don't know how to stop Mr. Beauregard from sending more killers to Ring Bit."

Viola poured the vinegar water over Tennie's hair. Putting the bucket down, she said, "I's tell you what to say if you do something for me."

Tennie nodded, and Viola continued. "The judge, he always had the respect. Everybody in town look up to him. But after his wife died, and his son and all his grandchildren die in a fire, it done something to him. He got this crazy notion he want to have another son. And the only way that gonna happen if he get a young pretty girl to help his body part achieve the maximum. Folks is starting to whisper about him. Pretty soon, that whispering gonna turn to laughing."

She paused, and Tennie thought she understood. If the judge's reputation suffered, Viola's would, too.

Tennie nodded.

"You tell the judge tomorrow you have to go up in the hills because you don't want to hurt Mr. Gid's or his folks' feelings by not being their houseguest," Viola said. "But when you get your horse business settled, you come back here and stay again, telling folks how nice the judge treat you, how polite and gentlemanly. After you leave the Beauregards, you spend the night here again while you waiting to leave on the train. You tell everybody you see how respectful and proper the judge treat you."

"Will it be okay?" Tennie asked, fearful of what might happen. "Will you—"

"He may nudge the gate, but he won't jump the fence. And I be right here. You do that for me, and I tell you how to handle them brain-addled Beauregards."

Viola talked all the while helping Tennie into her gown and robe, assuring her as she combed her hair that the plan would work. She ordered Tennie to bed, promising she would see that the boys bathed. Before leading Tennie upstairs to her room, she added more hot water to the tub, telling Rusty to hop in.

Exhausted, Tennie was glad to do as Viola said. Before leaving the kitchen, she reminded the boys to be sure and clean in and around their ears. Viola lit a lamp, and Tennie followed her upstairs into a bedroom as choke full of lovely furniture, thick wallpaper, and soft rugs as the rest of the house. A sturdy chair sat next to the door. Viola placed the lamp on a nightstand, and as she withdrew, Tennie thanked her again.

There was no lock, but Tennie tested the door to see if it would move with the chair under the knob, and it remained firm. Turning down the wick, she sank with relief between the crispest, smoothest sheets she had ever touched. She thought of her scratchy sheets in Ring Bit, and she began to cry. One day, maybe Wash would stop chasing outlaws long enough to give her a home with nice things.

A short while later, in a sleepy haze, she heard the boys coming up the stairs and entering another bedroom. She forgot to tell them not to jump on the bed, but she was too tired to get up and hoped they were so exhausted, they wouldn't think of it. She fell into a deeper sleep realizing Viola would make them wash their ears and not jump on the bed anyway.

She wasn't sure how much later a sound awakened her. She sat up, moonlight flowing in from the window by her bed. The knob on her door turned. Tennie held her breath, but the chair underneath the knob held fast. Her ears heard the soft sound of feet walking away, and she sank back into the pillows, staring at the doorknob for a long time before falling into sleep.

The next morning, Tennie worried the judge might be peeved with her. She found, on the contrary, he was even more genial. When he insisted she stay in town, she haltingly followed Viola's advice, which she believed to be true anyway. She did not want to hurt Gid's or his family's feelings by refusing to stay in their home.

"My dear girl," the judge said. "I doubt very seriously Nab will even realize you are there. If you don't drink out of a trough and aren't on intimate terms with a blacksmith, she considers you not worthy of a thought. But you are a sweet young lady to consider the Coltranes' feelings. I think the sheriff will be able to get rid of Gid's brothers, but if there continues to be trouble, I insist you return here."

Tennie agreed and it relieved her when he requested they stay with him again when they came down from the hills. She didn't want any kinks in her promise to Viola. She thanked him again profusely for his hospitality. Before they left the breakfast table, she asked his opinion of the Coltrane Farm.

"Oh, they've got good horses," the judge said. "Not Thoroughbreds, but excellent for short track racing and working livestock. Their grandfather and father had that magical way with horses that sometimes touches the Irish. Gid is good with horses, make no mistake about that, but he didn't inherit that special something Nab has. Nab's oldest grandson and I think one of the other boys has it, too."

All the intertwined relations of the Coltranes had Tennie confused. She should have listened closer to Gid's ramblings about his family. "But the father left for Texas?"

"Yes, Dings left for Texas," the judge said. "Dings Coltrane had the other habit that sometimes touches the Irish, a love affair with whiskey. Gid's brothers come and go as it pleases them. Nab can be tightfisted, pouring every cent back into the farm, but when their mother was alive, the other boys could always get what they wanted out of her."

Tennie still wasn't clear how the Coltranes could be related to the Beauregards, but the judge enlightened her.

"Raiford's great-grandfather was a lover of horses. He brought a horse and a young stableboy here from Ireland. Seamus, Gid's grandfather, stole the heart of one of the daughters, and they eloped. Raiford's branch of the family has never gotten over it."

"Mercy," Tennie said. "I hope I can keep up with all this. Thank you for explaining it to me."

As they were preparing to leave, Lucas stood near the judge, his eyes roving the house. "What's a person got to do to be a judge, anyway?"

"Lucas!" Tennie said.

The judge laughed. "A man should become an attorney first. We'll discuss it further when you get back."

As Tennie struggled not to laugh at Lucas, thinking he was a born entrepreneur, her eyes were caught by Badger's behavior. He seemed to be lurking behind Rusty as if he didn't want to be noticed. Tennie gave him a sharper look. His pockets were bulging. "Badger, what do you have in your pockets?"

He shuffled his feet and looked at the floor.

"Badger," Tennie warned.

"Biscuits," he muttered, still not meeting her gaze.

"Did you ask Miss Viola for those biscuits?"

He shook his head.

Tennie took a deep breath. "You take those biscuits back to the kitchen right now, young man. You know better than to take something without having it offered to you first."

Both the judge and Viola laughed, saying Badger could keep the biscuits, but Tennie insisted. Her skin flushed with shame, but at the same time, if that was the worst the Granger boys had done in the judge's house, she felt she had gotten off lightly. She was afraid to look at the back lawn.

They were to meet Gid, Hawkshaw, and the sheriff at the courthouse. Viola had stayed up almost the entire night washing and ironing their clothes, along with cooking so she could send a basket of food with them. Hawkshaw and Gid had rented a wagon and loaded it with more supplies. Tennie wondered if Hawkshaw had thought of it, or if it had been more of the judge's advice. The giant of a mule pulling the wagon had to be Gid's choice.

They said farewell to the judge, and after helping Tennie into the wagon seat, Gid picked up Badger.

"Come here, you little biscuit stealer," he said, and tossed him playfully into the wagon bed.

"Here comes the posse," Hawkshaw said when they reached the courthouse. The sheriff had half a dozen men riding with him.

"Do they expect that much trouble?" Tennie asked, worried over what they were about to ride into.

Hawkshaw stared at her with cool eyes. He shook his head. "Just curious."

Before they left, the sheriff introduced his men then asked innocently, "Did you sleep well at the judge's, Miss Tennie?"

If Tennie hadn't known better, she would have never suspected a thing. "Oh, yes, sir. The judge's house is beautiful, and he is the perfect host, so proper and respectful, yet so kind to put us up."

Hawkshaw gave her another long stare but said nothing.

They began their ride into the hills, Gid worrying and mumbling every few minutes over what Nab was going to say about the deal he had made with Hawkshaw. The boys began teasing Badger, quietly at first, about being a biscuit thief.

As the morning went on, the teasing and Badger's responses became louder. The sheriff's men took it up, asking Badger if he planned on whipping his brothers for besmirching his good name, offering to hold his shirt so it didn't get torn, giving him pointers on how to gouge, kick, and bite a bigger opponent.

Badger took the teasing as well as could be expected. Tears welled in his eyes, and he tattled that Rusty had told their playmate of the day before that all the black cowboys in Texas rode bucking horses that threw them so high in the clouds it left their hair snow white, and that Lucas had jumped on the bed after Miss Viola told him not to.

When the men riding with them eventually tired of their teasing and dropped behind them, Tennie turned to the back of the wagon, addressing Badger. "You shouldn't have done what you did, Badger, but I think you've paid enough for your sin. Why don't you boys sing some of the cattle songs Mr. Wash taught you?" She turned to Gid. "Would you like to hear them sing some cowboy songs, Mr. Gid?"

Gid looked startled. "Is they any about horses?"

"Old Paint!" Lucas said. "We can sing about Old Paint."

Tennie glanced at the men following the wagon. The sheriff and another man were deep in discussion; the others were openly watching her with interest. She blushed and turned around, quietly joining in the boys' singing.

Although Gid had been frantic the day before to get back to the farm, he was so worried about facing Nab with the agreement he had made with Hawkshaw, he didn't mind stopping halfway to give the mule a rest. Tennie got down from the wagon to stretch her legs.

Hawkshaw, who had been ignoring the sheriff and his men, caught her when no one could overhear. "How'd you escape the amorous judge?"

"A chair under the doorknob," Tennie confessed, not surprised he had guessed what would take place.

Hawkshaw gave a snort. "I knew you could handle it."

"With the housekeeper's help," Tennie said. "And I had to make a deal with her to preserve the judge's spotless reputation in exchange for a rock-solid plan to protect your life and Lafayette's from this Beauregard person."

His eyes bored into her. "What?"

She looked at the men standing with their horses on the roadside. "I can't tell you now." She was like Gid, who feared facing Nab. She was sure when Hawkshaw heard the plan, he was going to jump higher than Rusty's imaginary bucking broncs and come down with both boots planted on her head.

Although they saw no one on the rest of the trip, not even the farmer with the ratty hat, Tennie had the feeling they were being observed. The volley of bullets returned when they reached the gate. but it was the sheriff who yelled at the feuding Coltranes.

"Quit that shooting," he hollered. "I got a dang posse down here with me, and if bullets get to flying, every horse on this farm is going to become an easy target."

"This ain't none of your affair, Sheriff," Gid's brother hollered down the hill. "This here is Coltrane business."

"It is too my affair," the sheriff said. "Y'all hadn't paid taxes on this here farm, and now somebody else has done gone up and bought it."

"What?" was the next holler, but it was clear by the tone someone had the wind knocked out of him.

"You heared me," the sheriff called. "Now you release Nab and those grandsons. Gid's got a proposition for you."

They must have been so bumfuzzled by the sheriff's news, they decided getting Nab onto the front porch was the best recourse.

Gid looked as nervous as a bridegroom at the end of a shotgun when Nab came out the door, along with her two brothers, who, from a distance, did not look much like kidnappers anymore. Tennie hoped when Nab heard Gid's news, she didn't grab the rifle and start shooting.

"What's this here about the farm being sold for taxes?" Nab called.

"That's right, Nab," the sheriff hollered. "The county done sold that property to the first one who come along with the money to pay the back taxes."

Nab did grab the gun and took aim, but before she could fire, the sheriff interrupted her. "But he sold it back to Gid here. He sold it back to Gid with the provision he gets first pick of two of your mares and two stallions."

"You had no call to do that, Giddings Coltrane," Nab said. "No call a-tall."

"I had to, Nab," Gid yelled in a voice that

283

vaguely resembled a pig's squeal. "The judge done made me do it, Nab. The judge done told me I had to."

"That's right, Nab," the sheriff hollered. "He didn't have no choice."

The quiet from the porch lasted so long, Gid gulped at least half a dozen times before Nab responded.

"Gid!" Her deep voice boomed down the hill. "That there feller know a lot about horses?"

"A tolerable amount, Nab," Gid replied. "Enough to get by."

Lucas's eyes got big, and he tugged on Tennie's arm. "Mr. Hawkshaw knows a lot about horses," he whispered.

"Shhh," Tennie said. "Miss Nab will find out soon enough, and maybe she won't have a gun in her hand when she does."

Gid's brothers did not want to believe the sale, and it took the sheriff some doing before they gave up and came down the hill. Stout like Gid, they lacked his boyish charm and to Tennie looked more like big louts. Gid wasn't too charming with them, however, and disliked having to turn over almost all his money.

The sheriff insisted, nevertheless, and told them it would be best for all concerned if they never came back. "Try to make it to St. Louis without killing anybody," he advised.

After they left, the sheriff approached Tennie.

"Are you sure you don't want to turn around and go back to the judge's house?"

Tennie looked up the hill. Once Nab was freed from her captors, she had forgotten all about Gid and his friends. The horses needed her. There might as well not have been anybody at the foot of the hill as far as she was concerned. The prospect of spending even one night in the ramshackle cabin with a single-minded old woman filled Tennie with dread. She wasn't even sure she would be welcome. She looked at the sheriff. "I would love to go back to the judge's house, but I cannot spurn Mr. Gid's offer of hospitality."

"Suit yourself," the sheriff said. "Come on, boys. The show's over."

With the law and the lawbreakers gone from their presence, everyone visibly relaxed, except perhaps Gid, who remained on the jumpy side.

The cabin looked just as bad up close. Tennie tried to keep the dismay from her face. Nab had disappeared to the barns, and Gid began to unload the wagon, taking things into the house and hollering over his shoulder, "Come on in!"

Despite its disarray, the inside looked homey. Quilts covered old chairs and lamps sat on a little table and a tall buffet, both of which were covered in dust. The kitchen and dining table were on one side. Two bedrooms led off the living area. Upstairs was an open loft.

"That there is where I usually lay up at nightfall, Miss Tennie," Gid said, pointing to the loft. "But you can bunk there, instead."

"Mr. Gid," Tennie said, "I hate to take your bed."

"No, that's all right. I'll sleep down here on a pallet with the boys. Nab don't mind the heat, but that other bedroom over yonder is on the west side, and it's too blame hot to sleep in during the summer."

Hawkshaw would be on his own, but he had already drifted to the barns. Tennie looked at the stove with things cooking on it, and the pile of dirty dishes next to an overflowing dishpan. Her stepsons were looking around the room with curiosity, eyeing the loft with envy.

"Boys, you mind Mr. Gid and do what he says," Tennie said then turned to Gid. "Do you think Miss Nab would mind if I started in on the dishes? I would be in the way with the horses."

"Why, shorely! You just go right on ahead. Come on, you little taters," he said to the boys. "We got to help Nab with the horses." Before he left, he climbed the ladder to the loft with Tennie's bag.

As soon as he and the boys left the house, Tennie climbed up the ladder.

The loft contained a bed covered in quilts. The room was hot, but there was an opened window on one side giving it some air. A little homemade cabinet stood by the bed. Other than that, it was bare. Tennie folded the quilt down, running her hand over the sheets, bending to smell the bedding. Surprisingly enough, it smelled clean and sweet. She supposed Nab had prepared it in hopes of Gid's return.

Descending the ladder, she found an empty water bucket and went out the back door. She found a well in the yard and wished she hadn't sent the boys off with Gid so hastily. It would take her many trips to get enough water to wash all the dishes piled in Nab's haphazard kitchen.

Carrying the full bucket into the kitchen, she found a kettle containing hot water on the stove, looked in the bubbling pots, and found stew and greens cooking. Picking up a spoon that looked clean, she stirred the pots and tasted, surprised by the flavor. Whatever she lacked in the housekeeping department, Nab more than made up for in cooking.

On Tennie's fifth trip to the well she saw Lucas running up from the barns.

"Miss Tennie! Miss Tennie!" he cried. "A horse kicked Badger. Mr. Gid told him to stand back, but he didn't."

Tennie dropped the bucket and ran. She caught up with Lucas, and taking her by the hand, they ran together to the barn.

"It was just his hand," Lucas said. "But it might be broken."

They could hear Badger's bawling even before entering the cavernous barn. Everyone was crowded around Nab and Badger.

She sat on a short stool, comforting him. "Here now," she crooned. "Let old Nab see how hurt you be." Her large hands touched Badger's arm with the utmost tenderness.

She had dark hair and dark eyes like Gid, and a long, mournful face. Her faded black skirt was dusty, and the threadbare blue shirt she wore had mismatched buttons sewn up and down the front in different-colored thread.

Badger gave a fitful sob and tried to stop crying, letting Nab examine his hand and arm with gentle fingers.

"Old Bailey been cooped up for so many a day, he got plum cranky," Nab continued. "Animals got their habits, just like people, and when something throws them off, they shorely get upset. Old Bailey didn't mean to hurt you none."

Badger stared at Nab and nodded. In those few minutes, Tennie decided she liked Gid's sister very much.

"Father, Son, and Holy Ghost," Nab said, kissing Badger's hand lightly. "There now, boy"—she rubbed Badger's back—"nothing hurt but your pride."

Badger saw Tennie. He nodded to Nab and left to bury his face in Tennie's skirt.

"Come along, now," Tennie said, taking hold of

his unhurt hand. "We'll go in the kitchen and get one of Miss Viola's good biscuits."

In the kitchen, Badger sat on Tennie's lap with a biscuit in his hand. He began to cry again. "I want my Rascal. I want my doggie."

"Hush now," Tennie said, hugging him but being careful of his hand. "We'll be home before you know it, and you can play and play with Rascal then. You'll have lots of stories to tell Shorty, won't you?"

He nodded, and before long, he was asleep in Tennie's lap. She kicked a small rag rug to one corner of the kitchen and placed the sleeping boy on it. Looking around the cabin, she sighed, wondering if she had lied to Badger. She felt like they would never get home again. She wasn't even sure where home was anymore.

CHAPTER 17

Tennie had the table set for the adults with plates ready for the children. She worried Nab would be upset with her for making herself at home in her kitchen, but when the older woman entered the cabin with the others, she looked around and nodded. Tennie hoped that nod meant everything was okay.

"Nab," Gid said, finally remembering to introduce Tennie. "This here is Miss Tennie. She's betrothed to Wash, Colonel Lafayette's brother."

"Howdy-do," Nab said. "Never met Wash, but heared respectable things about him. Heared he was good winded."

Tennie wasn't too sure what good winded was, but she nodded and smiled, telling Nab she was pleased to meet her. She turned to the boys who had followed Nab in. Oddly enough, all were silent. All had blond shaggy hair and blue eyes. They were thickset like Gid. Tennie thought them thirteen, fourteen, fifteen, and sixteen, so close in age did they look. Gid rattled off names she probably wouldn't remember—Nestor, Virgil, Lundy, and Floyd. They carried the Coltrane name, too.

Gid explained Nab had married a distant cousin from Ireland. "Pa sent for him. Said he'd be good with the horses. Him and Nab made a good team till he got killed in the war fighting Sherman. Dang fool was too old to go to war but went anyway. Their young'uns got killed, too."

Tennie murmured her regrets, but Gid had already moved on to how happy he was to get some of Nab's cooking. "Colonel Lafayette's got him a new cook what puts peppers in everything. My guts don't do nothing but burn and churn all day long, Nab. All day long," he moaned.

It was the first Tennie had heard of it. According to Lafayette, Gid ate everything in sight with relish.

Unlike most people, who made the children wait until after the adults had eaten, Nab told the boys to help themselves and go out onto the porch to eat. She asked how Badger was, and having been awakened by the arrival of the others, he told her he felt better. When the boys cleared out, the adults sat down. Nab asked the blessing, and Hawkshaw, who did not bow his head, at least let his eyes look in his lap.

Gid and Nab began discussing their siblings, the shyster lawyer who helped them, and above all, the state of the horses.

When Nab accidentally spilled salt, she took some and threw it over her left shoulder, saying, "In your eye, devil. Begone."

Tennie hoped there wasn't some belief in the evil eye she would accidentally summon and cause Nab to get mad at her over. Unlike the priest, Gid didn't feel it necessary to warn her against anything, and he finally got around to explaining Tennie's and Hawkshaw's presence.

Nab shook her head in disgust as he talked about the Beauregards. "Maribel be a blatherskite, and he be so contrary, if you throwed him in a river he'd float upstream. Ain't neither one of them got the brains of a billy goat." She turned to Tennie. "You been a-studying on how to do it?"

Tennie flushed. "Miss Viola gave me a plan."

"Viola did?" Nab said. "Well, Viola got sense, so it ought to be a good 'un. Excepting around here, you might fall into trouble calling a darkie *Miss*. Ain't saying it's wrong, jest that some folks might not appreciate it."

Tennie swallowed, a little embarrassed. "I reckon it's because I've been in Texas. If a person's not polite, they are liable to get their head blown off."

"That's right, Nab," Gid said. "She's right there. They be so friendly, and then the next thing you know, they be mad and holding a grudge. Remember how quick Pa was to get mad? They's just like him, always getting riled about something."

"But the white folks call the darkies mister and miss?" Nab questioned.

"No," Gid said. "They treats them 'bout like everybody else does. Miss Tennie just got a natural politeness about her, that's all."

"You seen Pa in Texas?" Nab asked.

Gid shook his head, and the table fell silent.

Tennie decided it was a good time to change the subject back to the Beauregards. "Miss Nab, Miss Viola told me that Mr. Beauregard is in love with a cousin. I think she said the cousin's name is Helen."

Nab nodded. "That be right. They's wanted to wed, but being first cousins, her pa wouldn't allow it. Don't know why they don't now, since they be old and ain't got nobody."

Gid picked at a piece of meat in his teeth with his finger. When he got it dislodged, he said, "Can't. Maribel done told Beauregard if he married Helen, she was leaving her inheritance to the Catholic Church."

"Maribel always was powerful jealous of Helen 'cause the men folks liked her better," Nab said.

Tennie listened to their comments, grateful they weren't questioning her about Viola's plan. Hawkshaw, however, was staring at her.

Tennie asked Nab to let her wash the supper dishes, explaining she would be of little help with the horses but would like to pitch in another way. Nab consented, and although she was good at keeping her face deadpan, Tennie thought she saw a look of gratitude peeking out of one eye. While Tennie cleaned, Nab made a poultice of sassafras leaves and a hot compress to put on Badger's hand.

To Tennie's surprise and pleasure, after all the chores were done, one of Nab's grandsons picked up a banjo, another got on a washtub with a string attached to a handle, and they began picking and singing. She smiled in pleasure at Gid.

He grinned. "I can't tote a tune in a bucket. They all got it and them cotton heads from their ma's side of the family."

Nab found an old harmonica and handed it to Rusty. Lundy or Floyd, Tennie wasn't sure which one, began teaching Rusty how to play it. Later, the boys began singing the cowboy songs they knew, making up words and verses when they couldn't remember them.

When bedtime came, Nab placed quilts on the floor, and everybody found a place to sleep, including Gid. Hawkshaw went outside. Nab raised an eyebrow at Gid.

"Leave him be, Nab. He's bad about wanting to be by hisself. Can't hardly stand anybody sidling up to him. It's a wonder he done stayed in the house with us this long."

Tennie climbed the ladder to the loft. Before getting into bed, she looked out the window and saw a shadowy figure making its way to the barn to sleep with the horses.

For the next three days, Hawkshaw and Nab dickered over horses. When Nab heard Hawkshaw was from Kentucky, her eyes narrowed. When she found out he wasn't quite the novice Gid had made him out to be, instead of getting upset, she grew crafty. Hawkshaw wanted to take the best of the horses. Nab thought all her horses were good, but she wanted to keep the finest on the farm, and without telling outright lies, she tried to mislead him about a horse's strengths and faults depending on which one she wanted him to take and which one she wanted to keep.

"Is she a passive breeder?" Hawkshaw would ask when looking at a mare.

"No, not her," Nab would say. "She breeds positive every time. 'Course now, she's high-strung, and her dock there is little limber."

Hawkshaw would pick up the tail, and if it was limber, it was only by the most minuscule amount.

Trying to outwit Hawkshaw in the horse trade thrilled Nab like an inveterate gambler in a high-stakes poker marathon. A party of men had ridden a hundred miles to buy horses from her, but she turned them away, telling them to wait in town until she and Hawkshaw had finished their business. That she might lose a sale didn't appear to bother her at all.

Nab's grandsons were as adept as she at the art of trade. Under the guise of teaching Rusty and Lucas about stable work, the teenagers soon had them doing most of their chores. However, neither Rusty nor Lucas—nor Tennie—objected because they were learning so much, especially, just as the judge had said, from the oldest and the middle boy, who had unusual gifts.

In the kitchen, Tennie worked out a system with Nab that pleased them both. Nab would begin the cooking process, leaving Tennie to finish it while Nab tended her beloved horses. Impressed with Nab's skill, Tennie watched the older woman throwing ingredients into pots and bowls, trying to remember every step. In addition to taking over most of the kitchen duties, as discreetly as she could, Tennie created an improved sense of order in the chaotic cabin. Nevertheless, she still took time to escape to the barns and paddocks to look at the horses and watch the drama of the match between Nab and Hawkshaw.

Although Nab was good at keeping her face bland, Tennie recognized she had a favorite stallion she wanted to keep. She wouldn't have realized it, except Gid was incapable of keeping a poker face. By watching him get fidgety every time Hawkshaw neared Nab's favorite stallion, Tennie was able to surmise it. And if she knew it, she knew Hawkshaw did, too.

Although his hand still hurt, Badger lost his fearful anger and began to ride with the other boys.

Nab made them treat the stallions with kindness and consideration, but she wouldn't allow them to get playful with them. "You get too familiar with them, and they start getting sassy and think they don't have to mind you none."

Nevertheless, they were some of the gentlest horses Tennie had ever seen, appearing to catch calmness from Nab. It seemed odd to Tennie that horses with so many layers of muscles and such powerful hindquarters could be the easiest to get along with.

When she said as much to Hawkshaw, mentioning they were almost the equine version of Gid, he responded, "Just smarter."

Although he kept his face as unreadable as Nab, Tennie sensed Hawkshaw was pleased and excited about the bargain he had made. She didn't try to hurry him because she dreaded the day she would have to convince him of the plan of action Viola had advised. That he be in the best of moods was imperative to her success. She knew if his brain wasn't so filled with thoughts of horseflesh, she would have long before fallen under his suspicions.

When Hawkshaw did announce his final decision, he picked one of the positive breeder mares Tennie thought Nab really wanted to keep, but he bypassed her favorite high-strung stallion and choose a calmer one instead. He did not give his reasons for the ones he chose, and neither Gid nor Tennie asked, but Lucas, always braver than was for his own good, did question Hawkshaw about the stallion.

"I have to ship these horses a long way," Hawkshaw said, his willingness to explain surprising everyone. "I don't want some nervy stallion destroying himself and every other horse in the stock car."

Shipping the horses brought up more problems. Even though Gid would be with them, Nab didn't like her horses shipped unless her grandsons rode along to guarantee their health.

"Floyd and Virgil will ride in the boxcar with them," Nab said. "You'll have to pay them and pay their way."

Hawkshaw didn't see any reason why they should ride all the way to Texas. He wanted the horses to get off the train in Mobile, rest, then exercise a few days before riding the rest of the way to Texas. "If they leave now, the horses can be rested by the time we get to Mobile, and we won't have to lay over so long. I don't see any reason why your grandsons can't leave them with us in Mobile and go on back home."

Nab concurred it would be too hard on the horses to ride the rails all the way to Texas without a break. She wasn't thrilled about her grandsons being gone so long either, so she agreed they could turn the horses over to Hawkshaw in Mobile.

"Granny," Floyd said, giving Tennie another surprise because he rarely spoke. "Can Rusty go with us?"

Rusty gave a start. "Please, Miss Tennie?" he begged.

They were all looking at her, waiting for her to decide. Confused, Tennie tried to think. Lucas tugged on her arm, his face looking up into hers, begging to go along, too.

"You're not going," she told Lucas. At least, she knew that much.

Floyd and Virgil probably just wanted someone to help them shovel horse droppings out of the boxcar, but she knew Rusty probably realized that and didn't care. But what about the man who'd tried to throw her in a brothel when she was on her own? Hadn't Ozzie Milton made disturbing comments about liking little boys? What if someone like that tried to hurt Rusty? He was only thirteen, but there were fourteen-year-old boys in Texas after the war leading long cattle drives to market.

She rubbed her forehead, not knowing what to say. What would Ashton Granger want his boy to do? What would Wash advise? Three teenage boys loose in Mobile could get into a lot of trouble.

"I'll pay Rusty to ride with Floyd," Hawkshaw said. "No need in three of them going."

Tennie looked at Hawkshaw. Floyd was the one with all the horse sense, and Hawkshaw probably had more trust in Rusty than he did Virgil.

Nab nodded. "Floyd can teach Rusty the ropes."

Tennie sighed and looked at Rusty. "Stay with the horses and out of the saloons."

"Thank you, Miss Tennie," he said, his face alight with pleasure. "Thank you, thank you."

"It means you'll miss seeing a large old Southern plantation," she said, trying to make curious little Lucas feel better.

"That's okay. I don't care," Rusty assured her.

Virgil wasn't too happy. "Heck fire, Granny. I wanted to ride the train to Texas."

"When you get full-growed, you can go to Texas to visit your Uncle Gid," Nab said.

Tennie saw a funny look cross Hawkshaw's face, and she tried not to laugh. The thought of more Coltranes in Texas was too much for him. She hoped he never ran across the ill-tempered Grandpa Dings.

As she turned to go back to the house, she heard Hawkshaw say to Rusty, "I guess this will go a little way toward the balance I owe you."

"What?" Rusty asked, bewildered. "Oh, yes, sir. It sure will."

At the supper table that night, Hawkshaw asked Nab how easy it was to get a stock car.

"Sometimes takes a few days," Nab said. "Generally, they keep one a-resting nearby. They know I won't use no car 'cepting it's ventilated."

Because of the possibility Gid's truculent brothers might still be in the vicinity, Gid was elected to stay at the farm while Hawkshaw,

Rusty, and Floyd would drive the horses into town where they would await a stock car. Lucas heard and began raising a fuss, wanting all of them to go into town so he wouldn't be left out of the excitement.

"No," Hawkshaw said, cutting it short. "The less time your stepmother spends at the judge's house, the better off her reputation will be."

Gid's mouth dropped, and he stared, aghast. "Ain't nobody gonna say nothing like that. He's an old man. Why, he's the judge!"

Tennie spoke up. "It's okay, Mr. Gid. I'd rather stay here with Miss Nab and let the little ones get their fill of the country for a while. They'll be cooped up on a train soon enough."

Early the next morning, Nab readied the horses for travel, braiding their tails and doing them up in burlap. She was sending along enough hardtack and jerky for the boys to survive six months on a train, but Tennie made sure Rusty had some money.

"I'd like to buy a harmonica, if that's all right with you, Miss Tennie," Rusty said. "I haven't forgotten my promise to help with the stable fees for Apache when we get back to Waco."

Tennie nodded, thinking it a good idea. If he had a harmonica up to his lips, maybe there wouldn't be room for a whiskey bottle.

When Hawkshaw, Rusty, and Floyd rode out

with the horses, Lucas choked up, and Badger let a few tears flow. Neither had ever spent a night away from Rusty. Nab told her remaining grandsons to take them swimming in the creek. Lucas and Badger wanted to show off their *bagre* skills, but the water ran too fast and shallow for them to be successful.

That afternoon, the men waiting to buy horses returned, sent by Hawkshaw, and Nab's time was taken up with dickering once again.

Hawkshaw stayed gone three days.

In the meantime, Tennie enjoyed visiting with the men who came to buy horses and ended up staying the night. When Nab told them of Tennie's quest to change the mind of Raiford Beauregard, they shook their heads and wished her good luck.

Later, Tennie tried to help Gid explain to Nab about the taxes. He couldn't remember all the details, and asked Tennie to go over them.

"The farm is in Mr. Gid's name," Tennie said. "From now on the bill for the taxes will go to him in Texas, and he will pay them. The judge convinced him to make a will, leaving the farm to you if he passes away first. If you pass before he does, the farm would then go to your grandsons after Mr. Gid died, with the provision that none of them can sell any part of it unless the other three agree."

Nab, who thought somebody's word ought

to be good enough, didn't like the idea of the government interfering and all the paperwork involved but said she thought the part about not breaking up the farm was wise.

"Mr. Gid may want a few horses from you now and then to offset the cost of the taxes," Tennie said.

"Gid knows he can have any horse on this place any time he wants," Nab said. "He don't need to pay no taxes for that."

Tennie smiled. However, the thought of facing Hawkshaw when the time came, and later Raiford Beauregard, and the evidently jealous and conniving Maribel, ate at Tennie until she felt almost ill. She walked around praying so hard, she ironed a pair of Badger's overalls twice before she realized what she had done. Finally recognizing she could not count on Hawkshaw's cooperation, she accepted she would just have to find some other way if he refused to help her.

When Hawkshaw returned, he was pleased with the stock car and Floyd's knowledge of horses. At least, they all figured he was happy because he didn't look to be in a foul mood, and he said the railroad delivered the right stock car, and Rusty was learning. He slept in the barn again, and neither he nor Gid were in a hurry to leave the next morning. It was afternoon when they finally said good-bye to Nab.

Badger started sobbing. Tennie wanted to cry.

"Is there anything I can do for you, Miss Nab, for being so hospitable to us?" she asked. "Anything at all?"

Nab looked at Gid who was waiting by the wagon. "You look after Gid there in Texas. If he was to get down sick, he don't have nobody a-tall to look after him."

"I will. I promise to do the best I can for him." Tennie looked at her two unlikely friends. "I would have anyway, even without you asking."

Gid and Nab weren't demonstrative.

Gid got on his horse and said, "I'll be seeing you, Nab."

All Nab did was nod in return. As they left, she threw a handful of dirt behind them. Gid said it was to confuse any evil spirits about the direction they were headed. But she stood watching them ride away until they were out of sight.

The old neighbor with the hat full of shotgun holes came out onto the porch as they rode by. "Heading back to Texas, Gid?"

"Yes, sir, that'd be right," Gid said.

"Takin' the law back with ya?"

Gid nodded. "But I hear of any more varmints disturbing Nab, me and the Texas law is coming right back here. Kin varmints or the other kind."

Tennie shot a look at Hawkshaw and tried to smother a smile. He wasn't even looking in Gid's direction. His eyes were scanning the bushes and the trees around them, ready to strike if evil spirits in the form of Gid's sullen brothers reared their ugly heads.

They made it back to town without incident, however, taking the wagon and horses back to the livery. Gid said he would walk with Tennie to the judge's house, but Tennie wanted to stop by the courthouse first to see if it was still all right for her and the two remaining boys to spend the night.

As she waited for Gid to finish his livery business, Tennie walked down the street a slight distance. Someone caught her eye, a slender man with his back turned. He had his pants tucked into high boots, and he wore a large Stetson. Her heart leapt into her throat. Wash!

CHAPTER 18

Tennie began to run toward him, but when he turned around, she saw it was not Wash, but someone who looked nothing like him in the face.

She stopped almost in midair, embarrassed. He was understandably staring at her, so she gave him a brief smile of apology without looking directly into his eyes and turned back to the livery. Tears flooded her lashes and splashed down her cheek. She had no idea until that moment how much she had been hoping in the depths of her heart Wash would join her. She wiped her tears away so the others would not see she had been crying.

They said nothing about her appearance and began walking to the courthouse with her.

"I hope we can get this business with your cousin settled quickly, Mr. Gid."

He gave a heavy sigh, and Tennie realized he was dreading dealing with the Beauregards as much, if not more, than she was. She changed the subject and asked if he thought Hawkshaw was happy with the horses he had chosen.

By the time they reached the courthouse, Gid had everyone from all over the state of Texas flocking to Hawkshaw in droves to buy a colt from one of Nab's horses. He only stopped when they found the judge in his chambers.

He rose to greet them. "My dear"—the judge took her by the shoulders—"you look exhausted. Why don't you leave Lucas here with me and let me show him around? I'm sure Gid and young Badger will escort you to the house and find something else to do for a while so you can get some rest."

Tennie looked at Gid and he nodded.

Lucas said, "Please, Miss Tennie."

"All right." She smiled. "I do feel a little peaked."

The judge patted her shoulder as he followed her out of the office. "I confess I am being entirely selfish. I so enjoyed our visit the last time you were here that I want you vibrant and awake to share another conversation with me."

"I would like that," Tennie said with a smile. "I don't want my chin nodding at the table."

She wasn't tired as much as she was heartsick. Viola met them at the door, taking Tennie's bag from Gid's hand, which she insisted on carrying. Viola told Gid and Badger to go around to the back porch where she would serve them cookies and cold buttermilk.

After shutting the door, Tennie followed her up the stairs. "The judge told me to rest. He likes to talk and doesn't want me dropping off in the middle of the conversation."

"When I thinks he's said enough," Viola said, "I'll fetch you for a bath. You need to be fresh and pert for facing those fractious Beauregards. How was your visit with Miss Nab?"

Tennie thought about Gid making Nab happy by carrying on about the bad food in Texas, even though he ate it with relish. But she didn't want to say anything negative that would get back to her. "Miss Nab has a kind heart. Of course, she has to give so much time to her animals . . ." Implying the rest, she let her voice drop.

Viola opened the door to the bedroom Tennie had stayed in before, smiling and nodding in satisfaction. "That be right. Miss Nab, she be kind, but nothing get in the way of them critters."

Tennie removed her hat and placed it on the bed. Viola snatched it up. "Don't be doing that now. You'll be bringing bad luck on yourself." She placed the hat on the dresser. "You lay down now and have a good cry. Get your nerves out now, then tomorrow, they be gone."

Tennie thanked her as the door shut. Throwing herself on the bed, Tennie followed Viola's advice. After releasing her tears, she thought it would have been bad luck if she had left her hat on the bed. She could have accidentally wallowed on it in her misery.

For the most part, her evening with the judge was an enjoyable interlude. He allowed the boys to prattle about their day—seeing the courthouse, following Gid into almost every shop, visiting with the storekeepers in town. Tennie thought she would have liked to visit the shops, too, and decided to ask Gid to escort her if they had time. Whatever time they had left all depended on Gid's relatives.

The judge entertained her with stories about Rory Coltrane, Nab's irrepressible husband who had been such an influence on Gid. "He wouldn't have let Gid get into trouble with the law. It was too bad for all of them when Rory insisted on going to war and died.

"And what about this Hawkshaw fellow?" the judge continued. "What do you know about him?"

"Absolutely nothing except he's from Kentucky, and evidently, he made someone so mad, he's banned from going back," Tennie replied. "I've never heard him mention a father, a mother, a sibling, not so much as a dog from his childhood."

"And the war? Where did his allegiance lie?" the judge asked.

"The North," Tennie said. "I have no doubt he was a sniper and worked alone. I can't see him chumming up to other soldiers in a tent."

Tennie saw a look of intense hatred flicker through the judge's eyes. He gave a slow blink, and the look disappeared, but she thought it would do well for Hawkshaw to get out of town as soon as possible.

The judge touched her arm and patted her back, but Tennie wasn't worried with Viola and two boys in the house. She told herself if Lucas and Badger could save her from kidnappers, she didn't think a little old judge would present too much of a problem.

After they had talked alone in the parlor for some time, and he made an inquisitive comment about the kisses Wash had given her, Viola appeared at the door and announced her bathwater was ready.

Tennie again thanked him for his hospitality and followed Viola into the kitchen.

As she scrubbed, Viola gave more advice. "They is some sorry darkies that works for the Beauregards. Don't eat nothing. Don't let nothing touch your lips while you is there. When they get mad, they spits in the food."

Tennie paused and stared. "Spit in the food?" she repeated.

"That's right, and when they gets real mad, they liable to do something else that don't bear talking about."

Tennie's lungs expelled a long stream of air. "Okay. I promise I won't eat a thing."

"Or drink nothing," Viola said.

"Or drink anything, not even water," Tennie agreed.

She went to bed feeling like a character from an Arabian fairy tale who must engage in charming conversation night after night or be killed. Or have to eat food with spit in it.

Hawkshaw and Gid were waiting for Tennie, Lucas, and Badger in a surrey in front of the judge's house when they finished breakfast. The plantation would take an hour's drive. Nevertheless, Viola sent along food and water, taking no chances.

The judge placed a letter of introduction into Tennie's hand. "Given how Raiford and I feel about one another, it probably won't do much good, but it might get you in the front door."

Tennie glanced at Gid, wondering what kind of kinfolk he had who wouldn't invite him in. She thanked the judge.

"Good luck, my dear," he said, waving as they left.

Tennie waved good-bye and twisted around in the surrey. Hawkshaw sat up front with the reins, while Gid, Lucas, and Badger occupied the backseat.

"I've never ridden in one of these before," she said, looking around and making sure not to crowd Hawkshaw.

It had taken quite a bit of persuading on Gid's part to make sure Hawkshaw rode in the surrey and not on a horse so he couldn't ride off without them.

"Aren't we grand?" she joked.

"Not grand enough," Hawkshaw said.

"When we get out of town," Tennie said, "you'd better pull over so we can talk about the plan Viola gave me to get you and Lafayette off the hook."

Hawkshaw gave her an evil stare. "I'm waiting with bated breath."

They were on a tree-lined lane that was in surprisingly smooth condition. Hawkshaw took his time, and they passed by several suitable open spots until he found one he liked, beside a large embankment where the woods were the thickest.

"Out with it," he said, turning to Tennie.

Tennie swallowed and plunged in. "Miss Viola said the first thing to remember is that Mr. Beauregard is desperate to marry his cousin Helen. By all accounts, this Helen is a nice person, and why she wants to marry him, I have no idea. There is no accounting for taste. However, his sister, Maribel, hates her and vows to run off and marry one of their ex-slaves if Mr. Beauregard marries Helen. Miss Viola said she didn't think any of them would have her, except one or two who hate Mr. Beauregard so bad they might consider it just to get even with him.

"Anyway, until Mr. Beauregard gets rid of Maribel, he can't have Helen without a scandal."

"That story differs slightly from Gid's," Hawkshaw said, turning to give him a dirty look.

Gid looked embarrassed, shrugged his shoulders, and looked away. "I didn't want to upset Nab. She said marrying French is what got us Coltranes in trouble in the first place."

Hawkshaw grunted. "I've known men in the South who would have their sister committed to an insane asylum for threatening that."

"Mr. Beauregard tried," Tennie said. "But the doctor is a family friend. He claimed Maribel wouldn't do it, and he's not allowing her to be committed. He said it is hard enough for Miss Helen to hold her head up when they have an uncle who enjoys showing himself in town wearing women's underclothing and having everybody laughing at him."

Gid leaned forward. "He be from their other side, not us'uns," he said, shaking his head at Tennie to make sure she understood.

Tennie nodded and continued. "Now, when Maribel's husband died, she knew she'd have to wear black mourning and be a widow for at least a year. Except because of the way he died, and the bad feelings it caused, Maribel found she can't quit wearing the mourning or circulate around for another husband. No one will have anything to do with her—at least not those in her social sphere, which, frankly, is all she knows. She feels she'll never catch another husband. She blames Lafayette for that and has convinced her brother the only way she can get out of the vicious circle is if Lafayette is dead. But there is another way." Tennie took a deep breath. "That's where you come in," she said, looking at Hawkshaw.

"No," he said.

"You are returning the money and not instigating Lafayette into drawing his gun against you because I am your cousin and talked you out of it," Tennie said. "You want to leave that life behind and become a wealthy planter and horse breeder in Texas. You have the land, the money, but not the position. You need a wife from a better social circle in order to be respected among the wealthy Texans. That's hogwash, but they don't know it."

Hawkshaw leaned closer to her. "No," he said in her face.

Tennie ignored him. "The marriage could be in name only if that is what Miss Maribel wishes. You won't force your affections on her, and you will allow her to keep whatever dowry she has. Miss Viola said that is important—that you stress to Miss Maribel she will have control over her own money from the get-go."

"I am not marrying anybody," Hawkshaw said through gritted teeth.

"You don't have to," Tennie said. "That's the beauty of the plan. You will tell Mr. Beauregard you have a sister in Houston who you promised could arrange the wedding for you. Miss Viola said she could guarantee Miss Maribel will never make it past New Orleans before jumping the train and leaving us.

"Then you can write Mr. Beauregard and tell him what happened, but he won't care because Miss Maribel will be out of his hair, and he will have Miss Helen. You will have your reputation, and Mr. Lafayette will have his life, because Maribel will forget all about him when she is someplace else with a lot of money in her hand. And Mr. Beauregard is not going to send any hired killers after someone he has agreed to have as a brother-in-law. There are all these laws about breach of promise you could pursue if you wanted to, and he won't want to antagonize you into doing that."

They continued to argue over it for almost half an hour. "What if this crazy woman decides she wants to marry me?" Hawkshaw demanded. "What then?"

"It won't happen," Tennie said, refraining from reminding him just because Lupe wanted him didn't mean every other woman did. "Miss Viola said Miss Maribel only likes suave, sophisticated men. All you have to do is perhaps belch a time a two, or use a toothpick to clean your teeth, and she won't want to have anything to do with you."

Finally, Hawkshaw began to crack. "Would you swear to me on the Bible if she gets it into her head we should really get married, you will find a way to stop it without getting me killed by her insane brother?"

"Of course," Tennie promised. "But it may involve some sort of disease."

"I don't care. But you will have to do all the talking. I am not going to say a word."

"I promise," Tennie said, her eyes glancing at Gid, who sat behind Hawkshaw.

Gid gave her a short nod.

Hawkshaw got out of the surrey, pulled out his knife, and grabbed a small branch from a tree.

"Hey now, what are you doing?" Gid said.

"Get up front and take the reins," Hawkshaw said. "I have to make a toothpick."

The boys had already been schooled by Tennie not to interrupt or say a word about what was going on. They looked back and forth between her and Hawkshaw, their faces mirroring such little faith in her plan, she almost gave it up.

"You're going to be telling a lot of fibs, Miss Tennie," Lucas said when he decided the grown-ups had finished talking.

Tennie sighed, turned, and spoke to the boys. "What would make Jesus happier? For me to tell a few white lies these people want to hear to get them out of a fix? Or get on a high horse and pretend I'm better than everybody else by refusing to tell a fib or two that could possibly save the lives of Mr. Hawkshaw and Mr. Lafayette?"

"That's not what I meant, Miss Tennie," Lucas said. "I just meant you ain't a very good liar."

Hawkshaw snickered, and Gid nodded.

"Maybe listening to Miss Nab's horse trading all week was a blessing in disguise," Tennie mused. "God was priming me up."

"Oh, hell," Hawkshaw said. "My whole life hangs on a thread held by an ex-slave, a mountaineer horse trader, and an eighteen-year-old religious fanatic."

"I'm not a religious fanatic," Tennie said. "If I was, I wouldn't be associating with you."

"You haven't got sense enough to know who to associate with and who not to associate with," Hawkshaw said. "If you had a lick of sense, you would have laid the law down to that dim-witted fiancé of yours and told him he'd better forget about chasing outlaws and give you a decent home."

"Don't you talk to Miss Tennie like that," Gid said. "She does too have sense. She got more sense than any woman I knowed besides Nab."

"Well that's not saying a lot, is it?" Hawkshaw said.

"How'd you like for me to rip you out of this here surrey and break every bone in your body?" Gid said.

"How'd you like for me to pump you full of bullet holes first?" Hawkshaw returned.

"Always hiding behind a gun," Gid said. "What are you going to do when the day comes you don't have a revolver to hide behind?"

Gid reined the horses automatically to the right, and they entered the lane of the Beauregard plantation. Tennie and the others stopped fighting and fell silent. The ravages of war had not destroyed the stately oaks leading up to the mansion, nor the ancient tall shrubbery that softened the corners of the house. A large white painted brick home, it had tall white columns at least six feet in diameter spanning across a wide porch. Its stately beauty drew Tennie's breath away. She had expected a fine home, but nothing in her imagination prepared her for the heartbreaking loveliness of the Beauregard estate.

As Gid pulled up the drive, Tennie said while staring at the mansion, "Maybe I won't be your cousin. The judge already knows I'm not."

"Y'all get out here by the door, Miss Tennie," Gid said. "I'm going over yonder to those trees with the horses. I'm turning this here surrey in the direction we need to go in case we got to hightail it out of here."

Tennie turned to the boys. "Lucas, you and Badger stay close to the surrey and don't go off. If we have to leave in a hurry, we want you right there with us."

"Are we going to get shot at again?" Badger asked.

"I hope not," Tennie said, stepping down from the surrey.

Hawkshaw stood with her, looking up at the mansion. Tennie thought it odd no one came out to greet them. That wasn't like country people. Dogs ran around the house, baying at first, but were soon licking Tennie's hand. She knew whoever was inside the house had to have heard the hounds.

Gid left the boys with the surrey, joining Tennie and Hawkshaw. Gid looked pale, like his stomach was upset. Hawkshaw walked onto the porch and banged on the door. Tennie and Gid followed him. Hawkshaw had to knock three times before someone came to the door.

She was short, blacker than charcoal, and had a face like a bulldog. "What you want?"

Gid was incapable of speech—he looked too tongue-tied to even say his first name—and Hawkshaw had already warned he wasn't going to talk.

So Tennie introduced them. "You may remember Mr. Hawkshaw from a previous visit, and of course, Mr. Coltrane is a cousin of the Beauregards. I have a letter of introduction from Judge LeRoy. We would like to speak to Mr. Beauregard, please."

"He ain't here. He done took Miss Helen down to the lower forty and no telling when they be back."

"We've come a long way to see him," Tennie said. "We'll just wait."

"Suit yourself." The black woman slammed the door in their faces.

"Oh my." Tennie looked at Gid. "Are they always like this?"

"I don't know. I ain't never come up this far."

She sat down on the steps. "We might as well wait here. We certainly aren't going to be invited into the house until Mr. Beauregard gets here." She hoped he would invite them in when he arrived. She didn't want to conduct business on the front steps, but she would if forced to.

Hawkshaw and Gid sat down warily near her, knowing she meant to straighten out matters that very day, even if they had to sit on the porch for three hours.

Tennie expected Gid to start talking, but he remained unusually quiet, looking down at his clothes, taking his hat off and staring at it, as if he thought them not good enough to be seen on the front porch of the Beauregard plantation house. Hawkshaw made noises of impatience, wanting the whole affair over with as quickly as possible. A few small black boys found Lucas and Badger. Tennie could tell by their hand motions they wanted their visitors to go off somewhere else with them, but Lucas and Badger refused to budge. In addition to playing with the dogs, they ended up climbing all over the horses, but they were gentle creatures and didn't appear to mind.

Gid muttered that he didn't dare unhitch them.

Tennie, while remaining seated, began looking around. The cotton fields to the left were infested with weeds. The bases of the columns the mansion rested on were showing signs of rot. The beautiful white paint was beginning to peel in places.

She gave a start when she heard what sounded like Negro men and women screaming and scuffling, coming from around the other side of the house.

Gid shook his head. "No use interfering. We don't have a dog in that fight."

Tennie nodded and leaned back against a column, hoping it would hold her weight without collapsing. Despite the loveliness of the Beauregard plantation, she couldn't escape the oppressive feeling of crumbling decay. As the fight with its shrieking foul invectives continued, she stirred uneasily. "I wonder what they are arguing about?"

Gid shrugged, consumed with worries of his own.

Hawkshaw looked the other way. "Violence is only a temporary respite from despair," he murmured as if reciting a quote.

Tennie had never heard it before, but he didn't look inclined to talk about it. She stared at him, not totally understanding what he said or how close to the bone he felt it. She looked away and left him alone with his thoughts.

It was thirty minutes later, not three hours, when they saw a buggy coming up the lane.

"It's him and cousin Helen," Gid said, standing up, wooden with fear.

CHAPTER 19

The buggy stopped in front of them. A small man resembling a bulging toad alighted. He reminded Tennie of a picture she had once seen of John Quincy Adams, except Raiford Beauregard was much uglier. He came around the buggy and held his hand out to a slender woman with brown hair and a pretty, narrow face.

"Giddings! Hawkshaw!" Raiford said when he saw them, his voice hostile. "What are you doing here?"

Neither man spoke. Helen looked concerned. "Did Esther leave you out here?" She turned to Raiford. "Really, Raiford, you must do something with her. Of all the inhospitable things to do."

"I can't do anything with these slaves," Raiford said. "Ever since Lincoln freed them, they are surly and unresponsive. By God, in my father's day, it would have been thirty lashes for them."

Tennie stepped forward. "Mr. Beauregard? My name is Tennessee Granger. I am the marshal of Ring Bit, Texas."

"Marshal! Impossible!" Raiford said, staring at her as if she was a maggot on a dead cow.

"Yes, it is hard to believe," Tennie said, knowing most people did not understand the difference between a town marshal, a sheriff, a U.S. deputy marshal, and a U.S. marshal. "I assure you I am, and you may wire the U.S. deputy marshal in Texas to ask him. Mr. Hawkshaw has agreed to accompany me here." Tennie didn't know where that came from, but she continued to play it.

"Then why is he carrying a gun?"

"Because I don't carry one," she said. "He is with me of his own free will, and we are here to talk business with you."

"Business!" Raiford turned to Hawkshaw. "You didn't kill him, did you?"

"That's the reason we are here," Tennie answered. "Do you want to discuss it on these steps, or would you prefer to go inside?"

Raiford Beauregard looked about to explode, but brushing past them, he muttered, "Come into the parlor."

Helen looked upset as they followed him inside.

"Helen, leave us," he said.

"No," Tennie said. "It concerns her in a way, and I would prefer she stay."

Tennie was glad he didn't have a sword in his hand, or Raiford Beauregard would have skewered her to the wall. Instead, he glared and threw open the double doors to his parlor.

Tennie entered, trying not to let herself be overly impressed with the lavish furniture, the costly drapes, or the large fireplace with elaborate china urns on a carved mantel.

To show his displeasure, Raiford took a chair

and threw himself into it, not waiting for the women to be seated. Tennie sat on the edge of a sofa nearest him, while Gid reluctantly took a seat next to her. Hawkshaw sat in a chair away from them, while Helen stood with her hand on the back of Raiford's chair. Tennie looked down at the arm of the brocaded sofa and noticed how dirty the fabric was. The carpet in front of her had a bulge that told her the servants were lifting the edge and sweeping dirt under it.

"Can we get you something to drink? Perhaps some tea and other refreshments?" Helen asked.

"No!" Tennie said. Realizing she had been too emphatic, she tempered it. "No, thank you, ma'am. We are fine." She turned back to Raiford. "The judge sent along this letter of introduction." She rose to give it to him.

He stared at her, grabbing the letter and reading it quickly. Helen took it from him, scanning it before she let her hand fall, still holding the letter.

"All right. What is it?" Raiford said as Tennie sat back down.

"I am engaged to Mr. Lafayette's brother, Wash," she said. "I have used my influence to convince Mr. Hawkshaw to return the money you advanced him. He realizes he is leaving you in a rather bad situation, but together, we have come up with a plan we think will solve all your problems without risking the life of Mr. Lafayette or the reputation of Mr. Hawkshaw."

Raiford opened his mouth, but Helen put her hand on his shoulder. "Perhaps you should listen to her, Raiford," she said, looking at Tennie with an odd expression on her face.

Tennie didn't know how much Helen knew about Raiford's original plan. Perhaps she suspected it but was curious to see what Tennie had to say.

"Mr. Hawkshaw, as you can see, isn't getting any younger." She dared not look at him. "He would like to leave his violent profession behind and become a gentleman farmer and horse breeder in Texas."

"And what do I care about that?" Raiford said, his voice dripping in acid.

"Mr. Hawkshaw has the land, the plantation, the horses, the money, everything one needs to succeed, except for one thing," Tennie said. "To be accepted in the upper circles of Texas society, and by the people who would purchase his horses and allow him to circulate in their midst, he needs a wife of breeding and culture." She thought if they saw the run-down ranch Hawkshaw would be taking his horses to, they would kick her out of the house immediately.

Instead, Helen leaned forward, lips parted in hopefulness, while Raiford suddenly let his lids fall over his eyes, looking sly and devious.

"He's a Yankee," he said. "Yankees care nothing for those things."

Gid came to life. "Oh no, Cousin Raiford. He be from old Kentuck. You knowed how it was up yonder. Why the blue bellies just came in there and forced people to fight with them. Mr. Hawkshaw, he didn't have no choice."

Hawkshaw shot Gid a look that said he would like to kill him, but he looked away before the Beauregards could catch it.

"Certainly," Tennie agreed, hoping Hawkshaw would not murder her, too. "Mr. Hawkshaw would like to make a business proposition involving your sister, Miss Maribel. He would like to offer her his hand in marriage. In name only, if that is what she would prefer."

The double doors of the parlor flew open with a bang. A tall, handsome woman dressed in black entered. "What is this? Why is my name being bandied about?"

As Maribel stared at Hawkshaw, Tennie looked her over, realizing she possessed that deadly combination of black hair and blue eyes. She was not a young woman, but there wasn't a gray hair showing in her head. Her straight nose and full lips looked down on Hawkshaw.

"I thought you were going to kill him!" She threw the back of her hand to her forehead, and in a show of theatrics, she moaned. "Oh, God! Shall I never be free? Shall I never be loosened from this albatross around my neck? Should one youthful mistake be allowed to ruin my life?" She sank into a chair facing them, looking downward and sighing with overplayed emotion, covering her eyes with one languid hand.

Tennie wanted to curse Lafayette at that moment. Why did he always get mixed up with hysterical women? And why was she always stuck dealing with them?

"Maribel," her brother said, ignoring her performance. "Mr. Hawkshaw has come here with a proposition for you. He needs a wife of background and refinement to help him advance in Texas society. He would like your hand in marriage with no strings attached. It could be one in name only if that is what you prefer."

"I couldn't possibly consider it," Maribel exclaimed, meanwhile spreading the fingers over her eyes so she could peek at Hawkshaw.

"Mr. Hawkshaw realizes this is a surprise," Tennie said.

"Why doesn't he speak for himself?" Raiford asked in irritation.

"Because I am the law and the matchmaker," Tennie said. "Mr. Hawkshaw has asked me to speak on his behalf."

Maribel lowered her hand and was shooting glances in Hawkshaw's direction. "In name only?"

"Yes, ma'am," Tennie said. "If that is what you prefer. I cannot guarantee that Mr. Hawkshaw would not occasionally seek solace in the arms of

328

a barmaid, but I can assure you he would never embarrass you in front of friends." She wondered where all this information was coming from. Words just seemed to be flowing from her lips.

One of Maribel's eyebrows rose, and she began looking at Hawkshaw in arched interest. He stretched his legs out, took the toothpick from his pocket, and put it in his mouth. Maribel's eyebrow went down in distaste, and she looked away.

"Of course, Mr. Hawkshaw has plenty of money of his own," Tennie said, "and wouldn't dream of touching any dowry Miss Maribel might bring into the marriage. Any money she has would be in her control. In her full possession from the start."

Maribel shifted her attention to Tennie. "Really?"

Tennie nodded. "There is one thing. Mr. Hawkshaw's sister in Houston has begged him to wait and have the ceremony there. She wants to have a small elegant affair with just a few important guests." She wondered if anybody in Houston knew what a small and elegant affair was, thinking they only knew "get her hitched" or have a big blowout, but it sounded good. She continued. "That is where Mr. Gid comes in. Mr. Hawkshaw would never dream of pushing himself off on Miss Maribel, and he has asked her cousin, Mr. Gid, to be her male escort on the train to Texas."

A rich man with a plantation who didn't even want to touch his future bride or be near her until after the wedding was surely too much for anyone to swallow without suspicion, Tennie feared, but the Beauregards appeared to be gulping it down without a thought.

Gid leaned forward again. "That's right, Cousin Raiford. I'd be right proud to escort Cousin Maribel on the train."

Raiford and Maribel frowned, but Helen said, "That is so kind of you, Gid."

Tennie wondered what Helen saw in the unattractive Raiford. Was it the plantation that possessed her? Despite what Nab said, Tennie thought Helen still young enough to bear children. Perhaps she wanted it for them.

"The train for Texas leaves tomorrow at eleven," Tennie said.

Maribel waved her hand. "I couldn't possibly be ready by then. And my maid will have to go with me."

Esther burst into the room. "No, sir, no sir, no sir. I's not going to Texas. No sir."

"Don't be silly, Esther," Maribel said. "Of course, you're going."

"No, ma'am, I is not," Esther said. "I ain't going to that wild country. I be free now, and you can't make me."

Maribel gave her a long look under frowning eyebrows. She turned her head, raised her chin, and looked off into another part of the room. "Then I can't possibly go."

Helen's fingers were digging into Raiford's shoulder so hard, Tennie was surprised he did not cry out in pain.

He said, "What will it take to get you to go, Esther?"

Esther opened her mouth as if to imitate Maribel's histrionics, but thought better of it. "Ten acres of river bottomland for my grandson."

"Impossible!" Raiford thundered.

"Give it to her," Maribel said with the air of someone who couldn't be bothered with trifles. "You can take it out of my share of the inheritance Father left me."

"I certainly shall," Raiford said. Giving Esther a sulky look, he promised to prepare the papers that night.

"I still don't see how I can be ready so soon," Maribel said.

"Of course, you can, Maribel," Helen said. "I'll help you pack. It will be just like old times when we were girls going off to the academy."

For a minute, Tennie thought Maribel was going to tell Helen where she could go but evidently thought better of it. A free slave for the evening was not something to discard lightly, and Tennie had no doubt Maribel would make Helen do all the work and dance to her tune while doing it. What an unpleasant woman! Lafayette had no taste in women, except that they be beautiful.

"It's all settled then," Tennie said, rising. "We shall expect you at the judge's house at ten in the morning." She sallied out of the house while the going was good.

Hawkshaw stayed behind only a few seconds longer to press the money he owed him into Raiford's hand. Gid assured them he would take good care of Maribel, but it was clear they wanted him out of the house.

Tennie thought them awful.

The boys ran from around the side of the house where they had been listening under the window, beating them to the surrey. Gid helped Tennie in, and she put her hand to the side of her head, wishing to slow the blood pounding through her veins.

"Miss Tennie!" Lucas said. "That was the best lying I've ever heard in my life. Couldn't nobody beat that."

Tennie took a deep breath and tried to calm her jangling nerves. "Every time I looked into Helen Beauregard's pitiful face, I just lied that much more."

Hawkshaw's face showed he was still furious about the whole thing. He turned to Gid. "You keep her away from me," he said in a tone so menacing, Gid leaned back.

He nodded. They all nodded and rode most of the way in silence.

Before coming into town, Tennie broke the silence. "Maybe we should pull over and eat some of the food Miss Viola sent. I don't want to hurt her feelings."

Hawkshaw glared at her. "I don't care about her feelings."

"I'm hungry," Lucas said.

"Me, too," Badger said. "I want to eat something."

"You always want to eat something," Hawkshaw growled.

Gid had taken the reins when they got in the surrey, and he solved the argument by pulling over. "I could eat a little something, too."

Tennie divided the food in the basket. "Will the train we are taking to Mobile have first class on it? Maribel's going to want to ride first class. We can stick her and the maid in there and leave them alone."

"I got to look after her," Gid said, talking with a mouthful of bread. He swallowed. "I done promised Cousin Raiford and Cousin Helen."

"You can check on her, Mr. Gid," Tennie said. "She's not going to want you sitting right next to her the whole trip."

"She'll probably pretend she doesn't even know who you are," Hawkshaw said. "I'll get her a first-class ticket if they have it. Anything to get out of this town."

They finished eating, and Gid took up the reins

once more. Tennie began fretting about Rusty. "I hope everything is going all right with Rusty."

"It better be," Hawkshaw said. "I'll whip Floyd's and Rusty's asses if anything happens to those horses."

"Floyd ain't gonna let nothing happen to those horses," Gid said in a note so firm, it dared Hawkshaw to contradict him.

Hawkshaw didn't, and Tennie told Gid she wanted to stop by Viola's before taking their stroll through town.

"Let me out," Hawkshaw said when they arrived at the judge's house. "I'm walking to the train station to get a first-class ticket if I have to beg for it. I want that woman as far away from me as possible."

"You must not have seen her face when you started picking your teeth," Tennie said, "or you wouldn't be so agitated about it."

Gid helped Tennie from the surrey, and she ran up the perfect walk to the perfect house, wondering if life would ever bring her anything like it. She remembered all the losses the judge had suffered and thought he would give it all up in an instant to have his family back.

Tennie knocked on the door but didn't wait for Viola to answer. She opened it and was greeted by the aroma of mouthwatering cooking. "Miss Viola, Miss Viola," she called, heading toward the kitchen.

Viola met her in the dining room.

"It worked," Tennie cried. "Maribel's going with us on the train tomorrow."

"I told you it would," Viola said.

Tennie gave her a fast rundown on the events. "But what shall I tell the judge? He knows I didn't have a clue how to go about it when we first arrived."

"You tell him everything you told me," Viola said. "Excepting you say you and Miss Nab and Mr. Hawkshaw figured it out."

Tennie stared into her dark eyes. "But you thought of everything."

"Yes'um," Viola said. "But the judge might not like me interfering in other folks' business, so just to be safe, you don't bring me into it."

Tennie stared, searching her face. "All right. If that's the way you want it. I just hate taking credit for being the least bit smart when I know I'm not."

Viola laughed. "You smarter than you think you is."

Tennie smiled. "I'm going to walk through the stores with Mr. Gid," she said, excited at the prospect of shopping, even if she didn't have the spare money to buy much of anything. As she looked at Viola, a pall crept over her like a disconcerting shadow. "Will they let you go into those stores?"

"They will because I works for the judge,"

Viola said. "You run along now with Mr. Gid. And you be sure to keep your promise and tell everybody in town what a fine old gentleman the judge is."

"I most certainly shall," Tennie said with a gentle but determined smile.

As they finished supper that night, the judge wanted to hear about the events at the Beauregard plantation. Tennie, beginning in hesitation, soon found herself jumping from the dining room chair and mimicking with exaggeration the voice and movements of each person—Esther became even surlier; Raiford became impossibly pompous and ruder; Helen's voice dripped ever sweeter in a fevered pitch of desperation. Tennie pretended to be Hawkshaw turning loutish with the toothpick in his hand, and poor Gid trying to be nice and obviously feeling like he wasn't good enough to be in the room.

It was when she threw her hand to her forehead, imitating Maribel's dramatics in the hammiest way that the judge burst into laughter, and Tennie thought she heard giggles coming from a crack in the door leading into the kitchen. Lucas and Badger stared at her wide-eyed with mouths open, laughing whenever the judge did.

"My dear child," the judge said when she finished. "You are enchanting."

He looked at Tennie as if he wanted to eat her

up—she wondered if she had perhaps gone too far with her theatrics. She breathed heavily from her exertions. He breathed stronger and faster for perhaps another reason.

"I think I, and the boys, should go to bed now," she said. "We have a long trip in front of us."

The boys immediately began a clamor, but Viola entered the room and began urging them toward the stairs. "Miss Tennie be right. Y'all be having a big day tomorrow."

Tennie said good night to the judge and followed the boys up the stairs. After seeing them settled in another bedroom, she entered the room she'd slept in, shutting the door behind her. As she prepared for bed, she knew it would be the last and perhaps only time she got to sleep in such heavenly comfort.

She climbed into bed, lying on her back with her hair against the softest and smoothest pillow she'd ever known. There would be word from Wash in Waco. Perhaps he would even be there to meet her. She hugged herself in joy thinking about it.

The day had worked so perfectly, thanks to Viola. And later, she and Gid, with Badger and Lucas trailing along, had walked into shop after shop filled with treasures she never knew existed. Gid knew everyone, talked to everyone, while she looked. Sometimes the boys were rowdy and had to be made to wait outside, but whereas they knew they could get around her, they obeyed Gid much better, and she had been able to look to her heart's content. And at every place, when she was asked, she repeated in varying words how grateful she was for the judge's hospitality, how pleasant it was to stay in the home of such a nice gentleman.

She jerked up in bed, suddenly remembering she had forgotten to put the chair underneath the doorknob. Her feet hit the floor with a soft thump, and she practically flew to the chair, grabbing it and placing it under the knob as fast as she could. Only when it was safely in place did she breathe a sigh of relief.

CHAPTER 20

Before he left for the courthouse, the judge gave Tennie a letter to deliver to Winn Payton. "I'll come down to see you off before the train leaves," he promised. He took her hand. "This house is going to be so lonely without you. It's going to miss you."

"I've loved staying here," Tennie replied.

Viola entered the room with baskets filled with food for them to take on the train. The judge dropped Tennie's hand while she suppressed a sigh of relief.

"I'll see you at the station, Tennie," the judge said as he left.

Tennie turned to Viola. "Badger will be in heaven." She paused for a few seconds before saying, "Miss Viola, is there anything else, anything at all I can do to repay you for your kindnesses?"

Viola looked embarrassed. "They be one thing," she said shyly. "I ain't never had a letter. Could you . . . ?"

"Of course," Tennie said. "I will mail you a letter from Texas addressed personally to you in care of the judge at this address."

"I won't be able to read it myself, but the judge, he will read it to me," Viola said.

Tennie nodded and hugged her before going out onto the porch to wait with the boys and Gid for Maribel to arrive.

"Mr. Hawkshaw said he'd wait at the station," Gid said as they sat on the steps.

"I'm surprised he didn't decide to just ride out of here without us," Tennie said.

"He was going to, but I stopped him," Gid said. "That and he wants to get to them there horses as quick as he can."

They talked in a desultory way while they waited, but Maribel did not come.

Viola came out onto the porch. "Y'all best get on down to the station. If she's a-coming, she can meet you down there."

"But what if she doesn't come?" Tennie asked.

"Y'all done presented the case, and they done agreed," Viola said. "Now if they reneges, the fault will be all their own. You can just go on to Texas with a clear conscience."

They nodded, and as they walked away, they waved good-bye to Viola.

Just as they were almost out of sight, Badger hollered loud enough for the whole neighborhood to hear, "You make the best biscuits in the world, Miss Viola!"

Tennie hugged him. "Sometimes, Badger, you are such a little pest, and other times, you are like an angel from heaven."

"What about me?" Lucas demanded.

"Of course, you too," Tennie said.

They wanted to know about Gid, and to his embarrassment and pleasure, Tennie laughed and said, "Mr. Gid, too."

When she saw Hawkshaw waiting impatiently at the station, she thought she would have gladly said the same thing about him, too, but he wouldn't want her to even think it of him.

They sat on a bench next to the stationhouse, looking down the road, watching for Maribel's buggy. The judge arrived to see them off. From a distance, they could hear the sound of a train whistle blowing. The train pulled into the station, puffing black smoke and carting a long line of cars. The brakes screeched to a stop, steam blowing everywhere.

"Look!" Lucas said.

A buggy driven by Helen with Maribel on the seat beside her was followed by an old black man in a wagon containing a tight-lipped Esther wearing an old maroon velvet hat pushed down so hard on her head, it looked like it was giving her a headache. Behind Esther were piles of bags and trunks.

"I'll have to pay extra for all that luggage," Hawkshaw said, so furious he could hardly move his lips. He left to find the conductor.

When the buggy stopped and Maribel alighted, Tennie gasped. Maribel was wearing a new satin dress with wide white and black stripes. It had a wide red ribbon tied around the waist and flowing over the bustle in the back. Another red scarf was tied in a large bow around her neck. Her hat was red, with a black ribbon around it. Tennie had never seen a dress that looked less like mourning and wondered how long Maribel had secretly been hoarding it.

Maribel fluttered her handkerchief, making noises about being helpless while Gid hastened to assist her. The conductor came back with Hawkshaw, took one look at the wagon and said something to him that caused Hawkshaw to look even more cross, but he nodded before turning abruptly to enter the second-class car, taking his usual window seat in the back.

There was a problem about having Esther on the train, especially in first class, but Maribel insisted, and with the judge there to smooth things over, the conductor agreed. Esther, in the meantime, stood looking even more like a mean old bulldog, but Tennie didn't think she could blame her. She'd probably be spitting in people's food, too.

While Gid saw Maribel and Esther safely ensconced in first class, Helen took Tennie aside. "I know you think we are terrible."

Tennie murmured no and shook her head, but Helen continued as if she hadn't spoken.

"Our grandfather was a warm and generous man. He was known far and wide for his kindness and hospitality. The house was wonderful back then. I have so many happy memories of it."

Tennie nodded, realizing it was the house Helen wanted.

Perhaps Helen knew what she was thinking because when she spoke again, it was about Raiford. "Raiford's father was . . . a little unbalanced, like Maribel. Poor Raiford tries to live up to some imaginary standard he thinks his father had for him, and he can't do it. He's really not that bad."

"Yes, ma'am," Tennie said.

Helen smiled. "I really just wanted to say thank you." She squeezed Tennie's arm. "God bless you."

"And you, too, Miss Helen." Tennie hoped Helen found the house worth the price she was going to pay for it.

Helen left her, and the judge appeared at Tennie's side. Tennie smiled and told him again how much she appreciated his hospitality.

"My darling girl," the judge said. "It has been my pleasure. If things don't work out between you and your young man, you are always welcome here. I have no one, you know."

Tennie, feeling sorry for him, reached over and pecked his dry cheek lightly with a kiss. She took his hand and squeezed it.

The whistle blew, and the conductor yelled, "All aboard!"

"They won't let us ride in the caboose, will they, sir?" Lucas asked the judge.

The judge smiled and shook his head. "Sorry, son. That is reserved for the railway employees. You take good care of your stepmother, hear?"

"Yes, sir," Lucas said, taking her by the hand. "Come on, Miss Tennie."

They called and waved their farewells to the judge as Gid got on behind them.

"Did Miss Maribel ask to speak to Mr. Hawkshaw?" Tennie whispered to Gid as they walked to their seats.

"No, I asked her, but she give me this funny look and said no, it weren't necessary," Gid whispered.

"All for the best," Tennie whispered back, looking behind her at Hawkshaw sitting alone in the corner. She sat down in the middle of the carriage with Lucas and Badger, while Gid took up his usual spot by a window at the other end. He already looked bilious.

Tennie watched the picturesque town recede from sight, and all she could think about was getting home to Texas.

They continued to pick up passengers as they hurtled their way to Mobile. Two bachelors in their early thirties got on and sat on the other side of the aisle from Tennie. They dressed in nice suits, wearing new narrow-brimmed hats. When they tipped their hats to her, she saw pleasant faces with regular features. She gave them a nod and brief smile before turning her eyes away. Before becoming betrothed, she probably would have enjoyed talking to them. Now, she had little interest in anything but listening with half an ear to their conversation. Married or not, she would never tire of hearing the sound of men's voices.

They would be getting off the train before it reached Mobile to attend the wedding of a former comrade in the army. In between time, they talked about crops, politics, the weather, and horses.

Although Gid lurched when he walked and was so unsteady he had to hold on to the backs of seats to stay upright, he forced himself twice to walk to first class to check on Maribel.

"She told him she was fine and to leave her alone," Lucas whispered. "She sure isn't very nice to him."

Tennie made no comment. Instead, they ate supper out of the baskets Viola had prepared, with Lucas taking Hawkshaw his share. Badger took Gid food, but he could only eat a few bites. The men next to Tennie were some of the last to visit the dining car attached to the train.

Gid sat in the corner of the train car, staring morosely out the window. He had already held his head out twice and vomited, much to the disgust of his fellow travelers. Hawkshaw had tried to get him to buy another bottle of whiskey to help him sleep, but Gid refused.

"The colonel won't let me drink on the job, and I don't want to end up like my ole pappy, so I best not," he said, but Tennie thought the real reason was because he didn't want Maribel to see him drunk and think even less of him.

The light outside began to fade. Tennie didn't know why they were so tired. All they had done most of the day was sit and wait. She stood up, rousing the boys so they could fold down the wooden seats to sleep on. Hawkshaw had surprised her at the previous stop by buying handwoven blankets from a vendor and tossing them to her. She looked toward his corner and found a solitary figure, legs stretched out, arms crossed, and hat over his face.

After placing one blanket down as padding, she folded the other as sort of a pillow. They curled up on the seats, the rhythmic sounds and rocking motion of the train cradling them into sleep.

She was awakened by the sounds of boots scraping against the wooden planks of the train car floor. The two young men had returned from the dining car, laughing and whispering. Occasionally they spoke a word or two too loud, but they weren't disruptive. Tennie let them think she was asleep.

She caught snatches of conversation about a woman. As their voices rose and fell, and Tennie's ear became accustomed to them, she found their laughter and conversation increasingly derisive. She hoped they were not talking about Maribel.

". . . like a wild mare going to stud," one of the men said. The other laughed in agreement.

Tennie became afraid Gid would hear and feel like he had to do something noble to protect the honor of his cousin. Without looking at the men, she rose on one elbow and adjusted the blanket around Badger. The voices beside her became muted and stopped.

The facilities in first class were much better than those in the other cars, and Maribel wasn't required to make mad dashes every time the train stopped. Esther would alight alone, ignoring everybody. Not only did Maribel never step foot off the train, she sent word to Gid by Esther that until they reached Mobile, he wasn't to bother her. To Tennie's relief, Maribel did not request a visit from Hawkshaw.

The handsome young men had departed at the previous station, and the train had partially filled with more people headed the short distance left to Mobile.

Once the train began moving, Tennie walked to where Gid sat and took a seat across from him. "Don't fret about Miss Maribel, Mr. Gid. She's perfectly fine in first class. Mr. Hawkshaw says we are going to stay a few days in Mobile so he can tend to the horses. You'll see more of her there."

He sighed and looked out the window. "It's always been the same. 'You Coltranes jest get back now.' "

Tennie didn't know how to reply, so she changed the subject. "I'm thinking I need to send a wire to Mr. Lafayette telling him we are on our way back. I don't know if it would do any good to send one to Wash in Waco, or if he is still in South Texas roaming from place to place."

Gid drew his eyes away from the window to look at her. "I reckon the colonel would get word to him if there was any way of doing it. I'll help you send the wire."

When they tumbled from the train in Mobile, Hawkshaw said he was heading for the livery stable to check on his horses, telling Gid to see the ladies situated in hotel rooms. Lucas and Badger put up an argument to go with Hawkshaw; they wanted to see Rusty. Tennie didn't blame them.

Hawkshaw agreed they could, but issued dire warnings. "I'm not watching out for you imps. You better follow me, because if you get lost, I'm not coming to look for you."

They started off, but Tennie held on to Lucas for a second. "If you get lost, find a police station and stay there until Mr. Gid and I can fetch you."

"Yes, ma'am," he agreed before running to catch up with Hawkshaw and Badger.

"And take care of Badger!" Tennie called after him.

She turned to Gid, and together they walked to first class.

"We're going to have to rent a wagon to get all her trunks to the hotel," Tennie said. "I think people can check their luggage in at the station and pick it up later, but I have a feeling she's not going to let us do that."

Just as she thought, Maribel insisted on taking everything with her. It took a while before Gid could find a wagon to rent and load it. Maribel wasn't happy riding in a wagon and wanted a buggy for hire. Gid found one and helped her get in.

"Pay the driver now, Gid," Maribel ordered.

Gid did as she said without comment, emptying his pockets. "Gonna have to go into the boot money now," he grumbled.

When they arrived at the inn, Tennie found it charming, with architecture reminiscent of what she had seen in New Orleans. It didn't look like an inn to Tennie; it was more of a smaller version of a nice hotel. However, Maribel wasn't impressed and wanted to stay at a much larger, statelier hotel down the street.

Surprisingly enough, Gid put his foot down. "No, ma'am. This here is where Mr. Hawkshaw said we was to stay, and this is it."

Maribel frowned, sailed in to demand the largest available suite for herself, leaving Gid to pay for the wagon.

Once inside, Gid obtained two rooms with an adjoining door as they had before. He and Tennie carried their bags up the stairs. A porter and a loaded-down Esther struggled to carry Maribel's luggage into a room across the hall. Gid opened the door to their rooms and motioned Tennie inside, where he quickly followed her. He left the door open just enough for them to peek out. The porter stood at the door of Maribel's room, hoping for a tip, but was turned away. Gid hastily shut the door. He had already been burned twice. He wasn't going to be stuck with the porter's tip, too.

He took Tennie's things through the adjoining door and deposited them on the bed. "Are you wanting to stay here and get rested up?"

"No, I want to go down to the livery to see the boys and the horses. We can send Mr. Lafayette a telegram tomorrow when we know more about how long we'll be here."

"Sounds like a mighty fine plan to my ole jug ears." Gid opened the door and looked up and down the hall to make sure the porter wasn't lurking about waiting for him.

"We need to tell Miss Maribel, though," Tennie said.

Gid nodded and followed Tennie to Maribel's door. Tennie knocked, and Esther answered.

"We are going to the stables to look at Mr. Hawkshaw's horses," Tennie said. "Would Miss Maribel care to walk with us?"

"Certainly not!" came a voice from deep into the room.

Esther, looking like black thunder, closed the door in their faces.

Tennie didn't know what devil possessed her, but she knocked again. When Esther opened the door, Tennie called into the room, "If you don't need Miss Esther, perhaps she'd like to go with us?"

Maribel appeared at the door. "Of course, I need Esther here. Really, Mrs. Granger," she said, so forcefully Tennie blushed.

"Okay. We'll be back in time to see about supper."

"There is no need," Maribel said. "I will dine in my room. Now good-bye." And she shut the door in Tennie's face.

Tennie turned to Gid. "I guess she told us."

They began to walk down the hall. Gid looked so despondent, Tennie, as before, changed the subject. "I hope Lucas and Badger didn't get lost. Or we are going to be spending all our time trying to find the police station."

When Tennie and Gid arrived at the livery nearest the tracks where they thought they would be, Lucas and Badger were watching Hawkshaw examining the horses.

"They look fine to me," Tennie said.

"I told you Floyd would take good care of them," Gid said.

"Where are they?" Tennie asked, looking around.

"I sent them for lumber," Hawkshaw said. "We've got a stock car, and we're putting in a door and a platform on one end so Rusty and I can walk back and forth from the cars to check on them. I want to knock up some stalls inside the car, too, instead of just having them loose."

Tennie thought it was perhaps the most words he had spoken since they left the Coltrane farm. "Miss Maribel's at the inn. She said for us to eat supper without her."

"Good," Hawkshaw replied, stroking the neck of one of his horses.

"Are you going to need Mr. Gid to help you with the carpentry work?" Tennie asked, knowing how much Gid liked to gad about town. "If not, maybe he could escort me around Mobile and meet you back here later."

Hawkshaw looked up. "Not today. He can help tomorrow. It's better you get a feel of the town today if you think you want to roam tomorrow."

"I thought maybe Miss Maribel and I could take a carriage ride around Mobile tomorrow."

Hawkshaw stopped messing with the horses and looked at her. He turned to Gid. "Take her around to land agents and see if there is anything for rent around here."

Gid nodded, but Tennie could see he didn't totally understand what Hawkshaw meant. She grabbed his arm. "Come on, Mr. Gid. We've got to find a house agent, preferably a handsome one."

She stopped and asked the first policeman she came to in the business district. "We're trying to talk a friend into moving to Mobile, but we don't want her to think we are pushing her. She's a widow, and we thought she might be more receptive to a handsome agent."

The big policeman looked at her askance, shook his head, and pointed. "Go across the street there. He's not so fine, but the rest of them are older than dirt."

Tennie thanked him, and she and Gid walked across the street, entering the land agent's office. The policeman had been right. The house agent was a small man with a chin that hadn't kept up with the rest of him, but he was nice. She repeated what she had told the policeman and expanded on it.

At the same time, she realized she and Gid did not look entirely prosperous. "Perhaps you have heard of the Beauregard plantation. Miss Maribel is Mr. Raiford Beauregard's sister."

He looked about to deny any knowledge of them when a slow dawning crossed his face. "Oh yes, Maribel Beauregard. That was her maiden name." He looked at Tennie keenly. "And you say you are a friend of Judge LeRoy?"

"Yes, my stepsons and I stayed in his home. A

very kind man. A perfect host. His son was in a regiment commanded by a friend of mine back in Texas."

"Not Winn Payton?" he asked.

"Oh, yes," Tennie said.

It was a little scary how everyone in the South knew everybody else and all their business. They discussed the Paytons briefly.

"I think a little tour of the town tomorrow afternoon would be in order," the agent said. "I have a few homes that might pique Miss Maribel's interest."

Tennie walked to the door with relief. The agent turned to Gid. "I'm sorry, I didn't catch your name. You are Miss Maribel's cousin?"

"Yes, sir," Gid nodded. "Giddings Coltrane. The younger."

"Coltrane," the agent pondered. "Your sister breeds horses, doesn't she?"

Gid agreed with gratification as the agent's eyes lit up. "I've heard they are something special."

"Well, heck, yeah," Gid said. "We got a few of them down yonder at the stable yard right now. We'll be carrying them to Texas in a day or two. You ought to come on down and have a look at them."

The agent agreed, and instead of sightseeing in Mobile, Tennie got to endure standing around the livery stable again.

But the next day, hopefully, she would get a

tour of Mobile courtesy of the land agent. It was a fair enough exchange. She was glad to see Rusty again in any case. He looked excited, happy, and smelled strongly. He and Floyd had scrounged up the lumber Hawkshaw wanted and were eager to see more of the town. Tennie and Gid agreed, as long as they met them back at the inn in time for supper.

That evening, Tennie knocked on Maribel's door. Esther opened it, and Tennie asked if she might come in and speak to Miss Maribel.

Maribel came to the door before Esther could relay the message. "What is it, Mrs. Granger?"

"A gentleman wants to take us on a buggy ride and show us the sights of Mobile tomorrow afternoon, Miss Maribel. He's a friend of a friend of Judge LeRoy."

Maribel stared at her for a few brief seconds before saying, "All right," and shutting the door.

Tennie thought if she had just muttered "man, buggy ride" Maribel would have agreed.

That night as she prepared for bed, Tennie thought of all the lies she had told on Lafayette's behalf and hoped she didn't burn in hell because of them. She paused, thinking she heard the sound of Maribel's door opening. Going to her own door, she opened it a crack and peeked out.

Maribel was garbed in a red silk gown that pushed all the limits of what a lady should wear. The neckline plunged; the shoulders under her flimsy wrap were uncovered, and Tennie thought if she sneezed, a breast might pop out. Around her still lovely throat was a pearl necklace. Maribel sashayed down the hall, unseeing, with a mumbling Esther looking at the floor, trailing behind her. Maribel seemed determined to follow a headstrong path. Behind that determination, Tennie sensed desperation.

She closed the door, feeling guilty for being so judgmental of Maribel, yet at the same time, knowing nothing could excuse her treatment of Gid, or Esther either.

CHAPTER 21

After breakfast the next morning, with another nonappearance by Maribel, Gid walked Tennie to the telegraph office. After much discussion and advice from the operator, she sent a telegram to Lafayette saying in a shortened version that everything was fine, and they would be leaving Mobile for Texas in two days. The telegraph office in Cat Ridge was good about relaying telegrams to the stage drivers to deliver to Shorty. Her world in Ring Bit seemed a hundred years away. She wondered how all her friends were doing, how Rascal was getting along. She almost felt like sending Shorty a telegram saying how much Badger missed his puppy. Wash had promised they would go back for the puppy. *Wash . . .*

"Miss Tennie, I need to get back to the train yard to help Mr. Hawkshaw with that there stock car," Gid said.

Tennie was brought back to the present. "I'll stay around the inn. Do the boys need to come back with me? I don't want them getting into trouble in a train yard."

"Naw, naw," Gid said. "Them young'uns will be fine. If they get to pestering us, I'll make Rusty and Floyd bring 'em to you."

Tennie hung around the inn and Dauphin Street, trying to look like a visitor, not a prostitute. It must have worked—several men smiled and spoke, but nobody offered her money or tried to pull her into an alley.

Hawkshaw and Gid would find something to eat close to the train yard. Taking a small purse from her pocket, she opened it and counted her money, deciding that cheese and crackers would be enough to hold her until supper. After making her purchases, she went back to the inn to nibble on them. By the time the land agent arrived, she had been waiting in the lobby an hour.

Maribel wasn't ready, so Tennie had to spend another thirty minutes discussing horses and antecedents with the land agent, meanwhile hoping Maribel didn't come down the stairs wearing a repeat of the costume of the night before.

When she did arrive, she was wearing a close-fitting but much more demure dark blue skirt and jacket that showed her eyes and hair off to perfection. She carried a little lace parasol that had Tennie breaking the tenth commandment.

The land agent helped Tennie into the backseat of the buggy, putting Maribel up front with him. She was on her best behavior, being so pleasant to the agent Tennie wondered if she had been overreacting to Maribel's earlier deeds. However, as the afternoon wore on, and Maribel continued to ignore her, Tennie sat in the backseat, marveling at the beauty of Mobile all to herself as the horse clopped along brick streets, and the buggy wheels rolled them down sedate, treelined avenues.

"Now this lovely home belonged to one of the grand dames of Mobile society," the agent said. "She just recently passed, but the family is being very particular. They want to rent it to just the right sort."

Maribel agreed it was a gorgeous home but did not take the bait. On it or any of the others he presented so adroitly. Tennie was fairly sure it was not a question of money, and the agent had shown them a nice range of homes. Maribel didn't appear interested in setting up housekeeping and joining Mobile society.

Tennie didn't know what Maribel wanted. She had shown no interest in Hawkshaw and was just as glad to avoid him as he was her. She barely suffered Tennie and Gid's presence, and she had made no effort to make any contacts within Mobile's higher society, which she easily could have, given the network of old families in the South. They probably had heard of the tragedy involving Lafayette and her husband, but the farther away Maribel removed herself from the scene, the fewer people would have censured her about it.

That night, when Tennie heard the door across

the hall open and Maribel's voice murmuring something to Esther as they walked down the hall, she did not bother to get up and look. There wasn't a woman, with or without an escort, who could walk the streets at night in Ring Bit—it was far too dangerous. She could only hope for Maribel's sake that Mobile was safer.

Tennie did not know how she lived through the next day. Now that they were on their way back, all she could think of was getting to Texas and closer to Wash. She inspected the stock car Hawkshaw had altered. Boards with wide spaces between them for ventilation ran lengthwise across the long sides of the car. The door and platform on one end were sturdily done. Inside the car, he had put in boxed stalls. She wasn't sure how much he had to pay the railroad, if anything, to make the adjustments.

"Ain't that something, Miss Tennie?" Gid said, as proud as if he had helped build the Taj Mahal.

They would put Floyd on a train for home in the morning. It had been a wonderful adventure as far as he was concerned, but he was ready to get back to the farm, the beloved horses, and his grandmother's cooking.

"Do you think she'll stay here?" Hawkshaw asked as Tennie walked with him into the train station to buy their tickets on the train bound for Houston the next day.

Tennie shook her head. "She leaves her room

every night. I don't know where she's going."

Hawkshaw gave her a stare. "She's gambling at the casinos."

"Gambling? I thought her brother gave her a big dowry. Is she trying to gamble it all away? Does Mr. Gid know?"

"Probably," Hawkshaw replied, refusing to talk about it further. "They don't have first class on this route. She'll have to ride in second class with us, blast it to hell."

"Oh, Jesus," Tennie said, meaning it as a prayer, not an oath. "What am I going to do? Mr. Lafayette will kill me if I let her step one foot in Texas."

"*I* will kill you if you let her step one foot in Texas," Hawkshaw said. "I thought that black mammy promised you she'd jump the train before then."

Tennie nodded, pressing her lips together as she considered. "I don't think she was wrong. We still have New Orleans," she reminded him.

That night, Tennie felt too excited to sleep. She slipped downstairs into the dimly lit lobby, thinking she might find someone to talk to. To her surprise, Hawkshaw sat alone in a darkened corner, legs stretched out and crossed at the ankles.

"Are you waiting for the boys and Mr. Gid to go to sleep?" Tennie asked in a quiet voice.

He nodded, and she realized he had probably

done that every night. Lucas had told her he and Badger slept either in the bed with Gid or on the floor, while Hawkshaw took the other bed.

They heard the sound of footsteps on the stairs. Both turned and saw Maribel, again daringly dressed with the pearls around her neck and Esther at her heels. Neither turned their head to peer into the shadows of the lobby, and Tennie watched unobserved as they exited the inn. She rose and went to the window, peering out to see Maribel and Esther disappearing in the darkness.

"I hope she finds what she is looking for in that casino," Tennie said.

"I wish to God I'd never lay eyes on her again," Hawkshaw said.

Tennie turned away from the window and looked at Hawkshaw. "Quit complaining. At least it got Raiford Beauregard off your back. You don't have to worry about him sending any hired killers after you."

"If it's not him, it will be somebody else," Hawkshaw said. "For the rest of my life, there will always be someone after me."

Tennie swallowed. "Are you going to retire?"

He stayed silent a long time before answering.

"Yes. Now go to bed. I don't want have to deal with two crazy tired women tomorrow," he said. "I'm going to walk down to the livery to make sure everything is all right."

"Are you sure you aren't going to follow

Maribel to the casino?" Tennie asked, trying not to giggle.

"I am not in the habit of striking women, but you have brought me closer to it than any female alive," Hawkshaw said. "Now go to bed."

Tennie returned to her room and lay in a suspended state hovering between wakefulness and sleep. Hearing footsteps coming down the hall, she couldn't help herself. She had to see if it was Maribel.

Cracking her door once more, she put one eye to the opening. In the sliver of flickering light, she saw Maribel returning. The shoulder on her dress had been torn; a vivid red slap mark burned on her cheek. Tennie shut the door quickly, closing her eyes. The pearl necklace was gone.

That settled it. New Orleans was her last hope.

Maribel left Mobile with the air of a disappointed and angry woman. There was the ordeal with the trunks, and another one over Esther. Maribel refused to even discuss it with the angry conductor, and the only way they could get moving with Esther on the train was by Hawkshaw slipping him money.

Rusty and Lucas were in the stock car with the horses. Hawkshaw had taken his place at one end of the carriage, Gid on the other with Tennie and Badger in the middle. Maribel and Esther sat two rows up from Gid, facing Tennie, but she might as well have been invisible as far as the two women were concerned. Maribel ordered Gid to stay in the back and not bother her.

A stocky middle-aged man, prosperous and not too bad looking, sat across from Maribel. After the whistle blew, and the train began to roll and pick up steam, Maribel engaged him in conversation. Tennie couldn't, and didn't want to, hear all the words, but Maribel's gestures held a jarring note of vivacity that came across too strong. After a while he got up and moved.

A newly married couple sat across from Tennie, but they were so engrossed in one another, she did not even worry about making small talk with them. She glanced across the aisle at Maribel and saw her looking in Hawkshaw's direction, appraising him with cool and calculating eyes.

In one of those moments when everyone on the train fell silent, and all that could be heard was the sound of the wheels clacking and the engine chugging, someone in the back of the train cut loose a tremendous belch.

Tennie shut her eyes, took a breath, and reopened her eyes in time to see Maribel turn away from Hawkshaw in repugnance.

"Who did that?" Badger said.

"Hush, hush," Tennie said, almost crying in her effort to keep from laughing.

After a while, Hawkshaw got up and walked

through the carriage, heading for the stock car to relieve Rusty and Lucas.

When the two boys entered the carriage and sat down, Badger immediately told them about it. "Mr. Hawkshaw let out a big ole belch and everybody heard it."

"Badger!" Tennie admonished. "Keep your voice down."

Rusty and Lucas looked at one another and stifled giggles. Rusty looked at Gid. "I hope Miss Maribel doesn't turn around now," he whispered. "Mr. Gid is about to upchuck out the window again."

"Maybe he would feel better in the stock car," Tennie said.

Rusty shook his head. "He said he's so wobbly on his feet, he's afraid he'll fall off the train getting there."

"Do you want to go, Miss Tennie?" Lucas asked. "I can take you."

Tennie glanced around the train car. The couple on the other side looked as if they did not appreciate three boys crammed in the seat across from them with Tennie. She nodded her head, and Lucas took her by the hand.

"Badger, you stay here with Rusty and Mr. Gid," Tennie said.

"Don't be scared now," Lucas said, leading the way.

The train rocked back and forth, but Tennie

held her footing. They left the car, and outside, the wind blew Tennie's hair around her eyes. They stepped into another car, going through another second-class carriage.

"The stock car is next," Lucas told her, still holding on to her hand.

The door to the stock car wasn't pretty, but it was solid enough to keep a kicking horse from busting it down. Lucas opened the door, and Tennie went inside.

Hawkshaw was standing at one of the stalls, looking over a mare. Rusty and Floyd had taken the horses' tails down in Mobile, doing a good job of brushing them. Before he left, Floyd had braided and tied up the tails again for travel just as his grandmother had taught him. Every horse had a water trough and feed bucket in its stall. Straw covered the floor; the wind coming from between the boards whipped it into occasional flying wisps. Despite all the light streaming through the cracks, the roof of the car made it shady, with dark corners containing shovels, pitchforks, barrels of water, and feed.

Being nearer the engine made the ride smoother, but noisier. Hawkshaw looked up at Tennie and spoke when she stopped to look at the mare with him. "She'll be a good one if she drops her colts like Nab promised," he said raising his voice.

"I really don't know anything about horses,"

Tennie said, trying to talk loud enough to be heard, but not so deafening she scared the animals.

"I know that." He turned to scold Lucas, who had climbed up on the stall. "Be careful and don't fall in. These are gentle horses, but anything can spook a stallion into kicking your brains out. These mares aren't too happy riding in a train car either."

"They seem to be doing rather well," Tennie said.

Hawkshaw nodded. "Your friend Gid acts like he's a pint short of a quart, but he knows horses."

"He's your friend, too. You just don't know it," Tennie said. "When do you want Rusty back here?"

"When the train stops, he and Lucas can scat back here to help me take on water and shovel out droppings," Hawkshaw said. "Don't let Badger come back here. He'll climb all over everything and fall into the stalls."

Tennie nodded, and after a while of looking over the horses, she and Lucas returned to their carriage. The newlyweds had found seats in another car. Esther still looked mad and unhappy but had lost some of her surliness. Maribel stared out the window.

When they stopped at the next station, Maribel did not like having to step down from the car to use their facilities. It wasn't a particularly inviting station, sitting alone in the middle of a windswept sea of grass.

"I don't know why we couldn't have waited for a first-class Pullman," she complained.

"I don't think they ever put one on this side of the run," Tennie said. "We'll be in New Orleans sometime before dawn. We'll probably get off the train for a while there."

"You mean I have to sleep in that wretched seat?" Maribel demanded.

"They fold down," Tennie said, but Maribel only frowned deeper.

When they stepped back up into the car, Gid was there to assist Maribel, even though his face was pasty green. "Cousin—"

"Don't bother me," Maribel cut him off as she stepped up. "I don't want anyone to know we are related. Even in this godforsaken place."

Gid looked as if she had slapped him with a horsewhip, but he said nothing. Tennie didn't know what to say, except that Hawkshaw was exceptionally pleased with the way the stock car was working out.

"I told him it would," Gid said. "Suffering saints, my stomach is queasy."

Rusty and Lucas shut the sliding door of the stock car while Hawkshaw stayed inside.

"Here now, you boys help me up," Gid called. "My legs feel like calves' jelly."

They got him into the railcar, and Rusty took

the seat across from Tennie vacated by the newlyweds. Badger, mad because he wasn't allowed in the stock car, sat by Gid. Lucas sat beside Tennie and looked at cartoon drawings in a newspaper Hawkshaw had given him in Mobile. Esther kept her eyes looking straight ahead, apparently at nothing, while Maribel stared out the window, also apparently at nothing—nothing that took the discontented expression off her face, anyway.

Tennie began practicing scenarios. They would stop in New Orleans—Hawkshaw already said he wasn't taking Maribel any farther. He wouldn't have any compunction about getting back on the train to Texas without telling her, but Tennie would feel bad, and Gid wouldn't let them ditch her like that anyway.

They would probably put her up in a nice hotel, and Tennie would stand at the door of the room and tell Maribel that Mr. Hawkshaw had changed his mind about marriage, but they would help her get settled somewhere in New Orleans or put her on a train to wherever she wanted to go. Tennie was fairly certain it wouldn't be back to her brother Raiford.

She dreaded the scene because she feared Maribel would do just that, make a scene. Not that Maribel wanted Hawkshaw, she just wanted to be the dump-er, not the dump-ee.

Rusty leaned forward and whispered. "What

369

about her?" he said, motioning his head toward Maribel.

"I guess we best get to praying for a miracle," Tennie replied.

The sun beat down on them as they headed west, still daylight, but getting close to the time Nab and Gid referred to as "the edge of dark." The conductor had passed through a few minutes before and announced they were somewhere in Mississippi, leaving behind the flat grassland and entering hills dotted with stands of pines. It smelled clean and pure, notwithstanding the smoke from the boiler, but despite her prayers, Tennie's stomach was tied in small hard knots thinking about the trouble awaiting them in New Orleans.

She was so upset, it took a while for it to sink into her brain that the brakes were screeching, and the train was slowing dramatically.

"What is it?" she asked Lucas, who had his head out the window, looking toward the engine.

"It looks like trees fallen down over the tracks ahead," he said.

"Look behind you!" Rusty said.

Tennie turned and saw a masked rider coming up the edge of the car on a fast horse. He stood up in the saddle, and with one tremendous leap, grabbed the bars of the platform. Before any of them could react, he was inside the car, holding a revolver on them.

The train shuddered to a stop. Badger stood up in his seat beside Gid and cried, "It's the Daring Dandies!"

Tennie's mouth fell open. She shut it and stared. The man holding the gun was dressed in new black pants and a black leather vest with silver conchas, and he wore spurs with large decorative rowels. His hat was new and black, and underneath it, a black satin handkerchief was tied around his forehead, with holes cut out for his eyes, leaving a pencil-thin dark mustache visible. He walked down the aisle, looking for weapons. No one in their railcar was carrying a gun except Gid, and the masked man leaned over, pulling it from Gid's side and throwing it out the window. Badger stood on the seat next to Gid, his eyes wide and his hand resting on Gid's shoulder. Gid frowned, sick with fury and mad at himself for being taken unaware.

Other riders on horses stayed outside the carriage, and Tennie could hear another robber in the other car. She thought of Hawkshaw, who could easily pick off every single bandit from the horses outside, but he wouldn't do anything to draw fire on his own horses.

The robber held open a tote sack and demanded everyone put their money inside. To her relief, he passed by Tennie without stopping. He ignored Maribel, who was watching with excited animation, and Esther, whose eyes bulged wide and white against her black face. Tennie had never seen anyone who looked so scared and so mad at the same time. When the robber came back to Gid, he forced him at gunpoint to empty his pockets.

"That all you got, farmer?" the bandit said, his voice low and mean. Tennie thought him to be in his early to late thirties. He was not younger or older than that, she was sure.

"He keeps his money in his boot," Maribel drawled.

Gid gasped. Before he could utter her name, the robber demanded he remove his boot, waving his gun in front of Gid and Badger's faces. Badger had almost every cent Tennie possessed sewn into his pockets, and she could only pray he didn't suddenly spout, "You're not getting my money, mister."

Tennie thought quickly—Esther had seen her take her coin purse out of her pocket at the last stop, but Maribel hadn't. Neither Esther nor Badger spoke, however, and Gid drew out his stash from one of his boots and handed it over with none too much grace. The bandit backed up.

Rusty stared straight ahead, furious at being so impotent. The masked man paused in front of him, causing Tennie's heart to bang her ribcage with a series of thuds.

He put down his tote sack and pulled a rolled cigarette from his pocket, placing it between his lips, meanwhile keeping the six-shooter held steady against them.

He removed a match and tossed it into Rusty's lap. "Here, kid. Light my cigarette."

Rusty looked at him without expression, but Tennie knew even before he said anything he was going to refuse.

"My stepmother won't let me play with matches," Rusty said, staring at him without blinking.

The pause was so long, Tennie's nails dug into her palm. She tensed, ready to strike if the bandit's thumb pulled back the hammer on the pistol or if he raised a hand against Rusty.

He began to laugh. "All right, kid. I wouldn't want to get you into trouble." He picked up his bag and backed up, keeping the gun on them as he headed for the door.

To the shock of all the passengers, Maribel jumped up and ran toward him. "Take me with you!" she cried, hugging him. "Take me with you!"

"Maribel!" Gid hollered, his face white with shock.

The bandit looked at her and shrugged his shoulders. "Why not?" he said and pulled her roughly from the coach. They joined the other robbers on horseback, Maribel leaping onto the back of the horse of the leader in black pants like she did it every day of her life. The men fired a few shots in the air, making dire threats to anyone who tried to follow them, before turning and galloping away.

"Maribel!" Gid said, hanging his head out the window and hollering. "You're nothing but a hussy. You hear me? Nothing but a hussy slut! You're not fit to wipe the mud off Nab's boots!" He was so outraged, tears were streaming down his face. "Not even fit to *clean* Nab's boots."

Tennie shot up just as Maribel was almost in the piney woods and out of earshot and yelled out the window. "We'll leave your trunks in New Orleans, Miss Maribel!"

CHAPTER 22

Shock gave way to excitement and pandemonium. The conductor began yelling at the men to come out and help move the logs. Tennie grabbed Badger and asked him if he was all right. He was, but he had wet his pants. She hugged him and told him it didn't matter.

"I'm sorry, Mr. Gid," Tennie said.

He was enraged, but he said, "They only got the money out of one boot. I still got some in the other, dang that good-for-nothing Maribel."

"Mr. Gid," Tennie said, placing a calming hand on his arm. "You were right. She never was fit to wipe the mud from Miss Nab's boots."

He sniffed and nodded. "Yeah. Raiford neither, I reckon."

"I reckon so. Come on. Let's go outside and hear the damage."

Hawkshaw and the horses were fine.

"Did you see it, Mr. Hawkshaw?" Lucas asked. "Did you see Miss Maribel riding away with the robbers?"

He mimicked Maribel, clutching Rusty, and saying in a falsetto voice, "Take me with you, handsome! Take me with you!"

They all laughed, except Gid, who had left to help the men roll the logs off the track.

"That's right, Mr. Hawkshaw," Tennie teased. "Rusty, Lucas, and I were sitting in that train car just a-praying for a miracle, and what do you know? Angels arrived in the shape of the Daring Dandies."

"Oh, for pity's sake," Hawkshaw said. "I never met anyone so full of bull . . . corn in my life."

"It was a miracle," Tennie pronounced. "A plum bona fide miracle." She thought about teasing him over losing his fiancée but decided not to press her luck.

Dusk was settling when they finally got the tracks cleared. Hawkshaw told Rusty and Lucas it was their turn to ride in the stock car, and they did not object. Tennie felt bad people had lost money, but she heard many of them say they traveled with money pocketed in various places in case of just such an event. She tried to hide her elation at getting rid of Maribel. It didn't feel like the seemly thing to do.

Gid, once he'd calmed down, was embarrassed and didn't want anyone to know he had been in prison for train robbery, and they promised they wouldn't tell. Hawkshaw went to his corner of the car looking utterly relieved.

Another argument with the conductor ensued over Esther.

"You can't leave her out here in the middle of nowhere," Tennie said. "She can ride with me to New Orleans."

The conductor didn't like it, and Tennie got mad. "She can sit by me. And we are not greasing your palm a second time to let her do it."

Her frankness infuriated the conductor, but he held his temper. "All right, but see to it she sits by the window, next to you and away from everybody."

"Yes, yes, yes," Tennie agreed. "Come on, Miss Esther."

Tennie was glad she didn't expect any gratitude from Esther, because she didn't get any. Esther sat looking straight ahead in stony silence.

Once the excitement of the robbery wore off, and people quieted down, Tennie asked her what she wanted to do. "You can stay in New Orleans or go on to Texas with us. Or we can put you on a train back home."

"Can't go back," Esther said through tight lips, still not looking at Tennie. "Dang fool Beauregard will renege on his word if I's go back. Don't want to go to that heathen Texas. I got people in New Orleans."

"Are you sure you'll be all right?" Tennie asked.

Esther nodded, again repeating she had people there. She didn't invite further conversation, and Tennie didn't try to press anything else out of her.

When it grew dark, Esther got up without comment when Tennie asked her so she could put the seats down. She arranged the blankets as she had the night before, telling Esther to take her place by the window. Esther threw her a brief hard stare but did as she asked, and the two of them shared a makeshift bed.

Tennie couldn't sleep, and she knew Esther was awake, too. "I guess I'll have to write Mr. Beauregard and tell him Miss Maribel decided to stay in Mississippi with some new friends she made," Tennie said, talking low so as not to disturb the rest of the passengers.

Esther waited a minute or two before replying. "Better send the letter to Miss Helen, and let her break it to him."

"Yes, you're probably right," Tennie said.

Esther again did not respond right away. "She talked him into it," she said after a moment or two went by.

Tennie rolled over to look at her. "Talked who into what?"

"Her husband," Esther said. "She lied and told him Mr. Lafayette seduced her against her will. When all the time she was playing up to Mr. Lafayette so bad he didn't know if it was his feet touching the ground or the tops of his ears. Crying about how mean her husband was when that man done spoiled her, giving her everything she wanted."

Tennie took a deep breath. "Are you saying she purposely played it that way hoping Mr. Lafayette would kill her husband just so she could be rid of him?"

"Yes'um, that's what I's saying."

"Oh my," Tennie said. "Oh dear. I don't know if I should tell that to Mr. Lafayette or not. He thinks they just had a tragic love affair that went wrong."

"Wasn't no love on her part. She didn't know people was going to turn against her, making her stay in the mourning the rest of her life. And her having them fancy clothes made up on the sly and prancing around in her room at night, drinking and playing with herself," Esther said, making a spitting sound.

"Good heavens," Tennie said, hardly knowing how to take any of it.

"That man she run off with, he gonna knock her around to kingdom come. You see the way he shove her off this here train? She gonna get more than she done bargained for with that lowdown scoundrel." Esther said with grim satisfaction.

Tennie made a noncommittal reply, feeling guilty for being so happy to be rid of Maribel when Esther's words of prophecy were ringing so true in her ears.

They ceased their whispering, and the silence of the passengers, the repetitive noises the train made, and the weariness that comes after excitement soon had Tennie in a deep sleep.

She dreamed of Wash. He appeared, his face so near hers, smiling and full of tenderness. The waves of pure love emanating from him flooded over her. A stab of grief shot through her—that she had ever allowed thoughts of her own unworthiness to come between them appalled her. But in the dream, she put down every negative fear to delight in his love and happiness, returning it with her own.

Tennie opened her eyes. She was back in the noisy railcar with snoring passengers breathing in sooty smoke, but the deep emotion she'd experienced while sleeping stayed with her. It was some minutes before she realized the scar Wash bore across his lips from a violent sword fight had been missing. She thought perhaps she had dreamed of the true Wash, shorn of everything that did not matter. She only knew she loved him with all her heart.

She went back to sleep. She thought Esther nudged her once during the night, but she fell back into a deep and dreamless slumber.

In New Orleans the next morning, hungry and thirsty passengers exited the train. The station again teemed with people, and before Tennie could say good-bye, Esther had disappeared into the crowd. Tennie looked in the direction she had headed and silently wished her good luck.

As the crowd swirled in front of her, Tennie remembered the first warning Hawkshaw had given them about New Orleans. She felt in her pocket for the small purse she carried. As her fingers closed around it, she realized it did not feel right. Pulling it out, she opened it.

"What's wrong?" Hawkshaw asked.

"Esther stole my money," Tennie said.

He shook his head in disgust. "Well, you knew what she was like when you insisted she stay on the train."

"I couldn't help it," Tennie said. "We couldn't just leave her stranded in the middle of nowhere."

The conductor began calling for people to get back on the train. A Pinkerton agent had arrived and wanted to talk to some of the passengers.

"Quick," Hawkshaw told Gid. "Take Miss Tennie and the boys to the stock car and stay there."

Gid didn't question him, but Tennie did as Hawkshaw began impelling her in the direction of the stock car.

"Because Louisiana people don't always like Texans, and they especially don't like the Texas Rangers," he said in answer to her question. "All we need is for you to start babbling about your Texas Ranger fiancé or for them to find out Gid's been in prison for train robbery, and we're liable to never get out of this town. Now just let me do the talking."

They started up the side steps to the platform at the end of the stock car. "Don't let anybody in, no matter who they say they are, you hear me?" Hawkshaw ordered. *No matter who.* Tell them they'll have to talk to the owner of the horses later."

"I do not babble," Tennie said as she climbed the steps behind Badger.

"Get in there," Hawkshaw said.

The conductor was yelling, "Hey you, there. Come back here!" at Hawkshaw.

He hollered, "Coming!" at the conductor, and with one last thrust, got them all in the stock car, shutting the door behind them.

The horses began to neigh and paw, knowing something was happening and wanting out of the train car. Gid began to talk in low comforting tones to them.

"How are we going to keep people out?" Tennie said. The big sliding doors could be kept shut from the inside or the outside with metal bolts, but the side door couldn't be locked.

It opened from the outside in. Rusty took a pitchfork, turned it upside down, and jammed it under the doorknob. He searched until he found a hammer and a flour sack full of nails and pounded the nails around the handle of the pitchfork so it couldn't be moved.

While Gid and Rusty worked with the horses to keep them calm, Tennie and the younger boys looked between the gaps in the boards and tried to figure out what was going on. When a murder had occurred in front of witnesses in Ring Bit, the U.S. deputy marshal had sent instructions that

Tennie was to interview each witness and write down their statements of what happened. But the Pinkertons seemed content to question only a few people. She wondered what Hawkshaw was telling them and decided it was better she not know.

"Look, Miss Tennie," Lucas said, pointing. "There's some men coming this way."

Four men walked toward them, smiling, talking, and seemingly carefree. All had dark hair, some curlier than others, dressed in pants with suspenders over white shirts with rolled-up sleeves. They approached the car, looking entirely harmless and respectable. One of the men stepped forward, his jaunty hat cocked to one side.

"Bonjour!" he called. "Open this here door so we can see your horses."

"Can't do it," Gid hollered back. "Got orders from the owner to keep the door shut."

"But we are from *le commissaire*'s office," the man said. "We must inspect the horses. We have no desire to make the *misere*, my friend."

"Don't matter whose office you is from," Gid said. "I ain't opening that there door for nobody but the owner."

"But sir," the Louisianan said, "If you do not let us inspect these horses, we could impound them, and you would be tied up for weeks in paperwork trying to get it straightened out, man."

Tennie and Rusty looked at Gid. The man

outside sounded so friendly and reasonable. Would it hurt to let them inspect the horses? Tennie did not want to spend a minute longer in New Orleans than she had to.

"No can do," Gid said, taking out his gun.

Lucas had never taken his eyes off the men. Tennie looked between the cracks again. One of the men tried the door. Another walked around the side of the stock car. Tennie stared, the knob turned, but the pitchfork held. Still another tried the other big door in the back.

"I got a gun, and I don't mind firing it," Gid said. "I also got a woman and some children in here, so if you was to decide to fire back, that's who you'd be shooting at."

"We mean no harm!" the man said, looking truly contrite.

"Don't matter what you mean or what you say," Gid said. "You ain't getting in here without risking a hole in your stomach. And I'll be warning you, the owner of these here horses will be back directly, and he is mighty handy with a Colt revolver. One of them new ones. The ones with the big bullets."

The men outside huddled in a conference then came to a decision.

The man with the cocked hat who had been doing all the talking took a step forward. "*Pas mal*, my friend. We will return with *le commissaire* and *la* police."

"You do that," Gid said. "We'll be here."

The men left, disappearing into the crowded streets by the station.

Tennie took a deep breath and swallowed. "Mr. Gid?"

"Don't you worry none, Miss Tennie. They's all mouth."

Hawkshaw stayed gone for what seemed like an inordinate amount of time. Tennie kept waiting for the police to arrive, but they never did. Lucas was the first to see Hawkshaw approaching. He and Rusty ran to the door and slid it open. They all began talking at once.

Hawkshaw was not in a good mood. "Get back and hush. Gid, what happened?"

Gid explained.

Hawkshaw let out a mild oath, but dismissed every word spoken by the young men. "The police are going to keep Maribel's trunks at the station in hopes she returns with one of the robbers to fetch them." He looked at Tennie. "They congratulated you for being so quick on your feet to think of a way for them to capture the gang leader by yelling that you would leave her things at the station, but I explained you thought you were just being polite."

"Well, there went my reputation as a fellow law enforcer," Tennie said, patting her hair.

Hawkshaw didn't bother to give her a smart reply or even a curse word. "We can't leave until tomorrow. I found a decent livery stable just up the street. Word is already getting around that we're hauling some unusual specimens. I don't know how people here know stuff so fast, but they do. I'm just darn lucky those train robbers didn't know what we had."

He turned to Tennie. "We'll have to spend the night in the stable with the horses. I need Gid with me, and this town is not a good place for a woman, even one with children, to be roaming around by herself. Will you sleep in the stable with us?"

"Of course," Tennie said. "As long as we get some good Louisiana food to eat. These people know how to cook, anyway."

"What about the stock car?" Gid asked. "Is it safe to leave it?"

"I've hired some railroad bulls to watch it. We'll be safer in a public place than we would be stuck out here alone tonight."

While they waited for the men Hawkshaw hired to arrive, Gid and Rusty left to buy food. By the time they returned, and everybody had eaten their fill, the men Hawkshaw hired showed up, ready to work. Broad shoulders, with wide, thick necks, they looked as mean and tough as any man Tennie had ever seen.

She nodded and said, "Hello," glad she wasn't spending the night in the stock car with them.

They unloaded the horses, Hawkshaw and Gid

leading the stallions, Tennie and the boys leading the mares. Gid packed their things on the backs of the mares, and as Tennie walked near Hawkshaw on their way to the stable, a thought struck her.

"I'm glad Miss Maribel didn't have a very high opinion of Gid and Nab's horses," she said. "Or those train robbers would have gotten them, too."

"That's just now dawning on you, is it?" Hawkshaw said.

"You sure are grouchy, you know that?" Tennie said.

"I'm just trying to get out of New Orleans alive."

Tennie fell silent, and she didn't speak anymore until they reached the stables and turned the horses loose in a corral. Even then, she left Hawkshaw alone and concentrated on keeping the boys out trouble. She took one look at the big livery barn and wondered if she had made the right decision by agreeing to sleep in it. They weren't that far from the Mississippi River, and all she could think of was wharf rats running across her as she tried to sleep. It brought back memories of being kidnapped by the Miltons, and she had to fight an attack of shaky nerves.

Five cats, orange and gray tabbies, each weighing at least twenty pounds, sauntered out of the stable. Tennie was never so happy to see cats in her life.

Hawkshaw never left the horses as local men

drifted in singly and in bunches to look over them. Moving back and forth, he stayed in sight and always wary. He did not speak to anyone, and his appearance did not invite questions. Gid, on the other hand, never stopped running his mouth.

"Yes, sir, my sister breeds some mighty fine horses," he would agree with a stranger. "We had a big ole fight trying to save the farm. I got into it with my sorry, no-account brothers. They wanted to sell out and head for Californy. I said we ain't selling but by all means, inflict your presence on those Californy people cause we is plum wore out looking at your good-for-nothing phizes. Them boys is so lazy, they got calluses built up on their behinds that would shame a hog."

As he rambled on, Tennie came to realize he would not refute the quality of the horses, but he moved the conversation in every direction away from them he could. He didn't want to increase the incentive to steal.

At dusk, the stable owner and his helpers left to be replaced by a night watchman. The watchman was a skinny old thing looking to be at least eighty, wearing a straw hat, overalls, and a long salt and pepper beard.

"Name's Ebb," he said in a gravely, deadpan voice. "Ebenezer Parker."

"You don't talk like folks from around here," Gid said.

"I ain't. I'm from up around Roane County,

Tennessee. Got married and that woman talked me into moving down here to be close to her people. Soon as we got here, she run off with a feed salesman."

Gid made an appropriate comment, and Ebb continued, putting his thumbs in his suspenders, his voice as flat and pokerfaced as his expression. "That's what I get for marrying me a younger woman. Can't trust any woman under forty." He raised his eyebrows at Tennie. "Present company excluded."

Hawkshaw took one look at Ebb and shook his head. "We're on our own tonight," he muttered. "Might as well have stayed in the stock car."

Hawkshaw's cold personality did not appear to perturb Ebb in any way. He took Hawkshaw as he came, helping put the horses inside for the night, securing them in stalls. He pointed to the loft upstairs, telling Tennie, "You and them two youngest boys bed down up yonder. There's a shovel and pitchfork up there if you need it."

Tennie didn't know why they would need a shovel and pitchfork, but she saw them leaning against the wall as she climbed the ladder. Placing her blankets on a bed of straw, she looked out the opened window at the city of New Orleans, wondering about Esther and Maribel.

The urine smell wasn't as strong in the loft as it was down below, and the cats that had ignored her earlier decided to sleep with them, much to her thankfulness. With Badger and Lucas close by, Tennie lay with eyes open, listening to the sounds of the night—horses and people breathing, the occasional movement of hooves and whinnying.

"I don't want to live in San Antonio," Lucas said out of the blue. "I want to live in Ring Bit."

"Me, too," Badger agreed. "I miss Shorty."

"We'll be happy wherever Mr. Wash is. I promise you," Tennie said, thinking *no more jailhouses, no more drunks.*

She was almost asleep when she heard the hammer of a gun being cocked back.

CHAPTER 23

"Stop right there," Ebb said. "This shotgun pointed at your hide was oiled this morning."

Tennie and the two boys beside her stiffened. The shotgun roared.

In a matter of seconds, they heard the sound of boots rushing in, more guns firing, igniting flashes of light in the dark stable. A man shrieked. Lucas jumped up, knocking over a bucket that hit the wall with a clank. Tennie stood up, making Badger stand behind her.

The horses were going crazy—neighing, snorting, pawing the ground, and kicking the walls of their stalls. Cats screeched. Even in the din of gunfire and frightened horses, Tennie could hear the sound of someone running up the ladder.

Lucas grabbed the shovel and swung it at the shadow of a man, but he snatched the blade. The dark form swung the shovel around and the boy with it, because Lucas refused to let go. Tennie seized the pitchfork and jabbed it as hard as she could into the stranger's back. He screamed and stiffened, falling forward.

Lucas dropped the shovel and ran to Tennie, hugging her. Badger clung to her other side while she stared down at the figure of the man. She shut her eyes, trying to remove the image of the pitchfork sticking out of his back.

The sounds of gunfire ceased. Someone lit a lantern.

Tennie cried, "Rusty!"

"I'm okay," Rusty yelled back.

"You all right up there, Miss Tennie?" Gid hollered.

More lanterns were lit, illuminating the barn.

"Yes. Is everyone okay?" Tennie cried.

"Yes, ma'am," Gid said. "We all in one piece. You sure y'all are all right?"

"Yes," Tennie called. "But there is a man up here. I think he's dead."

Gid climbed the ladder. He removed the pitchfork from their assailant, tossing it aside, and pushed the body over the edge of the loft. It hit the floor with a loud thud. Tennie shuddered and drew the boys closer to her.

"You and them young'uns stay up here," Gid said. "Don't be coming down."

"We won't," Tennie agreed.

The police arrived. Tennie and the boys did what Gid said but scampered to the edge of the loft, lying on their stomachs, so they could look down below.

The police examined the scene, looking up to the loft but saying nothing about Tennie or the boys watching them.

As the stable filled with people, piece by piece,

everything began to come together. Hawkshaw and Gid recognized the black pants and concha-covered vest of one of the Daring Dandies. Not satisfied with the amount of loot from the train robbery, Maribel must have told them about the horses Hawkshaw was transporting. With bold impudence, they caught another train coming into New Orleans.

When the police asked about the holes in the back of the dead man, Gid spoke before anyone else could. "That there feller was heading up that ladder yonder, so I stopped him right quick."

The policeman questioning him nodded. Nobody said anything about going before a judge or having a trial. He didn't know where Maribel was, but said there was a reward for the capture of the train robbers. Ebb, Hawkshaw, and Gid could split it.

Several policemen began removing the bodies from the barn. Tennie scooted back and rolled over, putting the edge of the blanket into her mouth and biting on it to keep from crying. She just wanted to go home. She wanted to be back in Texas.

At dawn, the stable owner and his other helpers arrived, taking the horses from the stalls and putting them in the corral. Hawkshaw looked as if he had aged twenty years since leaving the Beauregard plantation. Gid looked tousled and worn. Ebb didn't look any different from the night before. They had to go to the police station to collect the reward. Hawkshaw gave instructions to Tennie and the boys to stay with the horses and scream bloody murder if anyone tried to remove them from the corrals.

The stable owner allowed one of his hands to fetch sausage and bread that Tennie and the boys shared. Several men came to look and talk about the disturbance of the night before, but no one made a move to touch the horses, much less take them.

When Hawkshaw returned with Gid and Ebb, he reported that the railroad men, knowing they were anxious to get back to Texas, had quibbled over the reward money, giving ridiculous reasons why it had been lowered. Hawkshaw and Gid yielded just so they could leave. Before going, the police strongly hinted if they did not want to be charged with manslaughter, it would be well to make a hefty donation to the New Orleans policemen's fund. They had been forced to agree to that, too. Ebb hadn't minded any of it, saying some woman would relieve him of his share eventually, anyway.

"Where'd y'all say y'all was headed to in Texas?" Ebb asked. "Ring Bit?"

"That's right," Gid said happily. Even with the reward reduced to a third of the original amount, and having to split it four ways, he was still coming out ahead in Louisiana.

"There lots of women there?" Ebb asked.

Tennie laughed. "Not really."

Ebb nodded. "I reckon I might look y'all up there one of these days. I just can't be going where's there's lots of females. Women make a fool out of me."

Hawkshaw grunted.

Gid laughed. "Thanks, old-timer."

They led the horses back to the train yard and the stock car, the sun beating down brightly on them. People walked the streets, smiling and laughing, as if saying all the thievery and attempted robbery the travelers had experienced in New Orleans had just been a simple misunderstanding, and the dead bodies in the morgue nothing more than an unfortunate accident. Such was the charm of "Little Paris."

The railway men put the stock car near the engine as they had the previous trip. Everything stood intact, and they waited for feed and water to be replenished before leading the horses up the ramp. One of the stallions hadn't wanted to get back in, and Gid had to pick up small amounts of gravel to throw at his rump to spook him into moving. Other than that, they had no problems at all.

Gid, free of Maribel, declared he was going to ride in the stock car the entire way to Waco. Hawkshaw again warned them to be careful of their money, and they had cash hidden in every shoe and secret pocket they could think of. He didn't look well, and Tennie wondered if his wound had reopened, but he assured her his leg was fine.

Besides the stock car, the train had two passenger cars, and behind them, two boxcars loaded with barrels and crates of goods headed from the port of New Orleans to Houston. Talk about the Daring Dandies' robbery and their subsequent capture filled the two passenger cars. Several people repeated gossip they had heard about a woman riding with the gang, but thankfully, no one knew who she might be.

Hawkshaw had already warned the boys not to brag they had anything to do with capturing the robbers. He didn't want anyone to know they were carrying reward money—although Tennie thought he had already wired his to a bank somewhere. She doubted it was to the one in Ring Bit.

· Once their seats were secured, and the train rolled at full speed, Rusty and Lucas headed to the stock car. They returned some minutes later, leading Gid, who looked as weak as a sick kitten. Tennie rose and helped them get him into his favored seat by a window.

"My innards done turned inside out," Gid said, panting. "I have to sit by a winder. The slats—they looked like prison bars. I couldn't help it."

"It's okay," Tennie said, trying to soothe

him. "Rusty and Lucas can trade off with Mr. Hawkshaw in the stock car."

Gid waved her away, not wanting her to see him so ill, and she returned to her seat. Hawkshaw saw what was happening and got to his feet, looking weary and tired. She sat down, and he passed her on his way to the stock car.

Tennie stared out the window. Home to Texas. Home to Wash. Would he be there anticipating her arrival? Would there be a letter from him? What would be waiting for her in Waco? They passed mile after mile. Worry over Wash and their future turned everything she saw into a continuous blur.

"Madam!" a voice seemed to be calling her. "Madam!"

Tennie started and saw an elderly woman dressed in dusty gray, her face as cloudy to match, standing above her. "Yes, ma'am?"

"Can you please do something about your boys? They've been arguing with each other at the front of the car for the last ten minutes," the old lady said.

"Yes, ma'am. I'm sorry." Tennie rose, but fortunately, it was time for another ten-minute stop. She joined the boys to rush off the train for a quick break.

"Stop fighting. You are disturbing the other passengers."

Badger began to wail because he wasn't

allowed in the stock car. Tennie looked at him crossly. "Go back on the train and help Mr. Gid. He's trying to get up."

Once back on the train, and at every stop thereafter where the train took on new passengers, Tennie searched for a tall woman with dark hair. It would be like Maribel to get back on the train and demand something from them. She wondered if that was part of the reason Hawkshaw looked so off-color.

Dusk came, and Hawkshaw asked Rusty and Lucas to spend the night in the stock car with the horses. "It's my stomach. The smell is getting to me."

"What's wrong with your stomach?" Tennie asked.

"I don't know. Dyspepsia?" Hawkshaw said. "Coltrane rubbing off on me? Who knows?"

Rusty and Lucas agreed, proud Hawkshaw trusted them. Before it became too dark to see, Tennie walked through the rocking railcars to check on them. The horses were in their stalls, the boys had made a soft bed of straw, and all seemed to be settled in for the night. Tennie went back to her seat, making a bed for herself and Badger.

They arrived in Houston at dawn, stretching as they exited the train car, trying to work the stiffness from their muscles. Hawkshaw said they would have a two-hour wait before they continued, and the stock car would have to be taken off and put on a smaller train heading for Waco.

Tennie's eyes roamed over the people, wishing Wash might be there to meet them. Although there were plenty of handsome men in boots and Stetsons, none of them was Wash. She hadn't really expected him to be in Houston. All her hopes were pinned on Waco.

Hawkshaw stayed with the stock car while Tennie and the boys went for food.

She looked around, thinking no one in their right mind would call Houston a pretty city. It was as if every man, woman, and child carried the attitude of "I have a gun and will use it if I have to." Nevertheless, it had an energy all its own that held an odd attraction.

"Miss Tennie, when we get home, will you fix me a sweet potato pie?" Badger asked.

Tennie nodded. She didn't ask, "Where is home?" She didn't know the answer.

Back at the station, they formed a line on the platform next to the tracks, waiting to board. Tennie gave surreptitious glances at the other passengers. Most of them were men, some in faded blue shirts with bright bandannas around their necks; others wore dark suits, making her wonder how they stood the heat and humidity already building in Houston. She caught her breath when she saw a tall well-dressed woman with her back to them. When she turned around, Tennie exhaled. Underneath her hat, the woman had russet-colored hair fluffed around her face. Unless Maribel had decided to henna her hair, it couldn't be her.

"I want to ride in the caboose," Badger whined.

"Me, too," Lucas said.

"I wish we could at least look inside," Rusty said.

"Go to work for the railroad, and you can ride in the caboose all you want," Tennie said, continuing her search of passengers. "In the meantime, quit moaning about it."

A tall woman wearing heavy mourning had joined the line near them. Tennie wanted to go to her and ask, "May I lift your veil to make sure you aren't Maribel Beauregard?" but turned away and gave her head a shake. She was acting as childish as the boys.

"All aboard!" the conductor called.

Hawkshaw said his stomach felt a little better, but he still would prefer Rusty and Lucas to ride in the stock car. They hopped aboard, and he shut the door behind them before joining Tennie and Badger. It took everything they had to convince Gid to get back on the train.

"I can ride horseback to Waco," he said. "Just wait for me there."

"We can't stay that long in Waco, Mr. Gid," Tennie said. "If Wash isn't there, the sheriff will make us leave town immediately. We'll be lucky if he lets us spend one night."

Gid stared at the train, twisting first one way and then the other, kicking his boots at the ground in front of him.

"Come on, Mr. Gid," Badger said, taking his hand. "This is the last stretch. Miss Tennie said so."

"We'll be in Waco before dark, Coltrane," Hawkshaw said. "I really need your help getting these horses to Ring Bit."

That Hawkshaw asked for his help motivated Gid enough to allow Badger to lead him by the hand into the railway car. Behind him, Tennie sent Hawkshaw a look of commiseration. "At least we have seen the last of Miss Maribel."

Hawkshaw shook his head in revulsion. "I still don't know how you talked me into that farce."

"It's over with now," Tennie said, feeling suddenly elated. "We are almost there."

Hawkshaw took his solitary place in the corner, stretching out and putting his hat over his face. The redhead and her male companion took seats across from him and a little farther up. Badger led Gid to his spot by the window at the opposite end of the carriage. Tennie sat somewhere in the middle facing them, placing her blankets on the seat next to her to save it for Badger, who would make numerous trips back and forth. A group of cowboys clustered around her but did not take the seat directly across from her, so it, too, was free. The woman in mourning took a spot across the aisle from Badger. Tennie felt sorry for her. If something happened to Wash, she would feel like covering her red tearful eyes, too, so she could hide alone in her grief.

The conductor walked up the aisle. The train gave a backward clank, lurched, and after a series of jerks, they left Houston. Last stop: Waco.

Tennie had bought a newspaper in Houston, thinking she would give it to Hawkshaw to read later. It would take a while for the demise of the Daring Dandies to make front-page news. Other passengers gossiped about the mysterious "woman in blue" who had been seen riding with the robbers, and Tennie did not enlighten them.

She wondered if Maribel had traveled with the Daring Dandies to New Orleans. If they had taken any of her money, she would be sure to show up at the chief of police's office to claim she had been kidnapped against her will, and the thieves had stolen her cash. Perhaps Maribel and Esther would find one another. Tennie thought it more likely Esther would end up in a voodoo shop buying a doll that looked like Maribel so she could stick pins in it.

She smiled to herself, thinking how silly she was being.

A cowboy sitting across the aisle from her with light gray eyes saw her smile. "What's so funny?"

Tennie grinned. "Nothing. I'm just happy we are almost to Waco."

The train picked up more passengers in Hempstead, and the car became crowded. Hawkshaw had to share the seats around him, forcing him to sit up. Gid had lost his Houston food out the window a long time ago. Tennie hoped Hawkshaw, who sat staring out the window, didn't lose his, too.

The cowboys, along with the redhead and her companion, left the train at Bryan, the last big stop before Waco.

Gid refused to get off. "Y'all might not get my pitiful hide back on again."

Hawkshaw and Tennie checked on the horses and the boys. They said everything was fine, but there was a slight bruise coming up around Lucas's left eye, and the knuckles on Rusty's right hand looked roughened and red. The horses were neighing and moving about more than usual, but Hawkshaw said he thought they could stand it until the train reached Waco. He inspected each one, soothing them in a calm voice.

The conductor called, "All aboard!"

Hawkshaw and Tennie moved back to the passenger car. With the train less crowded, he was able to stretch his legs out again. She found her place as the whistle blew and a blast of steam caused cinders to fly around the carriage.

Badger knew better than to bother Hawkshaw,

but with the train soon rocking at full speed, he kept running back and forth between Gid and Tennie, unheeding her commands to settle down. She was about to rise and search for the conductor to ask him how long it would be before they reached Waco when the woman in mourning rose, evidently in search of the conductor herself.

Tennie settled in her seat and looked out the window. The conductor walked by, but before she could stop him, he had already passed into the next car. In a little while, he came back again, followed by Rusty and Lucas, causing all questions to flee from Tennie's mind as worry over what her stepsons might have done took its place.

"Miss Tennie," Rusty said. "The conductor said we can visit the caboose and ride in it the rest of the way to Waco."

"Can I ride, too?" Badger said. "Please?"

Tennie's lips parted in surprise. Had the woman in mourning complained about Badger? Tennie half rose, looking first at Gid, whose eyes were almost rolling into the back of his head, before turning to Hawkshaw, who had his hat over his face.

"If you are sure it is okay," Tennie told the conductor.

He nodded, and she spoke to the boys. "Let Mr. Hawkshaw rest. He doesn't feel well. I'll go stay with the horses."

They grinned and exclaimed their thanks before following the conductor to the rear of the train.

Tennie picked up her blankets and canteen, not knowing why the conductor was being so obliging. She hoped her stepsons hadn't been pestering him behind her back.

She made her way to the front of the car and opened the door, the roar of the train and the wind hitting her in the face. She stepped over into the next carriage, almost empty except for a few sleeping men who smelled strongly of spirits. She opened the door, stopped to glance at the men behind her, but the increased gusts and noise had not awakened them. She stepped onto the platform, shut the door behind her, and crossed to the stock car platform.

Before she could open the door, the sound of frightened horses alarmed her. She pushed at the door and stepped inside.

The horses were out of their stalls, stomping wildly about the car. Some were snorting with their ears flicking back and forth. One stallion pinned his ears back and let out a roar, raising both front legs and crashing them back down.

Shocked, Tennie dropped her things and approached one of the mares prancing and curling her upper lip in anxiety. Hoping to calm her, she put out her hand, but before she could reach the mare, she felt an arm around her neck, pulling her back.

Someone was attacking her from behind. She struggled, looking down and seeing a black dress. She kicked, trying to pull the arm around her neck away, but whoever held her was incredibly strong. Her neck was wrenched so hard, she momentarily froze. When she did, something cold and sharp was placed against her throat. She looked up at the person who held her.

The black veil had been flipped back over the hat, exposing a feral face inches from hers. It wasn't the hideous purplish-red scar on the neck cut almost from ear to ear that immobilized Tennie, but the eyes above it—black empty holes that had nothing behind them. A person without a soul.

"I have a straight razor against your neck, Mrs. Granger," a voice said. "Move, and I will slice your throat just like mine was sliced, except I will go deeper."

"Inga . . ." Tennie breathed.

CHAPTER 24

The door to the stock car opened. Tennie gave a frightened, wild look at Hawkshaw as he entered, his gun drawn. The expression on his face did not change, not even a flicker. He stared at Tennie, but she knew he saw everything—Inga, the horses, the razor against her throat.

"Are you surprised to see me, Mr. Hawkshaw?" Inga said, taunting him. "You are truly not the man you thought you were. You could not bring yourself to cut my throat deep enough."

He said nothing.

His face revealed nothing but a cool lack of nerves, although Inga's malevolence was directed at him, glowing with glee that he would witness her making a frenzied slash at Tennie's throat. The revolver in his hand remained poised.

Tennie looked into his eyes. She lowered and raised her eyelids slowly, telling him to do what he had to do, then leaned her neck as far from Inga as she dared, right into the razor, and closed her eyes.

When the roar of the pistol came, it was as if it had blasted her eardrums away with it. Behind her, a horse screamed in pain. She pushed Inga's arm away from her as quickly as she could, but not before the razor dragged across her skin.

407

Jumping back, she felt warm blood seeping down the side of her neck. She stared at Inga, looking inhuman, crumpled on the floor with a bullet hole between her eyes. Tennie's whole body began to shake as the ringing in her ears and the blood rushing through her head unleashed a torrent of emotion. She began to weep, uncontrollable long, jagged sobs.

Hawkshaw replaced his gun. Breathing heavily, he examined her neck. "It's just a flesh wound." He put his hand on her shoulder, and she buried her face in his chest, unable to stop crying. He hugged her and murmured that she would be all right.

Gid lurched into the stock car, gasping for breath. "What the— ?" He looked around then down, saw Inga, and let out an oath.

Tennie tried to stop crying. She straightened, and Hawkshaw released his grip, but he did not back away.

"The horse . . . ?" Tennie asked.

"It's just a nick," Hawkshaw said.

Gid, unsteady on his feet, began to calm the horses, putting them back in their stalls. When he finished, he bent down toward Inga. Hawkshaw took Tennie by the shoulders and turned her away. A few seconds later, the sliding door to the stock car opened. Tennie looked over her shoulder and saw Gid kicking Inga out of the moving stock car, her body flying into the dirt and rolling away.

"I'm leaving this here door open partways till we get to Waco," Gid said. "If that's all right."

Hawkshaw nodded, and Gid got down on the floor of the stock car, laying on his side so he could breathe air from the opened door, without the slats in his way that reminded him of prison.

"But—" Tennie began.

Hawkshaw shook his head. "Don't worry about it. She probably bribed the conductor to let the boys ride in the caboose so she could get them out of here. I'll explain to him what happened, and that we don't want any trouble over it. He's not going to make any. He'll lose his job if the railroad finds out he let passengers ride in the caboose."

From his place on the floor, Gid rolled partway over, his face pallid and shattered. "He's right. Them jobs is hard to get. That there woman must have given him a right smart amount of money." He squeezed his eyelids, trying to shut out tears. "I promised Colonel Lafayette I'd take good care of you, Miss Tennie, and I sure been a failure."

"Don't say that, Mr. Gid. You've been with me every step of the way." She sank to the floor, exhausted. "I want to stay right here until we get to Waco."

Hawkshaw kneeled, placing his bandanna on her bleeding neck. He got up and looked over the horses, murmuring soothing noises to them. Once the horses had calmed, he sat between Tennie and Gid near the opened door.

It was only then she realized the battle Hawkshaw had just fought and won in what had been, and was, a very long war. She closed her eyes and let the rocking of the train calm every jangling thought.

The train rattled and jolted, slowing to a halt. Tennie opened her eyes, realizing she must have fallen asleep. She sat up and looked through the slats of wood. A sign that said WACO appeared and passed by. The tightness in her chest surprised her. She stood. Her legs feeling weak beneath her, she had to place a hand on the railcar to hold herself steady.

Hawkshaw stood by the opened door, looking out and steadying himself with one hand holding on to a slat of wood. Gid refused to move until the train came to a complete, shuddering stop. Sitting up, he eased his legs out of the stock car and let them dangle.

Hawkshaw slid the door open wider, dodged Gid, and jumped onto the station platform. "I'll be back in a little while," he said, walking toward the other cars.

Tennie did the same, except she stood in front of Gid and helped him from the train.

Rusty, Lucas, and Badger exited from another car and ran toward them, full of laughter and happy chatter because they got to ride in the caboose.

Lucas paused and stared at Tennie's neck. "What happened to you, Miss Tennie?"

Tennie put her hand up to the graze. "The train jolted and I fell, scratching myself on something. It's nothing." Dismissing the Miltons forever from her life, she looked down at her rumpled, dirty dress. "I look like something the cat dragged in," she mourned. "And I smell worse. Oh, God, I don't want Wash to see me like this."

Gid straightened, wiping the sweat and tears from his eyes with his forearm. "We'll get these here horses to a stable. Afterward, I'll take you to the hotel, Miss Tennie, so you can get cleaned up. While you are doing that, I'll be searching out news of Mr. Wash for you."

"Thank you, Mr. Gid," Tennie said, so relieved she wanted to cry. "But what about the sheriff?"

Gid gave a weak laugh. "We'll just have to hide them young'uns and Mr. Hawkshaw at the stables for a while."

Hawkshaw returned, nodded his head at Gid and Tennie to reassure them everything had been taken care of. He told the boys they couldn't ride the horses bareback to the stables. "It's better to lead them. Let them find their legs again."

They made plans while they walked the horses to the livery.

Gid explained his idea of taking Tennie back to the hotel to freshen up, while he went looking for news of Wash. "I'll come back to fetch you so we can find some out-of-the-way place to get something to eat. You and these here boys are

411

what the colonel calls 'persona non grata' in this here town."

The rest of the way to the livery, they teased Gid about knowing Latin. That Gid was back to his talkative old self relieved Tennie, but the excitement she felt over seeing Wash or hearing news from him blotted out almost every other thought.

At the stable, she could barely contain her impatience. She wanted to tell Gid she would be perfectly fine walking to the hotel by herself, but she remembered how upset he felt over his inability to protect her on the train. She swallowed her exasperation at having to wait while they settled the horses in and tried to keep the annoyance she felt off her face.

When Gid finally finished, she cautioned the boys. "Stay with Mr. Hawkshaw and don't cause any trouble."

They barely listened, so taken up with being reunited with their Appaloosa.

"We've got to exercise Apache," Lucas said.

"And groom him. They were sort of lax about that here," Rusty said in disapproval.

"Floyd and Miss Nab would be proud of you," Tennie said with a smile. "Come on, Mr. Gid. Let's go."

Despite her embarrassment over her appearance, Tennie asked Gid to stop with her at the post office. She ran up the steps, leaving Gid trailing behind.

"No, ma'am," the baldheaded postmaster said. "I'm sorry. There aren't any letters here for you."

Tennie's heart fell, but she refused to give up hope. She turned to Gid, who had joined her. "Maybe at the telegraph office."

Gid led her through a maze of streets to the telegraph office. The telegraph operator was a much sturdier specimen than the postmaster since he had to shut the office occasionally to travel miles to repair lines.

"Yes, ma'am, I have a telegram for you." He rummaged through a stack in a wooden shelf full of cubbyholes. "Here it is."

Tennie's hands shook as she took it, but as she read, her excitement ebbed away.

"What is it?" Gid asked.

"It's from Mr. Lafayette." She read it to Gid. "TENNESSEE STOP WIRE UPON IMMEDIATE ARRIVAL WACO END." She clutched the telegram to her chest, so disappointed.

Gid wanted to wire the Colonel right then and there.

"No, lct's wait until we know something else," she said. "There may be word at the hotel."

They left the telegraph office and headed for the square.

"I'll get you a room," Gid said. "And sneak Lucas and Badger in after it gets dark so the sheriff don't catch wind of them. Rusty can stay with me and Mr. Hawkshaw."

Tennie nodded in agreement. This time, she did not stay outside while Gid went into the lobby and up to the front desk.

"I can give you a room, Mrs. Granger," the hotel clerk said, "but there aren't any letters waiting here for you."

"Thank you," she said, trying to keep the disappointment out of her voice. She turned to Gid. "Mr. Gid . . . ?"

"Don't you worry none, Miss Tennie. I'll get you settled in your room, and I'll knock about town talking to everybody I can find to see if they is any word about Mr. Wash."

"Thank you," Tennie said. "You are a true friend. Would it help if I—?"

"No, ma'am," Gid interrupted, picking up her bag and heading for the stairs.

Tennie left Gid to the search, knowing there were places he would go that she couldn't, and men who would talk freely to him, but not to her. If felt good to clean the train grime off, but she wasn't sleepy. Full of the desire to do something, she decided to channel her energy into writing thank-you notes to the judge and Viola. She took her time, but even so, when finished, she still felt too wound up to relax. Instead of resting, she took the letters downstairs, leaving them with the clerk at the front desk. The porch beckoned to her, but afraid of attracting the attention of the sheriff, she sat down on a hard sofa in the lobby, watching the door and hoping Wash would burst into the room.

She knew as soon as she saw Gid's face when he entered the hotel he hadn't found out anything. She rose from the sofa and fought back tears. "There is no news, is there?"

Gid shook his head. "No, ma'am, but like my old granny used to say, 'No news is good news,' so don't you fret none. We'll go rustle up something to eat, and we can talk about what to do next."

There wasn't anything to do next except go back to Ring Bit, back to the jailhouse, and be thankful her job was still waiting for her. She would have a roof over her head and food on the table. That it was sometimes a brutal and noisy roof was something she would just have to deal with while she waited for Wash to return.

They joined the others at the livery stable. Gid had heard of a small inn on the edge of town where they wouldn't likely be seen by the sheriff. When they entered the crowded establishment, Hawkshaw went straight to a table in the rear, placing himself against the back wall with a clear view of the front door. Some things never changed.

Cornpone, bacon, and greens with side meat were the only things on the menu, but they ate without complaint.

"Dragging me and two little ones along on a

drive might be too much of a burden," Tennie said. "Lucas, Badger, and I can take the stagecoach back to Ring Bit. I know you'll need Rusty's help."

Lucas opened his mouth to howl a fierce protest, paused because he knew he shouldn't, and instead, gave beseeching stares to Hawkshaw and Gid.

Hawkshaw continued to eat, his eyes never leaving his plate. Gid opened his mouth, but Hawkshaw spoke first.

In between bites, without lifting his head, he asked, "Would you feel safer on the stagecoach or being with us?"

"Being with all of you," Tennie said.

"Then there's your answer," Hawkshaw said, sitting back and raising his eyes.

Gid exhaled in relief. "We can get a covered wagon. Load it with supplies, and it will be just like home. Them two mares will pull. Ain't no need in buying no mules."

Gid and the boys began to make a list of supplies. They wanted a tarp to sleep under if the weather got bad.

Tennie wanted Hawkshaw to know what the Granger ranch was like. "The house is falling down, and there is a hole in the roof of the barn where it looks like the moon fell through. Our two cowboy friends, Honey Boy and Two-Bit, work on a big ranch, but they run cattle on our land, too. Two-Bit is so lazy, his boss is always firing him, but he's likable in a funny sort of way, so he hires him back. In between times, he stays at the ranch in exchange for fixing the place up, but I don't think he's done anything."

"It sounds enchanting," Hawkshaw said. "The dream of a lifetime."

Tennie ignored his sarcasm. She knew he was worried about his future.

"Wash won't mind you staying there. He wouldn't want the boys to sell it, though."

"That's right, Mr. Hawkshaw," Rusty said, nodding. "Even falling down, it's still ours."

Gid wondered how Lafayette was coming along with the saloon. "I bet it looks jim-dandy by now."

"Better hope the next group of saloon girls he gets will be easier to get along with than the ones he had before," Tennie said. "I hope Wash returns before they get there."

The boys began kidding Gid, saying he was going to fall in love with all the new saloon girls and would probably get fired for mooning over them instead of doing his job. Gid played along with them, talking about finding a little Irish colleen, encouraging them to tease him.

Badger wasn't the least interested in talking to Gid about women. He turned to Tennie. "Will Rascal even remember me?" he cried.

"Of course, Rascal will know you," Tennie said. "We haven't been away that long."

"Speaking of dogs, I don't have a hankering

to wake one up," Gid said, "but I'm just a little perturbed thinking about cousin Maribel showing up down here in Texas."

"Clamp it, Coltrane," Hawkshaw said, standing and throwing money on the table. "I don't ever want to hear that woman's name again. Take Miss Tennie Marshal to the hotel so she can moon over her wandering boyfriend in private. You can sneak these little hooligans over there tonight." He left the café, the door swinging shut behind him.

"Is he mad at us?" Badger asked.

"Heck no," Gid said. "He spoke three or four sentences. Didn't you hear him?"

The men standing at the bar on the other side of the room were beginning to speak louder in brash, rough tones.

Gid rose. "Best get out of here before things get a little tetchy." He took the last piece of cornpone and stuffed it into his mouth as they headed outside. "Money's on the table," he hollered as he opened the door, spewing pieces of cornpone as he talked.

"You boys best catch up with Mr. Hawkshaw," he said once they were outside. "I got to escort Miss Tennie back to that there hotel and can't no little Granger mugs be showing up in downtown Waco during daylight."

Tennie wanted to dream of Wash again that night, but she didn't. Once the boys were back, they all fell into deep dreamless sleep, and Tennie had a hard time rousing them before dawn to get them out of the hotel and the town square before they could be seen.

Gid was waiting for them outside. "Hello, little partners." Turning to Tennie, he gave her instructions from Hawkshaw. "He said for you to get something to eat at the bakery next door. We'll get everything ready, and I'll come back and fetch you when it's time to go."

"We have to stop at the telegraph office and wire Mr. Lafayette," Tennie said.

"I ain't forgot. And I promise I'll swing by the post office, too."

Tennie waited until daylight before going next door. It was a Czech bakery, with flour all over the floor, all over the walls, and covering the arms of everyone who worked there. She'd never seen such pastries and felt guilty for spending money on something so unique and delicious looking just for herself. To ease her conscience, she bought treats for the others to eat along the way.

As she left the bakery and shut the door behind her, she turned and almost ran into the sheriff. She came to an abrupt halt, leaning backward. "We're leaving this morning. I have to send a telegram to Cat Ridge, and we'll be heading out."

"No word from Captain Jones, then?" he asked.

"No, sir." She wanted to walk away, but he

blocked her path, and something in his manner held her.

"You riding back to Ring Bit with that cold-blooded gunslinger and that musclebound bonehead? You're not taking the stagecoach?"

"No, sir. I'm not taking the stagecoach. I'm riding back with the cold-blooded gunslinger and the musclebound bonehead."

He remained silent for several seconds, making Tennie wonder if he was about to go into another apoplectic fit. But he had made her see how bad it looked, heading back to Ring Bit, not on a respectable stagecoach, but with a hired killer and a former convict.

"Don't go through Liver Junction anywheres near dark," he said. "It's a favorite place for bandits to rob people at night. Best time to pass is early morning, before the trash can shake off the previous night's drinking."

"Thank you," Tennie said, so surprised she could barely squeak the words out.

He stepped aside to let her pass. As she did, he spoke again. "I hope you hear from Wash Jones soon, Mrs. Granger. Me and Wash ain't always seen eye to eye, but he's a mighty fine man."

"Yes. Yes, he is," she said, and went back to the hotel. She climbed upstairs to her room, shutting the door behind her. As her eyes filled with tears, she turned and slammed her head against the door twice, upset that her actions might cause embarrassment and humiliation to Wash.

There was no word at the post office when she and Gid arrived, nor was there anything at the telegraph office. Tennie sent Lafayette a telegram offering the bald truth.

NOTHING FROM WASH STOP RETURNING RING BIT WITH HAWKSHAW GID BOYS STOP HERDING HORSES END TENNESSEE

The two mares were hitched to a small covered wagon. There was a fancy new saddle on the Appaloosa and an equally expensive sidesaddle thrown inside the wagon. Tennie opened her mouth to ask about them, remembered the few moments Gid had spent beside Inga Milton's body when her back had been turned, and decided against it. Instead, she asked how much her share of the supplies and wagon would be, but he and Hawkshaw wouldn't let her pay anything. She wished she had bought them more pastries. They told her they would catch and clean the game, but she would have to be the camp cook. She was happy with that.

Gid got up in the wagon seat with her. She had learned to handle a wagon and team on the way to Texas from Alabama, and she promised to trade off with him.

"That'd be fine, but them there boys need to take a hand," he said.

421

Later, Lucas traded places with Tennie, Gid placed the sidesaddle on the Appaloosa, and Tennie climbed up.

"I feel like Queen Victoria or somebody on this thing," she said, and Gid obliging laughed, understanding the effort it was taking her to pretend all was well.

About an hour outside of Waco, they spied two riders approaching. Gid and Hawkshaw, knowing of the outlaws who nested to the east, immediately took rifles in hand.

As soon as Tennie recognized the riders, she knew the news they would be carrying.

"It's Mr. Ben and Mr. Poco," Rusty cried, rising in the saddle and waving his hat to them.

"Who's that?" Gid asked Lucas.

Lucas likewise waved his hand. "It's Mr. Wash's men. They are Texas Rangers who ride with Mr. Wash."

Gid relaxed his rifle and looked at Tennie. He turned and told Lucas to stop the wagon. Tennie reined the Appaloosa to a halt as the men drew closer, a knot forming in her throat.

When they reached the caravan, the rangers nodded to the others in greeting but rode straight to Tennie.

Ben McNally and Poco Gonzalez-Gonzalez loved Wash perhaps even more than Lafayette did. Ben reached inside his shirt and pulled out a packet of letters and handed them to Tennie.

She took them, looking down at the firm handwriting spelling out her name.

"We were ambushed outside of Corpus Christi by raiders," Ben said.

Tennie barely heard the rest of it. As he talked, she looked down again at the letters and remembered the beautiful dream about Wash she had experienced. The dream where his love cut across all barriers, and the scars life had put on him were no longer there.

She already knew what the letters would say. She would save them, save them for a time when she could go off alone to savor and hold dear every word in them.

Poco was saying something about the stagecoach. "We can put you on the stagecoach, Señora Tennie. And escort you back to Ring Bit."

She blinked her eyes, surprised that so few tears were there. She would cry later. They were all staring at her, waiting for her to reply.

She had to swallow hard to get the words out. "Thank you. You are very kind, but I'll stay out here on the open range with the others." She looked down, her mind numb. What was it Lafayette had said? Remembering, she looked up. "These men are good to ride the river with."

Center Point Large Print
600 Brooks Road / PO Box 1
Thorndike, ME 04986-0001 USA

(207) 568-3717

US & Canada:
1 800 929-9108
www.centerpointlargeprint.com